Maria's Child

Bill Hearn

ISBN-13: 9798779712989

Cover art by Melanie Rabon

Acknowledgements

Excerpts from "The Infancy Gospel of Thomas" taken from a translation by Mark M. Mattison which he has graciously placed in the public domain. The full text is available on the web at: https://www.gospels.net/thomas/

Mrs. Baylor

Thanks for reading the book. Hope you enjoy it!

Bill [illegible]

Logos

"When I was first asked to speak I planned to give a brief account of the goals and accomplishments of the Brethren. But after spending a week here and seeing you at work, I've decided to tell a story instead.

"Imagine a lifeboat. Imagine too that when the ship it came from sank, all of the survivors were partly to blame. Twelve had scrambled on board carrying food and fresh water; twelve saved only themselves. Though islands can be glimpsed on every horizon, some of the survivors say one island is nearer, while others point another way, so the oars remain shipped and idle. When some of those with water share, their fellows call them traitors, and some of the thirsty curse the gift and its givers, saying they haven't given enough.

"By the third night those without water are mad with thirst, and those with water realize that what they've brought won't last much longer. So they fight, and as they fight the water bottles break, and the spilt water is ruined by the hardened salt spray in the bottom of the boat.

"After the battle, those left alive huddle in two groups: one in the bow, the other in the stern. They don't sleep, they don't row, they just wait, growing weaker and weaker, hoping someone will rescue them . . ."

—Joshua Grant, at a 2028 U.N. conference on world hunger attended by about 240 delegates.

Joshua Grant, founder of the Brethren of Charity — a small relief organization active in India and Bangladesh — was expected to provide the conference with one of its few non-political moments. But his one-minute "speech" — an Aesop's fable mocking the name-calling and public posturing that have marred the conference — was non-political only in that it offended the representatives of every government present.

— INN News

"Jesus Is Coming Soon!
(And This Time He'll REALLY Be Pissed!)"

— Popular bumper sticker, first seen around 2025.

Chapter 1

Five a.m., Atlanta, Georgia. December, 2032

Even before I see Joshua's face I know who's calling and why. He's acted quickly; it's been less than a week since we told him of his mother's illness. Leukemia is rarely fatal these days, but the diagnosis has pretty much guaranteed this call.

"Hello, Peter," my stepson says.

I turn on the video feed and take in his current incarnation: clean-shaven, short-haired, his skin a world-average light brown (a shade supposedly inherited from his Cuban mother). His expression is as gloomy and tired as the weather outside my window: a slow, sad drizzle that promises worse to come.

"You look exhausted," I tell him.

"You look a bit sleepy yourself."

"Well, it's five in the morning here. And raining."

His face lights up, rueful but amused. "I'm sorry. I thought it was seven there. You're usually up by seven."

"That's all right. I can take a nap this afternoon."

"How's Mom?"

"Much better. I'm going to see her in a few hours. How's Bangladesh?"

"Actually, I'm in New Delhi." He straightens, and in anticipation I sit up also. "I need to ask you something. I called Mom yesterday at the hospital but . . ."

". . . how did I miss that? I was there most of the day."

"I called while you were out getting a cup of coffee, I guess. But anyway, I couldn't ask her about this straight out; I didn't want to upset her. Even so, I have the feeling that if I *had* asked directly she still wouldn't know anything about it. How about you?"

"How about me, what?" I respond, a bit peevishly. "If you want me to answer a question you have to ask it first."

"All right," Joshua says, his eyes suddenly boring into mine. "Who am I?"

And there it is: the question I've been asking myself for thirty-three years.

"You're Joshua Grant," I tell him, knowing all too well that's not the answer he wants. "What do you mean?"

"Well, the problem is this: I wanted to donate my bone marrow — Mom's doctor said they might need to do a transplant and I'm an obvious choice for a donor. But the DNA test came back saying I'm not related to my own mother."

I say nothing, but the look on my face must be enough.

"I can see *you're* not surprised," Josh continues, "so why not let *me* in on the secret? It would make sense if I was adopted, but then how do you explain all the family photos of Mom quite pregnant?"

"You weren't adopted."

"Then explain the DNA test."

"It takes a lot of explaining. We'll need to talk about it face to face."

He sighs. "There's no way I can leave India right now. But I have to come to the States in two weeks. Can we talk then?"

"In two weeks? Sure. Shall I give your mother your best wishes in the meantime?"

This comes out with a bit of venom: when Maria's cancer was diagnosed I wanted Josh to come home right away, even when Maria said he had more important things to do than watch a sick old woman sleep.

"Don't just give her my best wishes," Joshua says softly. "Tell her I love her."

"I don't need to," I answer. "She knows that already."

I don't try to go back to sleep, instead, I fix some coffee and head into town. By 7:20 I'm parking outside Grady Memorial. Grady is an old hospital, grimy and run-down, but it's where Maria wanted to go. It's the only Atlanta hospital that still takes charity cases and they need paying customers. Since they need our money, Maria even consented to a private room.

She's eating breakfast when I come in, or trying to: she's still nauseated from the last round of chemo. We sit and watch the NetV for a while, but when I look over at 7:50, I see she's drifted off to sleep. I lean back in my chair, hoping to join her.

The morning's drizzle has changed to a driving rain, courtesy of Hurricane Wanda, which hit the coast late last night and is still at tropical storm strength even after travelling inland to Atlanta. The rain drowns the hospital noises, so I'm almost asleep when a new sound joins its monotonous drumming. Maria is dreaming. I lean close; chemo has made her prone to nightmares, and she likes me to wake her before they really get going. But this is no nightmare. She smiles, breathes deeply, murmurs, "Joe."

Joe was her first husband, Joshua's supposed father. Though Joe has been gone for some twenty-seven years, I still rank second in Maria's affections, and lately I've become quite calm about it. She dreams about me, too, but there's a lilt to her voice whenever she says his name.

Listening to *this* dream would be rude, so I grab the remote and cautiously turn up the NetV's volume. It's tuned to a news channel, and suddenly the story I've been ignoring is over and a new one begins. I see my stepson striding across the screen, followed by a large group in western and Indian dress.

"In New Delhi, India," the netcaster informs us, "Joshua Grant, founder of the Brethren of Charity, led a march to pray in front of the Golden Mosque, headquarters of the Muslim sect that recently called for the death of all Brethren members. Bani Sadr Akmeni, the sect's head, insists the Brethren's claims of pacifism and religious tolerance are lies; a ploy to lull good Muslims into complacency. The Brethren's reaction? They're praying for the continued health and happiness of Akmeni, and Grant has added further prayers asking God's wisdom, love, and 'good sense' to descend upon Bani Sadr.

"Despite warnings of violence, the prayer vigil was mostly peaceful, although a few rocks were thrown by hostile Hindus and Muslims."

As if on cue, three plum-sized chunks come whizzing at Joshua. Two miss, but the third strikes him a glancing blow. Josh winces, grabs quickly at his shoulder, then walks on. I'm more affected than he is. Or was. This is a news summary — it all took place hours before this morning's call. But even so, it's another reminder that a rock, bomb or bullet could nail Joshua any time, a thought I like even less than hearing Maria dream about Joe.

So I change the channel, but there's no escaping the news: Maria has logged her preferences into the remote. Altering her programming is beyond me, but I punch some random buttons anyway, hoping to find an old movie. Instead I get the usual mix of world misery: Sufi dervishes blocking construction of a new, Jews-only apartment block on the West Bank; Bangladesh suing the U.S., the European Union, India, and China for greenhousing their country into the Bay of

Bengal; Wanda ranking as the strongest December hurricane ever; and the U.S. planning to veto the U.N. CO_2 tariff for the seventh consecutive year.

But one button push brings a surprise: "God's Warriors," hosted by America's Number-One Internet Evangelist, Harold Pierpont Anthony. Maria claims my obsession with Anthony borders on psychosis, but this preset proves that she likes to keep an eye on our old nemesis herself.

Anthony's in his early eighties, but he could pass for fifty-five. Ever since stem cells got him out of his wheelchair he's been a covert consumer of every age-delaying treatment imaginable, including, if rumors are true, a replacement kidney purchased from a poor Mexican farmer, a transaction which would have been illegal as recently as 2025.

"Well Art," Anthony says to his genial sidekick, "I see that God's wrath has struck several Indonesian islands. Folks, this string of disasters is a clear sign. God's patience with those who refuse to see His glory is wearing thin."

"You jackass," I mutter, "They're dying because *we* fucked up their weather."

"These disasters upset some so-called Christians," Anthony continues, still beaming, "because the Bible tells us that pagans like most of those killed are going to burn in Hell. This has troubled me in the past as well, but I've prayed about it, and last night God gave me the answer."

"Oh really," I mumble.

"In these last days Our Lord has looked ahead and identified those who will never accept Him. He has caused more and more of these already-lost to be born in the godless and godforsaken countries of the world. Other faiths are lies of the Devil, and their members should and *will* be obliterated. Anyone who tells you different is no Christian."

Well! I think. The "heathen" are already goners in the great barbecue-to-come, are perhaps subtly less than human? How convenient to be absolved of all guilt ourselves! Anthony states this new spin on predestination with so little fanfare that most of his "guests" merely nod, but then, Anthony's disciples make an art of hearing without listening, speaking without thinking. And that's the problem. If they knew what I knew, I have little doubt that they would judge Joshua solely by how he was conceived, by who he "is," ignoring the good he's done since the day he was born.

One "panel" member does squirm a bit, a newcomer named Nicholas Preston. I suspect he's Anthony's token moderate, though Anthony's idea of a moderate is usually my idea of a lunatic. Crazy or not, this gentleman looks like he might be working up the courage to argue about Anthony's latest e-mail from the Almighty. But the show moves on to less flammable topics, and the man keeps his silence. As well he might, because even to a heathen like me, it's obvious that Harold Anthony has taken another small step in his very own *jihad.*

Chapter 2

. . . This was the third fatality this month on the Mount Lemmon Highway. However, a Department of Transportation spokesperson said that guard-rails or other planned improvements would not have prevented the accident, since police estimate Gluckmann's car left the road traveling in excess of 65 m.p.h. and the posted speed limit on the curve is 30 m.p.h.

—*Tucson Daily Star*, August 23, 1992

Many savvy investors think they've already found biotechnology's Bill Gates. Like Gates, Harold Anthony is an expert in his field and an astute and sometimes ruthless businessman.

Anthony Enterprises was founded in 1989 by Anthony and Jonathan Gluckmann, another pioneer in the field of genetic engineering. Renamed in 1992 after Dr. Gluckmann's death, Anthony Enterprises' assets have grown dramatically, and the company's roster of scientists reads like a biotechnology Hall of Fame.

Of course no stock is a sure thing, and some analysts warn that Harold Anthony's outspoken atheism is a public relations nightmare. Anthony has funded scientific investigations into such purported miracles as the Conyers visions of the Virgin Mary, the cures at Lourdes, the Shroud of Turin, and the Cloth of Orvieto. These "investigations" have been accompanied by surprisingly tactless comments about religious figures past and present. In highly public forums, Anthony has described Jesus as "a Hebe schizophrenic, brains baked by the desert sun," the prophet Mohammed as "the prototypical terrorist," and the Dalai Lama as "a guy who's smoked a little too much yak butter."

—*Investors' Monthly Digest,* May 1995

"I don't see any conflict in my position. I spent fifteen years in a wheelchair as penance for my sins, and the money I made in bio-tech does penance by funding God's work today."

— Harold Anthony, responding to an
interviewer's accusations of hypocrisy. 2025

When Joshua asked me who he was, he was right to demand more than just a name. Names tell little of underlying realities. For instance, considering the number of people Harold Anthony's had killed, I think he deserves a more dramatic label than those five bland American syllables. A more ominous name might bring Joshua to a proper fear of the man. Or maybe not; in thirty-three years I've seen little evidence that Joshua is afraid of anything. But after I come home and look at these old clippings, I'm more certain than ever that I need to change Joshua's mind.

I first met Harold Anthony when *I* was thirty-three.

Unlike Joshua, at thirty-three I was frightened by many things, but most of all by my ex-wife Beverly, a brain surgeon who lived in a ritzy apartment in downtown Chicago. When Beverly and I had married we'd both planned to be neurosurgeons, but I'd changed to obstetrics when I realized the mortality rate involved in cracking open people's skulls. Beverly was made of sterner stuff, in fact she once told me: "Surgeons operate on sick people. Good surgeons operate on very sick people. I'm planning to be a very good surgeon indeed." By 1996 (a year after our divorce) she was such a good surgeon that her name was uttered in hushed, admiring tones by half the doctors and nurses I knew. I don't consider myself a jealous man, but the more I heard her name the more I wanted to move my own operations somewhere else.

Not that I was doing badly in Chicago. I'd filled Beverly's place in our bed long before the divorce, my private practice was profitable if not glamorous, and I had a sideline-career that was threatening to become a main event, the result of two articles about prenatal genetic testing I did for the *Chicago Tribune*. I wrote the stories on spec, hoping to get some free advertising for my fledgling practice, but before I knew what was happening the newspaper wanted a series and radio talk shows were using me as a guest host. And then Harold Anthony called me out of the blue with a deal that seemed even better.

The position combined medicine and writing. In addition to its main research facility (the Anthony Bio-Technology Institute) Anthony Enterprises also ran a small fertility clinic in Tucson, Arizona. Many of its patients wanted an obstetrician blessed with the Anthony name, but the clinic's specialists were too busy doing strange things with Petri dishes to actually deliver any babies, so Anthony had "hired" one OB/GYN and wanted me to be the second. The medical job was routine, but Anthony was also offering a substantial five-year grant to write articles and perhaps a book about the social impact of bio-technology. I knew little about Anthony, less about Tucson, less about bio-tech than I let on, but I snapped at the opportunity because it would get me the hell away from my ex-wife.

Looking back, I wonder how I was ever talked into such a risky proposition. Anthony wasn't guaranteeing patients; he was just making me one of two obstetricians recommended by the Clinic. The "Clinic" itself didn't even fill a whole building: the first floor of its small office-park address boasted two dentists, a dermatologist, and a pediatrician. I was to have a suite of rooms on the second floor alongside Allen Deerborn, the Clinic's first OB/GYN. The third floor housed labs and examining rooms for the fertility specialists. I'd heard that the Anthony Institute occupied a more impressive building, but I'd be doing most of my work at the Clinic and local hospitals. And to top all that off, the grant and the Clinic recommendation were guaranteed primarily by Harold Anthony's goodwill, and I'd taken the "job" without ever actually meeting the man.

Our first face-to-face meeting was scheduled for nine a.m. at the Institute, four days after my arrival. This was years before GPS, and like most males then I was convinced I could find anything, so rather than getting directions I got out my new city map and left a little early.

I found the right street without any trouble, turned left, and headed towards the suburbs. Ten minutes later I came to what could have been a city park, except that city parks don't usually feature eight-foot-high, barbwire-crowned chain-link fences. Growing just inside the fence were olive trees and flowers, and further back date palms, islands of blooming oleander, and azaleas under tall pines. A minute later and I was driving by the centerpiece of this mysterious complex: a cubical concrete and black-glass building, six stories high.

I'd expected the Institute to be merely a larger version of the Clinic, so I kept driving. But within a mile it was obvious I was going in the wrong direction — the street numbers were too high. Gawking at the fence and the flowers, I'd missed the sign, an inconspicuous brass plaque that read: "The Anthony Institute. Visitors By Appointment Only." I noticed it only when I drove back and turned into the driveway.

The front gate was a bit more obvious. Boasting vertical bars that locked into the pavement and crossbeams thick as my waist, it might well have stopped an Abrams tank. A gatehouse was tucked alongside, and through heavy bulletproof glass I could see two guards. As the first walked out to ask my business the other watched intently.

"Can I help you sir?" the first guard asked.

"I have an appointment with Dr. Anthony," I answered. "At nine."

"Can I see some I.D?" he asked. I handed him my driver's license but he shook his head. "I'll need at least one more, sir." I added my doctor's pass from the Clinic, expecting him to wave me on through. Instead he walked back into the gatehouse, picked up the phone, talked for a moment, then dialed again. Finally he walked back out.

"Sir, could you get out of the car and follow me?"

"Is there a problem?" I asked.

"Standard procedure," he replied, with an unconvincing smile. I followed him into the gatehouse.

"Place your thumb on the screen, please," he said. I plopped my thumb down on what looked like a miniature document scanner, then watched as its ridges and whorls appeared on a nearby monitor. A second print was overlaid on the first and the monitor flashed: "Match within parameters, subject identity verified." Obviously, the computer had checked my thumbprint against its own digitized records. All well and good, except that I had never given anyone from Anthony Enterprises my thumbprint.

I decided not to think about that.

"All right, sir," the guard said, "I need to ask some questions."

"Questions?"

"Standard procedure, sir. Last four digits of your social security number?"

I gave them to him.

"Birthdate?"

"February 14, 1963."

"Place of birth?"

"Miami, Ohio."

"Mother's maiden name?"

"Mother or stepmother?"

"Mother."

"Uh, Taylor."

"Her birthdate?"

"Oh come on!"

"Do your best, sir."

I racked my brain. "Oct. 23, I think."

The questions rolled on — which high school I'd attended, marital status, my father's mother's name, my mother's mother's name, names of family pets, my nonexistent siblings' names, and my parents' current address, which he and I both knew was a cemetery; all dutifully verified from the computer's miraculous data base. Other than my social security number and birthdate, I had never told Anthony Enterprises any of it.

"Thank you sir," the first guard finally said. Both guards walked out with me out towards my car.

"Could you unlock your doors, sir?" guard number-one asked.

"What?"

"Unlock all your doors, sir. And open your trunk."

Grumbling, I reached for the power-lock switch, then leaned down to the trunk-release under the dash. The first guard walked back and swung the lid open, verifying, I suppose, that I hadn't hidden a dwarf back there. The second guard opened the passenger door and hopped in.

"Eddie will show you where to go," the first guard said, then walked back into the gatehouse. The bars retracted with a solid metallic thunk, and the gate slid back, smoothly and slowly; like the door to a bank vault, a missile silo, or a crypt.

Eddie was in his mid-twenties, heavily muscled, and friendlier than guard number-one, which was fortunate, because he could have knocked me senseless with his little finger.

"I like that," Eddie laughed as he hopped in. "Show you where to go! There's just one road."

One road, perhaps, but it took the scenic route. The main building was perhaps two hundred yards from the gate, but the driveway immediately turned away and began to wind through the grounds. The grass was dense and emerald-green, the space under the trees filled with luxurious vegetation.

"This is some landscaping job," I said. "How long has it all been here?"

"Eight or nine years, I think," Eddie replied.

"How'd they get it all to grow so fast?"

"The big trees were growing already; this used to be irrigated ranchland. But a lot of it's new; they come up with some strange stuff in here."

Strange? I had to agree. Besides the big scrub oaks, there were apple trees, pear, peach, and citrus; all bearing large burdens of fruit. Flowers bloomed everywhere, and small plots of vegetables were mixed in with the ornamentals. Somebody at Anthony Enterprises liked animals, too — we drove by three large enclosures containing monkeys, and another stocked with, of all things, pigs.

"I'm glad I don't have to pay the water bill for this place," I said.

"Fuckin' A," Eddie agreed.

We passed a tree growing fruit the size of soccer balls.

"Good Lord," I said, "what are those?"

"Mangoes, I think," Eddie told me. "But they're the biggest damn mangoes I ever seen, and I'm from Florida."

"Any good to eat?"

"Mister," Eddie laughed, "if you eat anything they grow here, you're a hell of a lot braver than I am."

We pulled into the parking lot and the dark cube of the building rose above us, blocking the sun. Eddie ushered me inside.

Nine o'clock came and went as I waited in a barren little reception area. At least I had company — Eddie sat reading a magazine, though his real assignment was obvious: he was there to make sure I didn't go anywhere unescorted. It was past 9:30 when a red-haired, rangy man in a lab coat walked over and extended his hand.

"Dr. Jacobson? I'm Eric Schroeder. Dr. Anthony wanted me to give you the grand tour."

I stood and shook his hand. Obviously, I wasn't going to see Anthony anytime soon, but since I had no idea who Eric Schroeder was I hid my annoyance.

"This is one hell of a building," I said as Schroeder led me out into the hall. "I didn't think gene-mapping equipment took up this much room."

"Well, the genome project is what gets in the papers," he replied over his shoulder, "but agriculture takes up the most space. In fact, I thought we might start with hydroponics."

"Hydroponics? Isn't that what people use to grow marijuana?"

"It certainly is," he said, eying me for a moment as if I might have a crop at home myself; then changing his expression to an arch grin. "Actually, in a way we are growing marijuana, but it's perfectly legal. We're trying to get corn to express the same fibrous qualities as hemp. Here we are."

We got into an elevator and came out on the first floor's lobby, empty except for a guard sitting behind a security console.

"Hi, Doc," he said to Schroeder.

"Could you buzz me into hydroponics, Jack?" Schroeder asked, walking to a door on the other side of the lobby. There was a buzz as the bolt was held back by a magnet, then Schroeder opened the door and motioned me into a large and disorganized reception area. At the back of the room was a door, and to one side a secretary sat at a computer.

"Hi, Marge," Schroeder said, "I'm showing Dr. Jacobson around." She grunted assent and went back to her work. We walked through the office, through the door, and into an empty hallway. Schroeder stopped.

"Marge is all right," he said, "and so is Jack."

"Jack?" I asked.

"The guard out in the lobby."

"What do you mean, all right?"

He paused, considering. "Nothing. I'll get you a lab coat." He pulled one off a rack on the wall and helped me put it on. "There's not time to see everything," he continued, "and that's kind of a shame."

We passed through what seemed like a dozen rooms crammed with plants in sand-and-water-filled containers. Corn was growing in one, the ears still tiny and unformed.

"This is the corn they've put the hemp gene in," Schroeder said. "The botanists won't know if they've succeeded until it's more mature, and they'll also need to keep an eye out for side-effects in the corn itself."

I gave a knowing nod, trying to hide the depth of my own botanical ignorance.

"Not one of our successes here," Schroeder said mournfully as we walked into a room featuring oddly shaped eggplants.

"Why not?"

"The botanists were trying to get eggplants to exude latex, since eggplants can withstand colder climates than rubber trees."

"What happened?"

"They got eggplants that bounced." He walked to a table at the back of the room, picked up a small eggplant and handed it to me.

"Drop it," he said. I did, and it careened across the floor like a manic football. He retrieved it and handed it to me.

"A souvenir. Take it home."

"This isn't secret?"

"The competition is welcome to it."

We came out into the lobby again, and Schroeder turned to me.

"You look like you keep yourself in pretty good shape. You like to swim?"

He opened another door and motioned me into a hall with glass walls. On one side was a small gym, on the other an indoor lap pool and Jacuzzi.

"Impressive," I said.

"Dr. Anthony likes it when his researchers spend a lot of time on the premises. Hell, he'd put in a dormitory if he thought anybody would stay in it. There's a dining room on the top floor, too. The architect wanted to put it down here, but Dr. Anthony thought we'd enjoy the view."

The tour continued to the second floor (administrative offices) then the third (dogs, rabbits, rhesus monkeys, and two chimpanzees). After the chimps we went up to the dining room. A small chalkboard listed entrees, and a buffet table was loaded with pastries, cereal, and fruit. We got drinks and pastries and sat down. As Schroeder had promised, there was a spectacular view of the Catalina Mountains north of town.

"You know, I was one of the people Dr. Anthony consulted before hiring you," Schroeder said after he'd wolfed down two croissants and a glass of sweet tea.

"Oh. Is there a board or something?" A naive question, perhaps, but I'd gotten the definite impression that Dr. Anthony did the hiring, although an "Anthony Enterprises Employment Consultant" had given me a battery of psychological tests.

"No, there's no board responsible for new hires," Schroeder said. "The chain of command is pretty simple here — Dr. Anthony speaks and we obey. But he did ask my opinion of your articles and résumé. I told him you seemed unusually well rounded for a doctor."

I laughed. "I guess that's my mother's genes at work. She died when I was three, but my father used to tell me she was interested in everything. She liked to write and draw, and apparently she played the violin pretty well, too."

"Really?"

"Some of it must have rubbed off; I wanted to be a classical guitarist when I was a teenager."

"Well, Dr. Anthony and I were impressed by your wide range of interests. Not many doctors or scientists cultivate that."

"Which are you, Dr. Schroeder?"

"Excuse me?"

"I mean, were you trained as an M.D. or a scientist? I'm sure there are plenty of 'doctors' here who don't practice medicine."

"Oh, I see. I'm both, actually. I used to be a thoracic surgeon, and I have a PhD in biology."

"That's pretty impressive, too."

Schroeder gave me an "aw-shucks" smile.

"How long have you been working here?" I asked.

"Oh, I'm one of the originals. I was a good friend of Dr. Gluckmann's; I came on when the company started up in 1989."

"Dr. Gluckmann?"

"One of our founders. The company was originally named Gluckmann Enterprises. Unfortunately, Dr. Gluckmann was killed on the Mount Lemmon highway back in 1992."

"Oh yes, I remember reading about that. What's Mount Lemmon?"

"It's a ski area north of here, about an hour-and-a-half drive. Beautiful country, but the road is treacherous. Dr. Gluckmann fell asleep and drove over a cliff."

"How long have you known Dr. Anthony?"

"I met him at about the same time I met Dr. Gluckmann. Back in 1987 or so."

"You know, we've talked on the phone, but I've never met Dr. Anthony face to face. What's he like in person?"

Schroeder waited a second before answering.

"He's easier to deal with over the phone," he mumbled, sipping his iced tea.

"Oh. Does he have some pet peeve I need to worry about?"

"No, nothing like that. But he does have quite a temper, and he's better at keeping it out of his voice than his face." He frowned, apparently came to some decision, then leaned towards me.

"Frankly, I was surprised he gave you that grant; your articles seem apprehensive about things Dr. Anthony calls 'doomsday hogwash.' "

"Really?" I said, also surprised. "Then why did he hire me?"

"Public relations convinced him that sponsoring you would be good publicity, whatever you said."

"That's not exactly encouraging."

"I'm sorry. Maybe I'm exaggerating. From your record you're obviously a good doctor, and it probably will be good for the company to support your writing. All I'm saying is that Dr. Anthony is . . . well, if you have the gift of tact, use it."

"Thank you for the warning."

"Perhaps Dr. Anthony feels that once you understand what we're doing here, some of your reservations will fall by the wayside. However . . ." Schroeder paused.

I looked up and saw someone else approaching: a portly balding man also wearing a lab coat. He leaned over our table. Schroeder and I stood up.

"My, my, aren't we formal," the newcomer said.

"Dr. Jacobson, Dr. Devaney," Schroeder made introductions.

"Call me Ed, please," the portly man said, shaking my hand, "and you'll also notice everybody here calls this bum 'Eric.' " He nodded towards Dr. Schroeder.

"Just don't call Dr. Anthony 'Harold,' " Schroeder said.

"Are you going to be working here, Dr. Jacobson?" Devaney asked.

"Uh, not exactly."

"Dr. Jacobson will be working at the Clinic," Schroeder explained, "and Dr. Anthony's also given him a writing grant."

"So Eric is giving you the grand tour?"

"Yes."

"Well I guess you'll coming to my lab soon."

"Ed is one of the researchers working on the human genome," Schroeder put in.

"Mostly I'm working on getting fat. What pastries are good today?"

"Croissants. I'll get you a couple and a cup of coffee. You talk to Dr. Jacobson." Schroeder got up and walked over to the buffet table. Ed Devaney sat down.

"Croissants," Ed said, turning towards me. "Light, flaky and full of cholesterol. Just what I don't need. So you're going to help Allen Deerborn deliver babies?"

"Well, I suppose so," I said. "Although I imagine there'll be only one obstetrician per mother."

"Not over there. Women at the Clinic don't have babies, they have litters. Do you have much experience with multiple births?"

"I've delivered several sets of twins and one set of triplets."

"You'll see some quads at the Clinic, believe me. So what do you write about?"

"Well, in a broad sense, the impact of biotechnology on ethics and society."

"You have some journal articles out?"

"Actually, no. But I've had three articles published in the *Chicago*

Tribune. One was reprinted in *Reader's Digest*. And I used to guest-host a radio talk-show in Chicago."

"Oh! You're that guy!" Ed exclaimed. I must have made a face, because he shook his head. "I'm sorry, that didn't sound very nice, did it? Actually, I read the thing you had in *Reader's Digest*; Eric was passing it around. It's not the sort of writing I do, but then again, *Reader's Digest* has never reprinted anything of mine. How do you like the Institute so far?"

"It's pretty impressive. And pretty hard to get into."

"Ain't that the truth."

"Why all the precautions?"

"Well, this is a paranoid industry. There's a rush to patent genes, which always seems strange to me, that you can patent something just because you've figured out what it does. The problem is: that information is easy to steal."

"I just deliver babies."

"Sure. I bet you really have a little camera in your tie-clip."

I turned and saw Eric Schroeder carrying a tray loaded with more croissants, coffee, and iced tea.

"What am I missing, gentlemen?" he asked.

"Dr. Devaney was just accusing me of industrial espionage," I said. Eric winced theatrically.

"That's not a topic for light conversation here. You better watch out around Ed. He's an inveterate prankster."

"You're a fine one to talk," said Ed.

After the coffee we finished the tour. The rest of the building went by in a blur, though I suspected there was a great deal I hadn't seen, maybe wasn't even supposed to see. Then Eric escorted me back down to the outer room of Anthony's office, where I waited some more. After a further half hour I began to wonder if Anthony was going to blow me off for the entire day. I was toying with the idea of leaving when the secretary walked over and said:

"Dr. Anthony will see you now."

She ushered me into his office. Anthony remained seated behind a large desk in a very large leather chair. I walked over and offered to shake hands. He grunted and motioned to a plain wooden chair placed so that the sun shone full in my face.

"Dr. Jacobson," Anthony began, "I enjoyed your articles. You write very well."

"Thank you, sir," I said. I hadn't sirred anyone in years, but some instinct warned me to revive the habit.

"Of course, the content is complete and utter horseshit, but at least your writing is entertaining."

I looked back at him, flabbergasted, trying to see if the remark was softened by his expression. But all I could see was his silhouette.

"You're probably wondering why I gave you that grant if I disagree with your opinions," he continued. "As I said, you write well. I think it's in the interest of the field that intelligent voices be heard, even voices I disagree with. But if I eventually convert you to my way of thinking, well, so much the better."

It seemed I was to be tested. "Your way of thinking on what?" I asked.

Anthony gave a soft huff, shuffled some papers. "Well, here's one example. Right here you talk about how genome alterations might affect average men and women. Why do you worry about *average* people? We have too many average people to begin with. I think biotech offers great hope in that area, particularly with some of our more disadvantaged cultural groups."

"Disadvantaged cultural groups?"

"Yes. Say you have a family, maybe Hispanic, with a history of welfare dependency. Soon it will be possible to identify the gene sequence responsible for that group's low intelligence, lack of initiative, and so on. We could replace that sequence with something more beneficial."

That group? This was blatant racism, barely hidden by scientific jargon. My third article had condemned far less offensive genetic tinkering, and I felt obliged to voice some objection now. After all, hadn't my articles gotten me this job in the first place?

"Well, even assuming that upbringing and environment aren't the larger factors . . ." I started.

"I'm firmly convinced they're not — I think the nature versus nurture debate has pretty much been settled."

"Well, even assuming that; wouldn't it make you uneasy to tinker with human genes that way?"

"Not really. What's wrong with being smarter and less lazy?"

"Nothing, at least in the abstract. But how do we know what other personality traits are affected by this supposed gene for intelligence?"

"Go on," Anthony said.

"What if you came up with a brilliant sociopath, for instance, or a brilliant manic-depressive? And if a little intelligence is good, is a lot better? What would a person with an I.Q. of 300 be like? How would he or she treat people of more routine intellects?"

Anthony seemed pleased, if not convinced.

"Not to mention religious concerns," I continued, and immediately realized I'd made a mistake.

"Don't tell me you have religious concerns," he muttered. "You sound like my goddamn mother."

"I meant other people's religious concerns," I hurriedly explained. "As a businessman, you need to take into account the beliefs and, uh, prejudices of most Americans."

"Now you sound like one of those public relations boneheads I hire."

"I'm sorry, sir."

He leaned back, and though I still couldn't make out his face, at least his body seemed more relaxed. "Now," he said, "other traits carried with intelligence genes; that's a legitimate worry. But what if we find that mostly positive personality traits are linked with intelligence?"

I was somewhat reassured. Perhaps Anthony was only playing devil's advocate. But then he continued.

"Let's discuss another undesirable trait. Since it seems there's a genetic component to homosexuality, we might find a cure for it in the same way we're hoping to cure sickle-cell anemia."

"But do most homosexuals want to be . . . 'cured'?"

He leaned forward, and for the first time I could really see his face. It wore a fierce expression.

"What's that got to do with anything?"

"Well, do you think something like that should be done against people's will?"

He considered this for a moment, leaning back. The sunlight was behind him again and all I could see was the outline of his close-cropped hair.

"No, of course not," he finally said. "I mean, if we could identify the trait in an infant, or even prenatally, then we could do something about it. The goddamn civil libertarians might let us get away with that."

"I've often wondered," I hesitantly offered, "why homosexuality shows such genetic persistence."

"What do you mean?" Anthony growled.

"Well, assuming that homosexuals have fewer children, one would also assume that the trait would gradually die out."

Anthony grunted. I continued.

"Perhaps it's linked to something positive. Maybe groups with homosexuals have survival benefits we don't currently understand."

"You can't be serious."

"Well, you were talking about sickle-cell anemia, and it has benefits as a recessive gene — it gives increased resistance to malaria."

"That doesn't mean every undesirable trait has good side effects," Anthony said. "And besides, malaria won't be much of a problem in the 21st century. We'll see to that."

I wondered if Anthony had a genetic scheme for mosquitoes also. Perhaps make all the males gay?

While I sat contemplating a sudden vision of nattily dressed insects engrossed in tiny copies of *Gentleman's Quarterly*, Anthony seemed to be thinking also. I hadn't been given an end-time for our meeting, but it was to be far shorter than I'd expected. Anthony sighed, then called his secretary.

"When's my next appointment?" he barked into the intercom.

"Five minutes, Dr. Anthony."

"All right," he replied, and then turned his attention back to me.

"Like I said, I don't expect you to agree with me — I just want to support intelligent discussion. Write what you want, just as long as Anthony Enterprises is mentioned prominently as sponsor. And the correspondence for publication goes through our offices and everything you write gets screened by our scientists — since you're not a specialist in the field we don't want you inadvertently giving away any trade secrets. We'll talk some more next month."

And he waved his hand towards the door and returned to shuffling through papers on his desk. I saw myself out. After keeping me waiting for hours, Harold Anthony had talked to me for about five minutes.

Eddie was waiting dutifully with his hot-rod magazine. He escorted me back to the gate, gave my car one final inspection, and sent me on my way.

Driving home, I took stock. On the whole I was pleased with my first visit to the Institute. But I wasn't quite as comfortable when I thought about Dr. Anthony himself.

Why had Anthony given me a grant? To encourage "a variety of intelligent voices"? Somehow I doubted that. I had the unpleasant feeling that my new "boss" considered both me and my articles idiotic. I also had the impression that, after sounding me out, Anthony had forced himself to end the discussion. But why?

About halfway home I began to wonder if Eric Schroeder had been hinting broadly at the real situation while we'd eaten our croissants. Dr. Anthony's opinions might smell of Mengele or Eichmann, but smells could be hidden with a suitable perfume. If selling Anthony's opinions was inherently impossible, then my more mainstream outlook (published with the highly visible support of Anthony Enterprises) would serve as a Trojan Horse for Dr. Anthony's brave new world. In essence, Eric was saying, I had two choices: I could either agree with Dr. Anthony and further his agenda, or I could disagree with Dr. Anthony and further his agenda.

Of course, I thought, a blunt exposé of Anthony's worldview would hardly benefit the company. And didn't I have Anthony's permission to do just that? "Write whatever you want," he'd told me. But then another phrase whispered in my memory, something about how everything I published would be screened by company scientists. It sounded reasonable, but could those "scientists" delete anything the company didn't like? I resolved to have a lawyer look at my contract.

Three-quarters of the way home, the exact wording of that document came back to me. I didn't need a lawyer to tell me what I'd signed; the situation was as clear as the Tucson sky, that endless washed-out blue that already made me long for a week of gloomy weather. If I ever published something that displeased Anthony, my "grant" would come to an immediate end, courtesy of a little clause allowing either party to cancel the arrangement at any time. I could also be sued for breach of contract if a negative article about Anthony was published without prior clearance, because prior clearance was a clear condition of our agreement. And I felt sure that anything negative I wrote about the Institute or Anthony would never pass through Anthony's hands without immediate and thorough castration.

And by the time I pulled up to my fancy new luxury apartment, rented with the first installment of Dr. Anthony's money, I felt rather ball-less myself.

Chapter 3

I'd like to say my encounter with Anthony made me rethink my outlook on life, but all it did was trigger a few nagging doubts. Since they happened mostly after midnight, I thought of these as *late-at-nights*, three words said very fast in honor of their short duration and small effect. For instance, *late-at-night* I might consider quitting my new job — but the next morning I'd consider my bank balance, and think of ways to ingratiate myself to my new boss. Or *late-at-night* I'd decide greed was the root of all evil (witness my current predicament) — but the next afternoon I'd wonder whether I could trade in my Miata for a BMW. And *late-at-night* I'd regret treating Beverly like an attractive genitalia-stroking household appliance — but the next two a.m. might well find me entertaining a young lady with nothing else in mind. My "new life" in Tucson was plagued by ennui, inertia, a boredom with medicine and a disinclination to write.

My boredom with medicine was particularly unfortunate. Allen Deerborn — the Clinic's other OB/GYN — had written a highly regarded study on multiple pregnancies, far better credentials for a fertility-clinic physician than my paltry résumé. But his arrival at the Clinic three years earlier had been unheralded, whereas mine was trumpeted loudly by a newspaper article that made me sound like a combination Jonas Salk and Shakespeare. Allen, understandably miffed, reacted by giving me unsolicited medical advice at every opportunity. Patronizing as this was, he knew his subject, and if I'd listened politely I might have made a friend and been a better doctor to this day. But I ignored him as pointedly as I could.

I ignored other opportunities as well. My practice was new so my medical schedule wasn't demanding. I should have used my free time to write or do research, but whenever I sat down at a computer I remembered that my soul was now owned by Anthony Enterprises. I would have gotten nothing done if it hadn't been for Eric Schroeder and Ed Devaney.

They knew my bio-tech knowledge was shallow, but instead of denouncing me as a fraud they pestered me to study, then got me access to some fairly hush-hush projects — Eric by making a fuss with Institute bureaucrats, Ed by sheer gall — he'd have me tag along with him as if we owned the place, and sure enough, the guards usually thought we did. Eric also e-mailed me a reading list, and Ed convinced some fellow scientists to fill me in on their latest experiments in layman's language, i.e., words containing no more than twenty-five syllables.

The two had very different habits. Ed practically lived at the Institute, and while we sometimes ate lunch or breakfast together on the top floor, I never saw him away from work. Eric was more outgoing, perhaps because he had no children and his wife had died of pancreatic cancer five or six years before. He invited me to lunch often, lunches pointedly eaten away from the Institute cafe, odd afternoons where he quaffed endless glasses of iced tea and talked a mile a minute. Much of what he told me was flattering to neither Harold Anthony nor his company, and some of it, including tales of industrial espionage straight out of James Bond, seemed beyond belief. But then, Eric was fond of things that were beyond belief. As I found out at our first lunch, when the discussion somehow returned to corn.

"So how is that experiment coming?" I asked.

Eric leaned across the table and said in a low voice: "Can you keep a secret?"

"Sure. What happened?"

"Well, you remember we were going to take the fiber gene out of hemp and put it into corn."

"I take it the botanists failed."

"They got the wrong gene." He paused theatrically, then whispered, "Instead of corn you can make rope from, they got corn you can make dope from."

"You're kidding."

"Hell, no! One of the botanists ate a few ears and got high as a kite. It was full of THC. And it's perfectly legal! I checked the statute myself. Marijuana is the controlled substance, not its active ingredient. Even the laws banning THC are written that way. They ban marijuana, hashish, or any other product distilled or manufactured from cannabis. This corn is like a designer drug — they can't touch you." He reached down towards his briefcase, opened it, and pulled out a small brown-paper bag. "You want to try some?" he asked.

"What do you do, smoke it?"

"I guess you could, but it would probably be bad for your lungs. THC is fat-soluble. Shell it and sauté the kernels in a little butter or oil. Take this, I've got plenty more at home." And he handed me the bag, which contained four ears of fresh corn.

I'd like to say I didn't believe him, but the truth is, I went home, prepared and ate the corn, then waited impatiently to get stoned. After two hours passed and nothing happened, I had a sudden inspiration. Rummaging around my apartment, I found Eric's "genetically engineered" eggplant. A careful inspection revealed the words "Made in China" molded into its dark underside. And at our next lunchtime meeting I found Eric sucking on an unlit corncob pipe, a wicked grin spread across his bony face.

But even with help like that I accomplished remarkably little my first two months in Tucson. I met with Anthony twice. I was half-expecting him to criticize my slow start, but he didn't. He seemed distant, his mind miles away, and apart from commenting that it might take time for me to settle in, he didn't remark on my idleness.

Disillusioned with both writing and medicine, I dusted off a teenage passion. My guitar playing hadn't been improved by twelve years of neglect, but now I had enough money to get a first-rate instrument. I bought an expensive Spanish guitar which needed some minor repairs. But when I asked about repairmen at Tucson music stores, I was consistently told:

"Well, there's only one good *classical* guitar guy in town. Joe somethin'. I can't remember his last name, but his card's here somewhere." Then the clerk would lead me to a bulletin board plastered with ads from local musicians, and I'd find myself gazing at a cheaply printed business card with the slogan:

"Whacked Your Ax? I'll Fix It Fast! / Joe's Guitarworks / Instrumental Repairs and Fine Lutherie." Across the card's middle were two badly drawn guitars — an electric and a classical — their necks broken and jagged holes sketched into their bodies.

The card sent a disturbingly mixed message — like a French restaurant advertised as "Joe's House of Snails." But I was assured time and again that Joe was the only local competent to repair my six-thousand-dollar toy, so I finally called him and arranged to drop the guitar off at his home workshop, which turned out to be located in a run-down stucco ranch house in an iffy neighborhood.

* * *

When I knocked, a Hispanic woman in her mid-twenties opened the door. She was short and stocky, but baggy jeans and a loose shirt couldn't hide an excellent figure. Jet-black hair hung past her shoulders. She wasn't unpleasant to look at, nor was she a woman to cause most men to stare. I wasn't most men, however, and it took me longer to speak than was strictly polite.

"I'm looking for Joe's Guitarworks," I said.

"You've found it," she replied curtly, and I knew she'd caught me staring. "Come on back."

She turned and I followed her through a short hall into what apparently doubled as workshop and living room. The workshop part was clean and organized — but the living area was a disaster; its only amenities a sawdust-coated TV, a ratty couch, and a haphazardly crammed bookshelf. A tall, bearded man with a ponytail was sitting at the workbench re-fretting somebody's Stratocaster.

"You must be Mr. Jacobson," he said, getting up and shaking my hand. The woman stood beside me, looking at Joe meaningfully. "Oh," he continued, "and this is my girlfriend, Maria Velasquez."

"Fiancé," Maria corrected him.

"Excuse me, my fiancé," Joe said. "We got engaged last month."

"Recently enough for *me* to remember," she mumbled, then turned and sat on the couch.

Joe ignored her; apparently this tone of voice was a common occurrence. Glancing down at my guitar case he asked, "You say you've got a buzz?" then gently put the case on his workbench, took the guitar out, and began tapping the top. When he tapped behind the bridge there was an ugly rattle.

"It's got a loose brace," he said. "I can glue it back for, oh, about eighty bucks." He sat back down and played a few chords. "Don't worry, it's nothing serious. When I'm done, this thing will sound wonderful. Man, Bernabe makes sweet guitars."

This was perhaps all that needed to be said, but I didn't really want to leave quite yet. His fiancé was still on the couch, and I made a show of looking around the room so I could look at her. In addition to Maria I saw two classical guitars hanging on the wall.

"What are those?" I asked, in a conversational tone.

"Oh, those are mine," he said softly, "I mean ones I made. Want to try one?"

He put my guitar in its case, walked over to the rear wall and took down the guitar closest to us. Then he pulled another stool over, dusted it off, and motioned for me to sit.

As I picked up his guitar I was preparing to be tactful, but after I'd strummed a few chords I realized tact wasn't needed. I must have looked pleased, because when I glanced up, Joe was smiling.

"Very nice," I said grudgingly. "How long have you been making instruments?"

"Oh, three or four years. That's my thirty-fifth guitar."

"Have you sold many?"

"A few. You make that one sound good. Play it some more."

Which I did. I remained impressed and decided to stick around for a while. Joe took down another guitar, and rattled off a few licks better than I would have expected from a repairman. Then he grabbed some music and we tried some duets. I was enjoying myself completely until I looked over and saw Maria still sitting on the couch, immersed in a book. Joe and I had made no effort to draw her into the conversation, but I don't like to be ignored, so I launched into "Asturias," a Spanish warhorse guaranteed to make any audience burst into wild applause, if one can actually play it, that is. My memory failed about twenty bars in — my fingers had given up long before that. Maria, oblivious, kept on reading her book. There was an awkward silence.

"I worked on that piece for six months and then gave up," Joe finally said. "You want some coffee?"

I glanced at a cup sitting on the floor. A furry mass floated on top.

"Joe," Maria said from the depths of her book, "you shouldn't expect people to drink your coffee if you leave moldy cups of it standing around." She looked at me for only the second time since I'd come in. "Don't worry, I washed some other mugs a couple of hours ago. The coffeepot, too. Joe was supposed to bring me the cups from in here but . . ."

Joe got the hint, began gathering mugs.

"Come on in the kitchen," he said, his long fingers now wrapped through about five handles. "I'll make us a fresh pot."

It took Joe two minutes to find the coffee scoop and another minute to remember where he'd put the coffee. We leaned against the counter as it brewed.

"So you just moved to Tucson?" he asked.

"Yes. I was living in Chicago."

"You like it here?"

"Well, I don't really know my way around yet. I understand the Mexican food is good."

"Where have you eaten?"

I mentioned two restaurants near the university.

"That's tourist food," he said. "I know some really good places."

"Are there other good restaurants in town?" I asked, "Besides Mexican, that is."

"Sure. Maria's family runs two great Cuban places. That's where she's from. You ever had Cuban coffee?" He glanced at the coffeepot. "It's good but it's strong."

"Stronger than what's in there?" He'd put almost half a can into the grounds-basket.

"Yeah. I watered this down a little. You'll love it."

"How did you get into making guitars?" I asked, partly to distract myself from Joe's coffee, which looked suspiciously like used motor oil as it dripped into the pot.

"I got interested halfway through college. I was studying engineering and I started making guitars as a hobby."

"What happened to the engineering?"

"I decided it might not be for me. I had . . . well, some unpopular opinions."

"Opinions about what?"

"Oh, politics. And the environment."

"Did I hear the word 'environment'?" Maria called from the living room. "You better look out, Mr. Jamison."

"His name's Jacobson," Joe called back.

"Well, Mr. Jacobson, don't encourage him — Joe can get a bit tedious when he talks about the 'environment.' Yesterday he lectured some poor customer for ten minutes because he didn't have enough air in his tires."

"Honey, I was carrying his guitar out and I saw he was driving around on four flats. You know how much gas that wastes? And I just happened to have a tire gauge in my pocket."

"My point exactly. How many luthiers carry around tire gauges?"

Joe didn't answer, instead he turned to the dish-drainer and got three mismatched mugs, then poured coffee, milk, and a truly shocking dose of sugar into each. "Shit," he muttered, looking up at me, "I hope you didn't want it black."

"I'll try it your way," I said. I grabbed one mug, Joe grabbed two, and we walked back into the living room. As Joe handed her a cup

Maria laid her book down: *Gravity's Rainbow*, a stream-of-consciousness "masterpiece" I'd tried to read in college. I'd given up after twenty pages; Maria was almost at the end.

"That's the book about V-2's, isn't it?" I asked.

"Among other things," Maria said. "Do you like Pynchon?"

"I can't really say," I said. "I only got three-hundred pages into that one. It was more than I had time for in pre-med."

"You're a doctor?" Maria said, catching my hint. But Joe wasn't impressed.

"You did better with that dumb book than me. I got about five pages into it. I prefer writers who use punctuation."

"You prefer dorky science fiction," Maria replied.

Joe tried a brief defense of his literary taste, so Maria turned the conversation from *Gravity's Rainbow* to several other good books Joe hadn't read, books she thought he ought to get started on soon, while Joe insisted that *Calvin and Hobbes* was at least as deep as Mr. Python or Piss-On or whatever his name was. I said nothing — I didn't want Maria or Joe to look over and see the growing bulge in my pants. Alarmed, I tried to get some relief by pondering the phenomenon itself: just what did I find attractive about this shabbily dressed Cuban girl? The tactic proved anything but deflating. After a while I sensed my silence might be more noticeable than my erection, so I decided to stage an exit. I glanced at my watch and was surprised to see I'd been there forty minutes.

"I have to go back to work," I interrupted. "But, listen, why don't we all get together this weekend, maybe eat at one of those restaurants you were talking about. My treat."

"Work," Maria said, "did you hear that Joe? He's got some work to do. Didn't you tell that guy you'd have his Stratocaster refretted by tomorrow?"

"Unfortunately," Joe said. "Oh, speaking of work, I didn't get your phone number. Where can I get a hold of you?"

"I work at a place called the Anthony Clinic," I said, getting out one of my new cards, which reminded me that the only thing I had from Joe was his phone number scrawled on a piece of scrap paper. "Do you have a business card handy?"

Joe reached for his wallet, but Maria was faster: she grabbed her purse and gave me one of Joe's cards inside of five seconds. I glanced at it. "You know," I said to Joe, "nobody at the music stores knows your last name, and it's not on your card, either."

"It's Anthony," Maria said quickly, "Joseph Anthony."

A slight tension had entered the room. I looked at Joe.

"That's funny," I said. "You have the same last name as my new boss."

"Well, I don't know if it's funny," Joe replied, "but it's perfectly natural. Harold Anthony is my father."

Chapter 4

Cuckolding the boss's son is rarely good office politics, and as I walked out of Joe's house I resolved to make no attempt to seduce Maria Velasquez. But by the time I got home, I'd thought of several good reasons to go right ahead.

For starters, Anthony hadn't told me he had a guitar-making son in town, though my guitar-playing had come up twice in our ten-minute, once-monthly "conversations." And Joe wasn't living like the heir of a multi-millionaire. Perhaps there was a bone of contention between father and son, maybe a brown-skinned young lady from a "disadvantaged cultural group," a young woman who would look far better lying nude on my satin sheets than she did in baggy jeans on Joe's battered couch. It bore looking into.

A few days later I met Eric Schroeder for lunch and coaxed him into outlining the Anthony family soap opera. Actually, "coaxed" is the wrong word. It was enthusiastically delivered, mixed with stray bits of masticated *chile rellenos.*

"I met Joseph Anthony the other day," I said, far enough into the conversation not to be too obvious.

"Harold's son? How'd that happen?"

"I went over to his house to get a guitar repaired. I had no idea they were related until we got to talking. Why didn't Dr. Anthony tell he's got a son in town?"

"Probably because they don't get along."

"Really? How come?"

"Family baggage, I'd guess."

"Like what?"

"Oh, nothing unusual. Joe's mom divorced Dr. Anthony when Joe was ten, and she took Joe with her to Minneapolis. From what I hear, after that Dr. Anthony alternated between ignoring Joe and putting long-distance pressure on him to be a great scientist. Joe got into MIT, but he dropped out last year to spend more time making guitars. Harold feels like Joe came back to Tucson just to rub that little career change in his face. And then, Joe's something of a treehugger."

"Why's that a problem?"

"Because Joe thinks genetic engineering is a potential environmental disaster."

"Dr. Anthony doesn't take kindly to that, I suppose."

"Nope."

"I thought Anthony was still married."

"He's on, oh . . . number three now. Pretty young thing without a brain in her head. Or maybe she's just smart enough to appear that way." He took another gulp of iced tea and sighed. "Poor old Harold, I bet he'll be on number four before too long."

"I met Joe's fiancé too," I put in, trying to steer the conversation towards Maria. "Pretty lady."

"She's another reason Joe and Harold don't get along." He shifted uneasily. "Tell me, what's she like?"

"I've only seen her once. But she seems nice enough."

"Does she speak any English at all?"

I looked at Eric, surprised. This Anglo assumption wasn't like him.

"She's fluent," I said. "Got a rather sharp tongue, at that."

"What's she dress like? Kind of wild? Sexy?"

"Like a frumpy college student. What on earth have you heard about her?"

Eric chuckled. "I should have known. My only source has been Dr. Anthony. Maria is really why Joe moved back here, and Harold hates her guts."

"What has he told you?"

"Well," he said, "it's probably all bullshit. Tell you what, I'll give you the party line from Harold the Great and you tell me how much of it's wrong."

"Well, fine. But keep in mind I've just met her."

"Sure." He motioned to the waitress for more tea. "Let's see, Dr. Anthony on the subject of Maria Velasquez . . . He says she can't speak any English."

"She speaks English quite well, thank you. And reads it well, too, judging by the books she likes."

"Okay, strike one for Harold," Eric said. "He also says that she and her family are all on welfare."

"According to Joe, her parents own *two* restaurants."

"I guess that's another strike." Eric said, then hesitated, perhaps embarrassed by his next bit of gossip. "Finally, Anthony says Maria is a 'Mexican wet-backed slut.' He says her back's wet because she stopped halfway across the Rio Grande just to get screwed."

"That's at least half a strike," I laughed. "She's from Cuba."

"Well," Eric said charitably, "geography was never Dr. Anthony's strong suit. I'm glad Joe's found such a nice girl."

I was glad, too. Though I planned to double-check Eric's report, it sounded as if Dr. Anthony would be ecstatic if I stole Maria from Joe. And Maria's supposed sluttiness sounded promising, too. Even Dr. Anthony couldn't be wrong all of the time.

My scheme for bedding Maria was simple. Step one: cultivate a friendship with Joe, which would give me an excuse to also become friends with Maria. Step two: pry Maria away from him. Step two would be easier if Joe proved to be a jerk, and I was encouraged by his 60's-era beard and ponytail. The hippies I'd known mouthed lofty slogans, but were really only interested in sex, booze, and marijuana. Only stupid women stayed with them long, and Maria seemed anything but stupid.

But as I got to know Joe I got a little worried. He didn't mouth lofty slogans, but he did seem to live by a few. He didn't smoke, didn't chase other women, was never drunk and rarely tipsy. He met panhandlers' requests for spare change with spare bills, and volunteered three times a month at the local homeless shelter. He sponsored two Guatemalan orphans via the Christian Children's Fund, kept their pictures plastered all over his house. Mr. Environment himself, he recycled every scrap of his garbage, owned a car but rarely drove it; refused to use endangered tropical hardwoods in his guitars. And despite her teasing, I soon realized that Maria loved and admired this overgrown Boy Scout.

I saw them both at least twice a week that fall — watching videos, hiking in the Catalina Mountains, or eating lunch at a Velasquez family restaurant. I'd hoped to get some help from Maria's parents, but I was disappointed there, too. Maria's mother always greeted Joe with a hug and a kiss, her father would come out of the kitchen and shake his hand, and her teenaged sisters would serve him lunch, dinner and suggestions. ("Hey Jooo . . . ey, if you don't like the dish at your table remember I'm off on Wednesdays.") Joe responded to their outrageous propositions with outrageous tips, and Maria would sometimes scoop half the money off the table and hand it back to him, saying "Joe, don't be ridiculous," or muttering something about "muerte" and "mis hermanas."

My flirtations with Maria were less obvious, mostly gallant comments and self-mocking chivalry. But though she often flirted back, I began to fear Anthony's calling her a "Mexican-wetback slut" was a moral as well as geographic mistake. Maria spent many evenings at Joe's, but she usually left before I did, and I never saw her there in the morning. And though I could only guess what they did when I wasn't around, her occasional warnings to an amorous Joe made me worry that Maria might be almost as chaste as her Biblical namesake.

But I soldiered on. Initially, I'd hoped to make a move on Maria after three or four weeks, perhaps a clandestine invitation to something Joe couldn't possibly afford, maybe an opera or musical in Phoenix, maybe even grabbing a morning plane to San Francisco and flying back that night. Or with luck, not flying back that night — and instead sipping champagne in a five-star hotel, sharing a balcony view of the moonlit harbor, and then at last feeling Maria's brown body surging wavelike beneath mine.

But for some ill-defined reason I delayed step two of my grand seduction, which was why I found myself over at Joe's house one night, doing nothing but talking, fully four months after we'd met.

"Is that so?" Maria was saying, a large glass of wine in her right hand and a smile on her face. "Well, let me tell you, your reasoning is every bit as screwed-up as theirs."

She was as tipsy as I'd ever seen her, and Joe also seemed to be feeling no pain, but I was reluctantly sober. My next "on call" started at six a.m.

"But they're nuts!" I protested, leaning over for the last piece of pizza.

"Do you think I'm a nut just because I go to Mass?" Maria asked.

"I think you're wasting your time."

"That's what I like about you, Peter. You're as tactful as you are logical."

"You don't think I'm any more logical than this?" I asked, waving around a small blue booklet. Earlier that evening, some amateur evangelists had shown up at Joe's front door. By the time they left, Joe had two of their tracts and they had five more dollars. A donation.

"I thought they were nice," Joe said.

"You think everybody's nice," Maria laughed. "If I was selling something I'd love coming to your house."

"You don't think I'm more logical than this booklet?" I persisted.

"Not when you're using the same so-called reasoning."

"How am I doing that?"

"Your gripe with that booklet is what? Tell me again."

"Well . . ." I glanced through some of the bold-faced headings. "How about this: 'Fulfilled Prophecies Prove Biblical Infallibility!'? What bullshit! The New Testament fulfills the Old because it was written by people who knew their Torah cover-to-cover."

"You mean scroll-to-scroll," Joe put in.

"All right, scroll-to-scroll."

"Look," Maria said, "if you had a medical text with a few errors, would you assume that everything in it was wrong?"

"If the errors all fit somebody's ulterior motives, I might. As far as Christianity's concerned, I think a bunch of Jews changed the life story of some wandering rabbi to fit their prophecies, then stuck all those claims of divinity in later. After all, if Jesus thought he was divine, why did he call himself the 'Son of Man'?"

"So you've actually read what we're discussing?" Maria asked.

"I took a course called the 'Bible as Literature' in college," I admitted. "I needed an elective."

"A regular religious scholar!"

"Well, whether I'm a religious scholar or not, I know the early Christians had a good motive to do a little embroidering. I mean, which line works better at reeling in the credulous masses? 'Our founder is a Jewish carpenter,' or 'our Founder is the Son of God, who just happened to *disguise* himself as a Jewish carpenter.' "

"You're still dodging my question. Why did those people from the church make you so mad?"

"Why? Because every time I write an article, I get dozens of letters from wackos like them. They act like they're reasoning, but they're utterly impervious to reason. And their letters are just like this little booklet."

"How?"

"Well, all this does is quote one part of a document as proof of a different part of the same document. You could quote the *Koran* that way and 'prove' Islam, or the *Torah* and 'prove' Judaism, or the *Book of Mormon* and 'prove' that Joseph Smith was a prophet instead of a schizophrenic con man."

"You've read all of those?" Maria asked.

"No, but I bet I'm right. It doesn't matter which religion you're talking about. People who believe in God love to turn off their brains and then act like they're proving something. What a crock."

"You sound like my father," Joe said quietly. I was a little taken aback. That wasn't a compliment from Joe's lips.

"How's that?" I asked.

"My father's not content with just being an atheist. He won't be happy until nobody else believes in anything, either. That's thanks to his mother, I guess. She taught him religion with a belt." He looked up and smiled, but it seemed a bit forced. "Maria's more reasonable. She's only gonna' lash you with her tongue."

"You think she's winning this discussion?"

"Not yet. But she will; I have faith in her. Though like all good faith, it's tinged with fear." Maria shot him a dirty look. "I mean . . . fear in an intellectual sense," he amended.

"I sense a challenge," I said.

"Just a warning."

"She can't win this one because she's wrong. Now Maria, are you going to tell me the people who wrote this booklet have proved anything logically?"

"No, because that wasn't what I said. I said you were no more logical than they were. As far as the booklet goes, I agree with you: they haven't proved anything. But the way you always 'disprove' anything religious works the same way."

"Like how?"

"Well, you told me earlier you don't think any of the miracles in the Bible could have happened. Why?"

"I've never seen a miracle. I don't know anyone who's seen one."

"I've never seen Paris, but I believe it's there."

"Come on Maria, that's hardly the same thing."

"What if you knew people who said they'd seen miracles? I know people who say they've been to Paris. Plenty of people say they've seen miracles. Even some scientists say they've seen things they can't explain."

"But they're deluded. Miracles don't happen because that's against the natural order of things."

"But that's exactly what a miracle is: something that's against the natural order. Your 'reasoning' is just as tautological as theirs. When you cut through the bull, that booklet says the Bible is true because the Bible says it's true. You believe there aren't miracles because you believe miracles can't happen. They quote from a document to prove the same document, you quote your beliefs to prove your beliefs."

"I think she's got you, Peter."

"And what do you think, Maria?" I asked, a little nettled.

"That wasn't the question," she said, then leaned forward and reached for her wine glass.

"I'm not going to take that for an answer," I shot back. "You've just jumped all over my tautological rear end; I ought to get a chance to jump all over yours."

"Watch it, buddy," Joe said. "This rear end's reserved." He patted Maria's hip.

"I think you've had enough to drink," Maria said, gently removing his hand. She took the jug away from his side of the table and poured its last remnants into her own glass. Then she turned to me.

"To answer your question, Peter, I'm a good Catholic girl. I believe what the priest and the catechism tell me."

"Oh, sure."

"Well, let's say I think that all religions are moderately true."

"That sounds more like it." But the line sounded familiar, and I wondered if my leg was being pulled.

"Just don't buy any used yaks from her," Joe warned.

"*Kung Fu*?"

"You are getting close, little grasshopper."

I had it. "*Lost Horizon*."

"The only decent book Maria ever made me read."

Maria didn't apologize. "Just because it's a borrowed line doesn't mean I don't believe it."

"Well Maria, you've converted me," I said. "As soon as I get off work tomorrow I'll go down to the Zen Baptist synagogue and get a prayer wheel and rosary. But I'm on call in the morning, and it's time I went home."

Maria looked at her own watch and winced. "I better go home too," she said, "it's getting late and I'll need to catch a bus."

"You didn't drive?" Joe asked.

"No, Mr. Air Pollution, I didn't drive."

"It's awfully late to be riding the bus," Joe said, sitting up slowly. "I'll take you. Let me get my keys."

"I don't think that's a good idea, Joe," she answered, eying the nearly empty jug of wine on the table. "Maybe Peter can take me. You go over that way, don't you?"

"Sure," I said, although I didn't. Maria picked up her purse, gave Joe a perfunctory kiss, and headed for the door. I followed.

* * *

Outside, the sky was clear but dark, lit only by stars and a sliver of moon. Maria was no more than a silhouette, but I didn't need to actually see her to conjure up visions of dancing eyes, brown skin, and long, black hair hanging almost to her waist. She'd given up her usual jeans that night for a peasant dress that showed off her fine legs, and a blouse cut just low enough to reveal the shadow between her breasts. Just above the shadow would be the cross she always wore on a thin gold chain.

At the car, I walked around and opened her door. She looked at me a little strangely and got in. I walked to the driver's side and got in myself.

"Thanks for the ride," she said as soon as we were underway. "Joe wasn't thinking, and he got a little pickled." She giggled. "I'm a little pickled myself."

"He seemed excited about something."

"Yeah. He's thought of some crazy new way to do the braces on his next guitar."

"He didn't say anything about it to me."

"That's my fault, I guess. He's been telling me all about it for days and I finally asked him if he'd please talk about something else."

I didn't answer. Though Maria usually scorned perfume, I'd just noticed the ghost of a fragrance, something she'd put on to go with the dress, and underlying that the scent that was somehow her own, an indefinable but enticing aroma.

But this was not the time. There was no opera, no romantic locale, nothing but my sudden need. So we drove; Maria gave directions, and the tension in my chest grew. I yearned to kiss her, to ravish her, to pledge undying love.

That final thought alarmed me. Maria had fallen uncommonly silent, so in desperation I tried to start a conversation.

"Is it true what Joe said about his grandmother?" I asked.

"Is what true?"

"That she taught Dr. Anthony religion with a belt."

For a moment Maria didn't answer. We were stopped at an intersection, and when I glanced over I could see her face clearly in the light from a gas station. She looked pensive, even sad.

"You know, Joe really likes you," she said, and I wondered if she'd heard my question. "He tells me you're like the older brother he's always wished he had."

I didn't answer. The light changed and I pulled away into the darkness. Maria's face was invisible when she spoke again.

"I guess that's why he said that about his father: he thinks you ought to know who you're working for. But he couldn't really talk about it. I've never heard him talk about his father with anybody, anybody except me that is."

"So it's true? Dr. Anthony's mother beat him?"

"If anything, Joe is sugarcoating it. I feel so sorry for his father sometimes."

"Dr. Anthony doesn't exactly return the concern."

"How do you know?"

"I see him once a month at the Institute. I mentioned that we'd met one time. What he said about you wasn't very flattering."

In fact, it had been brutally obscene. Eric hadn't been exaggerating.

"I know what he thinks about me," she said, "and I try not to hate him for it. The man's sick, and if you knew much about him, you'd understand why."

"All right, I'm curious. Why?"

Maria sighed. For a moment I thought she'd say nothing more. Then her voice came out of the darkness, curiously flat and bloodless.

"The story, at least the way I've heard it, is that Dr. Anthony's father ran out on his mother when Dr. Anthony was four or five. His mother started drinking, and then she got religion, and then she went back to the bottle. The whole cycle happened three or four times."

"How do you know Dr. Anthony isn't exaggerating?"

"Oh, we've never heard any of this from him."

"How do you know about it at all, then?"

Maria paused again, perhaps debating whether she should have told me as much as she had.

"Don't tell me if you don't want to," I said.

Maria made a hissing sound, something she often did when she was trying to make up her mind. "Look," she finally said, "this is kind of personal. But on the other hand, you work for Joe's father and you're friendly with my family, and that's not a good combination. Dr. Anthony scares me, and maybe it's only fair to warn you just what you're getting into."

The words seemed familiar, and then I realized that Eric often hinted at much the same thing.

"So how did you hear about this, if not from Dr. Anthony?"

"The usual kind of roundabout way. Joe told me, I suppose after he heard it from his mother; I can't see Dr. Anthony ever telling Joe about it to his face. So I guess Dr. Anthony told Joe's mother, back once when they still loved each other. It's hard to imagine they ever did love each other, seeing how relations are between them now, but they must have once — Joe wasn't spontaneously generated."

"How does Joe's mother know Dr. Anthony isn't making it all up?"

"Because Joe's Mom used to see Dr. Anthony's mother often — she ended up living in Tucson, and she talked about raising Dr. Anthony all the time. How they'd taken her boy away from her, how those awful Mexican families — he had Chicano foster parents at least once — how those awful Mexicans had ruined him. But the worst thing was that they'd send him back to her."

"Back to whom?"

"Back to his mother."

"Why?"

"Because he grew up in Southeast Texas, and that's a part of the country that takes being 'saved' pretty seriously. All his mother had to do was stumble down the aisle of some new church and her new minister would tell child welfare she was a lost sheep, that if God forgave her drunkenness the state should too, and back young Harold would go. It apparently never occurred to anybody that her religion was a worse problem than the booze. When he got back she'd blame her backsliding on the pressure of raising an evil child like Harold, and the rod would come out at the slightest provocation — I'm talking about a real rod, too: she used to beat him with a broomstick — accompanied with appropriate Old Testament excuses."

"Which explains Dr. Anthony's distaste for religion."

"That and the fact that she used to call him twice a week and tell him he was fooling with God's creation, and that he'd burn in hell for it."

"He kept in touch with her?"

"That's always amazed me. She finally kicked the booze, but never the religion, and she lived to the surprisingly old age of seventy. She must've had a liver made out of cowhide. She died about three or four years ago. Dr. Anthony not only kept in touch with her, he moved her to Tucson and supported her."

"And yet he hates you."

"He has to hate somebody, preferably a woman. I suppose he couldn't bring himself to hate his mother — for years she was the only family he had. So he hates me, and he hates God. But I never planned to take his son away from him. Poor Joe."

We made a turn and my hand brushed her knee as I shifted gears. It was hardly the first time we'd touched — Maria was free with hugs and friendly kisses, but I'd never touched her when we were alone.

"I talked to Dr. Anthony once," she said. "Did he tell you that?" Her voice had changed again — now it was girlish and frightened.

"You talked to him?"

"He called me not long after Joe and I started going out."

"Really?" I asked.

And suddenly Maria was crying, the words pouring out of her mouth in between gulps for air.

"Oh, what the hell am I saying! He calls me at least once a week; he called me this morning! And he always seems to call when I'm alone at the house. The first few times he started out very nice; but he always ended up asking me how much money I'd take to never see Joe again. So I started hanging up as soon as I realized it was him. But he keeps calling, and he always gets in a sentence or two. Sometimes he threatens me — once he told me he'd see me dead if I married Joe. And the names he calls me! He says I'm a whore or he asks me how many times I've slept with my father, or he tells me oh-so-kindly that I can get my gonorrhea cleared up at the county health clinic for free. Jesus!"

"What does Joe say?"

"I've never told him. I don't know why I'm telling you!"

"Maybe you needed to tell somebody."

"I should keep my big mouth shut! Promise me you won't tell Joe! I don't want him to hate his father!"

"Why shouldn't Joe hate his father? Dr. Anthony's one of the prime shitheads I've ever met."

She didn't answer, and in the dark I could hear her weeping.

"Come on, Maria," I said, "Dr. Anthony's not worth getting upset over. Anybody who met you would know you weren't marrying Joe for his money. Anthony's just an asshole."

"Promise me you won't tell Joe!"

"All right! I promise!"

She was still crying; I could just make out her bowed head. We drove on in silence for about half a mile. I was almost as depressed as she was — Anthony was the price she had to pay for Joe, but for what noble reason did I toady to the man?

Suddenly Maria raised her head and looked out at the street signs.

"Shit," she said, in a weary voice, the worst profanity I'd ever heard her use. "I've been making a scene and we missed my street. I'm sorry. You'll have to turn around and go back the other way."

I did as she asked, feeling a melancholy ache, a charged misery I wanted to savor. We passed more lights and I got another glimpse of her face. She'd wiped it with her arm, and there were no new tears coming. But she seemed older than she'd ever seemed before.

"I don't know why I'm telling you all this," she muttered. We drove on. I brushed her knee again at the next turn, this time intentionally.

"Okay," she said, apparently oblivious. "It's only about a mile away now. Take a left at the next light."

The next light was red. When it changed I started up, turned, and touched her knee again. My car was a wealthy bachelor's hotrod, and there wasn't much room for Maria to move. She shifted uncomfortably in her seat.

"Okay, now take a right at the Magic Market." Some tension had crept into her voice.

As I shifted gears for the turn I touched her knee again.

"It's on the right, about half a mile down this road." We were in a middle-class suburb now, a quiet residential street with no traffic at this late hour. In about a quarter mile, we came to a stop sign. I touched her leg one more time, but this time I left my hand there. Then I moved my fingers a half-inch towards her thigh.

Maria took my hand in hers and gently moved it back towards the gearshift. But I turned my hand over until her fingers lay in my palm and I stroked them with my thumb. For a moment she did nothing, and it was all I could do to keep from stopping the car and taking her into my arms, gearshift and bucket seats be damned. But she jerked her hand away. We were at her house.

"That's it! The one with the big palm tree!" She opened her door and jumped out almost before the car stopped moving. "Thanks for the ride, Peter," she told me, and started to close the door. Then she pulled it back open, and leaned down for a moment, staring at me, considering.

The dome light shone, bright enough to dull all the starlight and pity in the world, while the merciless door-open bell clanged a death knell for both my good and bad intentions. Maria's eyes were still moist, but when she finally spoke her voice was steely.

"Look, Peter," she said, "you're a nice man, but I'm engaged to Joe, and I intend to marry him and stay married to him for the rest of my life. I don't care if you are a big-shot doctor, I don't care if you are used to getting everything you want, I don't care if you drive a fancy car and make lots of money. I made a promise to Joe and I intend to keep it. And whether you know it or not, you made a promise to Joe, too. You let him think you were his friend."

She was crying again now, and she had a hard time going on. But she did.

"I ought to be really pissed, but that pass . . . don't deny it, that was a pass . . . that was about the politest damn pass anybody ever made at me. Maybe you just couldn't help it." She straightened up, and I could no longer see her face in the light thrown by the car. There was a long pause.

"But if you want to be my friend, you better keep your goddamn hands to yourself!" she said, and slammed the door so hard that the rolled-down window shattered, and milky little cubes of glass erupted from its frame and splattered across my outstretched arm.

Chapter 5

Maria never told Joe about that night, but for months afterwards my presence brought an animal wariness to her dark-brown eyes.

She needn't have worried; I'd given up all hope of luring her into my bed, although I was still plagued by dreams in which she visited me dressed only in a robe of her long, black hair. As for Joe, I enjoyed his company even more now that I wasn't plotting to screw his fiancé. Hardly surprising, but it felt so good that I forgot it was Maria, not I, who had kept faith with those she loved.

Impressed with my imagined self-control, I took a gorgeous thirty-year-old divorcé out for a fancy dinner, and afterwards made no attempt to bring the date to an erotic conclusion. Instead, I came home early, accompanied only by an unused erection and a certain monkish pride. Not long after that I purchased a little notebook to write down Allen Deerborn's constant medical suggestions, and actually read one of the books I knew previously only from *Bartlett's Familiar Quotations*. And since Dr. Anthony was paying me to write, I wrote; though I had to be content with carping about the sins of other bio-tech companies — over the next three months the least mention of Anthony Enterprises' dubious exploits was indeed purged from my pages in the name of corporate security.

But despite all evidence to the contrary, on Maria's wedding day I wanted desperately to believe that virtue was its own reward, that I would reap what I had sown, that I lived in the best of all possible worlds, that there was truth in these and a host of other inane platitudes.

And above all else, I wanted to believe that I had never fallen in love with Maria Velasquez.

The phone woke me that morning at 7:25. I rolled over and waited for the answering machine to kick in, but I'd accidentally turned it off the night before. On about the twelfth ring I gave up and grabbed the receiver.

"Hello," I said, a little groggily. I'd been up on a delivery till two a.m.

"Peter!" said a disgustingly cheerful voice.

"Joe," I mumbled, "why are you calling . . . so bright and early?"

"I woke you up?"

"Well, I needed to get up in about an hour-and-a-half anyway."

"You're coming to the wedding, aren't you?"

"Of course! Is that why you called?"

"Not really. I wanted to check on your new guitar."

In addition to buying a wedding gift, I was helping fund the honeymoon. I'd bought Joe's latest creation, the one with the new braces.

"You're a monomaniac," I said. "Are you taking a guitar to San Diego?"

"I decided to travel *a cappella* just this once."

"Smart move. So what did you want to tell me?"

"It's supposed to be real dry this weekend. Keep your humidifier going so the soundboard won't crack."

"You can relax; my humidifier's going right now. You know, you've still got time to skip town. I can take you to the bus station."

"No way. I'm looking forward to today."

"Yeah. What you're really looking forward to is tonight."

"That too," Joe admitted.

"Well, I guess I'll be there."

"What d'ya mean, you guess? Do you still have the map I gave you?"

"Yes. Don't worry; I know this city now like the back of my hand."

Despite my boast to Joe, I still often got lost in Tucson, and I gave myself so much extra time that when I got to the church I found only three other wedding guests inside. So I sat down and admired the old-fashioned sanctuary, complete with plaster saints and angels peering down from their own little dome-ceiling heaven.

Joe and Maria's wedding would be traditional too. Joe had told me about his two months of catechism classes; he'd even filled me in on some of the Catholic theology he now professed to believe. I'd thought it all patently ridiculous, but as Joe and Maria's friends and relatives trickled in, many crossing themselves as they faced the altar, I felt almost pious. Lost in lofty speculations, I was startled when the organist commenced Pachelbel's "Canon," and mothers, grandmothers, and flower girls trooped down the aisle. Joe walked around a corner at the front of the church, Maria turned the corner at the back, and the wedding march began.

She wore a simple white gown, its scooped bodice cut just low enough to reveal that cross necklace flirting with her breasts, while a crown of flowers and a lace mantilla adorned her long black hair. As she proceeded down the aisle the ache I'd felt while she wept in my car swept back, but this time it swelled into a fire in my chest — the same feeling I'd had the day I opened my divorce papers in Chicago. The most beautiful woman I'd ever known was marrying someone else, and all opportunity to stop it was long gone. So why was I here? Why wasn't I in a bar somewhere? Why wasn't I standing on a cliff with a pistol in one hand and cyanide in the other? Why wasn't I at the back of the church, banging on the windows and yelling, "Maria!"

And then I remembered my own wedding, a time when it was *me* standing beside a beautiful and intelligent woman. How seriously had I taken the promises uttered that bright morning? How much longer would it be before I got an invitation to Beverly's wedding? Would "recognition of the ex's" be a part of ceremonies soon, routinely scheduled just after "seating of the mothers"? Instead of rice or birdseed, maybe ex-husbands and ex-wives could throw rotten fruit at the newlyweds. Maybe the ex-husband could stand beside the bride's father, and when the preacher asked, "who gives this woman?" interrupt with his own bitter cry of "I do! And good riddance!" Maybe the ex-wife could dance down the aisle behind the flower girls, strewing thumbtacks from a gaily decorated basket. Marriage in the modern age, until boredom, petty inconvenience or a better offer do us part — those had been my real vows, whatever lies had tripped confidently down my tongue. "Go on," I thought, "marry him, Maria. You could have done a lot worse. You could have married me."

Stricken by a sudden fear that I was making a scene, I glanced at the people around me. A dumpy Hispanic woman with a pretty face was on my left, a polite tear running down her cheek; on my right was a little girl of about ten, overwhelmed by the romance of it all. Both were ignoring me utterly. With that small blessing to hold on to, I told myself that I was a fool, that I had no right to ruin Maria's wedding. I bit my lip and watched.

The ceremony seemed to take forever. Maria, Joe and the priest lit candles, kneeled, prayed, prayed and kneeled — and just when I thought it was all over the priest embarked on a sermon. All of it in Spanish, of course, so I had no idea whether I'd have to endure another thirty seconds or another thirty minutes. I kneeled and stood and kneeled and prayed with the rest of the congregation, remembering how a friend of mine had once described being in a Catholic wedding, how he'd tried to get the groom drunk the night before, but only succeeded in arranging his own dreadful hangover. He'd told me he now believed in hell — he'd been through it that morning, going through the endless rituals while trying not to throw up the beer and cocktail peanuts rotting in his stomach. I began to believe in hell too — I felt an agony of apprehension that something might cause me to lose control completely.

But nothing did. The sermon ended, rings were exchanged, bride and groom kissed, joyous organ music played as they walked quickly down the aisle. In thirty short minutes my life had been changed forever. Maria Velasquez was now Joe's wife.

I slid out of the church quickly. By the time I got to the parking lot I had a better grip on myself, but I still didn't feel up to driving. Instead, I got in my car and opened the windows, hoping the desert breeze would blow some sense into my brain. Trying to think calmly, I wondered if I'd been upset by losing Maria, or by the wedding ceremony itself. After all, this was the first wedding I'd been to since my own divorce, weddings always made me think of wedding nights, and I hadn't been to bed with anyone since I'd met Maria. Was it possible I just needed a good lay?

I was always happy to answer "yes" to that last question, and I was about to turn on the ignition and drive home when I remembered the reception, scheduled to start in a few moments in the building behind the church. I almost decided to skip it. But not going would mean surrendering to the spell the wedding had cast, and I'd promised Joe that I'd be there.

So I got out of my car and joined the crowd trailing out from the church. And in the back of my mind, even then, I knew the real reason I felt compelled to go. Though the sight pained me like alcohol on a fresh wound, I needed to see Maria in that dress once more, needed to imagine her as my bride, needed to dream that her loving gaze would someday be fixed on me.

My ex-wife's parents had rented a hotel ballroom for our wedding reception; Maria's parents had reserved the church gym.

Two windows opened into a kitchen at the far end, and basketball goals were cranked out of the way high above the floor.

Crepe-paper garlands decorated the steel rods reinforcing the roof; and a paper banner reading "¡Felicitaciones Maria y Jose!" hung over a large table bearing an equally large wedding cake. A smaller banner with stylized musical notes hung in a corner, where a Velasquez friend or relative had volunteered as disc-jockey. The music was barely audible over the din of rapid-fire Spanish and screaming children darting around, between, and through groups of adults. Maria and Joe, delayed by the photographer, were nowhere to be seen.

Convinced that I was back to normal, I got myself a plate of food and decided it would be polite to mingle. Among the Anglos gathered in the least noisy corner of the room was a woman I assumed to be Joe's mother. She had his height and wide shoulders; and she'd wandered in after I had, probably released from a round of wedding pictures.

I walked over and said, "Hello. I'm Peter Jacobson. You must be Joe's mom."

"Yes, that's me," she answered, and primly stuck out her hand. Then she seemed to place me.

"Oh yes, the doctor! Joe told me about you. You work with his father, don't you?"

"Well, not exactly. I'm a consulting obstetrician for the Clinic, and Dr. Anthony has given me a grant to work on a book."

"Oh," she said, "I remember now. Joe sent me a copy of one of your articles. I thought it was very well written, although I'm surprised his father liked it — it didn't fit his views at all."

"So he's told me."

"You don't do any actual research at the Institute?"

"No, I don't really work there," I said, which was almost true. She relaxed visibly. "Lovely wedding," I added.

"Yes, it was, and Maria is such a beautiful girl." She took a sip of her punch and looked out across the gym. "She's one of the most intelligent young women I've ever met, and so level-headed. And her family is delightful. Don't you think so?"

"Certainly," I answered. "Could you follow much of the ceremony?"

"A little, but I was at the rehearsal when Maria was still translating for Joe. I wish I spoke more Spanish. Maria has so many relatives, and I feel somewhat . . . overwhelmed." She paused, obviously hoping to move the conversation to another subject. "Tell me," she asked, "did you see Joe before the wedding?"

"No."

"I was worried last night at the rehearsal dinner; he was so angry."

"What about?" I asked. I'd never really seen Joe lose his temper.

"Something his father had done, he wouldn't tell me what."

"Was he upset that Dr. Anthony wasn't coming to the wedding?"

"Oh, I doubt it. His father was invited, of course, but I never dreamed he'd come, and I don't think Joe expected it either. This was some sort of a surprise, an unpleasant one apparently."

A teenager in a tuxedo appeared at her side. I recognized the best man, Joe's half-brother, about seventeen or eighteen years old.

"This is Ian, my other son," she said. "Ian, this is Dr. Jacobson. Joe's mentioned him, remember?"

He stuck out his hand. "Pleased to mee'cha'."

"Ian, you don't know what Joe was upset about last night, do you?"

"Naw. I asked him, and he just looked at me and growled 'never mind.' "

Joe's mother frowned, anger struggling with upper-class manners. "Joe's very thoughtful," she said. "I have no doubt his father did something thoroughly offensive and Joe won't tell me because he doesn't want to make a scene." She shook her head sadly, and then a good-natured mask returned. "Family squabbles," she almost bubbled, "I'm sure you really don't want to hear about all this, Dr. Jacobson."

"That's quite all right," I replied.

"If you'll excuse me, I think I'll see if I can break through the throng and have a word with my other son." I looked over towards the door and saw Maria and Joe making their entrance. I was left with Ian, who had little to say, perhaps because he had a mouthful of tamales.

"So how do you like Tucson?" I asked.

"It's okay," Ian mumbled. I waited. He continued chewing.

"You live in, where is it, Minnesota?"

"Uh-huh," he said, and chewed some more.

"You like the food, I take it?"

"Uh-huh!" he repeated between two more mouthfuls, then added, "I think I'm supposed to go do somethin' now."

Sure enough, the official reception line was forming, and as best man Ian was expected to stand beside the bride and groom. According to strict etiquette I was expected to get in line and pay my respects. I took a few tentative steps in that direction, and was surprised to feel my heart racing. Apparently I still wasn't up to facing Maria.

So I headed back towards the buffet table, loaded up my plate, then wandered over and watched the amateur disc-jockey shuffle through a mass of CD's spread out on a table. When his confusion grew boring I stood and watched a group of children trying to fly paper airplanes through a crepe paper loop. Then I left the building and took another look at the church.

When I came back the reception line was gone, the music had stopped, and Maria and Joe were preparing to cut the cake. Everyone watched quietly except for Maria's giggling sisters, who seemed to be expecting some sort of mischief. Joe wasn't the type to cram cake into his bride's face, but I wondered about Maria. After eating a bite offered by Joe, she swung her cake-laden hand back with a wicked grin, then reached up and daintily placed a dab of frosting on her new husband's nose. There was applause, and the music started again.

"So how are you doing, Joe's doctor friend?" a Spanish-accented voice asked. I turned and saw Maria's mother.

"I'm fine," I said, hoping I looked calmer than I felt.

"Joe is such a nice boy," she continued. "We think Maria is very lucky."

"Joe's lucky, too," I said.

"Of course. But he will have his hands full. Maria is a very spirited girl."

"Well, Joe seems to like her."

"Yes, he does. So, do you still work for Dr. Anthony?"

"Yes," I answered hesitantly, distracted by Maria's father, who'd come closer and was staring at his wife. Maria's mother noticed him too, and came to a decision.

"The man is a snake!" she hissed at me. "You should quit that job right away!" I took a step back as her husband strode up, speaking loudly in Spanish. She replied heatedly; he gestured wildly, then she crossed her arms and said "¡No!" to each of his next four sentences. Finally he shook his head and walked away. She took a deep breath before turning to me again.

"My husband thinks I should not tell you what happened. Normally I would not disobey. But you need to know what sort of man you work for."

"All I do is deliver babies," I said, afraid that her anger would somehow end up directed at me.

"I know that. What I mean is, you are Maria and Joe's friend, and you need to be careful. I think Joe's father is crazy. I've heard things around town, stories about what they do at that place. But I thought they might be lies; I didn't judge until now. Now I believe them. Not coming to the wedding was bad enough, but the gift he sent!"

"What was that?"

"They got it last night at the dinner; Mr. Anthony left it at the restaurant. Joe wanted to open it before the wedding when no one was around; he said he didn't trust his father and he thought it might be something insulting. He was right." She stopped for a second; lifted her lip in disgust. "I know Señor Anthony doesn't like Maria; I know he thinks we are just Cuban trash. But to send such a gift!"

"What did he send them?" I asked again. She paused as if she needed a moment's preparation, and then she spoke the dreadful words.

"A bag of tortillas and a gift certificate to Taco Bell!"

She watched me carefully, gauging my reaction. I was glad I hadn't laughed.

"Dr. Anthony is a snake," Señora Velasquez repeated. "I tell you this because Maria and Joe like you. If you can't find another job, at least you can be careful." She gave me a maternal pat on the shoulder and walked away.

After that, the rest of the reception could only be an anticlimax. I wandered around for at least forty-five minutes, sampled more food, had a dozen polite conversations. Finally, I felt ready to face Maria. When I saw her with Joe and some departing guests, I joined the small group.

"Peter!" she said, "There you are!" and raised her arms to give me a hug.

"Congratulations, Maria," I told her. Then I turned to Joe and shook his hand.

I'd felt nothing worse than a mild flutter, but for some reason I couldn't leave. I watched Joe toss Maria's garter, and Maria toss her bouquet. Then I joined friends and family lining the sidewalk, waiting to see the newlyweds off to San Diego. I showered birdseed down on Maria's head and felt fine when her eyes met mine. I laughed when I saw the bawdy slogans written on the car, reminders of how Joe and Maria would be spending their evening (and maybe their afternoon as well — San Diego was a long drive, but if the thought of Maria's legs wrapped around his bare hips got to be too much, Joe could always pull over at a motel in romantic Yuma or El Centro). I joked with the other guests as the car drove out of sight, tin cans clattering.

Then I drove back to the Clinic and took care of some paperwork, even though I wasn't officially working that Saturday. No rest for the busy and ambitious young doctor. Dinner at a nice restaurant, a quick stop at the video store, and I was home.

But when Maria and Joe returned from their honeymoon I found I was reluctant to see them together. I resolved to make new friends, but my resolution lasted only until their second invitation. They'd become the most important part of my life — and while seeing Maria as Joe's wife saddened me, the prospect of never seeing her again was worse.

And they were happy together — any fool could see it. Joe wanted no changes in Maria, and Maria was satisfied with only a few minor alterations of Joe. He still kept a workshop in their rented house, but it wasn't in the living room, and his housekeeping improved radically. But otherwise Joe remained Joe — amiable, easygoing, endearingly eccentric.

Maria had unwittingly changed my own life far more. After the wedding I made a brief return to my career as Casanova, but the thrill was gone. After adding a few more notches to my belt, I settled into a life of hard work and little else. Maria either sensed my romantic discontent or approved of my reform, because she sometimes played matchmaker. But her unattached female friends always paled beside her, and they were often literally beside her — I met most of them for the first and only time on thinly disguised double dates with Mr. and Mrs. Joseph Anthony.

A year and a half went by. I delivered more babies than I cared to count, including twins, triplets, and (with Allen Deerborn's help) two sets of quads. Once a month Harold Anthony called me into his office and discussed my literary efforts. He had won: I now wrote nothing negative about Anthony or his company; I knew it would never get past his censors. Though this made my articles dull, Anthony seemed satisfied, and I took the same liberal attitude towards the money he paid me.

As 1998 approached, Maria was working part-time at a day-care and starting her Master's degree in education, while Joe was beginning to earn a reputation as a guitar-maker far outside of Tucson. Their future looked good, and they wanted a child very badly.

Though they certainly never discussed it with me, I'm sure they worked at baby-making with gusto and determination. But no babies came. I knew they were anxious when Joe began asking discrete questions about male fertility. I knew they were desperate when Joe sent cautious feelers to his father for help. Harold Anthony's reaction was an immediate offer to pay for any treatment necessary, as long as it was all done at the Clinic. He even recommended that I be the obstetrician when Maria got pregnant. I was immensely surprised.

Chapter 6

"This is fantastic," Joe said, taking a swig of Dom Perignon. "Too bad you can't have any. How's the apple juice?"

"Wonderful," Maria replied sourly.

"Maria, the apple juice was a joke," I said. "A sip or two of champagne won't hurt you or the baby."

"Yeah, but I'd like more than a sip or two. What did you call this stuff?"

"Sparkling non-alcoholic cider."

"Sparkling cider it is. The first of many sacrifices." She held her glass high. "To the baby!"

Getting Maria pregnant hadn't been easy. Her Fallopian tubes turned out to be malformed, and Joe's sperm count was so low that the doctors said there was little chance of conception in a "natural environment." The Clinic's specialists saw only one option. In April of '99 Joe's sperm fertilized at least one of Maria's eggs *in vitro*. Three weeks later Maria was verifiably pregnant.

Of course, I just delivered babies; the various *in vitro* procedures were done by the fertility specialists on the Clinic's third floor. But Maria and Joe kept me informed, and when Maria was successfully stuffed I went to their house with my bottle of Dom Perignon and the aforementioned high-class apple juice. My intentions were mostly honorable — Maria was now my patient as well as my best friend's wife — but I have to admit that I still felt a nagging desire to stuff her myself.

Luckily, Maria didn't seem to pick up on this, so I was kept up-to-date on their future plans. Indeed, Maria phoned me often when Joe was out.

"He'll spoil the kid rotten," she complained one afternoon.

"You can't spoil a baby," I told her.

"Trust me. Joe will find a way."

Joe would soon be watching the baby because Maria planned to take only a semester off before finishing her Master's degree and finding a job teaching. Joe hoped to sandwich his guitar-making in between spells of changing diapers, heating formula, and cleaning up baby puke.

My own affairs had settled into a more predictable routine. I wrote, delivered babies, did some guest lecturing at the university. My only close friends were Maria and Joe.

And, in his own mind at least, Eric Schroeder.

It seemed to me we had little in common. He was closer to Anthony's age than mine, and though he often visited the Clinic's third floor, he was no longer a practicing MD; he concentrated on research. But apart from obligatory social outings with Harold Anthony and coffee breaks with Ed Devaney, Eric avoided his fellow scientists. He rarely had a good word even for Ed.

"Well," he said once, "at least he's better than the spooks."

"Spooks?"

"Ex-defense department, ex-CIA, call 'em what you like. At least half of the Institute researchers used to work in germ warfare."

"Really?"

"God yes! Where do you think Anthony got his training?"

"But Ed's not an ex- 'spook'?"

"No. But he doesn't think about what he's doing — and it doesn't bother him because he's trying not to think about it."

By early 1999 Eric complained often about disagreements with Dr. Anthony and other Institute scientists. And despite his constant complaints, I had the feeling he still wasn't telling me everything.

"Here," Eric said one afternoon at lunch. He handed me a newspaper clipping. It was an interview with Dr. Anthony.

"Anthony's giving interviews now?" I asked. "We better go sell some stock before word gets out."

"Read it," Eric laughed. Which I did, and to my astonishment, there was none of Anthony's usual master-race blather. His answers were moderate, well-phrased . . . and familiar.

"This doesn't sound like Anthony at all," I said. "Has he had a brain transplant or something?"

"No. I'm sure in private he'd say what he told them is complete and utter horseshit. But doesn't it give you a feeling of déjà vu?"

"I have a feeling I've read it somewhere."

"You ought to have a feeling that you wrote it some*time*." He handed me a photocopy of one of my old articles. Long passages highlighted in yellow matched several of Anthony's replies almost word for word.

"Shit!" I said. "Does he have a photographic memory?"

"No, not really. It's just that Anthony usually does his 'interviews' via e-mail. Much more convenient for a man with his busy schedule. It also gives him the opportunity to plagiarize." Eric laughed. "He probably didn't even type it. I bet he just had his secretary scan it into her computer."

Words failed me, though I guess my looks said it all. But Eric was amused.

"You should be flattered," he said. "Anthony has high standards for what he steals."

"But if he thinks my ideas are so ridiculous, how come he's using them?"

"Because he also thinks they're ideal for public consumption. You don't think he wants everybody to know what we're really up to, do you?"

"And what are you really up to?" I asked.

But Eric took a big gulp of iced tea, smiled nervously, and said nothing.

In April of '99 — the same month Maria got pregnant — I noticed a sudden falling off in my "friendship" with Eric. He quit calling me, and whenever I phoned him he was mysteriously busy. I couldn't imagine how I'd offended him — Eric was one of the most thick-skinned people I'd ever met — but when I called him at the Institute one Thursday morning in June he brushed me off so rudely I knew there was a problem. When I picked up my phone late that same afternoon I was surprised to find Eric on the line.

"Hey, Pete," he said, "What dya' say we go out and shoot some pool and drink a few beers?"

Something rang false in his voice, and I could hear traffic in the background. Evidently he was calling from a pay phone.

"Listen, Eric," I said, "I'm sorry if I interrupted you this morning."

"I'm the one who should apologize. My only excuse is that we had the original day from hell."

"You don't want to go someplace and eat dinner first?"

There was an overlong pause, as if Eric was considering something more complex than a simple change of plans. "No," he said finally, "I've already eaten. I'll pick you up in about twenty minutes."

Fifteen minutes later I heard him honking — another oddity: he usually came to the door. When I got in his car he seemed reluctant to speak in full sentences.

"What have you been doing?" I asked, "I haven't seen you much the past few weeks."

"The usual."

"Where are we going? University Billiards?"

"Bumpers."

Another surprise. Bumpers was a noisy bar favored by college students and young singles, not a good place for the serious pool Eric preferred.

"We can eat there too," Eric said, "if you haven't had dinner yet."

I noticed again that I hadn't been asked. Eric drove grimly on, and for the next ten minutes not a word passed his lips. When we got to Bumpers, he got out of the car and strode in ahead of me. When I walked through the door after him he was already looking around with an unusually critical eye.

"Let's sit over there," he said, pointing to a booth well away from the busier tables. We sat and a waitress came over immediately.

"I'll take a gin and tonic," Eric told her. I'd never known Eric to drink anything but iced tea, but I ordered a Heineken, just to be sociable. Eric said nothing until the waitress came back with the drinks. After she'd put them on the table and walked away, he seemed to come to a decision.

"Listen," he said, "I'm sorry, but I didn't want to talk in my car."

"What's wrong with talking in your car?"

"I was afraid it might be bugged. And I didn't want to talk on the phone this morning for the same reason."

"Bugged? You mean wiretaps? Some other bio-tech company?"

"No. I mean Anthony."

"Come on," I laughed. "Bugging's illegal. I've never heard of Anthony doing anything illegal." Eric looked at me and shook his head in disbelief.

"Well, nothing highly illegal," I amended.

"Listen," Eric said. "What Anthony's doing right now makes bugging his employees seem paltry."

"But I just deliver babies. Why would my phone be bugged?"

"It was my phone I was worried about. You may not realize it, but Anthony's installed video cameras all over the Institute, probably bugs in the labs and offices, and I know the phone lines are monitored. I'm pretty sure he's had most of the Clinic wired, too."

"Aren't you being a little paranoid?"

"And aren't you being a little naive?"

"About what? You've been beating around the bush with this for months."

He downed almost half his drink and motioned for the waitress to bring him another.

"I'm sorry," he said after a pause. "I shouldn't get mad at you." He sighed. "Before I tell you what's going on, I want to explain how I got involved. If I don't you'll think I'm just as much of a shit as Anthony."

"How could you be as big a shit as Anthony?"

"Because I've gone right along. I couldn't help myself."

"Why not?"

Another pause, another attack on his drink.

"It's hard to explain," he finally said, "at least to you. You went into medicine because you enjoy working with people, and it's something you're good at . . ."

"And I wanted to make a lot of money . . ."

"Yeah, but I doubt that was the whole reason. But with me . . ."

"But with you what?"

He paused a second, again almost at a loss for words.

"You want to know," he finally said, "the one and only reason I got into bio-tech?"

"Why?"

"Because it's so damn interesting! I never thought about what people would do with it. I was like the guys working on the A-bomb. You know, some of them worried it might ignite the atmosphere, kill every living thing on the planet. Did they stop? Oh no! They did some math and decided it *probably* wouldn't happen, then they went ahead and set it off anyway. Well, that's my excuse: I've been like a little kid, just wanted to see if my cherry bomb would really explode." He took another gulp from his drink and stared mournfully at the stranded ice cubes. "I used to think that was Anthony's excuse, too, but lately I'm beginning to wonder."

Eric's next drink arrived, and he immediately took a big swallow. I'd never seen him so upset. But was something concrete bothering him, or did he just want a liberally lubricated BS session? I couldn't decide.

And Eric kept on talking, mostly about hush-hush projects still in the planning stages: schemes to make oil-slick-eating bacteria, grow tomatoes the size of pumpkins, clone champion racehorses and woolly mammoths. Always he managed to turn talk of particulars back towards generalities, discussions of real situations into hypothetical scenarios.

We went on this way for almost an hour, then shot some pool, then sat down again. Eric drank steadily, and while I didn't match him drink for drink I didn't exactly stay sober, either. I'd almost decided he had no earth-shattering confession when he abruptly started talking about Harold Anthony's politics.

"The really bad thing about Anthony," Eric began, "is he not only has this reckless curiosity, he also mixes in some of the dumbest political and sociological garbage you can imagine. Did you know he's thinking of running for president?"

"No," I said, "I don't get around much with Dr. Anthony." In fact, I'd never seen him outside of the Institute.

"Well, you know Anthony assumes the average person is getting dumber, because the least intelligent people supposedly have the most children. But what really bothers him is, with the whole bell curve moving down there's a possibility that we don't get as many flat-out geniuses as we used to. He thinks the world needs to have a higher percentage of the *really* smart. Real people, he calls them."

The waitress came by and Eric ordered another drink.

"Anyway, the problem with his ideal world is there's no way to get enough 'smart' people to run it. So he thinks we should genetically manipulate intelligence, and also clone people of proven genius, like Plato or Leonardo da Vinci."

"Isn't Plato's DNA a little hard to come by?" I asked.

"Plato's may be, but we know where a lot of other famous people are buried."

Gulp. A large portion of his latest drink found its home in Eric's stomach.

"Look," I said, "you're not driving me home. And you damn well better call a cab for yourself, too. It's getting kind of late."

"We can't leave! I've got something really important to tell you." He took another sip of his drink, then continued on the same wild tangent.

"For his ideal clones, Anthony would need to get DNA from some very old human samples. He hasn't had a lot to work with; you can't just go digging up graveyards. But he did have one sample about 600 years old, and he was able to get it without raising an eyebrow. He had reason to believe it came from somebody extremely intelligent, a great artist, probably a great scholar and mathematician too."

"And who would that be?" I asked.

"Whoever forged the Shroud of Turin! The Institute has DNA from the bloodstains. Anthony's held on to it for eleven years now."

I remembered that Eric had told me part of this one before, how threads and surface particles from the Shroud were sent to the University's Physics Department for radiocarbon dating, how Anthony had gotten hold of a small sample and had it examined by some of his scientists as well. According to published reports, the Institute tests had found artist's pigments on the linen threads.

"I thought the bloodstains turned out to be paint," I said.

"Well, Anthony stretched the truth there. There were trace amounts of paint. Painters used to copy the Shroud, and when they were done, they'd press the copy against the cloth to sanctify it. But the sample also contained human DNA — a little fact Anthony downplayed as much as he could. Which brings us to the forger again. Some people think it may have been Leonardo. And think about this. The handiest blood for a forger to use would have been his own."

"Uh, Eric, I bet some Catholics have a more disturbing opinion on whose blood that might be."

"Aw come on, Peter! The U of A carbon-dated those threads to the middle of the fourteenth century!"

"You're losing me. Leonardo lived in the sixteenth century."

"Some people think that he may have taken the original forgery and substituted his own, using old cloth."

"That seems awfully complicated. Why not just a fourteenth-century forger?"

"Because whoever did it had an amazing knowledge of anatomy, and he invented a method of painting that left no brushstrokes. Leonardo's an obvious candidate."

"So what's the problem?" I asked. "Anthony has some crackpot visions of the far future, and he's stored some DNA from a fraudulent religious relic. Who cares?"

"The far future!" Eric exclaimed, "Anthony's working on this right now! Hell, what am I saying? I've been working on this right now!"

"Extracting DNA from relics is hardly scary, unless you really start trying to clone people."

Eric sighed. "Listen," he finally said, "cloning people is exactly what we've been working on."

"Oh come off it. Human cloning isn't illegal yet, but it's not exactly popular. Anthony's running a business; why would he do something so stupid?"

"Anthony only cares how public opinion affects him financially."

"But that would affect him financially. The company stock would do a nosedive. Anthony's very canny about that sort of thing."

"Who says the public has to know?"

"Aw, come on, Eric! You've got to have ova to work with, which means the donors have to sign consent forms. Women have to have the babies! How are you gonna' keep their mouths shut?"

"Who says the women have to know?"

"Really? How are you going to get ova from women without them knowing about it?"

"Why do you think Anthony started a fertility clinic? It's easy to get a few extra ova from some poor woman getting an *in vitro*. She can't tell how many they've taken."

"And what proof do you have?"

"I don't need proof," Eric said, "I've done it myself."

That brought me up short. Stealing ova from a patient could lose a doctor his medical license. But Eric was right. It would also be easy.

"Actually," Eric said, "borrowing the ova didn't bother me too much. But we've moved beyond experimenting on eggs. We have viable clone embryos . . ."

"Wait a minute. You're not talking twinning here? You mean viable embryos cloned from adult DNA?"

" . . . viable clone embryos in cryogenic storage at the Institute, and Anthony wants to carry one of the embryos to term."

"How?"

"The normal way. All he needs is a woman to implant the embryo in."

"Yeah, but who? And how can you be sure she'll keep it a secret?"

"Once again, who says the woman has to know? Anthony runs a fertility clinic, remember? You just implant one of the embryos in some poor lady who thinks she's getting her own fertilized egg."

"And when the baby doesn't look anything like Daddy or Mommy? How is Anthony planning to get around that one?"

"Why do you keep talking about plans? It's already happened! The perfect couple showed up two months ago."

"Right," I said. "Like who?"

Eric paused.

"Listen," he said, "whatever you do, don't take what I'm about to tell you to the press or the police. You might get Art Bell to listen in between calls about little horny aliens, but it's more likely you'd get yourself killed, just like poor Jonathan Gluckmann, and I'm sure you wouldn't be helping Joe and Maria that way."

"What do Joe and Maria have to do with this?"

"Well, Dr. Anthony thinks they're having his baby. In fact, Dr. Anthony thinks they're having him."

"What on earth are you talking about?"

"Dr. Anthony thinks Maria is pregnant with his clone."

I stared hard at Eric, memories of rubber eggplants and hallucinogenic corn dancing in my brain. Eric hadn't pulled a practical joke in months, but apparently that just meant he was overdue for a whopper. "Maria Anthony is pregnant with a clone of Harold Anthony?" I asked.

"The idea surprises you? It didn't surprise me when Dr. Anthony first proposed it. Joe doesn't have a low sperm count, he has a nonexistent sperm count. He's completely sterile. Harold's first reaction to that was to tell us to use his sperm to impregnate Maria's egg. Then lo and behold, we find out he's sterile too. I was surprised he hadn't checked — he and his latest young bride have been trying to make a baby for six months, but I guess Anthony couldn't imagine age had affected his mighty testicles." Eric snorted, took another gulp of his drink. "So what's left for our fearless leader? He's into his 'genetic legacy' as he calls it. Joe's his only child, so in an evolutionary sense, Dr. Anthony's a complete failure. But there's another possibility: a clone, a little Harold that Anthony can give the decent childhood he missed out on himself. And cloning fits Anthony's personality, too. Everybody always figured the first person to clone himself would be some crazed megalomaniac, and if that doesn't sound familiar then you don't know Dr. Anthony."

"But why Maria?"

"Anthony's first idea was to try it on his own wife. But we found out her mother took DES, which means the chances of Mrs. Harold Anthony miscarrying go up about 250%. And we don't have a lot of embryos to play around with. Meanwhile Anthony's pissed that his grandson won't have any of his genes, because the only way Maria will get pregnant is if they use a sperm donor. And for some reason he acts like that's all Maria's fault, that if she gets pregnant from a donor she'll be cheating on Joe. So he decides Maria will make a good broodmare for his xerox baby, and doing things that way will keep the family honor intact. And best of all, nobody's going to be surprised that Joe and Maria's kid looks a bit like granpa'."

"And what is Anthony going to do when this kid starts to look *exactly* like granpa'?" I asked, "Joe must know what his father looked like as a child."

"No, he doesn't. Anthony's mother was a lush; pictures weren't taken or kept. So I suspect Harold's not that worried about the baby having an uncanny resemblance to him, at least for a while. What Anthony worries about is Maria. And that's when I started to worry."

"You were all right with this so far?" I asked, trying hard not to laugh. "What could be worse?"

"What could be worse is what he might do to Maria. You know, I'm still pretty friendly with Anthony, at least, he talks to me a lot. He hates Maria with every bone in his body. And it's not just because of this Bell curve racial shit he's always spouting. I think she reminds him of some Chicano foster mother he secretly had the hots for. And he was upset with Joe before Joe met Maria; he thought that Joe was wasting his potential. Now that Joe's married, Anthony thinks he'll never change, and he thinks it's Maria that keeps him from it. Anthony wanted Joe to marry someone who could advance his career the way Harold's first wife advanced his. What does Harold get for a daughter-in-law instead? Some waitress Joe met in a cheap Mexican restaurant!"

"So what?"

"He hates her enough that I think he'd do anything to get rid of her. So when he talks like it's a done deal that Maria won't be a problem anymore, then you have to worry."

"You make it sound like he's going to take a contract out on her."

"That's exactly how he talks." Eric paused a moment, as if considering another possibility. "And of course," he continued, "Anthony's a brilliant guy. He might have a better way."

"Like what?"

"Do you remember that project we were working on last year, trying to deactivate oncogenes? Well, we didn't find a way to turn cancer cells off, but we got really good at turning them on. At least in rats."

"What's that got to do with Joe and Maria?"

"Bear with me. The rats would go along happily for months, but when we exposed them to one of the chemicals we'd tailored their DNA to react to, they'd develop these fantastically fast-growing tumors. Some of those old germ-warfare jocks were salivating at the possibilities. Shoot somebody full of retrovirus during a routine procedure, then months or even years later, expose them to the right carcinogen. Bingo! Cancer on demand!"

"Science marches on."

"Yes it does. Anyway, I don't know how Anthony's planning to get Maria out of the picture, but that little project certainly leaps to mind."

"And then what?"

"Well, as the baby got older, everybody would assume he resembled Anthony because he was Joe's real son, and Anthony's real grandson. Everyone who knew would be just as guilty as Anthony, and they'd keep their mouths shut." He took a big swallow out of his drink.

It took me a few seconds to process all this. It was certainly the most involved practical joke I'd heard from Eric, and the most tasteless, which was perhaps attributable to the fact that he was so drunk. I should have called him on it, but the writer in me was fascinated. Where was Eric going to take this outlandish tale next?

"Wait a second," I finally said. "You said Anthony *thought* Maria was pregnant with his clone. Whose baby is it?"

"Well," Eric said, "with a clone it's really more a question of *who* the baby is. When I began to suspect Anthony might hurt Maria, I decided I just couldn't go along anymore. I'd gone along before because, well, like I said, it was all so damned interesting. But with Maria out of the way, there isn't much doubt that Anthony would be a big factor in bringing up the baby. He could even have plans to eliminate other people who might get custody, like Maria's family, or Joe's mother. He hates her almost as much as he hates Maria. I could stand the thought of Joe and Maria raising baby Harold — who knows, they might improve the second version. But the thought of him raising himself?"

Eric finally seemed to have talked himself out, so I sat for a moment and calmly rated the story's plausibility. I'd never written any science fiction, but this had promise.

"Anyway," I said, in falsely awed tones, "you stopped Anthony from giving Maria his clone. So you put in her fertilized ova and she'll have the baby she's expecting. Right?"

"That was impossible," Eric said. "Joe's sterile, remember?"

"Yes, but they gave permission to use a sperm donor if one was needed. I thought you had one lined up."

"Well, that wasn't the only problem. Maria only wanted them to fertilize one egg at a time. She thought anything else was immoral."

I was impressed with Eric's research. Normally, *in vitro* doctors fertilized multiple eggs, and then inserted up to six. Usually, only one lodged in the uterine wall and the others spontaneously aborted. But sometimes *in vitros* resulted in quadruple and even sextuple implantations. The medical inclination then was to abort several of the pregnancies. Sometimes more than six eggs were fertilized *in vitro*. These extra embryos were often discarded, or even, with the parents' consent, used for experiments. Since the Catholic Church considered that life began at conception, it naturally objected to all these procedures. But none of these problems occurred when only one ovum was fertilized at a time. Maria might be an indifferent Catholic, even a heretical Catholic, but some Catholic thought remained, and she might well have opted for a statistically unpromising procedure rather than a morally dubious one.

"So you didn't have a fertilized ovum from Maria at all," I said.

"Right. As far as I know there was never any attempt to fertilize one of Maria's eggs. And I didn't really see any way to keep her from becoming pregnant; they'd discarded the embryos that weren't viable. At least if she was pregnant Anthony would leave her alone for nine months."

"You could have talked to me. I could have warned them to go somewhere else."

"Even talking to you was hard. You wouldn't believe the surveillance we've been under from the moment Anthony dreamed this scheme up. I was afraid we both might end up dead if I told you in April or May. But they think they're done now. I can't tell that they're watching me at all since sometime last week."

"So what did you do?"

"Well, I decided that if you're working for the devil, any change you make in his plans will be an improvement. I wasn't being watched as carefully at the Institute, which was where we'd prepared the clones. Embryos all look the same, so I switched the labels. Maria's going to have a cloned baby, but it won't be Harold Anthony."

I looked at Eric very skeptically, now that it seemed he was almost done. "So, to sum up this long and rambling story," I said. "Anthony thinks Maria is going to have a clone of himself, but you switched the embryos because you think two Harold Anthonys is one too many."

"Uh-huh."

"Additionally, you think Anthony may have a plan to do away with Maria, either by hiring the Mob or by inducing cancer with some biotech hocus-pocus."

"Right."

"So why are you telling me all this?"

"As far as the cloning . . . it just seemed to me that somebody honest needed to know what was going on, but that it might be best to keep it a secret from Joe and Maria. In all likelihood, they're going to have a normal little baby, and if they raise it thinking it's just a normal little baby, everything can still turn out just fine. As far as the rest, well, somebody has to do something to protect Maria."

"If you say so," I replied. "Anyway, if all this is true, you haven't told me one thing."

"What's that?"

"Whose clone is it?"

"I did tell you! We were only able to make two viable sets of embryos. One was from Anthony's DNA, and the other was supposedly from blood on the Shroud of Turin, but only Anthony believes that; the rest of us feel sure that DNA came from some recent contamination. Anyway, I switched the labels, so the Shroud embryo is what they put inside Maria. That's the baby she's going to have."

That did it. Eric was crazy to believe I'd buy this practical joke for even a minute. I looked at him and laughed.

"Right," I said. "Just what I would have done. Let's go home."

Chapter 7

It was raining hard the next morning, but rather than aggravating my already shitty mood, the downpour gave me hope. Sleeping-in during morning thunderstorms is a Tucson tradition because the rain can kill you; it floods streets and dry river beds, sweeping cars off bridges and dips in the roads.

Hoping it would rain harder, I grabbed a cup of coffee and two acetaminophen, turned on the radio, and crawled back into bed. Traffic bulletins warned of dangerously flooded intersections, so I reset the alarm, burrowed back beneath the covers and resolved to sleep another forty-five minutes. I had no appointments before 10 a.m. and my paperwork could wait.

But instead of sleeping, I began to think about Eric's wild story. His other jokes had been harmless, but this one was anything but good-natured. And then there was Eric's drinking, totally at odds with his usual behavior.

When I'd last seen him, Eric seemed almost too drunk to walk, much less drive a car. I'd left him leaning over in the booth, looking woozy and slightly sick, while I went to call a cab and ask the bartender not to have the car towed. But when I got back, Eric had disappeared.

Odder still, when I got home I realized I had Eric's keys. I'd taken them sometime during the evening; a detail I'd forgotten in my own alcoholic haze. But he must have driven off somehow — his car was gone from the parking lot when I went out to the cab. I could only assume he kept a second key handy for when do-gooders like me relieved him of the first.

However he'd gotten home, I hoped his head hurt as much as mine did.

At the Clinic, my day was almost as bad as my hangover. My first patient was a woman afraid her routine aches and nausea were signs of some rare and dangerous condition. I spent a half-hour politely refusing tests for everything from beriberi to Lou Gehrig's disease. I was on call from noon on, and I spent about four hours at the hospital, intermittently checking on a woman who should have been delivering any minute but for some reason was taking hours. The baby finally came a little after four, and I handed scissors to the father to cut the umbilical cord. He cut it, then promptly fainted and cracked his head on the bed. Mother and child were well when I left the hospital at 4:45, but the father had sustained a mild concussion.

I was back in my office when the receptionist rang me.

"I'm leaving, Dr. Jacobson," she said, "but someone's here to talk to you."

"Who is it? I don't have any more appointments."

"He says he's with the police."

A moment later a harried-looking gentleman in a suit came in. He offered his hand and I shook it.

"I'm Detective Martinez," he said. "We're trying to get some information about a Dr. Eric Schroeder. Dr. Devaney over at the Anthony Institute suggested we talk to you. You haven't seen Dr. Schroeder or heard from him today, have you?"

"No, I can't say that I have," I replied. "What's going on?"

"He's not a close friend of yours, is he?"

"Not what you'd call a close friend; but we often eat lunch together, things like that."

Martinez looked disappointed.

"In fact," I continued cautiously, "we went out last night and shot some pool."

Martinez looked up, much more interested.

"Could you tell me what happened," he asked. "Particularly what time you last saw him?"

"Sure. But what's going on? Is he all right?"

"Probably. Where did you go to shoot pool?"

"Bumpers. It's a billiards place near the University."

"About what time?"

"We got there about 8:30 or 9 p.m. I think we left at about 1:30."

"Did you leave together?"

"No. I'd had a little too much to drink, so I took a cab home."

"What about him?"

"He'd had a lot more to drink," I answered, "and he was supposed to take the cab with me. But when I got back after calling the cab company, he was gone. I assumed he'd driven home."

"Why did you assume that?"

"Because when I went out to get into the cab, his car was gone."

"How did you get to the bar?"

"He picked me up."

"Pretty rude of him to leave without you."

"Well, he was pretty drunk."

"Drunker than you were?"

"Considerably."

"You go out drinking with him often?"

"No. This was a first."

"Do *you* go out drinking often?"

"No," I said. "Look, isn't this getting a little in-depth for a traffic incident?"

"It may be more serious than that," Martinez said. "We don't know yet." He paused. "Can you think of anything else unusual about last night?"

"Well," I said, "I was surprised he'd driven off because I had his keys. I still have them."

Martinez looked up, now very interested. "So how did you think he'd taken his car when you got into the cab?"

"I assumed he had another set on him. Don't heavy drinkers do that sometimes, just in case somebody takes their keys?"

Martinez didn't reply; he just stood there waiting for me to continue. I didn't really want to get involved, but I felt I owed it to Eric to be helpful.

"Look," I said, "I told you Eric wasn't a close friend. But I like him, and you're getting me worried. What's going on?"

Detective Martinez tried to look ominous and succeeded admirably. "It's like this," he said. "You know the rain we had this morning? We found Dr. Schroeder's car washed up on a bank in the Sabino riverbed about noon. It was hidden by some cottonwoods or someone would've noticed it sooner."

"Is Eric okay?"

"We don't know. If he'd been washed out of the car, we like to think we'd have found him by now. He's not at home, he hasn't been to work today, and he hasn't called anybody, at least that we know of. When we found the car, we were hoping somebody had stolen it and left it in the riverbed as a prank. After what you've told me, I guess we should hope he abandoned the vehicle and walked to some girlfriend's house to sleep it off. The rain started this morning at six a.m., so it sure doesn't make sense that he was driving home from a bar he'd left at 1:30. But I guess he could have been coming to work. Did he come into work before seven very often?"

"I don't know. You'd have to ask over at the Institute. But I don't think so. He sets his own schedule, and I can't see him wanting to do anything today but eat aspirin and nurse his hangover."

"What really worries us . . ." he closed his notebook, "is the possibility that he pulled over near the river, then fell asleep in the car."

He didn't elaborate, but the implications were obvious. Martinez looked out my window for a second, perhaps contemplating the immense stupidity of the average civilian. Then he looked at me, as if something new and equally unpleasant had occurred to him.

"The other thing that bothers me," he said, "is this business with the keys. You're right about habitual drunks, they often keep a second set. But Eric Schroeder has as clean a driving record as I've ever seen, which is not what you'd expect of an alcoholic. And you're the first person we've talked to that's mentioned him ever drinking at all. Maybe he just kept a second key in case he locked himself out." He sighed. "And maybe he wasn't in that car. We may need to ask you some more questions later, Doctor. If you think of anything else, give us a call." He leaned back towards my desk. "Here's my card."

"What have you found out?" I asked.

It was Wednesday, five days after Eric's disappearance. The police had located neither hide nor hair of him, and I was a little spooked. I could believe that Eric would concoct an elaborate practical joke, but I found it harder to believe that the joke would involve the ruin of an expensive Japanese luxury car, not to mention numerous legal entanglements. Perhaps his disappearance was an accident, something that coincidentally occurred only hours after his dark warnings about Harold Anthony. But I found that hard to believe as well, which was why I was sitting in a small office in a suburban Tucson strip mall. Sitting across from me behind a cluttered desk was Valerie Weselesky, the private investigator I'd hired Monday.

As an old-movie buff, I'd half-expected Ms. Weselesky to look like Kathleen Turner, but the resemblance to V.I. Warshawski, Ms. Turner's sexy cinema private-eye, went only as far as the initials and Polish surname. Valerie Weselesky was dumpy, her mop-cut hair more brown than blond, and her thick glasses hinted at time spent looking over credit reports, not time squinting through the sights of a gun. Her office had concrete-block walls and a very small window, and you couldn't read her name backwards through the glass on the door because there was no glass on the door.

But I'd hired her anyway. There was no listing for Sam Spade in the Tucson yellow pages, and my new-found paranoia about Harold Anthony had steered me towards the least-obvious, least-known investigator I could find. I'd started at the back of the detective listings, and if there'd been any PI's with X, Y, or Z surnames Ms. Weselesky would have been out of a job.

"Well," she answered me. "It's hard to find out much of anything in three days. But I can give you my early impressions."

"Uh-huh."

"The first is: there's some connection between Dr. Schroeder's disappearance and your concern about this Maria Anthony, something you haven't told me."

"I did tell you. Harold Anthony. Her father-in-law." I'd told Ms. Weselesky that Eric's disappearance might be related to possible threats to Maria, threats Eric knew too much about. I certainly hadn't mentioned cloning. But Ms. Weselesky wasn't buying my incomplete story.

"Yeah, you did tell me that," she said, "and I'll tell you this. Just Harold Anthony's name isn't much to go on. If you feel that's all you can tell me, fine, you're paying the bills. But the less I know, the more inefficient and *costly* this investigation will be."

"I'll think about it," I said. My opinion of her skills rose slightly. At least she could tell when I was lying.

"Anyway," she continued, "my other two impressions. Number one is that Dr. Schroeder's disappearance fits a classic felony."

"Murder?"

"No, and you better be glad, since you're the last person who admits seeing him alive. It looks like an insurance scam."

This was not what I'd expected to hear. "In what way?"

"The lack of Dr. Schroeder's corpse. If he'd drowned, his body should be lying in the riverbed, surrounded by vultures. The police have checked downstream for about fifteen miles and they haven't found it. If he'd disappeared in the mountains it'd be a different story. But in the river? Somebody would have seen him by now."

"Couldn't some animals have . . . eaten him?"

"Coyotes are about the biggest scavengers around here, and they usually avoid human corpses. And even if they were brave enough to take a bite, they'd still leave enough to attract the birds."

"Okay. Tell me more."

"It would be an easy thing to set up. Let's say you're Dr. Schroeder. You hear from the weatherman that we're gonna' have a big gully washer the next morning, so you drive your car into the riverbed at five a.m. and walk away. You get on a plane or a bus with some fake I.D. and go off somewhere else. If you're smart, you've cashed in most of your bank account a few days earlier."

"Did Eric do that?"

"According to my friends in the police department, he's been making large cash withdrawals for some time now. Anyway, continuing with the assumption that you're ripping off your insurance company, when you're finally ruled dead, the honey who's the beneficiary collects, meets you in Las Vegas or Nogales, and you split the proceeds."

"I'm not buying it."

"Well, the police are having some trouble with it too. For one thing, no honey with a big insurance policy has shown up. In fact, no insurance policy has shown up. There is a will, a very recent one at that, but it leaves most of his assets to various charities. The bigger problem is that Dr. Schroeder isn't the type who pulls this sort of thing. He earns a lot of money. He'd have a hard time approaching his present income in another identity, even if he forged credentials so he could work as a doctor again."

"I see."

"So the motivation doesn't seem to be there. On the other hand, if he was in serious debt, or in fear of his life . . ." She paused, perhaps waiting for me to say something. I didn't. "Well, if that was the case, faking his own death might make some sort of sense."

"What about my other problem? What's your impression of that?"

"Frankly, I think you've been reading too many detective novels. I've made something of a specialty out of helping battered women, but I can't believe Harold Anthony's gonna' take a contract out on his daughter-in-law just because she's Cuban and he doesn't want her raising his grandson."

"I didn't specify a contract. I just said it was one of the possibilities."

"What other possibilities are there? Your cancer idea is straight out of the fuckin' twilight zone, if you'll excuse my French. I guess he could blackmail her and try to get her to leave her husband, but what's he gonna' blackmail her with? I've done some checking on the lady, and she's got no police record and her immigration status is perfectly legal. Besides, it sounds like the baby would be more important to her than any damage Anthony might do to her reputation. If she didn't give in to his threats, whatever the hell they might be, there'd be a lot of publicity. I don't know much about Anthony yet, but I already have the feeling he doesn't like uncontrolled publicity. I guess he could kidnap her, but unless he plans to ship her off to a harem in Afghanistan or something, kidnapping merely postpones the problem. Might as well just bump her off. And I can't see that. Not some bigwig like him."

"You're probably right," I conceded. "In fact, I hope you're right. But keep on looking into it anyway."

"It's your money. Maybe I'll have something for you in a week or two. But what I find will probably convince you to drop the whole thing."

"And what would you advise me to do till then, other than forget it and go home?"

"I guess you should sit tight and let me do my job."

But it was hard for me to sit tight. Visiting friends was no distraction; my only real friends were Joe and Maria. As for work: delivering babies made me think of Maria; writing about bio-tech made me think of Eric. After some agonizing, I realized I could at least disprove the wildest part of Eric's tale. Clinic policy was to do amnios on all *in vitro* fertilizations, amniotic fluid was routinely tested for gender, and if Maria's child was a girl, it obviously wasn't a clone of Leonardo, Harold Anthony, *or* Jesus Christ. Unfortunately, Maria's amnio was scheduled for her 16th week, three weeks away. Earlier amnios have a greater risk of complications, and I certainly wasn't going to move Maria's up just to ease my mind, particularly considering her already vigorous complaints about the Clinic's up-front, ass-covering insistence on the procedure. So I would have to wait. Finally, feeling like a credulous fool but unable to stop myself, I went to the University library to read about the Shroud.

An encyclopedia told me what I knew already: that the Shroud was thought by some to be the burial cloth of Jesus of Nazareth; that records of its existence dated back to the fourteenth century; that it showed a dim, life-sized image of a naked man, front and back. The reference also listed reasons to be skeptical, above all the results of carbon-14 dating done in the late 1980's.

I was more skeptical than the encyclopedia, and when I found my first book about the Shroud it only strengthened my attitude. More pamphlet than text, it earnestly theorized that Jesus's crucified body had been beamed towards Alpha Centauri, leaving the image as a kind of divine residue.

Two books by a man named Ian Wilson looked more scientific — a quick ruffle through the pages revealed graphs, charts, and scrupulous footnotes. I looked in the index of one and saw that several pages were devoted to the Leonardo theory.

I went home with three books and a photocopy of a recent article in *Time*, then parked myself in a comfortable chair. I started by just looking at pictures.

The Shroud itself surprised me. Fourteen feet long, it contained supposed impressions of both the front and back of Jesus's body, but apart from its size it was unimpressive, the markings on the cloth faint and singularly unbeautiful.

I guessed that the article in *Time* was my most objective source, so I read it first. After a brief synopsis of the Shroud's known history, it gave an account of the carbon-14 dating, which indicated that the cloth had been made somewhere between 1260 and 1390. Obviously, any date very far from 1 AD made the Shroud's authenticity questionable, but this date seemed particularly damning, since the first records of the Shroud showed up at about the same time. However, there were several theories about how the carbon-14 dating could be in error, and though they sounded like wishful thinking they didn't require supernatural intervention. One theory maintained that the sample's threads had been inadvertently taken from a patch sewn onto the cloth in the Middle Ages; another had something to do with a bacterial coating producing erroneous carbon readings.

Other scientific tests gave more hope to fans of the miraculous. Microscopic examination had found trace amounts of pollen native to Jerusalem. The linen was woven in a pattern supposedly unknown in 14th-century Europe, but common in Palestine since Biblical times. Cotton fibers were mixed in with the linen threads, even though cotton was rare in fourteenth-century Europe, but the threads contained no wool, a contamination typical of anything woven in Europe during the Middle Ages. Human DNA had been recovered from the Shroud, although not the complete chromosomal set needed for cloning. This briefly reassured me that Eric's story was impossible, until I realized that the recovery of mere fragments from one sample didn't preclude the discovery of a complete genome in another.

When I turned to the books I found more that was odd and

seemingly inexplicable. Areas of the Shroud that would normally be in shadow had no shading at all, while areas that would be the lightest in a conventional image were the most deeply shaded. Photographic negatives of the Shroud thus looked like developed photos, with light and dark in more normal places. There was no evidence that any pigment had produced the image, instead the fibers of the cloth were discolored as if by sunlight, heat, or some other form of radiation.

Reading further, I began to share Eric and Anthony's admiration for their 14th-century con man. The image's injuries were exactly what forensic scientists expected from a crucifixion. Nails had pierced the body's wrists, not the palms — as most paintings incorrectly depicted — and the back showed every sign of having been wounded by an authentic Roman scourge.

As I read, I became more and more uneasy. Oddly, the few facts bolstering the Shroud's authenticity didn't shake me; the carbon-14 dating seemed like irrefutable proof that the Shroud was neither supernatural nor even very old. But I kept coming back to one illustration, a photographic negative of the face.

When I used to leaf through my mother's art books, the old religious paintings always irritated me. In painting after painting, the artists had made Jesus the carpenter thin and effeminate, or given Jesus the peasant a patrician sneer. But the negative showed a man who'd known neither wealth nor luxury; beaten and tortured, with rough, Semitic features. As I read on, I wondered. Why did the likeness seem familiar? Why was it so unlike the Christ imagined by other artists? And why did its gaze leave me with a feeling of guilt, an apprehension of things undone, and a cold fear that all this world was a sad and pointless joke?

Chapter 8

Within a few days I'd read everything about the Shroud I could find. But Maria's amnio was still two weeks away, and I longed for some more immediate information. My chance came in a stone-gray envelope with embossed gold lettering, the return address reading simply: "The Anthony Institute, 22nd Avenue, Tucson, AZ." Inside was an invitation to a memorial service for Dr. Eric Schroeder, missing and now presumed dead.

I usually avoided funerals, but the possibilities inherent in this one intrigued me. Dr. Anthony was sponsoring a memorial for a man he'd probably murdered, and odds were the proceedings would contain at least a few references to God, a subject guaranteed to make Harold the Great uneasy. I opened my appointment book and penciled it in.

The service was at the Institute, in a second-floor room usually used for administrative meetings. About forty chairs were set up, with a single row facing the rest behind the lectern. There were no flowers, but somebody had brought in a few potted palms, presumably the same person who'd arranged to have lachrymose classical music playing in the background. When I arrived only nine people were there; all lower-grade Institute employees, including the dining room cook, his assistant, and Eddie the guard, who turned and waved, then got up and sat down behind me.

"Hi, Dr. Jacobson," he said in a cheery voice.

"Hi, Eddie," I said.

"I'm glad somebody came to this thing. I mean, jeez, where's everybody who worked with the guy?"

"I was wondering that myself. Did you know Dr. Schroeder well?"

"I didn't, but he was the nicest bigwig here — always real pleasant with us guards, used to give us Christmas presents and stuff like that. And what a sense of humor! He used to call to warn us about his practical jokes. Like the first time you came in, he said not to worry if you came out with a rutabaga or somethin', said it wasn't really from the labs, it was some sort of gag and he was gonna' get you good."

"It was a rubber eggplant. He told me it was genetically engineered."

"Rubber eggplant, eh? That's a good one. Hey, nice to see ya' Doc. I'm gonna' go talk to George." And he bounced off the seat behind me and went to perch behind another guard.

Just then Ed Devaney walked in, still wearing his lab coat. He glanced around the room in some bewilderment — perhaps thinking he'd mistakenly walked into an employee-appreciation brunch. Then his eye lit on me and he relaxed.

"Hi, Peter," he said, sitting down beside me.

"Hi, Ed. I'm glad to see at least one researcher show up."

"Yeah. I guess my associates were too busy. What a joke."

"I wonder if Dr. Anthony will be amused."

"I doubt it. Speaking of jokes, when do you think Eric will get here?"

I looked at him, baffled. "What do you mean?"

"I mean, if there was ever a man who might walk in on his own funeral, it was Eric. Here we are getting ready to tell everybody what a saint he was. Can't you just see him sneaking up behind us, leaning over and saying, 'Nice wake, boys'?"

"Very funny." I looked at him again. His smile was just a little tighter than usual. "You're serious, aren't you?"

"Let's just say it wouldn't surprise me. Eric was thoroughly pissed off with this place just before he went driving in the river. Playing dead has much more zing than a plain old resignation."

"What was irritating him?"

"I don't really know, and I didn't want to know. That's what I always told him when he started to complain. I came here to do science, not to get involved in corporate politics."

"What corporate politics?"

"Stuff I've done my damnedest not to know anything about. And if you're smart you'll remain equally ignorant. Which shouldn't be too hard, because you never come over here anymore. Where have you been?"

"I've had lots of babies to deliver. I'm an obstetrician, remember?"

"You're also supposed to be our science writer for the masses. Come by my lab and I'll tell you about the gene of the week."

I didn't really want to discuss why I'd been avoiding the Institute, so I didn't respond. We sat in awkward silence for about a minute, and then Ed spoke again.

"Say, speaking of babies, how's Dr. Anthony's daughter-in-law doing? Maria, isn't that her name?"

There was an odd quality to his voice, the same sort of play-acting I'd noticed when Eric asked me to shoot pool, except that Eric was better at it. And the question itself seemed out of character — Ed was rarely interested in office gossip, and he usually showed no interest in my obstetrical work. He knew that Joe and Maria were my friends, but other than that there was no particular reason to ask about Maria; her pregnancy — at least the official version of her pregnancy — wasn't the least bit unusual.

"Maria's doing very well," I answered rather formally, and then watched his face carefully as I framed my own question. "Why do you ask?"

And I could swear that he blushed a little.

"No real reason," he said. "I was just wondering."

There was a slight commotion at the back of the room. Dr. Anthony was standing in the doorway looking in at the crowd, or rather the lack of a crowd, and talking to some functionary still standing outside the door.

"Where is everybody?" he demanded.

"I don't know. We sent out forty invitations."

"You sent invitations to the cooks, the janitors, and the secretaries?"

"No, the invitations went to scientific personnel and administrators. And I sent one to Dr. Schroeder's personal secretary, of course. I suppose these other people just heard about it. Dr. Schroeder was always very friendly with the staff."

"Well, if they weren't invited I want them out of here!"

"Dr. Anthony, I really don't think that's wise."

"Why not?"

"Because the invitation wasn't worded so as to exclude anyone. And if they leave, there'll be no one here."

"Well, I told you that would happen. My people have better things to do than come to a service for a man stupid enough to drive into the river. This whole thing was your idea."

"Perhaps you're right sir. But now that we've announced it, we might as well go on. And you really should lower your voice, someone might hear you."

"I don't care who hears me. And listen, I want the name of everybody who's here without an invitation."

"I don't think that's wise, either, sir. You really have no grounds to discipline any of them; I assume they're all clocked out."

"I just want to have a private record of it."

"Sir, I'm no expert on labor laws, but I think that violates several of them. Any information you keep on an employee should be a matter of public record, in their personnel file . . ."

"So arrest me! I want a list of their names, and I sure as hell don't want my request in their personnel files. I want one copy, in my office, and just for me. Do you understand?"

"Yes, sir."

"Now let's get this carnival over with."

Dr. Anthony strode through the door and towards the lectern. With him was a short balding man wearing an expensive-looking dark suit, followed by a woman in her mid-fifties — the first person I'd seen today with the slightest air of being at a funeral. Dr. Anthony stood behind the lectern; the other two took chairs in the row behind it.

"Good morning," Anthony said, "it's still about five minutes before ten, but since everyone's here and we all have a very busy schedule, we'll begin. Mr. Sewell, our head of public relations, will speak first."

And with that tactful encomium the service began — all the funeral poor Eric ever got. Mr. Sewell (the bald man) stood up and spoke for about ten minutes. His eulogy was articulate but generic — he went on and on about "Dr. Schroeder's marvelous accomplishments," his "incredible devotion to Anthony Enterprises," his "scientific insight and experimental technique" — until I began to suspect he was reading from Eric's résumé.

The second speaker seemed more genuinely moved, though I wasn't sure if her emotion was inspired by Eric's assumed demise or a more longstanding grief. She turned out to be Esther Gluckmann, widow of the unfortunate Dr. Jonathan Gluckmann, and as she stood up I noticed that she had Dr. Anthony's complete attention.

Nothing she said was all that unusual, but she somehow made each of Eric's virtues seem like an unspoken criticism of Harold Anthony. She spoke of Eric's generous gifts to charity (Anthony often bragged that he never gave away anything). She recalled Eric's sense of humor (I could not recall ever having seen Anthony laugh). She praised Eric's sense of fair play as a businessman (Anthony had apparently studied business ethics with John Gotti). She remembered Eric's happy marriage (versus Anthony's bitter divorces and succession of trophy bimbos). No comparison was stated outright; it may have all been my imagination. But it wasn't my imagination that most of Esther Gluckmann's comments ended with a saccharine smile aimed at Anthony. And it wasn't my imagination that as she spoke he rose out of his habitual slouch, the tension between them growing with every word, a crackling electricity of ill will.

"In closing," Esther Gluckmann said, "I'd like to mention one of the most likable things about Eric. He was a man who treated everyone with respect, not only his scientific colleagues," here she nodded in Ed Devaney's direction, "but also those he met in other areas of life. I think it's the mark of a truly good man that he never abuses the power, talents or position that God has so graciously given him. I'm sure that Eric would have been pleased to see that such a wide variety of his friends came today to remember him, and also to grieve that yet another of the founders of this company has met his end in a tragic and bizarre accident. Thank you all for coming today." And with that parting shot she sat down and smiled sweetly at Dr. Anthony, who now refused to even look at her.

Mr. Sewell stood up at the podium and glanced over at his employer, now glowering at the audience of Eric's good friends — secretaries, cooks and guards. Perhaps Sewell thought of cutting his losses and bringing matters to a diplomatic close, but perhaps he was also a man who stuck to an agenda, and with a slight hesitation he announced the next speaker.

"And now Dr. Anthony would like to say a few words about his esteemed colleague."

Anthony stood. He had a few papers in his hand, doubtless some appropriate remarks that his secretary or Mr. Sewell had written, but as he came to the lectern he folded the sheets and put them in his suit pocket.

"I knew Eric for many years," he began, and then his bold attempt to wing it faded away into obvious impatience with the whole affair. He took a swig out of a glass of water sitting on the podium, swallowed, and continued. "He was a gifted scientist, a great attribute to Anthony Enterprises, and I for one will miss him a lot. Thank you." And he sat down.

A look of dismay shot across Mr. Sewell's face, but he was better at hiding his emotions than Anthony. He rose from his chair and took the podium again.

"I know that some of you still hope that Dr. Schroeder may still be alive," he said. "While I would encourage you in your hopes and prayers . . ." [at the word "prayers" Dr. Anthony scowled] "the police are now firmly of the opinion that Dr. Schroeder did indeed drown in the Sabino River, and steps are being undertaken to have him declared legally dead. In closing today, I think it would be appropriate to observe a minute of silence in honor of Dr. Eric Schroeder's passing."

So we sat, and thirteen of us tried to think about Eric instead of last night's baseball game or the day's waiting work. I succeeded with a sudden vision of Eric's bones bleaching somewhere in the Sonoran desert, their final joke gone sadly awry. And Dr. Anthony sat too — as subtle as Mount Rushmore on a clear Dakota morning. He was watching his Rolex, counting those sixty seconds away.

A week later we did Maria's amnio and I sent half of the sample off to the Clinic's lab. I also told my friend Jerry Williams at the University Hospital that I wanted a maternity test done, that I wanted it off the books, and that I'd personally pay him for his time.

"A maternity test?" he asked, puzzled.

"A maternity test," I reassured him. "M as in mother, A as in asshole, T as in twit, etcetera." Jerry had a rough sense of humor, and took an odd delight in being abused. "You'll be getting amniotic fluid samples and some blood tomorrow," I concluded.

"All right, a maternity test. You want to make sure some woman is having her own baby. I can get it done by the middle of the month. Soon enough?"

"Soon enough."

Chapter 9

An odd nightmare woke me on July fourteenth, and when I remembered that Maria's amnio results were due I realized I'd never get back to sleep. I rolled over and looked at the clock. It was 5:15.

"Happy fuckin' Bastille Day," I muttered, and got out of bed.

As I ate breakfast, I listened to the morning news in a vain attempt to forget about Maria. Kosovo was still simmering, but the economy was roaring along. Climatologists had announced that the 1990's was the warmest decade in 5000 years, and a mail-bomb had killed a professor at Penn State University — apparently someone felt the UnaBomber needed a replacement.

After breakfast I drove to work. Luckily, I had several appointments that morning. I'd resolved to stay calm while waiting for Maria's amnio results, but my good intentions would have come to nothing without some distraction. When the receptionist finally walked back to my office and said, "Lab reports," I almost yanked the envelope out of her hand.

I found the sheet with Maria's name, scanned quickly down the page, and with a sinking sensation saw that the baby was a boy. I sat at my desk for almost a minute before I thought to see if the test showed any problems. There was nothing; the fetus was completely healthy. That, at least, was good news, and I told myself that my reaction was ridiculous; after all, chances were a hair better than fifty-fifty that any given baby would be male. I decided to call Maria and Joe and tell them the test results were all normal.

The phone only rang once before Maria picked it up.

"Hello," she said.

"Hi, Maria," I said back, "This is Peter."

"Oh, hi," she said, sounding oddly apprehensive, and I realized that she was expecting to get the test results at her appointment later that afternoon. My surprise phone call must have her anticipating something dreadful.

"Listen," I said, "We got back the amnio results and everything's normal."

"Oh," she said, obviously startled. "I thought you were calling because there was something wrong."

"I'm sorry. I didn't realize calling would worry you."

"That's all right. I'm fine." She let out a long breath. "That's great, actually."

"Maria, amnios tell us something else. You and Joe said you wanted to know."

"Jeez. That's right."

"Are you okay?"

"Uh-huh. It's just that I've been sitting here all this morning. I've been so worried about the tests I couldn't go to class, and Joe's been so sweet, he wouldn't leave the house because I felt so bad." In her relief she was almost babbling. "But he's not here now, I haven't been shopping and neither has he, and there was nothing to eat for lunch, and he finally said it was bad for me to worry but it was worse for me to starve and he went to the store . . . but don't tell me! I want to be with him when we find out!"

"Well, call me when he gets back. I'll tell you if it's a boy or a girl then."

"Oh, come on Peter, we don't want to find out over the phone! We still have an appointment this afternoon, don't we?"

"Yes. You're at 4:30."

"Well, tell us then," she said, "and thank you!"

Five hours later Joe and Maria sat down in my office. The nurse had just checked Maria's blood pressure, and I waited for a moment so she could get settled. But it was hopeless; she was wiggling in her chair like an eight-year-old on the last day of school.

"Blood pressure's okay," I said, "and you're gaining just a little weight, which is good." I turned to Joe. "The amnio results were perfectly normal. Shall I give you the details or . . ."

"Come on Peter," Maria said, "Boy or girl?"

"You're gonna' have a baby boy."

My office phone rang. I was surprised — calls were usually handled by the front desk when I was with patients. I picked it up.

"Dr. Jacobson . . ." It was the receptionist. "I wouldn't have bothered you, but this Dr. Matthews said it was important."

Maria and Joe were coming out of a hug, and she was teasing him in a whisper, gently mocking his claim that he would have been just as pleased with a girl.

"I'm just winding things up with the Anthonys," I said, trying to remember just who the hell Dr. Matthews was. "Put him through."

But it was a female voice that came on the line. Formerly Beverly Matthews-Jacobson, my ex-wife was now de-hyphenated as well as divorced.

"Peter?" she said, "Are you there?"

"Beverly," I finally replied. "What a surprise! Where are you?"

"I'm in Tucson, believe it or not. I was here on business, and I thought it would be fun to talk."

"Well, sure, but now isn't a very good time. I'm with a patient. Let me at least get to another phone."

"No, don't be silly. I don't want to talk on the phone; I want to see you. Are you free tonight?"

"I'm not on call, if that's what you mean."

"But are you free? No dates?"

"I'm free."

"I hear there's a place called Tapas Tambien that serves wonderful Spanish food. Have you ever eaten there?"

I hadn't. Since meeting Joe and Maria my taste in restaurants had leaned towards the inexpensive, which Tapas Tambien was not.

"Peter?" Beverly said, and I realized I still hadn't answered.

"Sure. What time do you want to eat?"

"How about eight?"

"Okay. Where should I pick you up?"

"Oh, don't bother. I have a rental. I'll meet you there. I've already made reservations. You got all that? Tapas Tambien, eight o'clock?"

"Uh-huh."

"See you then. Bye."

"Goodbye."

I turned and saw Maria staring at me.

"Hot date?" she asked.

I purposely got to the restaurant at eight-fifteen. Beverly usually had her life scheduled to the second, and I felt the need to score some points. As I sat down I noted gleefully that she was fuming.

"Well, Peter," she snapped, "I see you've acquired a relaxed western attitude about being on time."

"That's a southern attitude, honey-child, not western." I put my napkin on my lap.

"Then what's your excuse?"

"I got an important phone call just as I was heading out the door."

"Medical or literary?"

"Literary." There hadn't really been a phone call, and I knew that to her, at least, medicine would be the more acceptable reason. We were off to a dandy start.

"Can I get you something to drink, sir?" the waiter interrupted.

"Sweetened ice tea, please," I said. Beverly looked at me, puzzled — I used to drink wine with my meals.

"In honor of a friend," I said, and then sat up straighter to continue the battle.

But apparently Beverly wasn't here to fight, and she could master mere emotion with an ease I'd once admired and loathed. She smiled.

"Peter, I didn't come here to argue. How have you been?"

I breathed deeply and thought about a line I'd read in one of my agnostic forays into the New Testament. Something about kindness being like coals of fire on your enemy's head.

"How have I been? All right, I guess. How have you been?"

"I'm fine."

"How's the hospital?"

"Good. I've just been promoted, and now I spend my time yelling at residents and wondering if I was ever that stupid myself."

"Maybe when you wore diapers. Do you still do a lot of surgery?"

"Oncology and the emergency room keep me busy. Of course I've got more paperwork and more administration, but on the other hand I've got more authority, which I certainly enjoy."

"How does the emergency room keep you busy?"

"Cranial gunshot traumas, usually. Not the best place in the world to catch a bullet, but we manage to pull most of them through."

"Sounds grisly. I think I'll stick to delivering babies."

"And how is delivering babies?"

"All right."

" 'All right,' isn't much of an answer."

"Okay. My new job hasn't been everything I'd hoped it would be, but then, what is?"

"What's disappointing? The medical part or the literary part?"

"The employer part."

"Oh? I thought Dr. Anthony's input into your practice was fairly negligible. You're free to take patients that have nothing to do with the Clinic, aren't you?"

"Yes. Actually, my work with the Clinic is fine. Dr. Anthony mostly leaves us alone over there, and I haven't had any major problems. No malpractice suits, not really even a hint of one. I've been very lucky."

"I'm not surprised."

"I am. Obstetricians are sued routinely."

"Yes, but you're a very good doctor."

"Oh really? That's not what you used to tell me in Chicago."

Beverly took a sip of wine and daintily patted her mouth. I sensed a prepared speech, and the prospect of receiving her charity weakened what little was left of my good intentions. I gulped some more iced tea and stared rudely over at the fountain gurgling in one corner of the room. She waited for me to look back, but I didn't.

"Peter," she said after a few more seconds, "that's one reason I wanted to talk to you. Some interesting things are happening in my life and I want to put some old resentments behind me. When we broke up I said some cruel things about you as a physician. I've been thinking a lot about that, and I wanted to tell you that I've never doubted you were a good doctor."

I was flattered in spite of myself. I looked back at her.

"So you'd trust me with your hamster?"

"What?" she asked.

"During one of our last fights you told me you wouldn't trust me with a pregnant hamster."

She laughed. "I'd trust you with my own baby." My eyebrows went up. "If I were having one, that is," she quickly amended. "Though I don't think I'd advise my husband — if I had one — to let you see me naked."

"Beverly, I don't put moves on my patients. I haven't been sued for that, either, I'll have you know."

"Of course not. Doubtless your patients *enjoy* your attentions."

"Beverly, I keep my professional life quite separate from, well, everything else. My patients don't get any of my attention. At least not that kind."

"Let's talk about something else," she said primly, an old ploy of hers. She liked to end an argument when she felt she was ahead. "If the Clinic is going well, what is it you don't like about your new situation?"

"I didn't realize how many strings the writing grant came with."

"What sort of strings?"

"Basically, I can't mention Anthony Enterprises unless I say something nice about them."

"Surely your contract doesn't say that."

"Of course not. It just works out that way. In order to do any observing at the Institute, I have to agree to let them do a pre-publication review. Supposedly that's just to keep me from inadvertently letting out any trade secrets, but I know better. Whenever I say anything remotely critical of Anthony Enterprises, they just take it out. I talked to a lawyer, and he says that if I violate the agreement I could be sued."

"Well, maybe you should write about something else entirely. Choosing that particular field was kind of an accident, wasn't it?"

"Yes."

"You've got a wonderful imagination. Maybe you should write some fiction. I bet you'd be good at it. I'll take back something else I said in Chicago, too. Your newspaper articles weren't disgusting."

I wondered what was behind this remarkable unburdening, although I had a guess. Now was the appropriate time for me to make some apologies as well, but I kept my silence.

"How's your love life going, Peter? Are you seeing anyone?"

"No, I'm not," I said, after a moment's reflection.

"Still playing the field?"

"Yeah, I'm still playing the field."

Beverly looked at me oddly, and I realized I'd spoken with a certain lack of conviction. She shifted uneasily and tried a new approach.

"You know, Peter, I promised myself I wasn't going to say anything negative tonight, but I'm going to break that promise. Our getting married was a big mistake, but I still like you, and to a certain extent I'll always care for you. So I'll be blunt. You're a lousy liar."

"Is that so?"

"It is indeed. I knew you were cheating on me almost from the first, and I didn't need anybody to tell me. All I had to do was look into your face when you gave me some cockamamie excuse for not getting home until three a.m."

"So I'm a lousy liar. Why are you telling me now?"

"Because I can tell you're lying again. You *are* involved with someone, aren't you?"

"No."

"Peter, I don't believe you. And I'd be glad to hear you were seeing somebody. We're not married anymore — I'd be happy to see *you* happy for a change. Who is she?"

"Beverly, I'm telling the truth. 'She' does not exist."

I was saved for a moment by the arrival of our waiter, laden with an order of calamari.

"I went ahead and ordered an appetizer when I got here," Beverly said. "I hope you don't mind."

"No, I love things with suckers."

"Are you ready to order?" the waiter asked, but I hadn't even glanced at the menu.

"No," I said, "I'll need a few more minutes." He left and I sat back and looked at the entrees, while Beverly looked at me, thinking about her last question. Over in a corner a guitarist was tuning up. A small sign at his side read: "Enrique Fernandez. Tips Gratefully Accepted."

"She's married, isn't she, Peter?" Beverly said in an icy voice, about the time I got to the wine list.

"Who's married?"

"The woman you're seeing. This woman you've fallen for."

"Beverly, I am not having an affair with a married woman."

"I don't believe you."

"Believe what you want — I'm not having an affair with anyone."

We locked eyes for a moment, then I looked ostentatiously down at my menu. At least two minutes passed before she said softly:

"You bastard. You complete bastard. You haven't changed one bit."

I didn't say anything; I just kept looking at my menu, amazed at how the two of us had picked up right where we'd left off in Chicago. I could have walked out, but that would be conceding my ex-wife another victory. And although she was right in her basic assumption, (women's intuition be damned!) I felt she was wrong in her moral condemnation. I might still have impure thoughts, but my recent actions regarding Maria were as clean as the new-driven snow. An apt simile, because the atmosphere at our table was now positively glacial.

"Peter!" said a voice to my left.

To my vast surprise, when I looked up there was Maria in the flesh, with Joe just as real beside her. Apparently they'd just come in, and Joe had seen me as they walked by our table en route to their own. Not knowing what else to do, I rose from my chair to make introductions.

"Beverly," I said, "this is Joseph Anthony and his wife Maria."

Beverly dropped her gloomy expression with some effort and leaned forward to shake hands. I paused, momentarily baffled as to how to conclude the introduction. "Ex-wife" suddenly seemed a totally inadequate label for this woman I used to sleep with. Beverly saved me the trouble.

"I'm Peter's *first* wife," she said sweetly — making it sound like I was planning a harem.

Maria made a grab at Joe's elbow, perhaps hoping to discreetly hustle him away. But I was suddenly feeling a perverse pleasure in the encounter. So you think I have a paramour, Beverly? Here she is, and watch how she hangs on her husband's arm. Read her body language if I get too friendly. And let's talk about how she's happily carrying her husband's child.

Well, maybe.

"Why don't you join us?" I asked. Joe was always a little dense when it came to unpleasantness, and he ignored Maria's signals and took my invitation at face value.

"Sure!" he said, and then turned to the hostess who'd been showing them to their table. "Can we sit here?"

"Certainly, sir," she said. "I'll get you some menus." They sat down, Maria on my right and Joe on my left. My ex, the soul of good breeding and manners, put on her party face.

"Joseph Anthony?" she asked, smiling at Joe. "Are you any relation to Peter's employer?"

"He's my father," Joe mumbled. I decided to change the subject.

"So what brings you two here tonight, Joe? I didn't know you liked Spanish food."

"Maria and I are celebrating, well, you know, healthy babies and all that. I told her to pick any place in town."

"So you picked a place with live flamenco guitar," I said to Maria. "That was nice."

"So you like flamingo guitar music, too, Mr. Anthony?" Beverly asked.

Joe took a second to answer; he was so unused to being called *Mister* Anthony. I helped out.

"You know, Joe, flamingo guitar. When you dress in pink and play standing on one leg."

I felt a slight pain in my shin. Maria had kicked me. Joe liked this joke, however, and played along.

"Yeah, but Enrique left his feathers at home tonight. What a shame. It's so much more authentic when you're dressed . . . Ow, Maria!"

I gathered that Maria had given Joe a little more energetic

reminder. Beverly was looking curiously in her direction.

"I'm so sorry," Maria said, turning and smiling earnestly at Beverly. "You must forgive my husband. He's something of a guitar snob. In Spanish it's called flamenco guitar, with a 'c' not a 'g.' This pink bird routine is one of his favorite jokes."

"A guitar snob, eh?" I asked.

"Yes, a guitar snob. He's almost as bad as you." Maria looked at Beverly. "Actually, I'm surprised Peter didn't tactlessly correct you several hundred times while you were . . . uh, married."

"I did," I said. "It never took."

But Maria was determined to have a pleasant conversation even if I was determined to sabotage it. She ignored my comment and pressed on.

"So Beverly, what do you do in Chicago?"

Beverly smiled brightly.

"I'm the head neurosurgeon at Chicago General. What do you do?"

"I'm studying to be a schoolteacher," Maria said softly.

"Oh, how nice," Beverly chirped. "And how about you, Mr. Anthony?"

Joe was less impressed by brain surgery. "I'm a luthier," he said proudly. "I build and repair musical instruments. Mostly guitars."

"And how did you two meet Peter? Did your father introduce you?"

Beverly seemed to have an unerring instinct for sore points tonight. I decided to help Joe out.

"I met Joe when I needed to get a guitar repaired. And I'm Maria's obstetrician."

"Oh, really," Beverly said. She looked at Maria with new interest. "When are you expecting?"

"Sometime in late December or early January."

"Are you hoping for a boy or a girl?"

"We found out today that it's going to be a baby boy."

"How nice."

We were interrupted by the waiter, come back for our orders. Joe and Maria hadn't even glanced at the menus, but apparently they'd had some recommendations, because Joe rattled off the names of two entrees with unusual assurance. As the waiter left, there was a lull in the music and the guitarist began to retune.

"Hey, everybody," Joe said, "Listen to this one."

"Listen to what? How do you know what he's going to play?" Maria asked.

"He's gonna' play a rondeña — that's the only flamenco piece you tune a guitar that way for."

I had never even heard of a rondeña but I was certainly tired of conversation — whatever startling revelation Beverly had planned for the evening seemed to be on temporary hold. We all sat silently and waited for the guitarist to begin — Joe with rapt attention, Maria with polite interest, Beverly with barely suppressed boredom.

As for myself, the argument with Beverly had made me reckless, and I forget where I was, or who might be watching. As the music started I was looking at Joe, who was staring intently at the guitarist, but I quickly found my eyes more and more drawn to Maria.

I'd heard tales of pregnant women's glowing faces, a magical radiance attributed to the growing soul in their wombs, but the pregnant women I saw every day looked tired, swollen, green with nausea. They never looked like Maria did that night. It seemed as if the light flowed not from the candles to her, but from her to the candles; while her face shone in a guileless and exalted expression straight out of a painting of the Virgin Mary or Saint Teresa. Visions of sex seemed suddenly blasphemous, but I could see myself on my knees in front of her, kissing her feet; or standing to one side and reverently touching my lips to her long, black hair.

The music came to a halt long before my reverie ended. I turned and saw that Beverly was no longer looking at Maria — she was staring intently at me. The entire restaurant seemed wrapped in a dead silence.

"Earth to Peter," Beverly cooed.

"What?" I said irritably.

"What planet are you on?"

"I was just listening to the guitarist."

"Well, he's not playing now." She turned to Maria. "How long have you and Joe been married?"

"Two years."

"I see. You must have gotten engaged about the time Peter moved to Tucson."

"About."

There was a vibration in my coat pocket and I remembered I had my pager with me. I took it out. It was displaying a number and a short message. "Jerry Williams. Please Call."

Beverly looked at me, annoyed.

"Literary or medical?" she asked.

"Medical," I said, in a low voice.

"Can't it wait?"

"I guess." I wished I'd had enough sense to not even look at the thing. My heart was hammering because there was only one reason for Jerry Williams to be calling, and I could hardly think of a worse time to find out about the "maternity test" than right now. The smart thing to do would be to call him back later; the news — good or bad — required no immediate action. Whether I could stand to do the smart thing was another matter.

"So why are you in Tucson?" Maria asked Beverly.

"They're doing some gamma-knife surgery tomorrow over at University Hospital. I'm going to observe."

"What's a gamma-knife?" Joe asked.

"Well, it's not really a knife at all. They focus gamma rays at a brain tumor. Since the beams are coming in from different angles they only destroy tissue at the focal point. It's less invasive than regular surgery, and it's the only way to get at some tumors."

"Why do they use gamma radiation instead of, say, X-rays? Do different types of radiation affect the tissue differently?"

"What a perceptive question, Mr. Anthony. What did you do before you went into making guitars?"

"I was studying to be an engineer."

"How interesting." Beverly stopped for a second and looked at me.

"Peter," she said, "I can tell you're dying to answer that phone call, you're fidgeting so. Just go see what it's about. We can wait."

I gave up. "All right," I said, "I'll be back soon."

I'd ditched my cell phone, unsure how easily its signal could be intercepted, and had Jerry call my pager instead. Unfortunately, that meant I had to find a pay phone. I'd assumed one would be up at the front of the restaurant, but they were at the back, near the restrooms. I dialed Jerry's number and stood fidgeting through five or six rings. Finally, someone picked up the receiver.

"Hello," said a feminine voice.

"Hi. Is Jerry Williams in?"

"He was here a couple of minutes ago. I think he just went down the hall to the coke machine. He should be back soon. Can I give him a message?"

"Can't I just wait on the line?"

"No, I don't think you should. There's only one line in here, and we're not supposed to tie it up for personal business."

I sighed. Of course, I could call Jerry's cell phone, which was probably in his pocket, but even that minor breach of security made me uneasy.

"Well, have him call me back the second he gets in," I told the voice at the other end. "I'll be at . . ." I glanced at the number on the pay phone ". . . 212-5489. Peter Jacobson."

So I hung up the receiver and stood there, trying to look slightly unfriendly so any talkative customers would steer clear and use the other phone. I was looking out into the restaurant when I heard Beverly's voice.

"Peter, when one makes a call it's customary to use a telephone." I turned and saw her looking at me. "Or do you have a new process that involves mental telepathy?" She must have just come out of the restroom.

"I'm playing phone tag, if you must know. He's going to call me back in a minute or two. What are you doing here?"

"Actually, I was hoping I might get a word with you alone. How did I beat you here?"

"I guess you knew where the phones were. What did you want to tell me that Joe and Maria couldn't hear?"

"It's her, isn't it?"

"What are you talking about?"

"The woman you've fallen for. It's Maria Anthony, isn't it? The lovely Latin lady having dinner with us."

"Of course not."

For a second, Beverly didn't say anything — instead she stood there looking into my eyes.

"I don't think you've even admitted it to yourself, have you?"

"Admitted what?"

"That you're head over heels in love with her, to use the old cliché. Oh, I can see some lust in your eyes — I don't think you could look at any woman without a fair degree of that — but there's more going on than a simple wish for a roll in the hay. I saw the way you were staring at her, any fool could see it; anybody but her *husband* that is, that big 60's throwback."

"Joe's my friend," I said heatedly, "and I haven't done anything I need to apologize to him for, at least not since they've been married. Why do I have to justify my love life to you, anyway?"

Beverly reached over and took both my hands in hers.

"Peter, I was looking for a tactful way to tell you this, and I thought it might be easier if I knew you'd found someone else, that's all. But I should have just come straight to the point. I'm getting married."

I didn't say anything.

"You don't look horribly surprised," she said.

"I thought it was that. That's really why you came to Tucson, isn't it?"

"Yes," she admitted. "I came to talk to you. The operation is my cover, so to speak. You know, I wanted to tar and feather you right after we separated, but when Jack proposed . . ."

"Jack, eh?"

"Jack Mathias."

"You'll sound like a legal firm. Mathias and Matthews."

"How funny. In fact, he is a lawyer. But anyway, when Jack proposed, I discovered that I wanted to see you one more time, just to make sure . . ."

"And what's the verdict?"

"It's over between us. That was pretty obvious from the moment your little Cuban Madonna sat down. I'm sorry."

"So this is it."

"Yes, this is really it. I notice you're not crying and beating your heels on the floor."

"Would it do any good?"

"No, because I'd know you didn't mean it. Can I have a hug for old times' sake?" I hesitated for a moment, and then gave her a quick, brotherly squeeze. But she didn't pull away — she stood there, loosely encircled in my arms.

"What are you going to do about little Mrs. Anthony?" she asked.

"I'm going to leave her alone," I said. "She's in love with her husband." And then Beverly did pull away.

"Ah, the sanctity of marriage!" she said. "It's a shame it's taken you this long to worry about it!"

"It is a shame," I admitted, "and I'm sorry I ever hurt you."

Another woman might have shed some tears, by way of accepting my apology, but not Beverly. I'd never seen her cry. She straightened up and I looked at her dispassionately. She was tall, beautiful, elegantly dressed, and as beyond me as ever.

"Come back soon," she said, "or your food will get cold." She turned and walked away as the phone behind me rang.

* * *

"Hello, Peter!" It was Jerry. "Have I got some news for you!"

"Really?"

"Is this line okay, my paranoid friend? Can I speak frankly, without fear of spooks?"

"Yes, you can. I'm on a pay phone at a restaurant."

"Well, your two samples are rather unusual, assuming they're really both from the same woman. You're sure you didn't make a mistake? If you didn't somebody else sure did."

"Quit playing around, Jerry. Tell me what you found out."

"I found out that this baby is *not* his mother's, at least in the normal genetic sense. Which would once have been downright impossible, but I guess now it's as easy as picking up the wrong Petri dish. Ain't *in vitro* grand?"

"Wonderful."

"No joke. Which is it gonna' be for the Clinic, Peter ol' pal? Lawsuit, out-of-court settlement, or a cover-up?" Jerry was ecstatic. Doctors enjoy proof of their colleagues' idiocy, particularly when the joke's not soured by an inconvenient corpse.

"None of your goddamn business," I told him. "And if you can't keep your mouth shut about this, at least keep my name and the Clinic's out of it. Okay?"

"Sure."

"Listen, I'm going to go eat."

"All right. And Peter . . ."

"Yeah?"

"It could have been worse. At least mother and child are gonna' have the same skin color. Well, close, anyway."

"You tested for race, too, eh? Nosy bastard."

"Couldn't resist."

"And what did you get on that?"

"Well, you know that's not the most precise branch of genetics yet. I'd guess the kid's parents were Eastern Mediterranean, Italian, or maybe Jewish. Might have an African great-great grandparent, too; can't be sure."

"Jewish, eh?"

"Couple of markers for that, yeah. Of course a lot of good WASPS have Jewish blood if you look back a few generations."

"Yeah, I guess they do."

"Hey, I'll talk to you later. Bye."

"Goodbye."

* * *

I stood for a moment staring at the receiver, wishing I could take this news and shove it back into the phone. Then I leaned against the wall and tried to think. It must be a foul-up, some Clinic technician mistakenly getting the wrong Petri dish from the incubator, just as Jerry suspected. Though even a mere mix-up would still create a grand mess. How could I tell Maria she'd unwittingly become a surrogate mother? If that was the case, *should* I even tell her?

And if Eric's story was true I could think of a whole world of reasons to hide it from Maria. To me God was nothing but a name pinned on human delusion, but Maria had been raised Catholic, she would never consider an abortion, and she had neither my faith in esoteric dating methods nor the skepticism I felt towards miracles. She had to carry this baby for six more months, and her reaction if I told her Eric's story might well be superstitious terror.

What if word spread further? Even discounting the lunatic fringe, (which I suspected was a pretty substantial portion of the religious anyway) the so-called mainstream worried me. What would they make of this story, particularly that little statement about a couple of DNA markers that might be Jewish? Assuming the most incredible possibility for the DNA's source to be true, what were the implications for anyone who *believed*? While the least radical Christians might only assume that God had crafted a new and merely human soul to fit the Shroud's DNA, fundamentalists might well assume Jesus's body had reappeared deprived of both soul and Holy Spirit, ripe to be inhabited by something from the opposite direction of Heaven. And a few oddballs on either side might consider the most sanity-toppling possibility of all: that God Himself had planned to come back this way since the dawn of Creation.

Given that, what if I told Maria about Eric's story after her son was born? What bizarre expectations might she have? What would the boy's childhood be like?

My legs took me back to the dining room before I'd come up with even the vaguest plan of action.

"Are you okay, Peter?" Maria asked me as I sat down. "You look like you've just seen a ghost."

"It's nothing," I told her. "Nothing at all.

Part II

Chapter 1

Zen Buddhism is fond of unanswerable questions such as "What is the sound of one hand clapping?" or "What did your face look like before you were born?" Questions like these are called *koans*. Meditation on a *koan* is meant to elicit *satori* — a mystical insight into the nature of the universe.

Unlike Buddhism, Western theology strives to be rational, but a *koan* lies at the root of Christian thought nonetheless. According to orthodox doctrine, God is omnipotent and eternal. He knows everything; cannot die, cannot sin, cannot act wrongly, because Rightness and Good are merely reflections of His nature. Compared to God human beings are powerless, our very essence at the mercy of our genes, our upbringing, the unforeseeable circumstances of our lives. But weak as we are, Christianity claims that every one of us is also damnably flawed. As St. Paul wrote: "All have sinned, all have fallen short of the glory of God."

So if we think in the traditional, logical Western way, the simultaneous deity and humanity of Christ means we must consider Jesus to be simultaneously omnipotent and weak, omniscient and clueless, eternal and transitory, perfectly good and inherently evil.

—from *Conversations with Joshua.*
Edited by John Baxter. 2032

At the hospital again, watching Maria. She doesn't know I'm here, but I'm glad to find her sleeping. I feel less guilty if I imagine she sleeps whenever I'm gone.

Tropical storm Wanda has left Atlanta, as has the rain, although a few clouds continue to scud through the sky. According to the weatherman, a new hurricane may be brewing off Africa, but it's unlikely it will hit the United States. It will probably go someplace else, someplace less prepared.

When Joshua was ten, Maria dragged me to church, and the minister prayed for a hurricane to miss the U.S. Afterwards, Joshua told me he thought that was a wicked prayer; that we shouldn't pray for bad things to avoid us when it meant that they would just go and hurt someone else. I told him that the minister didn't really want that to happen, that he was just praying without thinking.

To which Josh responded, "Should you try not to think when you pray?"

Maria stirs slightly, and I look down at what I brought with me today. It got me a few stares as I walked into the hospital, but I was expecting that. You could hide a pretty big bomb in a guitar case. I don't know why anyone would want to bomb a hospital, but I don't know why anyone bombs half the places that do get bombed. Plastic explosives have been much improved in the last twenty years; they've also become cheap and readily available. Plastíque is now even a weapon in gang disputes, more macho and less selective than tired old standbys like Uzis, AK-47's and Kalashnikovs. And that's just in the U.S. In the rest of the world, plastíque is as common as coconuts. As Will Rogers once said, mankind does progress: in every war they kill you a new way.

At eleven o'clock Maria wakes. It's good timing; in about a half-hour they'll be getting her up to eat anyway. She looks over, still half asleep, and sees me sitting in the chair.

"Hi," she says.

"Hi," I say back. "How are you feeling?"

"Hungry. And at the same time, full. Can you help me over to the bathroom?" She's still too weak to get there safely by herself, but she's also too stubborn to use a bedpan. I help her get up and walk her to the toilet. She swings the door shut, and in a minute or two I help her out again. On the way back to bed she sees the guitar case.

"Are you going to play for me, Peter?" she asks, puzzled. As I've gotten older I've become reluctant to play for anybody: bringing a guitar to the hospital is very much out of character. But Maria's dream the other day made me think: A little bit of Joe might help now.

"Well, I thought you'd like to see *this* guitar," I say. Maria is silent as I take it out of the case. Then she realizes which guitar it is.

"Do you think it was smart to bring that?" she asks. This is an instrument we never show anyone; it spends most of its time in a locked closet.

"Maybe not, but maybe we don't have that much to be careful about anymore." I realize too late that statement might be taken in an unpleasant way.

"Let me have it. I haven't looked at it for years." I take it out and gently hand it to her. Maria has never even learned to chord, but she holds it on her lap as she sits up in bed and gently strums the new strings I put on last night.

"Play something for me," she says, and hands the guitar back as carefully as she would a newborn baby. I try "Lágrima" for starters, a pretty piece, and also pretty simple, something Joe could have handled with ease. I stink, and the new strings keep slipping out of tune. But Maria smiles.

"Play something else," she says. And I try "Adelita," also by Tárrega, with slightly better results. Maria doesn't say anything this time, but she keeps smiling, so I continue. After a few more tries, old reflexes return and my performance becomes almost tolerable. And even in the hands of a hack like me, even after sitting in a closet most of the last twenty-six years, the guitar's tone is wonderful. The best and last guitar Joe ever made, this is an instrument most players would remember. Joe knew how good it was, and in a fit of pique he signed and dated the label by hand: "Joseph Anthony, 2005."

The label is the problem. By 2005 Joseph Anthony had supposedly been dead for six years.

"I've got good news and bad news," Valerie said as I sat down in her Tucson office. It was two weeks after I'd found out that Maria's child wasn't Maria's child.

"Aren't you going to ask which I want to hear first?" I said.

"Doesn't really matter. Here's the good news: It looks like you haven't been wasting your money after all."

"And the bad news?"

"It looks like you haven't been wasting your money after all."

For a moment I was bewildered, and then I got the joke.

"I'm glad there's something to laugh about," I replied. "Tell me how I haven't been wasting my money."

"There is indeed a rumor going around — at least among Tucson's morally challenged — that Harold Anthony tried to put out a contract on somebody."

"A contract on Maria?"

"The rumor isn't that specific. Actually, I'm amazed it's as specific as it is. Anthony may be a brilliant scientist or businessman or whatever, but he's been pretty stupid about this thing from the get-go."

"How?"

"The guy he tried to hire is the one spreading the rumor! You know, it's awfully hard to outrage the moral sensibilities of a hit-man, but your Dr. Anthony succeeded." She laughed and sat up to look at the notes on her desk. "Let's see, you told me that Anthony's something of a racist . . ."

"In a Mengele sort of way."

"Uh-huh. That seems to have been his downfall. He got the name of this Hispanic guy who knocks off police informants or people that welsh on dope deals, stuff like that. But Anthony didn't want him to shoot this victim. He wanted him to spray something in her face from a little aerosol can. Or maybe not in her face, the story gets a little fuzzy there, another version says he was just supposed to spray it in her general direction, so she'd breathe some in without realizing it. Supposedly, Anthony insisted he could put something in the spray that wouldn't kill her for at least a month, and that nobody could prove anything, because what was in the spray would appear to be harmless. So right off the hit man felt like he was being taken. He'd heard of Anthony Enterprises, so he figured he'd really be zapping her with some creepy unnatural bug, something he could catch, too."

"Her? The rumor says Anthony wanted a woman killed?"

"Uh-huh. He wanted it done next May. Nothin' like getting things planned ahead of time, is there? And that's where your Dr. Anthony really goofed. Hit men don't bump off many women, and some of 'em are a bit squeamish about it. So the guy starts making a little conversation with Anthony. First he asks him why he wants to wait till May, and he finds out the lady's pregnant, and that Anthony wants her hit after her baby's born and been breast-fed for four months. That gives our man another little jolt. So then he starts asking what this lady's done to make Anthony so mad."

"And then?"

Valerie was almost laughing.

"I'm sorry," she finally said. "It's obviously not funny. But I can't believe anybody would be this dumb. Anthony's probably lucky the guy didn't shoot *him*."

"What did he say?"

"The hit man asks why Anthony wants this lady done in. And Anthony gets real mad and starts yellin' about how he wants her gone because he doesn't want any 'syphilitic Mexican greaseball whore' in his family. Mr. Chicano Hit Man starts screaming back and kicks Anthony out the door. Literally."

Valerie was laughing now, but I wasn't amused. The story didn't mention Maria by name, but it might as well have, and I believed it.

Ever since Jerry Williams told me Maria's baby wasn't Maria's baby I'd had an eerie conviction that *all* of Eric's tale was true.

"If you wanna' look on the bright side," Valerie continued, "maybe the experience will bring Anthony back to his senses. He probably did come pretty close to getting his ass shot. He's lucky that hit-men don't usually off people without a little planning."

"So you believe this rumor?"

"If I'd just heard it out of the blue I wouldn't, but when it surfaces a month-and-a-half after you hire me to watch out for the same damn thing, right down to this screwy business about delayed-action diseases — what do you think? I think it happened."

"And you think Anthony will just forget the whole thing now?"

"It's a possibility."

"And if he doesn't?"

Valerie sat back in her chair. Her smile faded. She made a vain attempt to bring it back, but failed.

"Well," she sighed, "I don't think he's gonna' have much luck hiring anybody else in Tucson, but if he really means business, he'll just go to New York or Chicago and find some Anglo thug."

"Can't we go to the police?"

"You might, but I don't think it would do any good. The police arrest people after they've done something, not before."

"Anthony *has* done something! He's tried to get Maria killed!"

"But there's no way to prove it. The hit man won't tell the police. We might try to get the cops to set Anthony up, you know, have somebody pose as a hit-man and see if Anthony'll hire him, but I don't think they'll go for it; Anthony's an important guy around here, an upstanding member of the community and all that shit."

I looked at Valerie sadly, disgusted at our impotence.

"If we can't go to the police," I asked, "what the hell else can we do?"

Frowning now, Valerie tapped her pencil on the desk.

"I think first we need to tell this Maria lady what's going on," she finally said. "I can understand your not wanting to before now — I mean, if there'd been nothing to it you'd have gotten her all upset, which isn't a nice thing to do to pregnant ladies — and let me tell you, you've been a real philanthropist about this so far, I don't come cheap and it's not like you're married to the lady or somethin'. . . You don't look too excited about my advice here. What's the problem?"

"The prospect of telling Maria isn't appealing."

"What's she like? Meek, mild, and trusting would be nice."

"Cantankerous is more like it."

"Maybe her husband can help. Why don't you bring him in to my office next week, by *himself*. If we can convince him the three of us can work on her. When can you talk to him?"

"I can call him tonight. But why the rush? Anthony's not planning to do anything until Maria's had the baby."

"If Anthony's doing this to keep Maria from raising his grandson, he might go after some other people too."

"Like who?"

"How about Maria's parents? Don't you think they'd be an influence on the baby? Don't you think Anthony knows that and might want to do something about it?"

"I guess so."

"And in their case, he won't have to wait any five months. We need to act soon."

"Speaking of Maria, I don't see what telling her is going to solve. You still haven't told me what you think she should do."

Valerie reviewed the options one last time — I could almost see her ticking them off in her head. Then she gave me the answer she'd obviously thought of days ago.

"They should get out of town at the very least. Or better yet, disappear for good."

But how was I going to arrange a meeting between Joe and Valerie *sans* Maria? The only thing I could think of was to tell Joe I had a friend interested in his guitars. Unfortunately, since Joe's guitars were now popular and he was quite busy, Joe might well ask if my "client" could just drop by his house rather than meeting him somewhere else. Besides, lying to Joe was so easy it seemed unusually underhanded. I decided to tell him a small portion of the truth — which left me vainly trying to construct imaginary scripts. Seized with a sudden disgust at planning, I finally decided to just wing it and dialed Joe and Maria's number. Maria answered on the second ring.

"Hello?"

"Hi, Maria. It's Peter."

"Peter! I was just thinking about you." The sound coming through the receiver suddenly changed — Maria was covering the mouthpiece but making a bad job of it. I heard Joe say playfully, "Just thinking about Peter! I'll make you forget all about Peter!" then Maria's giggled protest, "Quit it!" Then she was back on the line.

"Actually, I need to talk to Joe," I said.

"But do you have time for a quick question from me?"

"Oh, all right. Shoot."

"Well, I know that when you're pregnant unusual things happen. Like you're supposed to crave pickles and ice cream, stuff like that." She sounded a touch odd, slightly out of breath.

"What strange craving do you have?"

"Actually, I don't have cravings."

"Wanna bet?" I heard Joe say. Maria giggled again, and then her hand must have returned to the mouthpiece, making a little better seal this time. But the situation was clear. My call had come at the end of a romantic interlude and Joe and Maria were lying in bed in post-coital splendor, perhaps even working up the energy for another round. I wondered what Maria wasn't wearing.

"All right," I said when she came back on the line, "you don't have cravings. What's the problem?"

"I have had some of the wildest dreams lately."

"Nightmares?"

"No! They're very pleasant. I'm way up high, there's lots of clouds and bright light and a feeling like I'm flying."

"You know what Freud said about flying dreams."

"You rascal!" she shot back. "Get serious! I've never dreamed much before, and now when I go to bed it's like the Late Show with Surround Sound and Dolby C, all telling me what a wonderful baby I'm going to have. Is there something wrong?"

I shook my head, trying to forget Maria's probable state of undress, or where Joe was fondling her. She was a patient, after all, and was owed an answer.

"I'm sure there's nothing wrong. Just be glad they're pleasant dreams."

"Oh, they are."

"I wouldn't worry about it then. Now, is Joe handy?"

"I'll say," she chuckled appreciatively. There were rattling sounds as she passed the phone over.

"Hi, Peter," Joe said. His voice had the relaxed tone of a man recently laid. "What's up?"

"Oh nothing much," I said cheerily, then more softly, "Can Maria hear us?" There was a slight pause, about five or six seconds.

"No, not now, she's going to take a shower," Joe replied.

"What are you doing Wednesday at three-thirty?" I asked.

"Working in my shop."

"You're sure Maria can't hear us?"

"Yes, I'm sure. What's going on?"

"Well . . . I've heard an unpleasant rumor, something to do with your father bothering Maria. On Wednesday I'm meeting with somebody who can explain the whole thing. Why don't I pick you up about three, and you can hear about it too. Come by yourself; I think it would be better if we left Maria out of this for a while."

Joe sighed. "If it has to do with my father, you're probably right. Maria's been after me to see him more often; she insists we can be one big happy family."

"Listen," I said, just to get a reaction. "This is just a rumor. Maybe Maria's right. Maybe your father's changed his mind about her."

"Like hell," he growled. "It would take a bomb to change that man's mind about anything."

"I'm sorry," I said, "I didn't mean to spoil your evening." Though that was a lie — spoiling the fun he'd just been having gave me great pleasure.

"Don't feel too bad," he said back. "My father's been screwing up my life for years. I'm used to it."

But when I knocked on their front door Wednesday my visions of a calm afternoon vanished. It was Maria who opened it, then stood blocking the entrance, feet spread a little apart, arms crossed like a mother addressing an obstinate and particularly idiotic child. Joe was standing behind her, his face set in a sheepish grin.

"Okay, Peter, what's going on?" she said, before I could even say hello.

"I have a friend who wanted to see one of Joe's guitars," I lied. "You can come if you want, but it'll be awfully dull."

"That's horseshit," she snarled.

"What do you mean?" I asked, trying to sound innocent.

"I mean you're almost as bad a liar as Joe is. You've heard some stupid gossip about his father, and now you're both out to protect me, and you're going behind my back because I'm in such a delicate condition! Well, let's go! I don't want to miss this dumb story for the world."

She strode past me towards my car, muttering something probably best left untranslated. Joe and I followed, almost running to catch her. When we got there Joe opened the car door and made as if to squeeze his six-foot frame into the tiny back seat, but Maria wasn't about to sit next to me. "Move!" she barked at her husband, "*you* sit up front. I know better!" Joe started to protest, but then good sense got the better of chivalry and he shut his mouth. We arranged ourselves as ordered and I drove off.

"Valerie Weselesky, Joe and Maria Anthony," I made introductions as we squeezed into Valerie's tiny office. Valerie looked at me across her desk and shook her head in disgust, as unhappy at seeing Maria as I had been.

"Well, Peter," Maria snapped the second she sat down. "You hired this lady to snoop into our affairs. Aren't you going to tell us why?"

I was terrified. I'd assumed Valerie would do most of the talking, and as Eric's story ran through my head, it suddenly seemed less than convincing.

"Why don't you tell them?" I begged Valerie.

"But you tell it so well," she replied.

Maria crossed her arms and glared. "I don't care who tells me," she said, "but I have a few billion better things to do, so one of you better say something or I'm going to call a cab and Joe and I will get out of here."

"All right, Maria," I said angrily. "It's like this. A few months ago I heard a disturbing story about Dr. Anthony. It concerned you and Joe, but since it could be checked out without prying into your personal lives *at all*, I thought I should see if there was anything to it before I got you upset. That's why I hired Ms. Weselesky."

Maria snorted, but I went on.

"What I heard was also so wild that I thought telling you about it would be unfair to Dr. Anthony, unless I had some proof."

"Why didn't you just ask *him* about it?"

"Because if it was true he'd certainly lie to me, and if it wasn't he'd probably fire me for even entertaining the notion."

"Must be pretty strange."

"It is, believe me. Listen, this will make more sense if I just start at the beginning, if I can do that without constant interruptions. You can yell at me when I'm through."

"Count on it."

Valerie was leaning forward on her desk now, hands cupping her chin and mouth, trying hard not to laugh — Maria was living up to the reputation I'd given her. I glared at my hired gun and began again.

"It all started with a conversation I had with one of the Institute scientists. He's a friend of mine, or he was a friend of mine, and he also did some medical work at the Clinic. Anyway, he knew Dr. Anthony pretty well. We went out one night, me and my friend that is, and we had a little too much to drink, and he told me some very disturbing things that are going on at the Clinic and the Institute. Most of that doesn't concern you," (I stumbled a little as I said that) "but he got to talking about one thing that did. You know he, well . . . Dr. Anthony doesn't like you very much, Maria."

"Oh come on, Peter. That's over and done with! If he thinks I'm so awful, how come he paid all our bills at the Clinic?"

"Because he wants a grandson very badly. But he doesn't want you raising his grandson, Maria, mainly because you're Cuban and he thinks Hispanics are . . . inferior. My friend said Anthony had some sort of plan to make sure you had nothing to do with bringing up the baby."

"And how was he going to do that?"

"Apparently Dr. Anthony never said it in so many words, but my friend got the impression that after the baby was born Anthony was going to have you . . . done away with."

Maria looked at me and burst out laughing.

"You hired a private investigator because somebody told you a story like that in a bar?"

Valerie finally came to my aid. "That's what I said when he walked in here and told it to me. I didn't say it too loud because he was paying. But it gets better. Let him finish."

I smiled appreciatively at Valerie and continued.

"I probably wouldn't have done anything about it except for what happened the next day. My friend was worried about his own safety, too; he was afraid that Anthony would realize he might talk. Anyway, we'd both had too much to drink so I went to call us a cab. When I got back my friend was gone. I'd gotten his keys away from him so he couldn't drive, but when I went out to the parking lot, his car was gone."

"So what?"

"It rained hard the next morning. That afternoon the police found his car in the Sabino riverbed. They still haven't found him."

"So he was driving drunk! He's not the first person to get drowned in a flash flood around here."

"He barely had a parking ticket on his record. And if he'd driven home he'd have gotten there a long time before the rainstorm. Something screwy is going on."

"Hold it, Peter," Joe said. "Your friend . . . you're talking about Eric Schroeder, aren't you?"

"Yes. I didn't know you knew him."

"I didn't. But I've heard my father talk about him. He was one of the original scientists at the Institute. They were friendly, at least more friendly than my father is with most of the people who work there. Maria, Peter's telling the truth, at least about that. I remember hearing about Dr. Schroeder. It was strange."

"Just because he disappeared doesn't mean this stupid story's true," Maria insisted.

"But it's got to make you wonder," Joe said. Maria snorted again.

"Listen, honey," Valerie said to her, "let me tell you what I found out. I didn't bug Anthony's office, but I do know some pretty sleazy characters around town. And about three weeks ago I started hearing a rumor that your lovely father-in-law tried to hire somebody to bump you off. And it's a very specific rumor, it talks about who, what, when, where, and even how."

"It mentions me by name?"

"Well, no, but it might as well. How many other pregnant Latina women are part of the Anthony family?"

"Maybe Peter got the rumor started, blabbing in a bar someplace."

"The folks I got this rumor from don't hang out with the likes of Peter. And Peter swears he's never talked about this with anybody but me."

"Well, who'd you hear the rumor from? Maybe I can talk to them."

"Lady, I can't tell you that. If I did those people would never tell me anything again. And they wouldn't talk to you anyway."

I realized we'd left one detail out. "Valerie, we haven't told her about the aerosol thing."

"Peter, I don't know if that's the most convincing part of the story."

"It was what convinced you, wasn't it?"

"I guess so."

"Maria," I said, "Eric told me the scientists at the Institute found a way to induce cancers in lab rats. Eric thought Dr. Anthony might use that as a murder weapon."

"Oooh, lab rats!" she said. "I'm so scared!"

"Part of the rumor Ms. Weselesky heard was that Anthony wanted this hit-man to spray you in the face with some sort of aerosol. It sounded just like the second part of the procedure Eric was talking about."

"And what was the first part?"

"Getting some of the rats' cells to incorporate defective DNA."

"So wouldn't I need to get sprayed twice?"

"Maria, I know all about *in vitro* fertilizations, and I know those doctors on the third floor must have stuck more needles into you than you could count. They could have done the first part of the procedure months ago."

Maria threw up her hands. "Peter, this gets sillier and sillier. Now I'm the bride of Frankenstein! You say Anthony tried to hire somebody to bump me off. How come he didn't succeed?"

"He got the hit-man mad at him," Valerie said. "He forgot he was talking to a Chicano and he said some pretty crude things about Mexicans."

"That much sounds like my father," said Joe.

Maria looked around the room for a second, obviously summing all this up in her mind. "So, let's see. My father-in-law loans us scads of money so I can get pregnant, then he wants to bump me off because he doesn't want his Cuban daughter-in-law raising his half-Cuban grandson. But he makes the mistake of hiring a hit man with a heart of gold. Maybe that's why he got turned down, did you think of that? Maybe your imaginary hood doesn't like what Dr. Anthony does to lab rats. Maybe he's an animal rights activist."

"Well, somehow when you tell it, it doesn't sound as good," I said, "but that's essentially the story. Except that last part about the lab rats."

"But Peter, it's the biggest pile of ratshit I ever heard. I certainly don't believe it, and I can barely believe you believed it. Joe, what do you think?"

Joe shifted uncomfortably in his chair.

"Maria," he began, "you don't know my father like I do. He's a very strange man, and lately he's seemed even stranger."

"How would you know? You do your best to avoid him."

"Now it's not true that I never see him — you're always after me to have lunch with him or call him on the phone. I've talked to him a few times since you got pregnant; you remember I took him out to lunch about two months ago, and he didn't make me mad like he usually does. He made me uneasy."

"And that's proof that he's trying to bump me off?"

"No, but if he's going nuts this story is more credible. Besides, this isn't the first time a rumor like this has circulated about him."

"What?" I asked. "That's news to me." I glanced at Valerie and realized it wasn't news to her. She looked at Joe and nodded, then turned toward Maria.

"I heard the rumor too, Mrs. Anthony, about seven or eight years ago. Joe's father started Anthony Enterprises with a business partner, Jonathan Gluckmann. Dr. Anthony had most of the ideas and Dr. Gluckmann had most of the money, and Gluckmann and he began to fight when the company got rolling. Just when things got really nasty Gluckmann was killed in a car crash, which was very opportune for Dr. Anthony since Gluckmann was heavily insured — he and Anthony both had business-life policies listing the other as beneficiary. The wreck was odd too — a one-car accident on the highway down from Mount Lemmon. There was some talk."

"So somebody's killed on what's probably the most dangerous road in Arizona, and that's supposed to be significant," Maria said. "And just for argument's sake let's say I'm stupid enough to believe this moonshine. What do you propose we do about it?"

Valerie turned in her swivel chair and grabbed some large file folders from the shelf beside her desk. I could sense she was trying to be upbeat, and when she turned back she put on one of her least convincing smiles.

"We thought you two ought to take a little trip," she said.

"It ain't happenin' Peter, and that's final," Maria said after we'd squeezed back into my car.

Joe wasn't so sure. "Maria, you may be right, but I'm worried about you. I think my father's quite capable of murdering someone."

"And I think you're blowing your childhood way out of proportion. Maybe your father was a royal bastard to your mother. That doesn't make him a killer."

"He's not my father, and I take it seriously," I said.

"That baffles me, too, Peter. You could make a better case for little green men in Roswell than you made for this stupid story. There's almost nothing to it, certainly not enough to chase me out of town. I like Tucson. My family lives here, Joe and I have friends, he has customers and connections. He's made a reputation for himself here. Have you thought about that, Joe? Even the most conservative plan that detective lady had will set you back two or three years. She wants us to change our names, move, and not tell anyone where we've gone. You'd have to build your business all over again."

"I thought about it," Joe said. "If it's what we have to do so you'll be safe, it's what we'll do."

"Well, it's sweet that you're worried about me, and I know that's why you let Peter get you all worked up. I'm sorry I was so angry. But the whole thing's silly. Believe me."

"Will you at least let Ms. Weselesky come over to your house and look for bugs?" I asked.

"She's an exterminator, too?"

"Knock it off, Maria. You know what I mean. Bugs, listening devices."

"Is she going to tear our house apart?"

"Of course not. She has some electronic gear — I don't know how it works, but it doesn't tear up anything. She's been checking my house once a week."

"Will it make you happy, Peter?"

"It will make me happier than I am right now, particularly if you don't talk about today's discussion inside until she checks your house out. And I'll pay, of course."

"Well, if you want to spend your money that way, you go right ahead — from the look of that office I'd guess the poor lady needs your cash. But she isn't going to find anything."

We got back to their house just in time for a desert sunset, clouds painted a thousand shades of vermillion against a cobalt-blue sky. Joe sat beside me, completely silent. With his beard and rugged face he looked ready to star in a John Ford Western. I glimpsed Maria in my rear-view mirror, hunched over in the back seat, her face glowing too in the auburn light. They belong in Tucson, I thought sadly, not in some sunset-deprived suburb of Normal U.S.A.

As I pulled into their gravel driveway, Joe sighed heavily. I knew he'd second-guess whatever decision he made about all this, so I'd burdened not only his evening with worry but in all likelihood the next few years of his life. He got out first and walked towards the house, too lost in thought to wait for Maria.

"I want you to remember one thing," I said softly as she wriggled her way out of the back seat.

"What's that?"

"Dr. Anthony's threatened to kill you before. You told me so yourself."

She glared at me over the headrest.

"Peter, I can't believe you're brave enough to bring up that night or that conversation. Besides, it was just one stupid phone call. He was angry."

"You said he threatened you several times, and always when you were alone. Which means he had someone watching your parents' house."

Maria didn't answer, she just stepped out onto the gravel and turned to close the car door. Then she pulled it back open and leaned down.

"All right; I'll think about it," she said. "And I'm sorry I got so mad. You're acting like an idiot, but you meant well."

And she shut the door, this time gracefully, gently, as befit the future mother of God.

On my way home I stopped at a pay phone.

"Let me guess — she wasn't convinced," Valerie said.

"I'm afraid not."

"Maybe that's for the best."

"I thought you were sure she was in danger."

"I am, but I've been wrong before. And your friend Maria said something that got me to thinking."

"Like what?"

"According to you, Anthony's so upset about her being Hispanic that he wants her killed to keep him away from his grandson. But if he's really into that Nazi bullshit, how is he managing to forget that his grandson is gonna' be *half*-Hispanic?"

"What do you mean?"

"The more of a racist he is, the less he should care about the kid, it being half-Cuban. The less he cares about the kid, the less he should want to bump off Maria. His supposed motive doesn't make any sense."

I didn't want to touch this at all.

"He's just crazy," I said. "Logic doesn't enter into it."

"Maybe. Or maybe his real motive has to do with whatever it is you're not telling me."

"I've told you everything," I lied.

"Then maybe we've been wrong and this rumor is just somebody's weird idea of a practical joke."

"Now *you* don't sound horribly convinced."

"Well, I gave it my best shot. I guess I'm not working for you anymore."

"No, you're still working for me. I don't think this is over yet."

"What do you want me to do? I can't think of anything else to investigate."

"You can sweep Joe and Maria's house for bugs every week, just like you've been doing mine. And I want you to keep your ears open. I'll pay you an extra . . . what do you call it? . . . a retainer."

"Money for nothin'. You got a deal."

Chapter 2

I didn't talk to Joe or Maria for two weeks after that — there didn't seem to be any point. Repeating my story wouldn't convince Maria her life was in danger, and seeing her while trying to avoid the subject seemed somehow absurd. Instead I nagged Valerie. One afternoon she exploded. Between expletives she said that if I had any bright ideas she'd be glad to hear them, and that if I wasn't satisfied I could hire somebody else. This sounded like a challenge, so I insisted she tell one of her friends in the Tucson police the rumor about Anthony and the hit-man.

"He said he'd look into it," she reported back, "right after he checked out a hot tip about Jimmy Hoffa."

But when the phone rang one night three weeks after our trip to Valerie's, for some reason I wasn't thinking about Maria. It was past eleven and I wasn't on call, so I picked up the receiver expecting a wrong number.

"Peter." It was Joe. "We need to talk. Can you come over?"

"Tonight? Right now?"

"If you can. Something's come up."

Joe answered the door quickly and took me into the living room. Maria was lying on the couch, wearing a very unsexy flannel nightgown. Dark circles underlined her eyes and her cheeks were hollow, as if she'd lost weight and hadn't been sleeping.

"Hi, Peter," she mumbled. "I'm sorry Joe hauled you over here."

"Don't 'Hi Peter' me!" I answered, then pulled up a small ottoman so I could sit close to her. "You look awful! What's wrong?"

"I'm all right. Talk to Joe first. That's more important. What's bothering me is just silly." But her nose was running, and I suspected she'd been crying.

"Talk to her first," Joe said. "It's not silly at all." He settled heavily into their battered old recliner. Maria sat up.

"It's the dreams I told you about. Actually it's just one dream. It's not so pleasant anymore."

"That's an understatement," Joe said. "You wake up screaming three or four times a night. You haven't slept well in two weeks."

"What have you been dreaming about?" I asked.

"Is that important? Can't you just give me something to get rid of it?"

"It would be better to take care of whatever's making you have nightmares. What are the dreams about?"

"They're about what your detective told us, at least I think so."

So much for my generous motives. Which was the bigger threat to Maria right now, Harold Anthony or my meddling?

"Listen," I said, "I can't give you any drugs. But hot milk is good if you can't sleep. I'll put some on and then you can tell me about your dream."

"You gonna' tuck me in and get me a teddy bear, too?" she growled.

"Sure. Did you have one of the dreams tonight?"

"Yes, about forty-five minutes ago. I fell asleep on the couch and then woke up yelling. That's one reason Joe called you."

"Well, why don't you watch something on T.V., just to get your mind off it, and I'll go talk to Joe." I handed her a remote off the coffee table and stood up.

Joe had already gotten out of the recliner and was heading towards the kitchen. When I followed him in he was taking the milk out of the refrigerator, so I went to the cupboard and got a cup. As he shuffled over and handed me the plastic jug, I realized that he looked almost as bad as Maria: slump-shouldered, his beard edging scraggily down his neck.

"How long has this been going on?" I asked.

"It got really bad right after we talked to . . . what was her name? The detective? Wendolowski?"

"Weselesky."

"It got really bad right after we talked to her."

"And what's bothering you?" I asked as I poured some milk in the cup and put it in their microwave.

"Later," he said. "Finish talking to Maria first." He sat down at the kitchen table and stared vacantly at the wall.

The microwave beeped. I took the cup of milk out, stirred it, poured a little in another cup, then tasted it to make sure it wasn't too hot. When I walked back into the living room Maria was watching T.V. with the sound off.

"Here you go," I said. "Drink this, and tell me about your dream."

She took a sip and made a rueful face. "Wouldn't hot chocolate work just as well?" she asked.

"Chocolate has caffeine. Ovaltine would be okay — you can get some tomorrow morning. What about your dream?"

"It seems silly now. There's really no reason for it to be so scary, I guess. It just is."

"What happens?"

"It's like the ones I told you about over the phone. I have the same feeling of being very high and small. There's a lot of bright light, and when it starts I feel like I'm flying or walking through the clouds. The colors are very vivid. You know it's funny, but I don't usually remember colors when I dream. The difference now is that I get frightened when I realize how high I am. And something, I don't know what, suddenly begins to speak to me, or to send thoughts into my head, because I don't really remember hearing it when I wake up — I just know what it's trying to tell me. If I had to put it into words I'd say it's warning me to run or hide. And then I do start to fall, and I keep on falling and I know the ground is getting closer even though I can't see anything but clouds and bright light. I'm always afraid I'm going to hit but I always wake up before I do."

"Sounds pretty scary to me."

"What's really frightening is . . . when I was a kid . . . we used to say that if you ever did hit the ground in a dream like that . . . that you'd die."

"Yeah, I remember hearing that. But it's nonsense."

"How do you know?"

"I hit the ground all the time in my dreams, and I just bounce."

That made her laugh, a first for the evening.

"You would bounce; you're the ultimate survivor. But about the dream . . ."

"What?"

"The funny thing is that I don't ever feel frightened when it starts. I don't feel like I'm in a bad place or that I'm around anything that wants to hurt me. It's like there's something very powerful that's scaring me for my own good."

"For your own good, eh? Well, I think you need to try and get some sleep for your own good, too. Maybe if you just lie down on the couch and leave most of the lights on you'll be all right. Joe and I will be in the kitchen. Can you try to do that?"

"Sure." Joe had already brought a couple of blankets out, and

Maria pulled one over her and lay down on the couch. I went back into the kitchen. Joe had made some tea in the microwave and was drinking the tepid brew with the bag floating in the cup, still staring at the wallpaper.

"Thanks for coming over," he said. "It was my idea; she didn't want to bother you until tomorrow. But I can't calm her down anymore, and I think having you here helped. How is she?"

"She'll be all right. But she needs to be sleeping. Stress isn't good when you're pregnant."

"I know."

"I guess I'm to blame for all this. I mean, I could have kept my big mouth shut. At least until after the baby was born."

Joe looked at me and shook his head, but I pressed on.

"Well, anyway, I apologize."

Joe sat up and pushed his tea away. "Oh, Peter, come off it! You heard somebody wanted to kill Maria, and you think you could just keep that to yourself? I wish I'd known about it sooner."

I had a feeling more serious news was in the works.

"What else happened?" I asked.

Joe didn't respond at once. He seemed to be getting up the nerve to ask me something.

"Peter," he finally said, "I know you think this story about my father and Maria is true. You haven't been doing anything creative to convince us, have you?"

"I don't understand."

"I mean, you haven't hired some actor, anything like that? Trying to fool us for own good?"

"No."

Joe stared at me a little longer, obviously trying to decide whether he believed me or not. "Maria's dream isn't the only thing we've heard," he said. "I've gotten two phone calls, late at night. I got them after we talked to Ms. Wendolowski."

"Phone calls? From whom?"

"It's like some dumb Godfather movie, only with Chicano gangsters. The phone rings at two in the morning and this guy says something like: 'Hey amigo, I don't bump off ladies, but I think you oughta' know your asshole father wants to do in yours.' You swear you've got nothing to do with that?"

"I swear. I didn't hire anybody to call you."

"Shit. But that's not all."

"What else is going on?"

"I hate to even mention this part; it just sounds like superstitious bullshit. But Maria's not telling you the scariest thing about her nightmare."

"What's that?"

"I can see how your story about my father could set off Maria's dream. But she had the scary version at least twice before you hauled us over to Valerie Wendowski's. And I've had the same dream, and I know dreams aren't contagious."

"They might be if somebody tells you about a dream they've had," I said defensively.

"How does that explain her having it before she knew any of this was going on?"

"I don't know. Coincidence, I guess."

"That's one too many coincidences for me, and I haven't even told you the worst part."

"Which is?"

"First, tell me again about this crazy scheme my father has to give people cancer. How does it work?"

"Well, you alter a few cells so that they're unusually susceptible to specific carcinogens, probably by inserting new genetic material via a retrovirus. Later, if the cells are exposed to one of the carcinogens they become malignant."

"And these cancers are very fast-acting once they're set off?"

"Eric said they were unusually aggressive, yes. What's that got to do with anything?"

"Ian called me from Michigan a few hours ago. They had to rush our mother into the emergency room; she started hemorrhaging from her lungs. They did some CAT-scans and found out she's full of tumors — they've spread everywhere. The doctors doubt she'll make it through this month."

As always, I stopped for a second to think of something good to say, and what came out of my mouth was fatuous.

"Oh my god, Joe," I finally croaked. "I'm sorry."

"And the funny thing is," he continued in a voice that was calmer than my own, "she had a full check-up just six weeks ago. The only other time she's seen a doctor recently was here. She was visiting us in March and she didn't feel well, something about hot flashes. I told her she ought to make an appointment with you, but you were out of town. Your office referred her to Dr. Deerborn, but when she showed up, he'd been called out for an emergency. Mom told me she talked to Dr. Deerborn's associate instead, and that he gave her a shot of something."

"Dr. Deerborn doesn't have an associate."

"Maybe I have his title wrong. I remember one other thing though — my mother said that when she got there the receptionist told her Dr. Deerborn's associate didn't work in the same office; that she'd have to go up to the third floor of the Clinic."

The cancer killed Joe's mother a week later, and on the flight back from the funeral Maria gave in to Joe's urging that they leave Tucson. She was worried about her own parents, so worried that she decided in favor of Valerie's most radical scheme: a fake accident that would make it appear she and Joe were dead. I was expecting something dramatic: an empty car off a cliff or a fake drowning similar to Eric's; but Valerie's plan was simplicity itself. Maria and Joe would go for a walk and not come back.

"All you gotta' do is tell some friends you're going hiking. I know a trail off of the Mount Lemmon highway that should do nicely. You park your car, hike about five miles, and then come back out on the highway lower down. Peter will pick you up there."

"Wait a minute," I said. "Shouldn't you pick them up? What if Anthony's got a tail on me?"

"If Anthony's had you tailed, then he knows all about me," Valerie said. "This way I can follow you and see if anybody's tailing either one of us." She turned back to Maria. "When your friends 'miss' you they'll call the rangers, who'll find the car and start to worry, 'cause you can do three things on this trail. You can take one turn and make a loop back to where you started, or you can take another turn and go back to the highway further down the mountain — which is what I want you to do. But if you take a wrong turn at another fork, you can hike into some serious trouble. When you don't show up, that's where the rangers will think you've gone."

When I looked at the map, I realized I'd once hiked this very trail. It started about halfway up the road to the ski area, where the trees grow tall on rain that never gets to Tucson. Most of the route was fairly easy, but I remembered one or two steep pitches and several rugged side trails, tough terrain for a woman starting her third trimester.

"After you pick them up," Valerie told me, "I want you to drive them over to Willcox, where they're gonna catch the bus."

"I hope they're not going far," I said.

"Where they're going is none of your business, Peter. What you don't know you can't accidentally tell somebody."

"But a bus! Why can't they fly?"

"The bus will be safer. Most people buy Greyhound tickets with cash, and nobody'll want to see ID's. And they'll blend right in, particularly Joe. He looks like lots of people I've seen on the bus."

I would have been mortally offended, but Joe looked up and smiled.

And so the first Saturday in September found me parked on a small dirt road just off the Mount Lemmon highway. I'd rented a minivan with heavily tinted windows; Joe and Maria had left their battered old Civic at the trailhead further up the ridge. They were supposed to show at my end of the trail around 2:00, and I was beginning to get worried by 2:30. I called up Valerie on the cell phone she'd loaned me, a digital model whose signal was supposedly difficult to tap.

"They're still not here!"

"Don't get your panties in a wad," she said back. "The guy who wrote the trail guide wasn't six months pregnant. I probably didn't add enough time to his estimate. They'll be along, and we'll still have plenty of time to catch that bus."

At 2:45, just when I was beginning to wonder if Joe and Maria would really need rescuing, I saw Maria in my rear-view mirror, coming out of the woods. I did a double-take as she and Joe climbed in the back seat of the van. Joe had shaved off his beard.

"Interesting new look," I told him.

"That was the idea. I took some shaving stuff and a thermos of hot water and did it on the trail."

"How was your hike?"

"Not too bad."

"Speak for yourself," Maria said. "I think I'd rather be dead than do that again. I'm getting too fat for this sort of nonsense. Hey, Joe?"

"Uh-huh?"

"My feet hurt. Could you rub them?" She plopped her legs up on his lap.

"I bet they smell real good."

"You'll survive. And you can untie the laces for me too — get some practice for when I'm too big to see my toes."

Joe did as she asked, then slipped her hiking boots and socks off and dropped them on the floor. Then with a sudden smile he took his thermos, a can of shaving cream and a washcloth out of his day-pack.

"You gonna' shave my feet?" Maria asked.

"Shaving cream is just soap and air. It'll make 'em smell better." He squirted a little on the washcloth and began rubbing.

I got on the phone again and called Valerie. "They're here," I told her, and pulled out and down the road. A mile or so later I saw her pull out behind me.

It was a quiet trip. For the first half hour I concentrated on my driving; the minivan sat so high I felt like I was steering a giraffe. I tensed again as we came back through Tucson, half expecting a car full of Anthony's hoods to force us off the road. I'd seen so many movies where that happened when you tried to leave town, and the idea seemed no more unlikely than any other event of the past few months. But Tucson was oblivious to our escape, and I finally began to relax when we left the suburbs and headed for the little desert town of Willcox. Every fifteen minutes or so I checked with Valerie.

"See anybody?" I asked her on our last call.

"No. As far as I can tell, we're being completely ignored."

"That's good."

"Interstate through a desert's not a good place to tail somebody. It's probably a stupid thing to worry about. But I look at the bright side. I get to put it on your bill."

"Thanks."

"I'll be hanging back here somewhere until the bus pulls out, but I'm not gonna' call you unless something goes wrong big-time. See ya' back in Tucson."

A few minutes later I pulled the van up to the bus station, a small building just inside the Willcox town limits. The open desert started not fifty yards away, an expanse of wind-blasted mesquite, cactus, and low shrubs that stretched all the way to the horizon. The desert was so big it made the little town seem like a set from *The Twilight Zone.* Leaving Joe and Maria there frightened me — I felt they might vanish the moment I turned my back.

"We're here," I announced. I turned in my seat and saw that Maria had fallen asleep on Joe's shoulder.

"Time to wake up, honey," he said. She mumbled something but didn't move. Joe rolled up a sweater and put it between her head and the window for a pillow. Then he slid over towards the door. "I'll go get the tickets," he told me, and got out.

And so I was alone with Maria. I had no idea when or if I would ever see her again, and I turned halfway in my seat to stare at her lovely face, then, for a few agonizing seconds, a little lower down, where I imagined the cross necklace rising and falling with each sleeping breath. In fifteen minutes I'd have nothing left of her but a few snapshots I'd taken and hidden away in my dresser drawer, and the negatives, which I'd squirreled away with other odd treasures in a safety-deposit box downtown.

She shifted, and the sweater slipped from beneath her head and fell to the seat. "Where's Joe?" she asked sleepily, then opened her eyes and looked at me and beyond, to the empty desert that seemed to stretch across half an eternity.

"Getting the tickets," I answered. I felt sure she'd been awake, sitting there with barely opened eyes, watching me watch her. I started to look away, then turned back, wanting to tell her everything and knowing it would be best to say nothing at all. She laughed softly.

"Gee, Peter. I'm breaking a promise I made to myself."

"What was that?"

"Not to be alone in a car with you ever again."

There was no malice in the remark; Maria's face showed only wry humor.

"You're safe," I said. "I've reformed."

"Well, don't reform too much. If it wasn't for Joe, I might find you kind of appealing."

Before I could answer, she slid to the door and jumped out. A moment later the tailgate opened and I saw her grab the small daypack she'd taken on the hike. I'd picked up their other "luggage" that morning: two large backpacks — Joe was traveling without a guitar for the first time in years. Perhaps Valerie had some plan to get more possessions to their new home, but it could also be that they'd be carrying everything they now owned. It occurred to me that Maria might be pig-headed enough to unload the packs by herself, so I jumped out to help.

I'd finished wrestling them onto the pavement just as Joe walked out of the building, tickets in hand. He came around to where Maria and I were standing, easily picked up both packs and set them down out of the way. Then he held out his hand for me to shake. I felt a sudden and desolate certainty that I'd never see him or Maria again.

"Got everything?" I asked. The wind was blowing so hard I almost had to yell.

"Uh-huh." He looked at the empty landscape. "I guess this is it. Thanks for all you've done for us, and be careful around my father. He's not a nice man."

"So I've heard."

Maria was standing slightly off to one side, a sad look on her face, but no tears. I imagined her hardest goodbyes had taken place earlier, when she'd left her family. She stepped towards me.

"Goodbye, Peter," she said, and gave me a sideways hug; she was pregnant enough now for her stomach to get in the way. "We'll miss you." She looked at me a second longer, and then thought of something else. "You're a good man," she told me, "when you try to be."

Valerie had said not to hang around, so I got back in the minivan and drove away. When I last saw them, they were holding hands on the bench outside the station, Maria's long black hair whipping Joe's face in the harsh September wind.

Chapter 3

Somehow it had never occurred to me that Harold Anthony had any real fatherly emotions. When it came to Joe, I'd written him off as a cardboard villain, an evil automaton with no heart to break. I'd never been more wrong.

He found out his son was gone when the forest service called. Instantly alarmed, he told them he had no idea why Joe and Maria's car had been abandoned, and then insisted upon an immediate search. When the forest service found nothing, Anthony brought in help at his own expense: planes and helicopters, extra search teams on foot, bloodhounds and two famous Navajo trackers. But the trackers had no luck because parts of the route were too heavily traveled; and the bloodhounds did no better, perhaps because Maria's family provided their handlers with clothes that actually came from her sisters' closets and my own.

After two weeks the wilderness search was called off — even Anthony admitted that if Joe and Maria were still out there, they were either dead or hiding. But the excitement was only beginning. From the outset Anthony thought Joe had been abducted, and when the police disagreed Anthony hired half the private detectives in Arizona to take over. After a week-and-a-half more went by with no ransom demand, Anthony lost all fear of upsetting his imagined kidnappers and began badgering reporters and announcing press conferences until the media were almost sick of him. By then Joe and Maria's faces were plastered over newspapers and magazines nationwide. Of course there was reward money: ten thousand dollars at first, then twenty-five thousand, then fifty. The numbers would have gone higher, but each increase brought in more fanciful and bogus leads. At least that was what Valerie heard through the detectives' grapevine. And something else she heard made me feel a little better about what we'd done to Joe's father.

"You know he's been doing this public grief thing real good," she told me, "and he's been careful to express concern about Maria as well as Joe. But you know what's going on behind the scenes? He's told all those detectives to investigate Maria's family — he thinks *they've* kidnapped Joe and that Maria's in on it. The detectives keep telling him that the Velasquezes are completely legit, but he won't listen."

"Do you guys often trade stories like this?" I asked. "Isn't your business supposed to be about keeping secrets?"

"Being a private eye is also about finding out secrets, so we tell each other *little* stuff all the time. Secrets also get kept better if your P.I. likes you. Anthony gets people pissed — word is he's the client from hell. I've never even met him and he pisses me off, so you can quit worrying about my being tempted by all that reward money."

"The thought hadn't occurred to me," I said, although it had.

"You're a lousy liar; that's one thing I like about you. But, like I said, the guy gets me pissed. I don't want his stinking money."

By November the furor was finally dying down, and so was hope that Joe and Maria might still be alive. I spent a lot of time at the Institute, ostensibly doing research on a new writing project, in reality keeping tabs on Anthony. There wasn't much to watch. Once Anthony had made all the business decisions at the Institute, but now he seemed to care only about his son, and Anthony Enterprises wallowed, rudderless. His secretary, genuinely concerned, told me that Anthony spent hours sitting in his darkened office, looking through the few family photos he'd kept after divorcing Joe's mother, or staring out at the mountains that had swallowed his son.

Joe and Maria wrote several times during the next two months, but I had no idea where they were. Valerie kept that information to herself, insisting that I couldn't accidentally spill anything I didn't know. I would have been more offended if Valerie hadn't also hidden the information from Maria's family, who knew only that Maria had fled Tucson because of Harold Anthony. Valerie herself only knew the city Joe and Maria had moved to; she had no residential or mailing address. All of Joe and Maria's mail now went through one of Valerie's colleagues back East. Before Joe and Maria left Valerie gave them her friend's P.O. box number and instructions — they were to rent a box themselves and mail her friend its number as soon as they got situated. All communication would first go through this private detective, who would remove Joe and Maria's new address from their letters before sending them on to Valerie in Tucson.

"It's not foolproof," Valerie told me. "Anybody who finds out I have a connection with Joe and Maria could look into my background and investigate my friends. And this lady back east . . ."

"Another lady P.I.?" I said.

"I don't trust men. They're too easily led by their dicks."

"Why, thank you."

"Well, you're a perfect example, aren't you? Or is your interest in Maria Anthony purely altruistic?"

"It's as altruistic as I can make it."

"Dammit, you've gotten me off track. What were we talking about?"

"Your scheme to send letters without knowing where the hell Joe and Maria are."

"Oh, yeah. Like I was saying, an investigation of me would turn up my friend's name, and once they found her . . . well, she doesn't know anything about Joe and Maria other than to send mail marked 'Grant' to their new P.O. box, but she's only forwarding mail to fifteen or twenty boxes. They could all be checked out."

I gathered from Joe and Maria's first letter that money was already a problem. They hadn't had much in savings and they hadn't taken it all with them — a cleaned-out bank account, even on the dawn of Y2K, would have been too suspicious. I'd pressed a small loan on Joe, but he'd refused all but a few hundred dollars. Valerie's contrived identities were good enough to survive a burger chain's background check, but they weren't yet good for much else. There was no way for Maria to make use of her almost-completed master's degree, and Joe had no references he could use to get a job repairing instruments, though in their second letter he wrote that he'd found some work framing houses. And of course they had no health insurance, so they'd have to bear the cost of Maria's delivery themselves.

Their letters were joint efforts. Joe was more honest about their difficulties — Maria hadn't called him the worst liar in the world for nothing — and he often let clues slip about their new locale. Comments about humidity, traffic, and people's accents gave me the impression they were in a big Southeastern city; maybe Charlotte, Nashville, or Atlanta.

January approached, and I worried more about my one absent patient than any of the women I was actually delivering. Obsessed with Maria, I also ignored the dozens of gloomy predictions about the upcoming millennium. Apparently I was right not to worry, because New Year's Day came and went, no comets appeared in the heavens, the seas didn't boil, and airplanes did not rain from the sky. If God had anything dramatic to say, we all missed it.

Two weeks later Valerie gave me a short note from Joe. It announced the birth of Joshua Manolo Grant, eight pounds, four ounces, delivered shortly after midnight on January 1, 2000. Maria and the baby were fine.

Chapter 4

Though I'd anticipated missing Maria, I'd also assumed that one day that longing would fade. But as January moved into February I felt no hint of recovery. Maria's absence had left a huge hole in my life, bigger even than the emptiness I'd felt when Beverly left me. The only woman I felt like talking to was Valerie, and that was definitely not a romantic relationship. Nonetheless, I went to see her frequently, and in true Sam Spade style, she'd usually break out a bottle.

And what did we talk about as we drank? Maria, of course.

"A phone call is a bad idea," Valerie told me.

"I want to talk to them. How is that more dangerous than letters?"

"Lots of ways. Let's assume the worst possible scenario — that your Dr. Anthony is on to us and is intercepting my mail. With the system I've got going, he still has no easy way of finding out where Joe and Maria are. But if she starts calling you and he's got your phone tapped . . . well, there's plenty of gizmos that'll give him her phone number. And if he gets her phone number, he'll find out where she lives in no time."

"So I'll call them from a pay phone."

"Then she's got to send us her phone number through the mail, which I don't like, either. I set up this whole scheme so somebody who got hold of a letter still couldn't find them."

"But Anthony won't think to check the mail. He's a computer geek."

"I still don't like it. For that matter, it would be better if you didn't know her phone number. You're obsessed with the lady; you'd call her all the time."

"I am not obsessed with Maria."

"Sure. Here, have another drink. Did you know your hands sweat when you talk about her?"

"They do not!"

"They do too! Look at that glass! Tell you what, how about they send us a video?"

"How would that be safer than a phone call?"

"Because it won't show where they are unless Joe points the camera at a sign that says 'Welcome to Saskatchewan.' Would some pictures of Maria calm your lustful heart?"

"What lustful heart?"

"Hah! I bet your palms are sweating just thinking about it. Would you like to see some home movies?"

"Sure. When can they make them?"

Valerie reached into her desk and handed me a videocassette.

"They already did, and they mailed it to me to give to Maria's parents. I made you a copy."

So later that day I got my first look at Joshua, just another wrinkled baby with a squashed-in nose. His skin was lighter than Maria's and darker than Joe's, and like most newborns, he resembled a prune more than anything else. But I didn't look closely at him until my third viewing of the tape. My eyes were all for Maria.

She'd cut her hair. I was angry for a moment — I felt she had no right — and then I had to laugh at myself and feel a little sad. Maria's long hair had been her one vanity, but her new pixie hairdo was an even more effective disguise than Joe's newly naked face — I might have walked past her on the street with little more than a bewildered glance. She looked hard and calculating with her hair short, but being clean-shaven changed Joe's face even more. Bearded, he'd had a philosophic calm, now he looked naked and defenseless, an Isaac ready to lie down on an altar of his own making.

The tape was precisely what one would expect — long jerky views of the baby sleeping; of Maria holding the baby; of Maria changing the baby; of Maria feeding the baby (I viewed that over and over in slow motion, tantalized by the fleeting view of Maria's breasts). Because of the haircut and shave, Joe and Maria's voices seemed to come out of the mouths of two strangers. But I played it three times, and then went to bed feeling more lost and abandoned than I had before.

What I needed was another project, something combining virtue and revenge. Exposing Anthony's theft of human ova would fit the bill nicely. But to do that I had to find another doctor or researcher with a guilty conscience, another Eric. I didn't expect to find my stoolpigeon at the Clinic (they had more to lose by talking) but I did no better at the Institute, though I spent a lot of time there, poking my nose into current projects and doing my best to befriend those in charge.

Dr. Anthony was no longer the worst obstacle. Dealing with sheriffs, Indian guides and bloodhound trainers had loosened him up considerably, and the Institute's Orwellian security was gone too, overwhelmed by a constant stream of outsiders consulting with Anthony about the search for Joe. The Institute scientists, however, were still the same close-mouthed bunch: techno-geeks terrified of human contact, or cold-war germ jockeys who answered questions with ice-cold eyes and masterful evasions. I finally decided to try and crack Ed Devaney, who at least liked to talk. Ed took a coffee-break in the Institute cafeteria every day at 10:45, as regular as clockwork, and I started meeting him there once or twice a week.

My first tactful appeals had no effect. I tried being a little more obvious, then finally went for broke and told him I'd heard that some nameless bio-tech company was stealing ova from patients and using them in cloning experiments. A strange look passed over his face, but it disappeared when I asked his opinion of this hypothetical project.

"That story's too dumb to have an opinion about," he said. "Where'd you hear it?"

For a moment I panicked — I hadn't prepared my own story very thoroughly — but the shade of Eric came back and saved me.

"It was on the Art Bell show."

"The Art Bell show?"

"You know, that radio talk-show guy who's on after midnight."

"You mean the UFO nut?" Ed exclaimed. I nodded, and he laughed.

"I can't believe you listen to that bullshit!"

And that was as far as I got with Ed.

But Art Bell's name gave me an idea. If unsubstantiated lies on a radio show could sway public opinion, wouldn't the unsubstantiated truth be even more effective? Via the Internet, I might be able to sink Anthony Enterprises without bothering with evidence.

I've never been any sort of computer expert, but I knew I shouldn't just log into chat rooms from my office. Instead, I had Jerry Williams get me a university account under a fake name. But when I began looking for forums to leave my planted leaks I found I was too late. Green Party web pages in Europe were already full of rumors about

Anthony Enterprises, and some of the accusations were spilling over into the more moderate American sites. Anthony's ova-stealing scheme was spelled out in detail, as was the fact that he planned to use the ova for human cloning. I found myself breathlessly waiting to read about the Shroud of Turin, but that, thank God, was never mentioned.

Something else struck me about the Anthony stories. The rumors about other bio-tech companies could have been written by a Trekkie who'd managed a C+ in high school biology. But the stories about Anthony were either couched in flawless industry jargon, or expressed in lucid, precise language geared towards the educated layman. Indeed, whoever was spreading the rumors about the Institute wrote as if he'd recently worked there.

February 29 found me eating a late breakfast in the Institute cafeteria. Ed Devaney walked in at 10:45, as usual.

"Hi Peter," he said, "How's the baby business?"

"I have the day off."

"Must be nice to have Tuesdays off."

"Well, I'm working this weekend."

"Poor boy." The sympathy was feigned: Ed often worked weekdays and weekends.

"Have you tried one of these things?" he said, pointing to an outlandish pastry on his plate. "Man, working here is making me fat."

It was almost as if his last word triggered the explosion. As Ed said "making" there was a rumble, and with the word "fat" came a low roar, mixed with a sound like ten-thousand shattering wine-glasses. The far wall disappeared, then part of the ceiling, followed by the floor, the line that marked its five-story descent advancing rapidly towards us.

To my right was the end of a long buffet table, perpendicular to the north wall. I fell over in my chair and grabbed its leg with my right hand just before the floor collapsed under me. Ed was sitting closer to the missing wall, and I saw him clutching desperately at the table where we'd been sitting. As it began to slide, I grabbed one of its legs with my left hand. The explosion was over, but as I hung there the crash and clatter of falling furniture, dishes, concrete and glass came to an incredible climax. And then everything was quiet, the only sound an occasional thud as a few precariously balanced objects careened down into the wreck of the building below.

I was lying on a section of linoleum tilted at about sixty degrees. Beneath me was the hole into which two thirds of the Institute had just collapsed. The only thing keeping me from sliding down five stories into the rubble was my grip on that buffet table, which still sat on undamaged floor. My life now depended on it being too heavy to slide — I didn't think it was bolted down.

Ed Devaney's life depended on my grip on our dinner table. His lower torso was over the edge, and there was no way for him to get a purchase on anything and climb higher. All he could do was cling to one leg of the table while I clung to the other.

"Jesus, Peter! Hang on!" he said. He was probably screaming, but I could only hear from the ear pointed away from him. My left eardrum had ruptured. Through my right ear I heard other sounds: people crying, screaming in pain, begging for help. Some sort of alarm went off, and above its clanging I heard running water from the sprinkler system. I tried to pull the table leg and Ed up the slope, but I wasn't strong enough.

"Ed!" I yelled, "Can you climb up? I can't hold you much longer!"

"I don't think so!"

"You've got to try!"

I could see his efforts through the corner of one eye. A young man in good shape might have managed it, but not a pudgy scientist in his early forties, not someone who was doing his level best just to hang on. He managed to pull himself up slightly, but to climb he would need to hold all of his weight with one arm so he could find a higher hold with the other, and there was no hold other than the one he already had.

Water from the sprinklers started to spill over the edge, drenching the tilted floor and both of my handholds. Worse still, something hot and greasy had sloshed out of the buffet and was running down the table leg I held with my right hand.

"Peter!" Ed yelled, "This isn't going to work, is it?"

"Just hang on!"

"Peter! Let go of me! It's no use!"

"Somebody will help us! Just hang on!"

"You're gonna' fall in a minute!"

"Somebody will help us!"

For a moment, Ed said nothing else, and I hung there listening to the clanging alarms, hoping I'd soon feel someone's strong hand pulling us to safety. Instead I felt an ominous burning begin in my right bicep.

"Peter!" Ed said. "I've gotta' tell you something!"

"What?"

"Whatever Eric told you, it wasn't a joke. If you ever see him or Maria Anthony again, tell them I'm sorry."

I twisted my neck and looked at Ed. He made a last frantic attempt to climb — I could see his legs pumping, trying to get a hold on something, while his face turned red with the effort. It was no use, and he quit trying and hung almost motionless again. "I'm sorry," he repeated. "Just tell everybody I'm sorry."

Then he bit his lower lip, closed his eyes, and let go.

It surprised me so much that I held on to the useless dinner table for at least ten seconds more. Finally I let it slide over the edge, trying to push it off to one side so it wouldn't land on whatever was left of Ed. With my left hand free I was able to swing around and grab the buffet leg with both hands, then hook my foot around another leg. Somehow I ended up wedged under the table, cramped but momentarily safe. In a moment or two I worked up the nerve to get out from under, move back from the edge, and survey what was left of the Anthony Institute.

It looked like Godzilla's big brother had come and taken a bite out of the building. Part of the ceiling hung down in front of me, but other than that the entire north side was gone. Most of the sixth floor was gone, too, with the worst damage in the center, near where we'd been sitting. As I came slightly out of shock I realized the scene was familiar; it looked like pictures of the Murrah building in Oklahoma City, and for the same reason. A truck bomb had gone off on the north side, blowing out a large portion of the first four stories. With nothing to support them, most of the fifth and sixth floors had then fallen to the ground.

I don't remember the next few minutes very clearly. I think I wandered around looking for someone I could help and trying to get out of the building. I succeeded in the latter: I found the one intact stairwell and went down it quite normally. But with the best will in the world, I wasn't much help to anybody else. Most of those who survived walked or crawled out themselves, and most of those who couldn't walk or crawl were already dead.

By the time I got outside the first ambulances and fire trucks had arrived. Though I heard it through only one ear there was noise everywhere: sirens wailing, firemen yelling, the building's alarms clanging, and a fire truck honking desperately to get past a car an idiotic Good Samaritan had left in the middle of the street. Some survivors were screaming or crying hysterically, some sat down on the curb or had the presence of mind to head towards an ambulance, others, like me, were wandering around zombielike in front of the building.

As I looked at the destruction I thought about Ed. Was it possible he'd survived the fall and that I'd then dropped the table on his head and killed him? I suddenly felt that I had to know. I started towards the rubble. I'd gotten up to some of the shattered concrete when a fireman gently took my elbow.

"You can't go up there!" he said.

"My friend's in there. I couldn't hold on to him!"

"You can't go up there. The whole building might come down."

"You're going up there," I objected.

The fireman didn't answer, though afterwards I wondered what reply he might have made. Maybe, "Yeah, but I'm getting paid to be stupid"? Stupid perhaps, brave certainly, but I saw that firemen were swarming all over the rubble, looking for people who might be alive and buried only lightly, people who might be bleeding but savable in the first thirty minutes or so before heavy equipment arrived on the scene. But if more of the building fell, it would take most of the rescuers with it.

"Look mister," the fireman said again, "you can't go in there. You're hurt and we can do it better."

"Look for him, will you? He won't be under anything; we were up on the sixth floor."

The fireman winced. Everybody who wasn't under anything would have fallen thirty or forty feet. Everyone who hadn't fallen would be under the rubble. He was almost certainly risking his life to rescue corpses.

"We'll look for him. Here you go."

He handed me over to a policeman who walked me to an area that was beginning to fill with ambulances and paramedics. As we walked I told him about Ed, how I'd tried not to drop the table; that I just couldn't hold on to it anymore — but he wasn't listening. One of the paramedics came up, looked at my ear and shone a light in my eyes, and then yelled something to another one with a clipboard. I must have been a low priority, because they sat me on the curb and told me to stay there.

By then I was crying, and every time I sobbed it sent shooting pains through my ear, which only made me sob some more. I wanted to make a scene, make somebody help me, but then I thought of Ed. A scientist to the end, he'd done his calculations and calmly taken the only logical step left. I wondered if I'd do as well when my time came.

Chapter 5

Several terrorist groups have taken credit for the Tucson bombing, but police consider a previously unknown organization calling itself The Wrath of God the prime suspect. The group claimed responsibility in a five-page manifesto mailed to a Tucson newspaper before the explosion.

In the manifesto, The Wrath of God claims the bombing was carried out to discourage genetic manipulation of natural organisms, particularly the manipulation of human genes and DNA. Unconfirmed reports say the manifesto particularly objected to the Anthony Institute's supposed propagation of human clones, although spokespersons for Anthony Enterprises have denied that any research in human cloning was taking place.

Police say this incident and last year's mail-bombing at Pennsylvania State University may be related, since both targets were involved in genetic research. In any case, the two attacks have done real damage to the biotechnology industry. Since the casualties include many of the top genetic scientists working in the United States, research in the field has probably been set back five to ten years.

—*Newsweek*, March 12, 2000

It was two hours later that I thought about Harold Anthony.

It seemed likely he'd been killed — his office was in the front part of the building, and most of the remaining survivors were being pulled from pockets in the rubble further back.

Ed Devaney wasn't among them. The firemen found him quickly, dead from a thirty-foot fall onto broken concrete. A table was nearby, but it hadn't hit him. At least that's what I was told later, although I wonder to this day whether the firemen actually noticed a detail like that in the chaos.

I'd survived relatively unscathed. My ruptured eardrum would heal itself, as would several small cuts I hadn't even noticed in the excitement. Nonetheless, the ER personnel insisted on checking me over thoroughly, but since they had a host of more serious injuries to deal with first, I sat in the waiting room for four hours, trying to ignore the pain in my ear, trying not to think about Ed.

When I finally did remember Anthony I'm afraid I wasn't very charitable. If he was dead Maria and Joe could come home, and I became positively giddy at the thought. In my quick wave of joy I forgot about Ed, forgot about the others who'd died, forgot even the mundane fact that I might well be out of a job.

After being examined I caught a taxi back to the Institute and drove my car home from there. Then I took a short shower, and got on the phone to reassure friends and relatives that I was all right. Next I called the Clinic to see if anyone had arranged for another obstetrician to fill in for me the next day. Somehow I suspected that I wouldn't be at a hundred percent for a while. Then I took a much longer shower and went to bed at five in the afternoon.

I woke in a haze at about six-thirty the next morning. My phone was ringing, but it seemed very far away. When I turned my head the sound got louder, and I remembered vaguely that there was a good reason for this, related somehow to the awful pain in my left ear and the horrible dreams I'd been having. I let my answering machine pick the call up, and ignored the voice leaving a message until I heard the word "emergency." Then I grabbed the receiver.

"Hello. This is Dr. Jacobson."

"Oh, good! This is Dr. Bryant. I'm a surgeon at Tucson Medical. Sorry to bother you so early, but we have a patient here who insists on speaking to you before he'll give us permission to operate. Could you come to the hospital and see him?"

"Sure," I said, a little groggily. "Who is it?"

"His name's Harold Anthony."

It's strange, but in a roundabout way I saved Anthony's life. Before Joe's disappearance, when Anthony wasn't in his office he could invariably be found in one of the laboratories; and both his office and the laboratories were completely destroyed. But Anthony had changed his habits since Joe's disappearance: he'd begun spending more time in Security, which was located toward the back of the second floor, away from the center of the blast. The explosion was too far away to cause that part of the building to collapse, but it did take out most of the interior walls, shattering metal-and-glass partitions and sending their fragments rocketing into the rooms beyond.

They found Anthony under the chief of security. The two men had been listening to a surveillance tape when the bomb propelled a small piece of metal into Anthony's spinal cord and a larger shard of glass through his employee's aorta. Anthony lay there in total darkness for the next eighteen hours, unable to move his paralyzed legs, barely able to shield his face from the drip of the dead man's blood. A maze of sheet rock, steel doors, and twisted metal beams delayed the firemen's search, as did fear of a further collapse, and Anthony wasn't rescued until early Wednesday morning.

Other than the paralysis, he'd suffered only a broken leg and some contusions. But the piece of embedded metal was razor sharp. If Anthony moved the wrong way it might cut into something else, perhaps more of his spinal cord, perhaps his right kidney, the only good kidney Anthony had. The fragment had to be removed. At least that was the story Dr. Bryant gave me when I got to the hospital.

"I wish he would have let us go after it right away," Dr. Bryant said as we stood outside Anthony's room, "but he was adamant that he wanted to see you first. If he'd been in immediate danger we would have gone ahead, but he wasn't and I decided I'd rather have him cooperative. He seems to feel he might not survive the operation."

"Is it that dangerous?"

"Not really. I'd put the chance of surgical mortality at about one percent, but Mr. Anthony said what he has to tell you is so important that even a one-in-a-hundred chance of your not hearing it isn't acceptable."

"I see. I'm just wondering why he wants to talk to me."

"As to that, you're a better judge than me. But whatever it is, I want you to remind him not to move. We've given him a dose of zemuron to immobilize the area around the fragment, but there are so many muscles in that part of the back I can't be sure we've gotten them all. Keep him from getting too excited."

"Peter! You're alive!" Anthony greeted me as I walked up to his bed. I was surprised he remembered my first name, much less used it, but his friendly tone was even more startling. I'd expected fury over the bombing, perhaps a new revelation about Joe and Maria, perhaps some threat or curse. Instead, he seemed elated.

"Dr. Bryant told me to tell you . . ."

"Not to move, not to even try to move. I know."

"It's very important. He says the metal fragment could . . ."

"Enough already! What I need to tell you is more important, and if you don't shut up and listen I'll wave my arms around until you quit blabbering. Pull over a chair. This may take a while."

I did as he asked.

"Have you heard why the Institute was bombed?" he said.

"No, not yet. I wasn't aware anyone knew."

"Some police detective zoomed over here as soon as they brought me in. The doctors weren't going to let him talk to me, but I insisted. He said some religious group did it. The police have a letter from them, a letter that was mailed the day before."

"The world is full of nuts," I said.

"But they weren't nuts! By God, they were right!"

I sat still, wondering if I'd heard him correctly.

"Peter," he continued, "I wanted to talk to you because you're one of the few employees that's ever objected to what we were doing. And I want to apologize for lying to you, or at least for misleading you for so long."

I was baffled.

"I can see you're confused," he said, "so let me start with something I'm sure you've wondered about: Why do you think I paid you to write for me when you disagreed with so many of my opinions?"

"You tell me."

"I picked you *because* you disagreed. I thought your articles would let us do our research with less public attention."

"And how would that work?"

"Well, having you write articles expressing concern about genetic research would make the public think we were concerned too."

I'd figured that out long ago, but I smelled an additional rat. "I see," I said. "Was that the only reason you hired me?"

"That doesn't really matter now, does it?"

"I want to know anyway. What was the second reason you hired me?"

Anthony didn't answer.

"Look, Dr. Anthony," I said, "tell me the second reason or I'll go home."

"All right. Do you remember the psychological tests we had you take?"

"Yes."

"I wanted a front man, not a whistle blower. The tests showed what I suspected from your personal history: that you weren't the sort of man who'd put himself or his career at risk to prove a moral point."

"I see."

"I'm not saying you're a coward, Peter. It's just that you're obviously a person who, well, a person who acts in his own best interests. A man who prefers talk to action. And we decided that you wouldn't have the . . . well, let's say that you wouldn't have the confidence to really look into what we were doing. Or to just up and quit if you found out we were using you."

I was silent, trying to decide how much truth there was in Anthony's description.

"But Peter," Anthony continued, "I see now that you were right. Whether you had the courage to act or not, you were right. And whoever bombed the Institute was right, too."

This was getting to be too much. "What do you mean they were right?" I practically spat in his face. "Was it right to kill sixty or seventy people!"

"If that's what it took to stop us."

I thought of Ed Devaney, of the mangled corpses I'd glimpsed as I walked out of the building. I thought of the woman who'd lost her arm, and then stumbled down four flights of stairs with somebody's tie strapped around the stump to stop the bleeding.

"I'm not buying that," I said. "I know I didn't agree with some of the things you were doing, but . . ."

"Ah, Peter! I underestimated you! You knew we'd moved from plans to action! Where did you hear about what we were doing?"

"I've heard rumors."

"Is that so?"

"Yes, I've heard rumors about things that were going on, but I would never have killed anybody to stop it. And a lot of good might have come from some of your research. I don't know what's come over you, but I think you're full of shit."

"Full of shit, eh?" Anthony said, still with a curiously congenial tone. "Is that any way to talk to a dying man? A man who will probably never walk again?"

"I'm sorry. I know you've been hurt. I'm just not going to condone bombing and murder."

"Don't apologize for me getting hurt. I deserved it. This is God's punishment for my sins. This and His taking my son away from me."

Anthony gazed heavenward with a curious look of exaltation. I wondered what eighteen hours of darkness and blood-soaked solitude had done to him, what it would have done to me. Had Anthony had a change of heart about Maria?

"I thought you didn't believe in God," I said.

"I didn't, but God has never stopped believing in me. Have I ever told you about my mother?"

"No."

"I've hated my mother for years. There! I've said it! You don't know what a relief it is to admit that. She was an alcoholic, but she was also deeply religious. Drunk, well she'd whip the fear of *her* into me. Sober, she used to whip the fear of God into me. And she didn't go to namby-pamby churches with homosexual preachers; she went to a church that believed in the Bible!"

"Is that all you wanted to tell me?"

He went on as if he hadn't heard.

"Have you ever thought you were going to die?" he asked. I shook my head. My brush with death the day before had been over too fast for reflection.

"I have," he said. "I sat there in the dark for . . . they tell me it was eighteen hours or so . . . I sat there in the dark for eighteen hours and thought about dying. And I thought about my mother, and I thought about Joe, and I thought about what we've been doing at the Institute, and that's when I realized this was God's punishment for the abominations we made. That's what I wanted to warn you about."

"What abominations?"

"The soulless creatures we were making. Oh, they'd look human, but I always knew in my heart that they wouldn't be."

"What soulless creatures?" I pressed him, wanting to hear the word beyond all doubt or refutation.

"The clones!" he hissed softly.

"Clones," I repeated, "you were making human clones?"

He nodded. "Thank God they're gone now, destroyed in the blast. They were all just fetuses, frozen embryos. All but one, that is. That's what I need to warn you about."

"What?"

"Maria Velasquez's baby. That was our first clone. Joe didn't know."

I tried to look shocked.

"Maria is probably dead," I said, "and the baby along with her."

"I don't believe that for a second! Oh, I think Joe's dead; I think they killed him. But that whore is still alive, and her child has been born. I know it in my bones. And what's worse, it wasn't the child we planned on; it was something infinitely more evil. We were betrayed by someone on my staff; we discovered it a few weeks back. The reason I wanted to tell you is that I need your help. I know you were Joe's friend; I know you'll help me avenge his death. Money is power, and I'm going to be powerless for a while. Anthony stock has already fallen like a stone, and it won't come back soon — my primary assets, my scientists, they've all been killed. Without money I have no way to find her, and I won't have a way for a long time. God has had to destroy everything I possess to show me the error of my ways. In the next few hours He may even destroy me. It may be that I've accomplished my mission just by warning you."

"Your mission?" I asked. "What mission?"

"I've sinned greatly, so God has given me a great task as penance. I've made it possible for the Beast to be born, and it will be my destiny to destroy him as well. I will find that child, I will denounce him, if needs be I will murder him in his bed."

Anthony had grasped my hand, was looking into my face with earnest intensity. For some reason he thought he'd found his first ally in this new crusade. If I'd been thinking clearly, I would have played Claudius to his Caligula; I would have smiled and said: Oh, yes! I see! You've been transformed! Let me be the first to bow down before you! And then I would have gone home and plotted against him, all the more effective for seeming weak and compliant.

But his description of me, that I was a man of all talk and no action, a man whose convictions extended only as far as his next paycheck, all these truths infuriated me. I spoke for once without fear or much thought.

"I don't know what's come over you," I said, pulling my hand out of his. "But if you think I'm your ally you've finished losing your mind. You may *think* you've undergone some great rebirth, but I don't think so. A week ago you judged good and evil by how they benefited your miserable self. And you know what? Nothing's changed! You've just switched sides because you think it's expedient. Well, it won't do you any good, because the real beast is in your puny little soul."

"You must help me!" he said.

"I know why you think I've got to help, but you're wrong there, too. Sure, I didn't like your playing God. But that doesn't mean I'm going to turn around and help you wipe out the poor suckers you were playing with: clones or painters or resurrected rabbis or whatever. I can damn well be in the middle, whether you think there is one or not."

" 'Because you are neither hot nor cold I will spit you out of my mouth!' " Anthony recited.

"That may not be a problem much longer," I said. "You're making me pretty damn hot right now."

I stood up, habitually moving my chair back against the wall, out of the way. I suppose it was the doctor in me; I didn't want it interfering with the crash cart if they needed to bring it in. If I'd been thinking a little more clearly I might have forgotten my Hippocratic Oath and tossed Anthony out of his bed. Of course he lay there still, his earlier look of exaltation replaced by an expression I knew better: a pinch-lipped crabbiness made daunting by the fire in his eyes. As I reached for the door, he called after me:

"So the real beast is in my puny little soul? How does that make me any different than you?"

"At least I know what I need to be fighting," I said, then walked out, ignoring the glare of Dr. Bryant, who'd come back just in time to hear the volume if not the substance of our exchange. No doubt he was furious at me for upsetting his patient. I didn't care.

"Go easy on the anesthesia, doc'," I told him as I strode out, "a little more pain will do him good."

Driving home, I cursed myself for a fool. Now was not the time to openly oppose Anthony, or hint at how much I knew. Resurrected rabbis indeed! I could only hope he hadn't noticed that glaring clue that I already knew everything he'd told me, in fact knew even more than he'd told me, that I'd been in league with some Judas in his organization from the very beginning.

Luckily, Anthony was probably right: he'd come out of this debacle a financial wreck, at least in the short term, and his ability to track down Maria would be significantly hampered. But I knew Anthony wasn't permanently ruined; his company still held patents that would bring in money whether its scientists were alive or dead. Unless he had another startling change of heart, Anthony would emerge as a bigger danger to Maria than ever. And not just to Maria. I was now his enemy too, one of the few people alive who knew what had been going on at the Institute, perhaps the only one with any motive to tell.

I came to a decision. I pulled over to a pay phone and called Valerie. Luckily she was in.

"Peter!" she said, "You lucky devil! Aren't you glad that you work at the Clinic and not the Institute!"

"Actually, I *was* at the Institute."

There was a long pause on the other end. "Jeez," she finally said, "I hope you're all right."

"I've been better, but I'll survive. I'm not in the hospital or anything. Listen, I need to talk to you. When can I come over?"

"So Anthony's got religion?" Valerie asked.

It was a little after three. We were sitting in her office, discussing the events of the past two days.

"Anthony's got religion, and I opened my big fat mouth."

"Not the brightest thing you've ever done, but nearly getting blown up might make anybody a little irrational. Speaking of which, what do you think the chances are that Anthony's conversion will stick?"

"How should I know? What worries me are the implications if it does."

"Well, I'm a little lost about the implications. I certainly don't understand why Anthony has it out for the baby now. It doesn't seem to be a necessary consequence of finding God, not even of finding a thoroughly screwy God." She looked at me slyly. "Does it have anything to do with what you've been hiding from me?"

Like all liars, I hadn't kept my stories straight. I'd been smart enough to omit all mention of cloning from my explanation of Anthony's conversion, but it hadn't occurred to me that conversion alone didn't explain his newfound hatred of Maria's child. For the equation to make any sense, one had to know about the cloning.

"Come on," Valerie persisted, "I'm getting into this thing up to my eyeballs. I deserve to know what's going on."

I didn't answer immediately, and Valerie said nothing either, just sat there staring as she rocked back and forth in her swivel chair, tapping her pencil slowly on the desk. I thought a long while.

"Before I tell you," I finally said, "can you promise me this isn't going to be one of your 'little' secrets? It won't be something you tell some other P.I.?"

She sat up eagerly. "Scout's honor."

"You a girl scout? I don't believe it."

"Poetic license, but binding nonetheless."

"You once asked me why Anthony cared so much about Maria's baby, seeing that it would be half-Cuban."

"Yes. And I still wonder about that."

"The child isn't half-Cuban. Anthony thinks that its genes are lily white."

"I don't get it. How could the kid not be half-Cuban if its mother is all Cuban?"

"Maria isn't the child's mother."

Valerie looked puzzled for more than a moment, then she put part of the equation together.

"Okay, they got Joe's sperm and somebody else's egg together and put it in Maria. How does the result end up being the Antichrist?"

"They didn't do it that way. Sperm wasn't involved."

That one took her a moment longer.

"The kid's a clone?" she finally asked, a little hesitantly.

"Uh-huh. Which is why Anthony now considers him soulless."

"Do Joe and Maria know?"

"They don't, and I think it might be best to keep it that way."

She considered this for a moment as well. Then she moved on to the inevitable question.

"A clone of who?"

"Let's just say I don't know for sure, but the implications of who it might be are very disturbing. To me as well as to Dr. Anthony."

Valerie didn't say anything for a little while more. She shuffled a couple of papers on her desk, tapped her pencil again, and then came to some decision.

"Okay. This all makes some sort of sense now, though I must say it's the wildest thing I ever heard, and I'm in a business where you hear some pretty wacky stuff. What are the implications for you?"

"I think that by opening my big mouth I've put myself in danger, though I can't really say how much. If nothing else, I can't be much use to Joe and Maria as long as Anthony is keeping an eye on me. And if it turns out that there's something to my paranoia . . . well, I'd like to be able to react quickly if I have to."

"What do you think Anthony's going to do: have you bumped off?"

"I'm more worried that he might have some thugs pick me up for questioning. In which case everything I know about Joe and Maria might be something he knows too."

"In which case he might bump you off when he's done, just to keep things neat and tidy."

"That, too."

"So how do you think you can avoid this?"

"By disappearing down the same sort of rabbit hole that you sent Joe and Maria into."

More silence from Valerie. In fact, she was treating me to more silence this afternoon than the total she'd given me since I met her. Finally she looked up.

"Well, Doc, I'll let you in on a little trade secret. You've picked a good time to shuffle off your mortal coil. Y2K didn't screw up things as bad as everyone was predicting, but it screwed up a few government databases royally. They were running on shitty patched-up COBOL programs written back in the mid-60's. If you're unlucky enough to be on one of those programs the government isn't real sure right now if you're dead or alive."

"What do you mean?"

"Well, the federal government likes to keep track of dead people, because one of the best ways to become somebody else is to borrow the identity of a corpse. County courthouses rarely check death certificates against birth certificates, and if you write 'em and say you need another copy of your birth certificate, they'll send it to you. Get a birth certificate, then you can use that to get other I.D., a passport, drivers' license. None of 'em forged, everything quite legit-looking. The big sticking point used to be social security; those guys had a pretty good idea of who'd croaked. But Y2K has done some amazing things to that little government operation. Right now if they come up with a live dead person, so to speak, they're likely to think that it's just a computer screw-up and gloss right over it."

"I haven't heard anything about this."

"You think the government is advertising it? Hell, no! But let me tell you, things at Big Brother and company are currently one fucked-up mess. We might even be able to find some dead doctor whose shoes you can fill. I've been thinking about doing something like that for Maria, finding some teacher who doesn't need her credentials anymore because she ain't breathing."

"Can you do anything like that for Joe?"

"Not a chance. What percentage of the population do you think makes a living selling handmade guitars? He should have picked something a little more normal if he wanted to have a prime a'hole like Anthony for a father. But doctors and teachers are a dime a dozen. I think it could be handled."

"What about recommendations?"

"Well, you can try to get them from people who don't know your new self has died, so to speak. You can even recommend yourself."

"What?"

"Start job-hunting before you disappear. List your new self as a junior partner in practice with your old self. Write a letter and try not to make it *too* complimentary."

"That's kind of funny."

"Isn't it though? Listen, I wouldn't have tried it in '99. But this is the new millennium. What better time to invent a new you?"

"Sounds inviting. At least more inviting than worrying about Harold Anthony. But what if I'm worried about nothing?"

"Listen, I can get this ready to go and then not use it. It'll cost you money though."

"That much I counted on."

Chapter 6

In the weeks after the bombing I enrolled in a karate class, applied for a concealed weapons permit, and had Valerie debug my house *twice* weekly. I quit eating at my regular restaurant and stocked up on Perrier so no one could poison me by bribing chefs or sneaking cyanide into my tap water. Finally, I started marking my BMW's trunk and doors with scotch tape to foil potential car bombers. But six weeks passed serenely by, then six months; and Harold Anthony remained silent, recuperating behind the locked gates of his Catalina foothills estate. I'd heard he was lifting weights for two hours every other day, building strong arms and shoulders so that no one would dare call him handicapped.

He coped equally well with the departure of wife number three. Frightened by Anthony's new obsession with religion, she'd sued for divorce without contesting their pre-nuptial agreement: a parsimonious document that gave her a paltry two-hundred grand for five years of marriage.

My own visions of being broke and unemployed proved pessimistic — Anthony never bothered to cancel my writing grant, and the Clinic still attracted patients, although I noticed that many of the third-floor "doctors" now wandered the hallways looking lost and bereft. Perhaps they missed their glory days as apprentice Frankensteins.

What was left of the Institute's ominous black cube was brought down at the end of April by a Dallas demolition firm. I went to watch, and found the unwatered gardens brown and withered, the animals sent off to God knew where. As the ruined building collapsed I felt a moment of intense fear, then a surge of vindictive glee, and lastly, a twinge of regret. Unfortunately, watching the Institute's fall did nothing to end my nightmares, dreams that recalled Ed Delaney's death, though sometimes it was Maria, sometimes Joe, sometimes the baby Joshua that slipped from my fingers and fell slowly towards a smoking pile of rubble hundreds of feet below.

Unable to hold on in my dreams, I made it a waking obsession. I filled my house with Maria's image — snapshots I'd had enlarged and framed, and a few paintings I paid to have made from the snapshots.

And as a sort of homage I began remaking myself into Joe. I joined the Sierra Club and recycled my Perrier bottles. I sponsored two more Christian Children's Fund orphans (I'd already picked up Joe's Guatemalans), then looked around for other worthy charities. I read science fiction.

As for the baby Joshua, since Maria and Joe loved and protected him, I felt driven to do the same. And as his protector, his possible parentage still frightened me. After Eric disappeared I thought that I alone knew of the connection between Joshua and the Shroud. But Anthony knew about the switched embryos, and the strangely accurate Internet rumors had me wondering if Eric was still out there, stirring up more trouble than he'd ever bargained on. Besides myself, there might be two men who knew the real story of Joshua's conception, and I wondered what the world's reaction would be if that story was ever revealed.

So I started going to church. I hadn't converted, nor did I expect Joshua to someday sport a halo or pointy little horns. But I was curious — if the average congregation believed that Joshua was Christ or Satan re-appeared on this Earth, what would they do about it?

At first I only went to church services themselves, singing hymns at nine a.m. with one congregation and 11 a.m. with another. I quickly saw a pattern. The liberal churches featured gently smiling ministers, women as often as not, preaching about the Third World and social responsibility to rows of empty pews. The conservative churches featured ministers with tight-lipped smirks, exclusively male, preaching hell and Falwell in packed auditoriums.

It was Hell that made me worry about Christians: smiling people who praised their Divinity's infinite love and forgiveness, then calmly related His plan to condemn billions to torments that would have appalled the Marquis de Sade. I could see a religion believing in some punishment. An unrepentant Hitler didn't belong in Paradise, and I liked the idea of demons thrusting a few red-hot pokers up Dr. Anthony's supercilious nose. But eternal damnation? Not an eye for an eye, but a trillion eyes for an eye? And according to many churches, most of those suffering this endless temper tantrum would be nowhere near as wicked as Adolf. Some would be people like Albert Schweitzer, who, in between acts of loving charity, wrote books questioning the divinity of Jesus; or Mohandas Gandhi, as Christ-like as any man I could think of, but also one who apparently never uttered those magic words, "I accept Jesus as my personal savior."

Not everyone bought into the idea of Hell. It certainly wasn't featured in the sermons of the earnest young women just returned from Nicaragua and Honduras, nor was it emphasized in moderate churches. But if there were Christians who viewed Hell as something their religion could do without, a few trips to Sunday School convinced me there were many others who were quite fond of the idea. After all, they knew they weren't going there — not unless they offended the Almighty by asking inconvenient questions.

To make matters worse, I foolishly paraphrased my hospital conversation with Anthony (minus any mention of cloning) in a letter to Joe and Maria. To my horror, Maria found the idea of Harold Anthony spouting Bible verses encouraging; she felt sure he'd achieved some spiritual and moral epiphany. I asked if sporting a button that said "Jesus or Hell" was a moral advance over merely chasing a buck, and whether any religion that relied on conversion by threats of eternal torment was to be trusted. She wrote back that in her opinion the good Lord had nothing to do with Hell, that those things had been put in the Bible by the worst elements of religion. I wasn't surprised at her benign views, but I was frightened when she wanted to know why she, Joe, and Joshua couldn't return to Tucson, now that Anthony had at least partially seen the light.

"After all," she wrote, "even those nuts who kiss rattlesnakes don't condone murder. Certainly Joe's father won't walk straight out of a church and hire a hit-man. It has some inherent contradictions."

"Don't be too sure," I wrote back. "Plenty of Christians used to believe that their good and just God sent unbaptized babies straight to perdition. What about the contradictions inherent in that?"

A weak argument perhaps, but I was stranded on my own lies. Joshua might end up dead if Anthony found him, but I couldn't tell Joe and Maria why without revealing all of Eric's story, a step that frightened me almost as much as their returning to Tucson.

"You could be wrong, you know," Valerie told me during one of our frequent afternoon cocktail hours. "It could be all right for them to come back."

"She might be safe, but I'd have my doubts about Joshua."

"You really think the baby would be in danger? I know you heard Anthony threatening him, but after all, that was just after the guy had almost been blown to kingdom come. I'll bet now he'd rather find another sweet young gold-digger and try out his Viagra prescription."

"Why do you think he's suddenly become sensible?"

"Well, for one thing, he hasn't tried to have you killed. Weren't you worried about that, after your last heart-to-heart with him? But it's been six months since then, and you're still breathing."

"Proving you wrong doesn't sound very appetizing when you put it that way."

"Don't sweat it. I've been watching your tail, and I do more with your retainer than buy us whiskey. I've got contacts, and they tell me Dr. Anthony is just sitting up at his nice house, pottering around in his wheelchair and chasing that pretty nurse he's hired. And he goes to church *a lot.* I'm surprised you haven't run into him."

"I don't go to his sort of church. The ones I've been to already are bad enough."

"Well, you won't catch me in any of 'em. They don't approve of my choice of drinking companions. You excluded, of course."

"Why not?"

"Because most of my drinking companions are gay as a three-dollar bill."

I must have looked shocked.

"You're gay?" I asked hesitantly. Valerie laughed.

"Yeah, I'm gay. You haven't noticed me chasing your tight little buns around, have you? But getting back to Dr. Anthony, I think he's reformed. At least I know he doesn't have any plans to do you in."

But there, unfortunately, Valerie was wrong.

Chapter 7

My imitation of Joe was far from complete; I hadn't become a slob. So when I got home one September night and sat down to look at my mail, the dining table in front of me was freshly polished and shiny. All except for one corner, that is, which was covered with a fine white dust mixed in with a few grains about the size of breadcrumbs. Puzzled, I looked at the dust for a moment, then looked directly above it to the ceiling. The dust was under a small fire alarm. There was one in almost every room in the house, and when several had started beeping the month before, I'd had my cleaning service change the batteries in all of them. The one above the dining table looked a little strange, and I realized it was hanging askew on the ceiling. A dry-wall anchor had pulled slightly out, and the dust on the table was from the ceiling.

Well, I thought, the battery was defective, and the maid replaced it again today. But the little specks of white dust made me uneasy — they were the sort of thing a maid would notice. So I took my shoes off, stood on a chair, and pressed the alarm's test button.

Nothing. The small red light which usually glowed was dark as well.

I took my chair around the house, pushing the test buttons on all the other smoke detectors. Four of them didn't work.

Thirty minutes later Valerie pulled into the convenience store parking lot where I was waiting. I'd driven there straight from my house and dialed her pager from a pay phone. When she called back she seemed less than pleased to hear my voice, but when I told her that someone had been fooling with my smoke detectors she said she'd be right over.

Her car — a dirty, aging, red Chevette — was as glamorous as the rest of her. She parked next to me, got wearily out of her car and hopped into mine.

"Okay," she said, "tell me again about your screwy smoke detectors."

"Four aren't working, and I think somebody's been tampering with them."

"Why?"

"There's white dust from the ceiling under one, and they should all be working. I had the batteries changed last month."

"Had the batteries changed? You mean you paid somebody to change some batteries?"

"Sure. Don't you?"

Valerie just looked at me for a moment, shaking her head. "How come you didn't choke on that silver spoon growing up?" she asked.

"Oh, be quiet. Don't you think it's worth looking into?"

"I guess. But the most likely explanation is that your maid put the batteries in wrong."

"Then how do you explain the dust?"

"Oh! Who knows? Maybe there was a spider web on that one, and she swept it with the broom and knocked it a little loose."

"All right," I said, "maybe I'm being jumpy. You want to go home?"

Valerie thought about it. Then she looked at me again, a little less skeptically.

"I want to go home, but you might be right," she said. "Listen, let's go in my car, and don't talk to me once we get in your house. If somebody's been in there, they may have planted some bugs. I've got a couple of note pads and pencils in the glove compartment: if you've got something to say when we're inside, write it. If you've got a lot to say; write me a note that says: 'Let's go outside.' Understand?"

"Now who's being a little paranoid?"

"Look Peter, if you're gonna' get paranoid, you might as well go the whole nine yards. There's nothing more useless than being a *little* paranoid."

I hopped into the passenger seat of Valerie's creaky econobox and we were off. My house wasn't far, but to my surprise Valerie drove by without stopping.

"That was it!" I said.

"I know!" she hissed. "Why don't you slide down in your seat a little, so you're not quite so easy to see. I'm gonna' go around the block and make sure nobody's keeping an eye on anything."

We circled three times before Valerie was satisfied. Finally she pulled to the curb a good hundred yards away from my front door.

"Why do you always park so far away?" I asked.

"So people won't associate my car with your house."

We walked in and I quietly showed Valerie the smoke detectors. By the time we got to the third she was scowling at me in obvious disapproval. When she looked at the fourth she gestured at me to follow her instead of bothering with the pad. We went out to my back yard.

"Smoke detectors?" she hissed. "Those aren't smoke detectors!"

"Well, what are they?"

"They're CO detectors, carbon monoxide. It says so right on the outside. You've got four of them and six fire detectors, and guess what! Only the CO detectors are dead. Don't you even know what you've got in your own house?"

"I had an electrician install them."

"I should have known."

"Why is the fact that they're carbon monoxide detectors so suspicious?"

"Because you only have four of those and none of them are working. Did you just tell them to change the batteries in the smoke detectors?"

"I can't remember exactly what I said."

Valerie shook her head. "I don't know, maybe they didn't change those batteries because they're not really smoke detectors — though I have a hard time believing your cleaning service would be that literal. And the alarms should have beeped at you before the batteries went. You didn't just put up with that for a few days and then assume everything was okay when it stopped, did you?"

"No."

"Well, I don't know if you're just dumb or there's something really going on. What do you have that runs on natural gas?"

"Well, the heat is gas, but it's not on yet. And the water heater is gas, I think."

"Is your water heater inside?"

"Yes, it's in the utility room."

"Let's go take a look."

We went back inside and I showed Valerie the way to the water heater. She knelt down and looked at the gas line. There was a small box there I'd never noticed. Two insulated wires ran from the box towards the ceiling, where they met the vent-pipe running above the heater. From there the wires apparently continued on into the attic. Valerie took all this in and motioned me outside again.

"When did you have the timer put on your water heater?" she asked as soon as we were away from the house.

"A timer? Why would anyone put a timer on a water heater?"

"The cheapest way to run a regular water heater is to have it heat up the water just once a day, that's why. I'm surprised Joe never preached to you about it. But anyway, you don't remember having that installed?"

"No. I'm sure I never had one installed."

"Which proves precisely nothing. Maybe it's been on there since you moved in and you've just never noticed it. Are you working tomorrow?"

"No, I'm not."

"Shit! I was afraid of that."

"Afraid of what? What's going on?"

"Probably nothing. I'll go in and take another look. You just wait out here and look at the stars and think about Maria or something. Jeez! How many pictures of the lady do you have? . . . Oh, never mind."

Valerie went inside again and returned about five minutes later.

"Well, what's the verdict?" I asked.

"That timer is set to do something at 10 p.m.; either blow you to kingdom come or heat water for your nightly bubble bath. Since it's after 10 now it seems we're safe for at least twenty hours or so."

"If it was a bomb wouldn't it have already gone off? I called you about 9:45."

"Not necessarily. It might be set to blow the second or third time the timer goes around."

"So assuming Dr. Anthony's behind this, what's he up to?"

"Maybe he had somebody come in here posing as a plumber while you were at work today. They could have slipped dead batteries into your CO detectors, and fixed your water heater to start putting out carbon monoxide about an hour before it blows up."

"Then why wait twenty-four hours?"

"I don't know. Maybe he's going to send somebody else out to kidnap you tonight. After they'd asked you questions about Maria, maybe given you some sodium pentothal, they could deposit your drugged ass back here just in time to be put under again by the CO and then blown to smithereens. You're not working tomorrow, so nobody would miss you. Or maybe that gadget is supposed to be there. I'm gonna' have to call somebody who knows more than me to figure this one out."

"A plumber?"

"No bonehead, not a plumber. Even you couldn't get a plumber out here at eleven p.m. I have a friend named John who used to work on the LA bomb squad. He can tell whether that box is supposed to be attached to the water heater or not. Probably it is, and he'll just have a good laugh at your expense."

"My expense?"

"I'd guess three or four hundred dollars."

"Oh."

"There's only one thing that worries me."

"And what's that?"

"If I was Anthony, and I wanted to rig something like that, my friend is who I'd hire to install it in the first place."

We returned to the convenience store in Valerie's car. She got out, made a quick phone call, and hopped back in beside me.

"We're in luck. He wasn't out at some bar getting blasted."

"Reliable fellow you're hiring. How much is this gonna' cost me?"

"Three hundred and fifty."

"Wonderful."

"You got any better ideas? He's going to meet us here — he ought to be able to make it in about twenty or thirty minutes. You mind if I listen to the radio?"

"Be my guest."

Valerie picked a blues station, not my first choice, but at least she wasn't fond of polkas. Halfway through some mournfully obscene number she began laughing softly.

"What's so funny?"

"Give me a second, I gotta' think this through." I waited and she began to laugh a bit louder.

"Yeah, it'd work," she mumbled, "and it'd serve him right."

"What would work?"

"Letting Anthony kill you."

Valerie waited by the pay phone while I went to a twenty-four-hour-a-day discount store and picked up a large gas can and some batteries. Her friend had arrived by the time I got back, and I stood to one side and watched him smoke a cigarette while she filled the can and put it in the trunk of her car.

"Okay Peter," she said when she'd finished, "we've got it all figured out. You'll drive your car back and park it wherever you normally park it."

"But I park it in my garage! It'll burn down with the house!"

"Tough shit! I told you to sell that German roller skate two months ago, but you wouldn't listen. You can't take it with you."

"All right." I said. After all, the car was leased.

"After you go in, wait for John to come in too, then come back out to my car. My guess is that they wouldn't be coming to get you until about four in the morning, but I might be wrong, so don't dawdle. Grab your spare cash and a couple of other things, and try to get back in under ten minutes. John's gonna' take the gas can and batteries with him when he looks at your water heater. If there's nothing wrong he'll put the gas in your garage, put new batteries in your CO detectors, and then come out and laugh at our silly asses. If the water heater's rigged, he'll change the timer so it blows tonight at two a.m. and he'll leave the gas can in the utility room to help things along. With luck we'll have a bad enough fire that the police won't be totally surprised to find no trace of your body, and Anthony will think whoever he hired to do you in fucked up and didn't set the timer right. If the fire isn't that bad, most-likely police scenario number two is that you were kidnapped by the same fuckers who blew up the Institute, and they buried you out in the desert somewhere and then torched the house to hide the evidence. Either version will allow the police to close their books on you, and I'm betting they'll happily go with one or the other. Unfortunately we'll need to hang around to make sure nobody decides to walk their dog on your front lawn at two in the morning, but once the house blows you can come sleep at my place. In the morning I'll get your cash and new I.D.'s from the safe-deposit box and Peter Lunsford will be on his way."

"Peter Lunsford?"

"The new you. As Peter Lunsford, OB/GYN, you met an untimely end when you put an aluminum ladder on a power line. You were playing handyman because you worked for peanuts in an inner-city health clinic."

"Couldn't you find a less noble M.D. for me to impersonate?"

"The less noble M.D.'s all had big life insurance policies, and insurance companies that write big policies get upset when ex-clients come back from the dead. Dr. Lunsford's life insurance was just enough to bury him — I'm betting his insurer wrote that check and promptly forgot about him. I'll tell you more later. We need to get going."

We went back by the convenience store, where I picked up my car and then drove it back to my house. After the garage door slid down behind me, I hopped out and unlocked the front door for John. Then I went to my bedroom, where I pulled down my biggest suitcase and hurriedly began packing clothes, shaving gear, deodorants and two thousand dollars in cash I had hidden in an old shoe. Then I walked around the house and grabbed a few of my favorite pictures of Maria. I was about to leave when I thought about the guitar Joe had made me. Valerie would probably prefer that I let it burn, but I grabbed it anyway, then headed out the back door, through my back yard, and out to the street, trying to stay in the dark as much as possible.

Valerie was parked down the street — not directly in front of my house but closer than usual so she could watch for Anthony's men. She popped the hatch release, I threw my load in, and then hopped in beside her.

"You had to bring that guitar?" she asked.

"It's a work of art; I can't let it blow up."

"You can't travel with it, everybody will remember you. They'll say: 'Yeah, there was a guy with a guitar on my bus, I remember him; he bumped me in the head with the damn thing.' You're gonna' stick out on Greyhound as it is."

"I have to take the bus?"

"If you go, you'll have to take the bus."

"Shit!"

"Don't get your panties in a wad yet. John went in the front door about the same time you came out the back. I bet he'll be done in a minute or two. The longer I sit here the more I think he's just gonna' have a good laugh at our expense."

"You mean my expense."

"Well, if it's all a false alarm I'll give you a discount on my overtime."

"Very generous of you."

But it took John considerably more than a minute or two, and when he came out he kept to the darkness the same way I had, so that Valerie and I didn't see him coming until he was about twenty feet from the car.

"This don't look good," she muttered.

John hopped into the back seat and let out a long tense sigh.

"What's the verdict?" Valerie asked.

"Well, what's on that water heater ain't been approved by Consumers' Union."

"You mean it's a bomb?"

"Unless you wanna' get fussy with your terminology, yeah. I got up into the attic and looked, and somebody's attached an extra ventpipe that'll send CO right into the bedroom when a little valve is triggered. About forty minutes after that the same timer shuts the gas off for 60 seconds — which douses the pilot light — then turns it on again and starts flooding the house. Five minutes after that it'll start generating sparks. It's a pretty sweet way to bump somebody off: the CO will knock 'em out, and when the natural gas blows it'll destroy all the evidence."

"Did you reset the timer?" Valerie asked.

"Yeah. And I gotta' say, I'm starting to feel bad about that. Lettin' the place blow is arson, you know."

"You didn't plant the damn thing in the first place."

"Ah, you try tellin' that to a judge. You know, the one flaw with that setup is that somebody can find it *before* it blows. I was damn careful not to put any fingerprints on anything, I'll tell you. Why not just call the police and have 'em take a look? With any luck, whoever did it is gonna' end up in jail."

Valerie turned and looked at me in the back seat.

"Well, Peter, how brave are you? If the cops get Anthony, you'd be home free, and so would Maria and Joshua. Of course if they don't he could keep trying to kill you. In fact, he could also try to kill you before the thing ever went to trial; there's no doubt he'd get out on bond."

I thought for a moment. The possibility of keeping my BMW was tempting.

"Give me some numbers," I finally asked. "What are the odds that Anthony will land in the state penitentiary?"

John looked at Valerie and shrugged.

"Honestly, now," I prompted.

"About one in five," he said, after a moment's pause. Valerie shook her head.

"The odds that somebody goes to jail might be one in five, but the odds that Anthony would get convicted are probably about one in fifty. The fact that you and Anthony are connected is actually going to hurt your case — somebody tried to blow up Anthony just a few months ago, and the police may think those same people are out to get you."

"So I'd probably be safer playing one or two rounds of Russian roulette than staying in Tucson."

"I think you're exaggerating," John said.

"I don't think so," I replied. "Let it blow."

"It's gonna' cost you," John said. "I want two grand, or I'm going back in there and turn the gas off."

"How convenient," I muttered. "Just what I have on me."

After John left with my entire supply of ready cash, Valerie and I sat in the car and waited for the explosion. I thought the odds of someone coming out at two a.m. to let Fido poop were slim to none, but Valerie felt we should stay until the fireworks happened — just in case. Just what she planned to do if someone was on my lawn at 1:55 I didn't know, and I didn't want to know — I couldn't think of any way of warning a prospective bomb victim without landing in jail ourselves.

We had some coffee to keep ourselves awake — Valerie had bought a couple of big cups at the convenience store and poured them into a thermos she kept in her car. The coffee tasted eight hours old, which it probably was. We also had the radio, and after an hour of blues I was ready to beat B.B. King with a stick. At about 1:20 I couldn't take it anymore, so I leaned down and shut the radio off. Valerie wasn't amused.

"Turn that back on, Peter! If I just sit here I'll fall asleep for sure."

"Can't we listen to some classical music?"

"That orchestra shit puts me to sleep worse than nothin' at all."

"Then why don't you tell me about my exciting new life as Peter Lunsford. Where am I going? What am I going to do for food when I get there?"

"Peter, you've got enough money socked away to live for five years. At least at a normal person's standard of living."

Valerie had moved most of my assets to some numbered accounts in the Cayman Islands, via financial manipulations I didn't begin to understand. She'd assured me I could still draw on that money in my new identity.

"Besides," Valerie continued, "I've been checking into jobs for you. I think I've found some people who'd be glad to hire you, people who won't look into your credentials very carefully, either."

"Oh sure."

"Really. These people will be glad to get anybody. It'll be a pay cut, though."

"Wonderful. What is it, house physician at a car wash?"

"No, an inner-city health clinic in Atlanta. You'll be their token white M.D., and you'll be doing prenatal care, probably for a bunch of teenaged welfare mothers."

"The job of my dreams. Maybe I should just walk back into my house and take that nap."

"I've got some other things you could look into, but in terms of not blowing your cover, I think this one's the best. If you do it for even six months you'll have a legitimate employment history."

"They'll want to know about my old jobs too."

"That's another reason I picked this Lunsford guy. He'd just switched jobs before he fried himself, and his next-to-last employers apparently haven't heard that he's croaked. You can just leave out his last job on your new résumé, and explain the gap with a six-month vacation to the Virgin Islands or something."

"I thought this new me was broke. How'd I go to the Virgin Islands?"

"They won't worry about that; they'll probably just assume you had family money. Listen, we still don't have to go through with this."

"It's 1:30, you know, which means the CO will already be filling up my bedroom. Are you going to go in there and shut that thing off?"

"No, but if your house blows, you could still show up as Peter Jacobson tomorrow morning and claim you spent the night with a girlfriend. The house is insured."

"And then wait around for Anthony to try and bump me off again? No thanks. I'll say no thanks to this Atlanta thing, too. I'll try and set up a private practice somewhere."

"I know something that'll change your mind."

"What's that?"

"Atlanta is where I sent Maria and Joe."

My mouth suddenly felt very dry. Valerie leaned down and turned the radio on again.

"You poor horny bastard," she chuckled.

At 1:55 Valerie turned the radio off and sat up nervously in her seat.

"Any minute now."

"Are you sure we're far enough away?" I asked.

"John said this was plenty." We both sat and stared nervously towards my house. "Kind of sets your teeth on edge, thinking it's gonna' go any second, doesn't it?" Valerie said.

"It makes me want to cry. I've got a lot of money invested in that time bomb."

A nondescript American sedan drove slowly by, only the fourth or fifth car we'd seen in the last hour.

"Oh shit! Have you noticed that car?" Valerie asked.

"What car?"

"The one that just went by. That's the second time it's been around the block."

"So?"

"What do ya' bet that's Anthony's welcoming committee? What am I gonna' do if they walk up there and break into your house?"

"Why would they do that?"

"We figured they were planning to question you before they did you in, remember? I figured they'd be by later — you used to be such a night owl I thought they'd wait until at least three."

"It's just a car," I said, "calm down."

But Valerie was right. A few minutes later the sedan came around the block again. We slid low in our seats and watched as it pulled to a stop in front of my house. A tall, beefy-looking man got out from the passenger side and headed towards my front door.

"We gotta' stop him!" Valerie hissed.

"So they can kidnap me right now! Forget it!"

The clock on Valerie's dash read 1:59. Valerie opened her door and started to get out, so I grabbed her arm and held her in her seat. She tried to wrench away, but the cramped interior of the Chevette gave her no room to fight me. I looked up and saw that the man who'd gone to the front door of my house was doing something to the lock. Suddenly he stood up, waved to the driver and put his hand on the knob.

There was a sudden flash of light, and the house exploded. The door came flying out over my front lawn, propelling the man ahead of it like a sideways flying carpet. I clapped my hands over my ears just in time to dampen the sound, but I felt it in my stomach, a tremendous "whump" that made Valerie's car rock as if an eighteen-wheeler had just zoomed by on the Interstate. I took my hands off my ears, and heard the sound of falling debris, airborne a full two or three seconds after the explosion. Flames were already licking through the shattered windows.

My front door had come to rest about five feet shy of the sidewalk, on the soft Bermuda-grass lawn I'd insisted on planting, desert or no. The man in the car went over and lifted it off his comrade, who got groggily to his knees.

"So I'm not a murderer," Valerie muttered, "though that's no thanks to you, you asshole!"

The two men got into their car and sped away.

"Time to go," Valerie said tersely, and we were off.

Part III

Chapter 1

1 I, Thomas the Israelite, thought it necessary to make known to all the Gentile brothers all the things done by our Lord Jesus Christ in the village of Nazareth, after he was born in our region of Bethlehem. This is the beginning.

2 The child Jesus was five years old. After it rained he was playing at the ford of a flowing stream. And stirring up the dirty waters, he gathered them into pools, and he made them clean and excellent, ordering them by word alone — and not ordering them by a deed. Then, having taken soft clay from the mud, he formed twelve sparrows from it. But it was the Sabbath when he did these things, and many children were with him. But a certain Jew saw the child Jesus with the other children doing these things. He went to Joseph his father and slandered the child Jesus, saying that, "he made clay on the Sabbath, which isn't permissible, and formed twelve sparrows." And Joseph went and rebuked Jesus, saying, "Why are you doing these things on the Sabbath?" But Jesus clapped his hands, ordering the birds with a shout in front of all, and said, "Go, take flight like living beings!" And the sparrows, taking flight, went away squawking. And having seen this, the Pharisee was amazed, and he reported it to all his friends.

3 And the son of Annas the high priest said to Jesus, "Why are you doing such a thing on the Sabbath?" And having taken a willow twig, he destroyed the pools and drained the water which Jesus had gathered, and he dried up their gatherings. But having seen what had happened, Jesus said to him, "Your fruit will have no root, and your shoot will be withered like a scorched branch in a violent wind!" And immediately that child withered away.

4 From there he was going with his father Joseph, and someone running struck his shoulder. And Jesus said to him, "Cursed be you because of your leader!" And immediately the boy died. And the people who saw that the boy had died immediately cried out and said, "From where was this child born, that his word becomes deed?" And when the parents of the dead child saw what had happened, they blamed Joseph his father, saying, "Because you have such a boy, you can't live with us in this village. If you want to be here, teach him to bless and not to curse, because our child has been taken away from us."

— *The Infancy Gospel of Thomas*
Non-canonical, ca 2nd century

"And his mother treasured all these things in her heart."

The Gospel of Luke, 2: 51

"And now let's go to Joshua in Ellenwood, Georgia. Good afternoon, Josh; you're on the Rush Limbaugh Show!"

Alarmed, I sat up in my car seat. Luckily, any amount of alarm was perfectly safe — I was tooling down I-75/85 at a blistering five miles an hour, stuck in the lunchtime traffic jam, which by 3:30 would blend almost imperceptibly into the rush-hour traffic jam. It really was blistering outside, the temperature still in the mid-90's even though August 2005 was almost over. I'd been at Grady Memorial Hospital since three in the morning, finishing my shift by delivering two cocaine-addicted premature babies. It was one in the afternoon now, and I needed an invigorating dose of righteous anger — hence my choice of Rush Limbaugh for radio companionship.

"Good afternoon, Mr. Limbaugh," piped a familiar voice, "and anti-dittoes from us environmentalist whackos." It was indeed Joshua Manolo Grant, Maria and Joe's son, one of the most unnervingly precocious five-year-olds you could ever hope to meet.

"Well Josh," came Rush's mellifluous baritone, "it says here that you're five years old. Why aren't you in kindergarten?"

"My school doesn't start until next week."

"Is your mother home watching you?"

"No, my daddy is. My mother's at work."

"A true liberal family, folks — Dad's at home while his wife works!" said Rush. Actually, Joe often worked fifty-hour weeks, but he'd taken a few days off because Maria had several teacher work-days before her students arrived. The following week Joshua would begin kindergarten at the same elementary school, and Maria could finally start pursuing her chosen profession.

"Folks," Herr Limbaugh continued, "I put young Joshua on because Bo was very impressed by him. Joshua, where's your father right now?"

"He's making a lute."

"Is that his hobby?"

"Making instruments is what he'd like to do, but he builds houses for money."

"Does he know you're on the phone with me?"

"I'm not sure. But I have his permission — he said I could try and call you but I probably wouldn't get through."

"Why did you say 'environmentalist whacko anti-dittoes'?"

"Because that's what my father always says when you come on."

"So you don't know what an environmentalist whacko is?"

"Not exactly, but my daddy says you'd call the captain of the *Exxon Valdez* an environmental moderate."

There was a slight pause from the golden EIB microphone. I found myself sympathizing with Mr. Limbaugh — doubtless this wasn't the level of repartee he was expecting from a five-year-old. But Rush recovered quickly.

"Your father can't be a liberal!" he said in mock amazement. "He has a sense of humor! Do you like the jokes on our show?"

"I don't like the ones about poor people. My daddy says that you make jokes about poor people all the time because you think you're better than they are."

"But Josh, I am better. I've worked hard, and I've earned the money I've made."

"Well, I have a question. What made poor people lazy and you hard-working?"

"My parents taught me that you can't ever accomplish anything without hard work. Poor people have been taught by liberals that society owes them something, that they're entitled. Do you know what entitled means, Joshua?"

"It means the same thing as owed, doesn't it?"

"Yes, it does, Josh."

"But that makes me wonder about something else, Mr. Limbaugh. If poor people are poor because they weren't raised right, why do you make fun of them? My daddy says it's not right to make fun of people for something that's not their fault."

There was another pause, as if Mr. Limbaugh had become slightly uneasy. "Well, Joshua," he said with something less than his usual cocksure enthusiasm, "the world needs a little humor now and then. I don't really dislike poor people. I'm just joking."

"My daddy says that when you tell the same type of joke over and over, it's because you really believe what you're saying as a joke, but you don't want to admit it."

There was another pause, as if Rush sensed that he was entering new and dangerous territory. "Without admitting that your father's right," he said slowly, "what does he say I really believe about poor people?"

"He says that way down deep you think poor people are poor because they're stupid. He says you think it's stupid to try to help them, that it's just a waste of time because they're too dumb to be taught any better. But if you said that without making it a joke people would call you a . . . a . . . I forget the word."

"A bigot?" said Rush in a tired voice.

"That's it! A bigot! If you said poor people were born stupid and didn't make it a joke people would call you a bigot."

"Does your father think I'm a bigot?"

"My Uncle Peter says you're a bigot, but my father says you're just . . . I can't remember that word either."

"Prejudiced?"

"Yes, that's it. He says you're prejudiced. He says that's when you don't realize you're being unfair."

Herr Limbaugh had made several irritated noises during Josh's speech, and now he resorted to one of his favorite tactics. I heard a heavy sigh and the rustle of papers.

"Well, Josh," he finally said, "if your father has so much to say about me maybe he should call himself. Can you say anything your father hasn't said first?"

"I have a couple of questions. Is that okay?"

"Sure! Ask away!"

"Why is it that when somebody's said something you don't have a good answer for, you always rattle your papers around and make that breathing noise?"

Silence from Rush. Josh continued in a guileless voice.

"Do you do that so that people will think you've thought of a really good answer that'll make the other person look stupid, and that you're just too polite to say it?"

More silence from Rush, answered this time by silence from Joshua. When Rush replied his voice was lower, a threatening bass instead of a soothing baritone.

"Joshua, how old are you? Really?"

"I'm five. I'll be six in January."

"I think you're really in your twenties, and that you've carefully scripted this whole encounter. You know, if your arguments need to have a cute and cuddly voice behind them, they must not be very persuasive."

"This is the only way I know how to talk."

"Is that so? Well, does your five-year-old brain have any other trenchant questions to ask me? And I don't want to hear about your father anymore — if he wants to talk he should call himself."

"I did have one more question."

"All right! One more question by Joshua from Ellenwood, boy

genius or ingenious actor! What is it?"

"My question is about the earth getting hotter."

"Global warming! Ask on, oh youthful sage!"

"You say that we can't prove all the pollution is making the earth warmer."

"That's right. We need much more data before we can be sure that the past few hot summers are anything other than a random climactic fluctuation. Can you say that, Josh? Random climactic fluctuation?"

"Random climactic fluctuation."

"You know, I never had that phrase in my first-grade reader. You see, a warming trend might just be like . . . well, I'll try to explain it in a way a five-year-old boy (or a twenty-five-year-old liberal) might understand. Let's say your parents were driving along in their car, and you were looking out the back window. If you couldn't see forward, every time your parents started up a big hill, you might think you were going into the mountains when you were really on the way to the ocean, because you'd have no way of knowing if the hill kept on going. You'd only know for sure after you went up lots of hills, and they kept getting higher and higher. The weather is the same way. A few hot summers don't prove that the climate is getting hotter, no more than going over one or two hills proves you're heading towards the mountains. You'd have to look at the weather for many, many years to say there was a real change in climate."

"But couldn't it work the other way, too? Couldn't you really be going into the mountains all along? I mean, can you prove the earth isn't getting hotter?"

"Not really, but I don't think there's much proof that it is."

"Well, if you turn out to be right, and we make less pollution, how does that hurt us? Wouldn't that be the safest thing to do even if we aren't sure?"

"My boy, if you really are five years old I think you're too young to understand all this. If, as I suspect, you're really in your twenties, I want you to listen carefully. Cutting pollution is a facade: what the liberals really want is to attack property rights; to require that the productive countries in the world pay money to the inefficient ones. They also want to take steps towards a single world government. Did you get all that?"

"But if the scientists who are so worried about the earth getting hotter are right, and we don't do anything, wouldn't that be a lot worse?"

"Son, they're not right."

"But if they are, couldn't a lot of worse things happen than what you were talking about? My daddy says that scientists think that whole cities could get flooded, and that lots of places where we grow food could become deserts, and that hurricanes could get really awful and happen all the time. Wouldn't it be smart to at least drive smaller cars and take the subway and stuff like that just to make sure nothing like that happens? Aren't we taking an awful chance if we don't do anything?"

Another long silence, with no answer from Rush. Joshua went on.

"And since we make most of the pollution here in America, is it right for us to decide for the whole world that it's nothing to worry about? Aren't we doing something that's good mostly for us but could hurt everybody?"

Rush rattled his papers again, and started that patented sigh, then cut it short in mid-exhalation.

"Joshua," he said, "on my show callers who get on the air under false pretenses are cut off. If you really are five years old, I apologize, but I think you're a college drama major putting on that boyish voice. I'm going to move on to another caller."

"Well, thank you for talking to me, Mr. Limbaugh, and maybe another day you can think of an answer to my questions."

"I have answered them, son," Rush said, although he hadn't. Then he plowed ahead. "Let's talk to Dave from Des Moines. Dave, you're on the Rush Limbaugh show!"

Poor Rush — somebody should have warned him. Not that Herr Limbaugh didn't recover quickly, within minutes he was telling callers that he knew all along that Joshua from Ellenwood was no five-year-old, that the call was a typical liberal ploy, appealing to the emotions rather than the intellect by airing the pleas of children, the poor, abused *chil'ren* (he did his Jesse Jackson imitation), to please stop the pollution and the guns and the Republicans and all the other mean, nasty things in the world.

I could understand Mr. Limbaugh's skepticism. I'd fled Tucson and my old identity four-and-a-half years ago, and I'd kept an eye on Joshua (and his mother) ever since. And from the day Josh began to talk most adults reacted with a certain sense of disbelief.

Many adults also disliked him, even though he was a cheerful boy who never whined, was always helpful, and always told the truth.

Perhaps that last trait was the problem: the truth wasn't always what adults wanted to hear.

I also felt uncomfortable around Joshua — though admittedly I had the knowledge of his unconventional conception to add to my unease. In the last five years I'd been a frequent guest at Joe and Maria's south metro apartment, and as I watched Joshua grow I often wondered: is this young Leonardo's twin at play, or Eric's anonymous 14th-century con man, or someone else? But Maria and Joe had no such misgivings — Joshua was the one bright spot of their new life.

Little else had gone well. Before he received a "Call from the Lord" to become a minister in a rabidly fundamentalist Tucson church, Harold Anthony had taken a quick look at his son's innovations in guitar strutting. He patented Joe's design in 2002, and then sold production rights to a major guitar manufacturer. The patent was under Joe's name, but since Dr. Anthony was a beneficiary of Joe's estate he ended up making more money from Joe's guitars than Joe ever had.

He also succeeded in shutting down his son's incognito Atlanta instrument business. After leaving Tucson, Joe had hoped other makers would borrow his strutting pattern; that way he could sell his guitars without drawing an obvious connection to his old identity. But with the innovations patented, guitars made with his unusual bracing ran the risk of attracting attorneys as well as musicians. So Joe was reduced to framing houses, while Maria stayed home days and went to night classes to get a Bachelor's degree under her new name. Meanwhile, Joe spent his meager free time trying to find some way to sidestep his father's patent. He'd begun making other plucked instruments three years ago, lutes and Baroque guitars, but as of yet his best attempts were only promising.

"The damn things are strung with cobwebs," he often complained. "I can't seem to get the knack of it."

But he liked working as a framer far less. Joe was a perfectionist, but his bosses wanted work done fast and sloppy. And though Atlanta's air was beginning to resemble Mexico City's, as a construction worker laden with power tools Joe had little choice but to contribute to the general miasma. He drove hundreds of miles every week, and he sometimes talked about taking his old pickup and converting it to run on propane or natural gas, both supposedly less polluting than gasoline. Maria was afraid that he'd blow himself up in the process.

"I'm reading *The Mosquito Coast*," she told me over the phone one afternoon. "It reminds me of the new Joe. My husband, lunatic tinkerer."

As for my new life, I'd taken Valerie's suggestion and applied for a position with an inner-city health clinic. My duties were just what Valerie described — prenatal care to welfare mothers, many of them teenagers, and delivering their babies at Grady Memorial downtown.

What Valerie hadn't mentioned was that working at this job was almost as dangerous as staying in Tucson. The clinic was in a "depressed" neighborhood, and my skin color put me decidedly in the minority among its clients and staff. In my first year on the job I was relieved of my wallet three times by small gangs of young hoodlums. (Excuse me, "small groups of morally challenged adolescents.") The first two times they relied on mere intimidation; the third time they had a gun. I quickly put aside my liberal reservations, got a concealed weapons permit, and began carrying a gun myself. Then, to advertise the fact I framed an enlarged copy of my permit and hung it on my office wall. "Here are my diplomas," I'd say, pointing to the row of Peter Lunsford's credentials, fraudulently obtained. "One from Washington State and one from Case Western, and here's my concealed weapons permit." After I started giving this little spiel I was rarely even hassled; the "predators" (as local radio talk-show hosts dubbed them) preferred easier prey. Luckily no one ever found out that my gun frightened *me* so much that I kept the damned thing loaded with blanks.

At first, I was determined to spend just six months at the clinic before starting my own practice, but at the end of those six months I'd taken no steps to find other work. I felt that I wasn't accomplishing anything there, and that feeling somehow made me even more reluctant to leave.

I spent a lot of time getting mad at my clients. In my second year I realized how many "repeat customers" I had, young women who would probably bear four or five children before they hit forty. They also missed prenatal appointments, ate poorly and didn't take their vitamins. The worst cases did drugs and turned tricks, avoided all medical attention until labor began, then went to the nearest emergency room, often giving birth to premature babies with HIV or addictions to cocaine or heroin.

One day I was mentally raging at a patient. "How can you bring children into the world like this?" I was thinking. "Didn't your parents teach you anything?" A perfectly obvious question, but the answer was obvious, too: deprived children grow up into lousy parents, who raise deprived children who grow up into lousy parents, who raise deprived children who grow up into lousy parents; forever and ever, amen. And the solution? I had no idea.

But I knew what wasn't needed: another classy Buckhead practice specializing in the problem pregnancies of aged yuppies. So I stayed at the clinic for four years. I would have stayed longer, but after four years I was an emotional, financial and social wreck. One afternoon I realized I was so burned out it was only a matter of time until I screwed up and killed somebody. That was the sop my conscience needed, so I ran.

For the past year I'd been the "junior" partner of an obstetrician younger than myself, in a practice catering to middle-class women in south metro Atlanta. But I still donated two days each month to my old employers.

The crack baby I'd delivered this morning had even worse prospects than usual, and halfway through my fifty-five minute, twenty-two-mile commute I knew I needed cheering up. I decided to drop in and see the Grants' reaction to young Joshua's latest outrage.

"Uncle Peter!" Joshua screeched when he opened the door. Then he grabbed my legs in what was meant to be a hug. Bearing Joshua with me, I stumbled into the living room. Joe was sitting at the dinner table with a magazine and a cup of his tarry coffee.

"Hi, Peter," he said. "Did you hear Josh on the radio?"

"Sure did. I was stuck in traffic."

"No MARTA for you?"

"Not when I went in at three in the morning, thank you." I finished freeing myself from Josh, then walked over towards Joe.

"Can I get you some coffee?" he asked, "I just made a fresh pot."

"Thanks, but don't get up. I can help myself." I went into the kitchen and returned a moment later with what looked like a cup of black mud, then sat down in the chair across from Joe.

"So. Did you hear your son?" I asked.

"Yeah. I knew he was trying to call, and I had the radio on in the other room. I about fell down when he got on the air, though."

"Why didn't you go in and talk to Rush yourself? You've been itching to give him a piece of your mind for years."

"Because my father doesn't need to hear my voice and start wondering who Joe from Ellenwood is. And I thought Josh was holding his own."

"I did too. Josh, did you like talking to Mr. Limbaugh?"

Joshua looked up. He was playing with an enormous Lego set Maria had picked up at a garage sale, making something that looked for all the world like a gigantic igloo.

"Yes, I liked talking to him," he said. "He was nice. But he didn't really answer my questions."

"That's because they were such good questions."

"Then why didn't he answer them?"

"Because he's an evasive son of a . . ."

"Peter . . ." Joe growled.

"Because he doesn't like answering hard questions, and I don't think anybody's taken that particular line with him before. What are you building?"

"A pleasure dome."

"A what?"

"Mom read me a poem the other day, all about Kubla Khan's pleasure dome. What's a pleasure dome?"

"A dome is a building with a round roof."

"Oh, I know what a dome is. What's a pleasure dome?"

"Maybe it's a dome where you pleasure yourself," I mumbled to Joe. He grinned. To Josh I said, "I don't know. But building a dome is pretty hard with Legos, I bet."

"I'm finding that out."

I took a sip of my coffee and grimaced.

"Too strong, eh?" Joe asked. I nodded. "You should drink it anyway," he said, "if you've been up since three you need some caffeine."

"You look pretty tired yourself. What's *your* excuse?"

"I want to make instruments this week, not sleep."

"So now you can't wait to get back to work and get some rest?"

"Hardly. My foreman's got it in for me."

"Why's that?"

"Because he's a jerk."

"Now Daddy, he's not that bad, is he?" Joshua said from behind a wall of blocks.

"Well, he sure doesn't like me much. You know what silt fences are, Peter?"

"Haven't the foggiest."

"They look like little plastic fences, and they keep dirt from washing down into the streams. Anyway, at this site they put them up all wrong. I complained about it and the foremen's been on my case ever since."

"You ought to keep your mouth shut, Joe. What's a little dirt in the streams gonna' hurt?"

"You wouldn't say that if you were a fish," Joe said, then looked over at his son and continued in a whisper: "You're probably right, though. I don't wanna' lose this job, and they're already pretty mad at me for taking the week off. I'd never have gotten away with it if they weren't so short on framers. But it's hard to keep my mouth shut, and this foreman is so suspicious. We've got some Mexican guys on the site, and I was joking with 'em the other day, and he's made up his mind I was calling him names in Spanish."

Joe's Spanish was once the butt of jokes, but now he sounded like a native. And Joshua was every bit as bilingual as his parents.

But then, there wasn't much Joshua couldn't do. His drawings hung on the refrigerator; they looked like Raphaels in Crayola. He'd gone through a craze for building mobiles — and now string, paper and wood twirled gracefully in the kitchen, living room, bathroom, and his father's workshop, which also doubled as Josh's bedroom. He'd helped Joe put together a tenor ukulele, then learned to play it with astonishing ease. Josh also listened to a surprising range of music, and he was starting to compose. His new obsession was Renaissance vocal polyphony, which he'd heard for the first time on public radio. I wondered how many other Atlanta children had requested a CD of Ockeghem and Dufay masses for their fifth birthday.

Evidence of Josh's other budding interests was visible elsewhere in the room. Next to a small TV was a small bookcase, filled with Joshua's favorite reading — middle school books about science and animals; *The Hobbit* by J.R.R. Tolkien, *The Black Stallion* by Walter Farley, and George Orwell's *Animal Farm.* Beside the fiction was a large copy of illustrated Bible stories for children, as well as an adult Bible.

Over in another corner was the family computer, an aging IMac on which Joshua surfed the Internet, played chess, and occasionally did his homework. (Josh could print legibly before the age of four, but now preferred to type.) He'd mastered every piece of software Joe and Maria owned early in 2005, everything, that is, except the violent games that had come with the computer. Joshua possessed neither toy guns nor a typical boy's love of mayhem.

"It's amazing, isn't it?" Joe said to me in a low voice. I'd drifted off, staring around the apartment at the casual display of Joshua's kindergarten genius.

"What?" I said, although I knew precisely what Joe was talking about.

"All this stuff Josh does. It's amazing, isn't it?"

"Maybe not. He has two smart parents, and your father's no dummy either."

"None of us were smart like this. He's almost supernatural. And you know what the really scary thing is?"

"What's that?"

"Sometimes I think he hides just how smart he really is."

Though Joe was still my best friend and Joshua my honorary nephew, Maria's reaction to my sudden appearance in Atlanta had been confusing.

On one level she'd seemed genuinely glad to see me. On another level she seemed racked by guilt — after all, if I hadn't concerned myself with Maria's welfare, Dr. Anthony wouldn't have tried to kidnap and kill me. Then again, my tale of water heaters and destruction seemed to *ease* some of her guilt — she'd wondered before if she and Joe were fleeing from nothing, but the destruction of my house seemed to say that they were right to run, and right to stay hidden. On still another level, my appearance apparently made her feel like a scarlet woman — a wanton flirt whose remarks in the van in Willcox worked all too well, since here I was again, chasing her through three time zones and two identities.

And I was impossible to avoid; an understudy lover who also happened to be her husband's best friend. So sometimes Maria treated me like an incontinent stray dog; sometimes she was coldly polite, and on rare occasions I became her confidante — she'd tell me how she worried about Joe, how she worried about money, how much she missed Tucson and her family. These confessions always took place over the phone when Joe was out, and at our next meeting she'd be prickly and distant. Maria had given me just such a call two nights before, and I was planning to make my exit before she got there.

"You can't go yet," Joe said. "You haven't played my new guitar."

"I thought you hadn't finished it."

"What gave you that idea?"

"I talked to you two days ago. You said you hadn't finished it."

"Oh. I meant I hadn't put the finish on it. It's ready to play now:

French polish dries pretty fast."

"Where is it?"

"In Josh's bedroom. I'll go get it." He vaulted up the stairs.

"It's a good one," Josh whispered the moment his father was gone, as if conveying a great secret.

"What?"

"Daddy's new guitar. He says it's the best one he's ever made."

"Your father's made some pretty nice guitars. This one would have to be awesome to be his best. What do you think?"

"I think he's right."

Joe came down the stairs carrying a case, which he put gently at my feet. I opened it, took the guitar out, then played a few chords.

"You're not kidding, Joe," I said. "It is good." Then I laid it flat on my lap and noticed the label. It read: "Joseph Anthony, 2005."

"Joe," I asked, pointing into the soundhole, "do you think that's wise?"

He frowned back at me. "It's got those 'effin patented braces, so there's no way I can sell it. So I figured I'd put my own damn name on the thing."

The obscenity startled me — Joe didn't usually curse in front of his son. But Joshua hadn't noticed; he was staring in at the label.

"Who's Joseph Anthony, Daddy?" he asked. "Why'd you put somebody else's name on your guitar?"

"It's just a joke," Joe said. "I'll change it later."

"Can we play some music, Daddy?"

"I'm not playing real well right now, Josh. I smashed my finger with a hammer yesterday, remember?"

"How about you, Uncle Peter? Can you stay and play some music with me?"

"Sure," I said. "Can I play your Dad's new guitar?"

"Of course," Joe said, with an unconscious scowl. "Or try another one. I've got fifteen more upstairs."

When Maria came home thirty minutes later I was still sitting on their sofa, a book of simple duets parked on the coffee table, accompanying Joshua as he plucked melodies (his fingers were still too weak to handle much chording). My unexpected visits usually brought a swift sequence of expressions to Maria's face: a quick and beaming smile, then a guilty look — as if enjoying my presence was a dangerous indulgence — followed by a second smile identical to the first, except that it never reached her eyes. But today when she saw me sitting there, the first smile remained.

"Hello, Peter!" she said. "Can you stay for dinner?"

"Sure," I answered. It was twenty or so hours since I'd last slept, but dinner with Maria was worth drinking more of Joe's coffee. Joe would probably need some more caffeine himself: he'd fallen asleep in their battered recliner. Maria walked over and kissed him on the cheek. He looked up groggily.

"Was I asleep?" he asked.

"Looks like it."

"Did you hear Joshua this afternoon?"

"I heard about it, that's for sure."

"How was work?"

"Boring. But I can't wait until the kids show up next week. Hey, I've got groceries in the car; let's get them out before the ice cream melts." Joe struggled out of the chair and followed her outside.

"I'll put the guitars up, Uncle Peter," Joshua said, staring meaningfully at the door. I took the hint and got up to help with the groceries.

For the next few minutes we were all quite domestic. Joshua came outside and helped, but that was hardly unusual: Joshua was unfailingly helpful, just as he was unfailingly kind, cheerful, and considerate. Soon there was a pile of groceries in the kitchen. I would have left them to Maria and Joe, but I was shamed again by Josh's example.

"I can put the groceries away, Mom," he offered. "You and Dad go sit down."

"Thanks, but no thanks, Joshua. You're still a little short to get to the high cabinets."

"I can stand on the stool."

"Yes, I've seen you do that, and it scares me to death. You can take things out of the bags for me."

"Did you hear me talk to Mr. Limbaugh today?"

"Just a little, honey. One of the other teachers was listening, and she came running in to my room squawking, 'Is that your son?' But by the time I got to her room you were almost done."

"I taped most of it," Joe said. "You can listen later."

"You taped it?"

"Yeah. I never dreamed he'd really get through, but when he came on I ran in and popped a tape into the stereo."

"Did you mark it?"

"What do you mean?"

"You've got a jillion old tapes sitting in there, and not one of them has a label that tells what's actually on it."

"A slight exaggeration."

"Only slight. Why don't you go upstairs, find that tape, pop out the record tabs, and put a new label on it? I don't want you to goof and record something else over it."

"I wouldn't do that."

"Oh yeah? What did you tape over when you recorded Josh?"

"I'm not sure."

"I rest my case. Get going." She turned to Josh next, handing him a large package of toilet paper. "Can you take that upstairs and put it in the bathroom?" she asked. Josh followed his father out of the room, and I found myself alone with Maria. She spoke to me over her shoulder as she put cans on a shelf.

"Thanks for listening to me whine the other night, Peter."

"What do you mean?"

"When I called you Wednesday."

"You didn't whine."

"Yes, I did. I've been doing it for almost five years now, and I want to apologize. I call you up to complain, and then I treat you like dirt for weeks afterwards."

"It's been a hard five years for you."

"Yes, it has, but it's been even worse for Joe. Now that I'm working and Josh will be in school maybe he can go back to doing something he really wants to do. Banging together shoddy houses and strip malls isn't what he was meant for. I've always known that, but I haven't been very understanding lately."

"The situation is hardly your fault."

"Yes. Harold Anthony and his damn patents. You know, I got a letter from my parents yesterday about Dr. Anthony."

"So it's Dr. Anthony again, eh? I thought he'd dropped that title."

"Apparently he just finished a degree in theology."

"He has a doctorate in theology now?"

"Yes he has, although I have no idea what lunatic seminary gave it to him. My father says his church is getting to be quite a force in Tucson."

"That little place?"

"That little place now has upwards of 2000 members, a new

sanctuary, a small orchestra and rock combo, excuse me; they call it a praise band . . ."

"You mean 'Rock of Ages' with a trap set?"

"More or less. Anyway, my father didn't complain about the music. It's what people from that church are *doing* that has him upset."

"Like what?"

"Well, let's see. They're picketing the gay bars . . . and Anthony's given sermons about how gay men should be jailed because they're a public health hazard. And my father says there are rumors about worse things."

"So why are your thoroughly straight parents worried about all this?"

"Because Anthony also gives sermons about Catholicism, and New Age religions, and Islam, and how the U.S. is God's new Israel. Right now the rhetoric is mild, but my mother says she remembers when what he said about homosexuals was mild, too. Now he's practically encouraging his church members to go out and beat up gay people. She wonders who's next."

"How does your mother know about all this?"

"One of her neighbors goes to Dr. Anthony's church, and she comes back and tells my mom about it."

"Well, look at the bright side — we don't know any gay people in Tucson, except . . ."

"Except what?"

"Well, your father does wear some strange clothes — those Hawaiian shirts he has are out of this world . . ." Joe had walked up behind me, but I continued teasing Maria anyway. "Maybe he's getting ready to come out of the closet."

Maria turned and smiled at me, then rattled off something in Spanish. I looked at Joe, who was chuckling.

"Translation please," I asked him.

"You sure?"

"I can take it."

"She said your pregnant mother must have been scared by a jackass."

Maria was leaning back against the sink, chuckling herself, and despite the fact that her husband was standing beside me, despite the fact that she wasn't getting any younger, despite the fact that I knew I wasn't going to do it — I wanted desperately to kiss her.

Chapter 2

Though I'd never admit it to Joe, I tended to agree with Rush Limbaugh about C02, climate change, and my deodorant burning holes in the ozone layer. But that fall I wondered if Joe was right. Of course there was Katrina, not to mention twenty-five other named storms. In Atlanta, a drought that had begun in July continued through October, then in November the heavens suddenly sprang a leak. It rained for days on end, and rivers throughout the South rose out of their banks. Rain was still pouring down the Saturday before Thanksgiving, when Maria brought bad news to my front door.

Obviously upset, she'd forgotten to raise the hood on her poncho, and my first thought was of her cold breasts in that soaked blouse, my second that she and Joe had just had a huge fight. Then I saw Joe striding up the sidewalk after her, holding an umbrella in one hand and Joshua in another.

"Can we come in?" she asked.

"Sure," I answered. She stepped inside while I held the door for Joe. He came in without a word of greeting, and put Josh down on the floor.

"Can he go upstairs and read a book or something?" Joe asked.

"Sure," I said.

"Can't I help?" Josh asked.

"No," Joe said. "Go upstairs." Josh started up.

"You can watch T.V. in the spare bedroom," I called after him. Joe just grunted and walked into my living room. I turned and followed. Maria was already sitting on the couch, her dripping head in her hands. Joe sat down beside her.

"What on earth is going on?" I asked. Maria looked up, but Joe spoke first.

"Here," he said, reaching into his pocket and handing me a sheet from the national section of the Atlanta paper. He'd circled one small story.

Murder May Be Latest In Series of Hate Crimes Against Gays

Tucson police are investigating the possibility that the murder of local private investigator Valerie Weselesky may be related to attacks on patrons of gay bars in Arizona, New Mexico, and Utah.

Weselesky's body was found Monday, tied with baling wire to the driver's seat of her 1998 Volkswagen Beetle. An autopsy revealed that Weselesky was drugged and beaten prior to being placed inside the car. According to police, the car was driven to a dirt road in the Sonoran desert near Nogales, doused with gasoline, and set on fire with Weselesky inside. Police will not confirm rumors that Biblical verses condemning homosexuality were found pinned to her body.

"It is a possibility that Ms. Weselesky's death was the work of a killer or religious group targeting gays," said Cynthia Harris, public affairs liaison for the Pima County Sheriff's Department. "It's also possible that the murder was related to Ms. Weselesky's work, or was the work of a copy-cat killer or killers." Harris said that police have found no evidence to support rumors that Weselesky was involved in drug trafficking.

Meanwhile, as Tucson's gay community points a collective finger at the Church of Biblical Truth (whose members frequently picket gay bars) the reaction of the Reverend Harold Anthony did little to calm matters. When asked to comment on rumors of a paramilitary "God Squad" recruited from his congregation, Anthony told reporters:

"That's nonsense. I've never advocated violence against homosexuals. However, Ms. Weselesky's death, while regrettable, is just a foretaste of the torments unrepentant homosexuals will suffer in the flames of hell."

There was more, mostly criticism of Anthony's statements from other Tucson pastors, but as I read about the flames of hell I had a vision of Valerie's flesh stuck to a car seat's red-hot coil springs. I jumped up and made a quick trip to the bathroom, where I lost my breakfast. When I returned Maria and Joe were still sitting, staring into space.

"When did you find out?" I asked.

"This morning. There was a blurb about it on CNN. I went out and bought the paper hoping I hadn't heard the name right."

"She was such a nice lady," Maria said, fighting back tears. "How could somebody do that to her just because she was gay?"

I didn't answer; I was thinking of the night I tried to keep her from rescuing Anthony's henchmen.

"You really think she was killed just because she was gay?" Joe asked Maria.

"Why else?"

"Because she was connected to us. Maybe my father had her kidnapped to get information about you."

"That's stupid! Your father thinks we're dead."

"According to Peter, my father just thinks *I'm* dead. He thinks you're very much alive, and he'd like to change that."

"That's stupid, too. If we hadn't broken a dozen laws when we left, I bet we could fly back to Tucson and stop this charade once and for all."

"If we did you'd be dead inside of six months, just like my mother. What *would* stop this charade is if someone from that Wrath of God group flew back to Tucson and shot my father."

"Joe!"

"Unfortunately, I'm too chickenshit to do it myself. But I wouldn't cry if somebody else did."

"You don't have any proof that he's murdered anybody!"

"But bodies sure pile up around him, don't they! Jonathan Gluckmann, Eric Schroeder, my mother, and now this! And do you remember what almost happened to Peter?"

"There's no proof your father had anything to do with that."

"Who the fuck else could it have been?"

"Watch your language; Josh might hear you!" Maria said. As if in confirmation, Joshua called down, "Daddy, is everything all right?" Joe leaned back and glared at his wife, but said nothing. Maria went on: "And you're not going to shoot anybody. You wince when you smash a cockroach."

"He's right, you know," I cut in.

"Right about what?" Maria snapped.

"About Valerie. She was one of maybe five people in Tucson who know you're still alive. She was the only person there who knew what city you'd gone to. What do you think the odds are that she'd get murdered and Harold Anthony would just happen to be a suspect?"

A stinging retort seemed ready to burst from Maria's lips, but she quelled it, then leaned back on the sofa too, mulling things over. After a few moments Joe took her hand.

"You said Valerie was one of five people who know I'm still alive," she finally replied. "My parents and sisters are the other four?"

"Unfortunately."

"Then maybe they should leave too."

"Maybe. Maybe the three of us should move again. The only problem is that I don't have the slightest idea how to arrange it."

"There's Valerie's friend," Joe said.

"What friend?" I asked.

"The woman we send our mail to Tucson through. Isn't she an investigator?"

"Yes, but all we know about her is that she picks up the mail at a post office box in Durham."

"Maybe one of us could go up there and watch the box. When we find her we'll see if she has any ideas."

"How would you find the right post office?" Maria asked.

"There's only one per zip code. And you can get a street map to it on the Internet," Joe said. "At least I think so."

I frowned. Shooting Harold Anthony sounded a lot simpler.

Joe volunteered to go to North Carolina, but we dropped that idea an hour later. A CNN news clip covering the attacks was followed by a story on Harold Anthony, complete with an account of Joe and Maria's disappearance. With Joe's picture on national TV, I was the one who flew to Durham.

I was at the post office by nine a.m. Monday, complete with my alibi: a large stack of letters on which I could pretend to put stamps. Though it was the only ruse I could think of, I knew my "disguise" would be pitifully obvious if I had to stay longer than fifteen minutes, and to make matters worse, I might have to repeat this act for several days, since I had no idea how often Valerie's friend picked up the mail.

But none of that proved to be a concern, because at 9:10 a tall, stunning brunette strode in and walked quickly to the general area of the box. I watched out of the corner of my eye as she unloaded its contents into a leather document bag and walked away. As soon as her back was turned I rushed towards the box, checked the scotch tape I'd put on it, then moved quickly towards the exit, hoping to catch her in the parking lot.

But instead she caught me. After appearing almost magically behind me as I came around a corner, she leaned forward and whispered, "I have a gun in my coat pocket and it's aimed right at your spine. Head outside, or I'll put you in a wheelchair like your goddamned boss."

I started to protest, but she whispered, "Not a word, mister, don't say a word."

We walked outside into the nearly empty parking lot, and I saw a large, muscular man waiting inside a Lexus. He jumped out and opened the back door as we approached.

"Put your hands behind you," the brunette said, then snapped a pair of handcuffs to my wrists. Her friend shoved me into the back, then slid in alongside. She walked around the car and got in the driver's seat. We pulled away.

"My friend has a gun, too," she said as soon as we were out into traffic. "You can call him Bruce. It's not his real name, but you probably think all gay men are called Bruce. As for me, how does Gertrude Stein sound?"

"I'll call you anything you want if you'll let me go. Why are you kidnapping me, anyway?"

"Because you were staking out my box, and that means you work for Harold Anthony. Don't bother denying it, I saw you go over and check that piece of tape."

"I don't work for Harold Anthony!"

"Sure. And I'm Miss America."

I quit protesting, then realized after a minute or two that my silence made me seem even guiltier.

"What are you going to do?" I asked.

"We're working on that. For starters, I think we'll go to a private place and beat the holy shit out of you. Just like you did to Valerie."

Forty-five minutes later I was sitting on the bed in a room at a Red Carpet Inn, unbeaten but still handcuffed. "Gertrude" was slapping a nasty-looking leather blackjack against her palm, but "Bruce" didn't seem anxious to beat anybody. After I explained that I was an Atlanta obstetrician, he pled my case better than I had.

"Look Jennifer," he said, and the woman fixed him with a fiery stare. Apparently that was her real name. I pretended not to notice.

"Look," he tried again, "he says he's a doctor in Atlanta, and an old client of Valerie's. It can't be too hard to check that out."

"Why would he be casing the post-office box?" she asked.

"I told you that already," I said. "I wanted to find you and get your advice."

"All right!" she finally said, speaking directly to me for the first time since we'd gotten to the motel. "Where do you work?"

"It's called DeKalb Obstetrics. The number is . . ."

"I'll get the number myself, thank you."

She called directory assistance, then my Decatur office. When she got the receptionist she launched into a cock-and-bull story about mistakenly picking up my briefcase at the airport and wanting to return it. In the car I'd pegged her as Midwestern, but now she launched into a flawless Southern drawl that made her sound like a 21st-century Scarlett O'Hara on the prowl.

"You can't give me his phone number in Raleigh? . . . Oh, I understand perfectly . . . Well, let me give you my number here, you can call him, then he can call me and come get it himself . . . You know though, I'm just a little worried; I'm alone in town and I don't want to let the wrong person into my room. Could you give me an idea of what he looks like? Thank you; that's so sweet . . . Five-eleven, athletic build, dirty-blond hair, blue eyes? Really? I believe I saw him at the airport! He looked nice. Is he married?"

When she hung up the phone she looked at me and shook her head, then looked over at "Bruce."

"The description fits, damn it! Plus that Lunsford is out of town, and his receptionist says he flew to Raleigh. You say he doesn't have a gun?"

"No way."

"What do his hands look like?"

"Like a doctor's. Manicured nails, no calluses, except on his left fingertips. I'd guess he plays guitar or violin. They sure aren't the hands of somebody who hits people for a living."

"Give me his wallet." Bruce complied and she rifled through it. When she got to a snapshot I had of Maria and Joe she looked up abruptly.

"Bruce," she said, "take a walk. Come back in about ten minutes."

"You're not gonna' hit him, are you?"

"No, I'm not gonna' hit him. Get out of here."

As soon as Bruce left she got up, motioned for me to stand, and unlocked the handcuffs. I put my hands in front of me and rubbed them to get the circulation going. She tossed my wallet back on the bed.

"Your real name isn't Lunsford, and that picture's of Maria and Joe Anthony," she said. I didn't respond, but I don't think she was expecting an answer. "I remember now — Valerie had me sending any mail marked Lunsford to a P.O. address in Atlanta."

"That would be me."

"I guess apologies are in order. I just wanted to get whoever had done this to her. Valerie, that is."

"I take it you two were pretty close."

"Yes, and before you ask, the relationship wasn't platonic." She sat down, looking surprisingly vulnerable for someone who'd just been planning to break my skull. "I'm really sorry I didn't believe you at first, it's just that I never thought Valerie would be hiding a man."

"Valerie hid a lot of women?"

"Yes, that was her specialty: hiding women from abusive husbands, shit like that. We split because I wanted to make money, and Valerie wanted to help the downtrodden. So she ended up in Tucson and I ended up in California. I got rich, she got killed."

"California? I thought you lived here."

"No, of course not. Until two days ago any mail that went to that P.O. box got forwarded to my box in California, and I took it out of the old envelopes and put new addresses on it. I guess Valerie didn't tell you how the whole scheme worked. I came here because I thought Anthony might have gotten this box address from Valerie. I was checking it every three hours, hoping I could catch whoever'd been sent to catch me. Instead I got you, Mr. Innocence. Shit. I really wanted to take a pound of flesh out of somebody."

"Indeed. And how does 'Bruce' fit into all this?"

"I needed some muscle. Bruce knew Valerie too; he was pissed off about the way she died, and he's strong as an ox. Unfortunately, the only thing he's ever actually assaulted is a weight machine." Mentioning Valerie had brought tears to her eyes, but she saw me looking and angrily wiped them away. "Speaking of illegal activities, what are you going to do now? Have me arrested?"

"I can't hire you if you're in jail," I said.

"Hire me to do what?"

"Let's talk about that in a second. Why do you think that's Maria Anthony's picture?"

"Because it is. I've seen her photo in half the papers in the country."

"Maria Anthony had long black hair."

"Which she could have had cut. I look at faces, not decoration. Look, if you're worried about telling me something I don't know, forget it. I've suspected that Valerie had something to do with their disappearance for a long time. It's the sort of thing she arranged, and two weeks after it happened she had me forwarding mail to somebody new in Atlanta, one of Valerie's favorite destinations for Hispanic women. If I didn't know this had something to do with Maria and Joe, why would I be here at all? Why would I be mad at Harold Anthony?"

"So you don't think Valerie was killed because she was gay?"

"I don't think Valerie was killed *only* because she was gay. I figured Anthony was trying to get some sort of information out of her. But I suspect the fact she was gay made it a lot more enjoyable. The bastards!" She paused. "You said you wanted to hire me. What on earth for?"

"To get Maria's family out of Tucson. That's why I came looking for you. I don't think Valerie got killed because she was gay, either. I think Anthony was trying to find out where Maria is."

"Listen, I don't have my license anymore, and I haven't done any of that sort of work for years — I'm hopelessly rusty."

I sighed.

"All right," she said, "I can see your problem. If you hire somebody else that's one more person who knows that Maria Anthony is still alive."

"But you can't help me."

"I didn't say that. I'm not going to try and fake anybody's death; I'd screw it up. But I do know how to move someone and make them unusually hard to find. That'll have to do."

"Great. When can we get started?"

"Later," she said, looking at her watch. "If you can wait here, that is. I'm going to the post-office again. I've been going for the past five days. Who knows, maybe one of Anthony's goons will show up after all."

"And then what?"

"Then I give them a taste of what I was going to give you."

"Will that solve anything?"

"I'm not sure, but I figure it's worth a try." She lifted the blackjack off the table, then stood up and grabbed her purse.

"Toss me those cuffs, could you?" she asked. I did as requested, then watched as she slid out the door.

Chapter 3

When I returned to Atlanta I had to go straight back on call: handling deliveries from three in the morning till four in the afternoon. But the sun was shining for the first time in weeks, the air was warm, and my patients all delivered fat, healthy babies with indecent ease. I was off-duty and back at DeKalb Obstetrics by five. The staff and other doctors had left, the building was quiet, and as I signed insurance forms I found myself daydreaming about how pleased Maria would be with my trip. Though Jennifer had caught no one but me, we'd come up with a plan to relocate Maria's parents and sisters to Miami, while leaving a paper trail that led to Veracruz, Mexico.

The silence was broken only by the intermittent ringing of the telephone at the front desk. The only way to reach the phone on my desk was to dial the extension, so I was surprised when it rang at about a quarter to six. I put the call on the speaker rather than picking up the headset.

"DeKalb Obstetrics," I said, "Dr. Lunsford speaking." Then I picked up another form, glanced at its contents, and signed it.

"Dr. Peter Lunsford?" a female voice asked. Something about her tone made me put down my pen.

"Yes, that's me."

"Thank God you're in. I'm Patricia Collins, one of the teachers at Ellenwood. You're listed as an emergency number on one of Joshua Grant's forms; I'm here at the school watching him right now. Maria's been gone for two hours, and I'm getting so worried — nobody knows where she is. Somebody should have stopped her from driving off, but it all happened so quickly."

"What happened?"

"Oh! Of course you don't know." She paused, then spoke with guilty self-importance. "It's her husband, Joe. There was a construction accident, and, well, he's dead."

I shudder thinking about the way I drove in the next half-hour, tearing down city streets to the beltway, then hitting ninety-five in the first open stretch, slamming on my brakes when I hit the inevitable slowdown near I-20, honking my horn and flashing my lights, leaving a wake of bird-flashing, cursing commuters behind me.

I could have seen the clogged highways as a blessing. Joshua probably hadn't been told about Joe, and if I was delayed someone else might do it. But worry and anger drove me on: worry that Joe's "death" might be a ruse, anger at a persistent voice in the sewers of my brain, a voice that whispered, "If Joe's dead, you can have Maria."

Despite my insane driving, it took me a good fifty minutes to make the twenty-six miles to Ellenwood Elementary. All my panic accomplished was to hasten my arrival to a point near I-675 where traffic slowed to a crawl. No amount of banging on my steering wheel could make it move any faster, and other assholes like myself had already clogged the breakdown lane, so after a while I sat calmly, wearing the same zombified look as the other commuters.

It was dark when I pulled up to the school, but Mrs. Collins had been keeping an eye out for me. I banged on the front door for less than thirty seconds before she arrived and opened it.

"I'm sorry," I said as I walked in. "I got here as fast as I could."

"That's all right. I know how bad the traffic is this time of day. Listen, I hate to ask you, but you are listed on Joshua's form. Can you take him? I told Maria he could stay with me tonight, but I barely know him, and he's such a . . ." She stopped, as if embarrassed by what she'd been about to say.

"He's such a what?" I prodded her.

"He's such an eerie child. I don't like to say it, but he makes me very uneasy."

We were walking quickly down the darkened hall, and I was glad that Mrs. Collins couldn't see the look which crossed my face. There were times when Joshua made me uneasy too.

"What happened today?" I asked. "I can't believe the police would tell Maria news like that and then let her get in a car."

"The police didn't tell her. They called to see if she was in and apparently let the news slip to our principal. He called her to the office and told her himself, but I think he tried to soften the blow so much that Maria thought Joe might still be alive."

"Are you sure he's not?"

"I hope to God that's so, but everybody here says he's dead. The principal called Maria in just after the children went home, all the children except Joshua, that is — he goes to Maria's room every afternoon until it's time for her to leave. Maria dropped Joshua off in my room before she went to talk to the principal, and the next thing I know she comes running in here, asks if I can take Josh home with me for the night, and then goes running out to her car. A policeman got here just a few minutes later. He was going to try and track her down but a call came in about a bank robbery over in Forest Park."

"Do you have any idea which hospital they took Joe to?"

"No."

More bad news, but then I remembered that I knew where Joe had been working, and hence the most likely hospital. They'd probably taken him to Henry General, unless they'd called in a helicopter and flown him up to Grady. Unfortunately, the good weather made that more likely. I looked heavenward and cursed the cloudless sky — if it were still raining Joe would have spent the afternoon at home.

When we got to Mrs. Collins's room Joshua was expecting us.

"Hello, Joshua," I said.

"Hello, Peter," he said calmly, his voice sounding shockingly adult to be coming from such a small child. "What's going on?"

"You're coming with me. Grab your stuff and let's go; I'll tell you more on the way."

After I buckled Joshua into the back seat, I grabbed my cell-phone, walked a few paces away, and started making calls.

My first guess was correct — a Joseph Grant had been checked into Henry General. But that was all the information I got — they wouldn't tell me Joe's condition, nor would they delegate someone to look for Maria. So I drove to Henry General and looked for myself, towing Joshua down the halls like a rag doll. Maria was nowhere to be found, but I did locate a young ER doctor who told me what had happened. We conferred in a corner of the waiting room, while Josh lay down across two plastic chairs and appeared to sleep.

"He was dead on arrival," the doctor said softly. "The brain waves were totally flat."

"What the hell happened?"

"He was down in a ditch, laying sewer pipe, and the ditch collapsed on him. It was probably because of all the rain we've been having."

"Couldn't they dig him out?"

"That's what's so horrible. They got to his head in about two minutes, but that's never enough. When you're buried like that you can't breathe — it's like being crushed by a boa constrictor. He could see they were trying to help, but by the time they got the rest of him out he was gone."

"What in hell was he doing down in a ditch, anyway? He was a carpenter."

"Well, I heard about that too. A couple of his co-workers came in with him, Mexicans, I think. They were yelling that they wanted to have the foreman arrested. The paramedics didn't have time to listen to that, and I'm the only doctor around here who speaks any Spanish, so I told them to tell me about it. Not that I can do anything, you understand, but I thought it might calm them down.

"They said your friend never got along too well with the foreman. They'd already had a big argument about something called silt fences — the foreman had come by and found your friend replacing some instead of working where he was supposed to. Then later that day your friend came by and saw these two Mexicans working in the ditch. He told the foreman that if he didn't brace the walls he'd call OSHA. The foreman told Joe that if he didn't want to get fired on the spot he'd better get in the ditch and work with them."

"Why didn't the Mexicans get buried too?"

"They did, but just up to their waists. Your friend was working lower down in the ditch; they were standing on top of the pipes. Apparently he asked the two Mexicans if they had any life insurance, and when they said no your friend said he did and so he'd better work on the bottom. They all thought that was a good joke until the ditch caved in."

"Did you see his wife? Her name's Maria."

"No, I never saw her . . . Hold it. Maria? Does she look Hispanic?"

"Most people would say so. She's from Cuba."

"Shit. There was a Latin-looking lady here, but I assumed she was with the Mexicans. She came in just as I started talking to them — they were so mad they were shouting in Spanish practically at the top of their lungs. I didn't tell them to be quiet — they needed to blow off some steam, and I thought she was married to one of them anyway. They ran through the whole story just like I told it to you, and right when they finished she got up and left. I haven't seen her since."

"So she knows Joe is dead."

"If she speaks Spanish, she does, and she knows exactly how it happened. The Mexicans were screaming that the foreman ought to be arrested for murder. Since your friend was white, it didn't occur to me that she might be related to him. I guess I should have asked." He looked up guiltily.

"You did the best you could," I said. A few years before I might have reamed him a new asshole, because it was obvious he'd told the Mexicans that Joe was dead, information he was only supposed to release to relatives. For that matter, he shouldn't be talking to me, even though he knew I was a doctor. Unfortunately experience had taught me I wasn't exactly infallible either. "Do you have any idea where she went?"

"None whatsoever."

"What will happen to the foreman?"

"OSHA will fine the company, that's all. And I guess your friend's widow could sue."

The word "widow" was like a blow, and I thought for the first time of Joe's body, somewhere nearby, growing colder by the minute. I didn't want to see it.

"Is that your boy?" the young doctor asked hopefully, pointing to Josh.

"No," I said. "His." The doctor winced and stood up. Somehow I felt he wouldn't last long at this business.

"I'm going out to try and find his mother," I told him, standing up myself. "Thank you for talking to me."

"You're welcome," he said. "I'm sorry that's all I could do."

I carried Joshua back out to my car. He was fast asleep, and kept falling over as I tried to buckle him in. It was almost ten now, long past his bedtime, but as I got in the driver's seat I realized I had no idea where to look for Maria. I needed his help.

"Joshua," I said softly, then turned and shook him lightly.

"What is it, Uncle Peter?" he said after a moment, eyes still closed.

"Joshua," I repeated, "Are you awake? Can you think?" Joshua opened his eyes.

"What is it?" he asked again.

"If your mother was really upset, where would she go?"

"What would she be upset about? And where's my dad? It's late. Why didn't he come get me?"

"First tell me where your mother might be. Every place you can think of."

"I think she'd go to our church."

"Where's that? What's its name?"

"St. John's. I think she'd go there."

I pulled out my cell phone, called directory assistance, and got the phone number and address for a St. John's Catholic church near Ellenwood. I called the number, and as I expected, got an answering machine.

"Uncle Peter," Joshua said from the back seat. "You promised you'd tell me what was happening." I was silent — the words wouldn't come. But they didn't need to.

"My father's dead, isn't he?" Joshua asked. I didn't answer, but he understood my silence, and began crying softly.

"We need to find your mother, Josh," I finally said. "I'm going to the church, and then we'll both take you home."

When I got to the church all the lights were out, but there was one car in the lot: the ancient Nissan Joe had bought for Maria. Maria was nowhere to be seen.

"Where is she?" I wondered aloud.

"She's inside," Josh said, with an odd certainty. We got out of the car, and as we walked up to the entrance I could see a dim glow of candlelight. I wondered how Maria had gotten in until we got to the front door. It was flanked on either side by small panes of glass, and one on the right was shattered. I reached my arm inside, carefully avoiding the jagged shards in the frame — and pushed the door open.

We walked into the foyer and then into the nave. Scores of candles flickered, and in their soft light I saw that we were not alone: wooden statues of saints and martyrs peered sadly into the gloom, all seeming to gaze at Maria, who was kneeling in front of a statue of the Virgin Mary.

"Momma!" Joshua cried, and ran to her. She turned in surprise and nearly fell down as he rushed into her arms.

"Joshua! I thought Mrs. Collins was taking you home with her!"

"She called Uncle Peter to pick me up," he said, then buried his head against her chest and began to cry.

Maria looked at me for the first time.

"So you told him?" she asked in an icy voice.

"He seemed to know anyway," I said.

"And here you are, just like always."

"I was worried about you. Listen, just because you can't hear it doesn't mean you haven't set off a burglar alarm. The police may be here any minute. We need to go."

But Maria didn't move. "So you're worried about me," she said, at the same time looking back towards the statue. "Did you ever worry about Joe? You know, I've been sitting here thinking. Joe loved everybody, and see where it got him? I thought about that in the hospital and it bothered me so much I couldn't even go say goodbye."

I glanced down beside her and saw the tire iron from their Nissan; she must have used it to smash the glass beside the front door. I also saw that she'd cut her arm reaching through the broken pane.

"Maria," I said, "you're hurt."

She turned away from the statue, looked at me again, and eased Joshua out of her arms and onto a pew. Then she went on talking.

"Of course this lady behind me is supposed to prefer people like Joe. Do you think Joe is in heaven right now? Gee, I hope so, because marrying me just fucked up his life. He was a brilliant man — a hell of a lot smarter than you are — and because of me he ended up dead in a ditch." Her right hand closed around the tire iron, and she rose slowly to her feet.

"Maria," I said.

"Lovely name, isn't it? I'm named after her, of course." She pointed at the Virgin Mary. "According to the church, she and all the saints are giving Joe his reward. But you! You want payment in this world, and you're hanging around to collect like some goddamned vulture. You think I haven't seen you staring at my boobs since the day you met me? Maybe Joe never noticed your interest in my cleavage, but I sure did. I'm sad to say I liked it most of the time, but suddenly I know better." She turned back and addressed the statue. "Here's what I think, Maria." She strode towards the Virgin.

"Momma, no!" Josh said, but he was too late.

"Stupid bitch," she said, and swung the tire iron at the statue's head. It popped off cleanly and came to rest on the floor, eyes gazing mournfully heavenward.

"And as for you, Peter . . ." She turned away from the statue and came at me. I raised my arm to block the blow, and a moment later felt a shocking pain. Maria had thrown the tire iron down, and it landed point first on my foot. She continued the attack with her fists, pounding them hard into my chest.

"Get out of here, you bastard, get out of here right now!" I tried to grab her flailing arms, tried to back away, but the only result was that she connected a few blows to my face as well. "Momma, stop it!" I heard Josh say, and suddenly I was blinded, as somebody turned all the sanctuary lights on at once.

"What's going on?" said a loud voice, and I turned, expecting to see a couple of policemen, pistols drawn. Instead, there was a young man holding an enormous bronze candlestick.

"Just get him away from me!" Maria screamed. "Make him leave! I never want to see him again!"

"Listen, buddy," the young priest said, "I've already called the police, and I can always pop you with this." He waved the candlestick. "If you don't want to get in worse trouble just get away."

I backed slowly away from Maria.

"Now lie down on your stomach," he said, and pulled a short length of velvet altar rope out of his pocket. Apparently he planned to tie my hands, but Maria spared him further heroics.

"Leave him alone, Father." She sat down wearily on a pew and picked up Joshua, who'd fallen to the floor.

"Mrs. Grant!" the priest said, "And Joshua! What's going on?" But Maria was beyond answering, and it was left to Joshua to tell the priest.

"My father was killed today," he said in a calm voice, "and then Uncle Peter picked me up and we came to look for my mother. She got mad at him; I really don't know why — he didn't do anything wrong."

The priest turned and looked warily at me again. After a moment he felt safe enough to lay the candlestick and rope gently on a pew.

"Is that true?" he asked me. "Is Joseph dead?"

"Yes, it's true," I said. "I'm a friend of the family, and Josh and I were worried about his mother."

"What happened?"

"It was a construction accident."

"Oh my God," he said, slowly, "how horrible." Then he turned to Maria.

"Mrs. Grant, why didn't you call me, or Father Harding? I would have been glad to come down and open up the church, and someone could have stayed with you."

"Listen," I said, "I can pay for the damage."

"Oh, Peter, shut up!" Maria snapped. "You think your damned money can fix everything!"

The priest turned to me. "We're not worried about the damage, Mister . . ."

"Lunsford."

"We can fix a few panes of glass and . . ." His eyes lighted on the decapitated statue. He walked over and looked sadly at its head lying on the floor, then picked it up reverently and tried to replace it on the body. It wouldn't stay, so he laid it on a pew instead.

"Mrs. Grant," he said, "Don't worry about the statue either. It's natural to be angry at a time like this. I'm just glad no one was hurt." He looked doubtfully at me, then he saw Maria's arm. "You've cut yourself! We need to get you to a hospital!"

"Let me look at it," I said, "I'm a doctor."

"Keep him away from me," Maria growled.

"Come now, Mrs. Grant," said the priest, "be reasonable. What harm can it do for him to look at your arm?" Maria nodded reluctantly and I walked over and examined the cut. It would need several stitches, maybe as many as eight or ten, but the bleeding had almost stopped.

"She'll need to get it sewed up," I said, "but it's not an emergency."

"Well, let's go to the office. Mrs. Grant, do you have any relatives in town?"

"No," she said weakly.

"Close friends?"

"No," she said, and I felt hurt, despite the fact that she'd almost brained me a minute before.

"Well, let me get on the phone and see if any of the ladies of the church can sit up with you. And maybe someone can help out with your son." He turned and looked oddly at Josh, who was sitting quietly beside his mother. I could tell the boy's calm unnerved him.

"What about the police?" I asked, "Hadn't you better call them and tell them it was a false alarm?"

"They aren't coming. I saw cars in the parking lot and stopped to investigate, and right when I got to the door I heard Mrs. Grant. She sounded upset so I grabbed the first things I could find and rushed in. I didn't have time to call anyone."

"No burglar alarm?"

"The janitor must have forgotten to set it when he left." He beckoned us out of the nave. "This way."

We sat in the church office while the priest made a few phone calls, brewed tea, and offered Joshua hot chocolate. Maria's unease in my presence was painfully obvious, and after a few minutes I went and sat in the adjoining room and thought how handy it was to be a priest: a symbolic eunuch, supposedly immune to any impure thoughts about the grieving woman in his office.

To my surprise Joshua came out and sat with me. He still seemed almost as calm as the priest.

"Is your foot hurt, Uncle Peter?" he asked.

Suddenly it hurt abominably, and I eased off my shoe and peeled away a bloody sock. Maria wasn't the only one who'd need to visit the emergency room. I had a deep gash where the tire iron had cut through the leather before bouncing off onto the floor.

"I'm sorry," Joshua said. "Momma didn't really mean to hurt you."

"I'll be all right. Josh, I'm sorry about your father."

"I'll miss him," said Joshua, "at least for the little while until I see him again." He turned and went back in to his mother. A moment later the priest came out.

"I think you can go home now, Dr. Lunsford," he said. "Thank you for your help."

"Fat lot of help I was."

"Oh, I don't know. Grieving people often need someone to get angry at. You've been a good target at least." He looked down. "What happened to your foot!"

"She dropped a tire iron on it. It's still lying in your church somewhere."

"Is that what she hit the statue with?"

"Yes."

He frowned.

"I didn't dare call one of the older nuns to be with her — if they found out she did that they'd be horrified. And some of them are very uneasy around Joshua."

"How's he holding up?"

"Almost too well. He says his father is in heaven and so he's not worried about him. It's the sort of reaction you usually see in someone quite old and quite religious. I'm stunned to see it in a five-year-old."

"So you know Josh and his mother well."

"Joshua sticks out, and so of course I've noticed his parents, too. Have you known Mr. Grant for long?"

"For many years. He was my best friend."

"I'm so sorry. Will you be all right? Should I get someone to drive you to a hospital?"

"No. I can handle it."

"I'm also sorry I screamed at you. When I first came in, that is."

"That's okay. Appearances were against me."

And so I limped back to my car and drove to an emergency room, where a doctor put three stitches in my foot. Once home I spent a wretched night, tormented by visions of Joe in a cold, muddy grave — and Maria lying naked in warm, tangled sheets.

Chapter 4

Out of necessity I saw Maria often in the weeks after Joe's death — but she would accept no comfort from me. No doubt she regretted tossing a tire iron on my foot, but there was more to her unease than embarrassment. She acted almost as if we'd been having an affair — one she was determined to end and I was not.

Her family should have been with her, but we were afraid to bring anyone to Atlanta without thorough preparation. Long ago Valerie had set up an emergency system involving code phrases, wrong numbers and preselected Tucson pay phones, but Maria talked to her parents only twice, and even that made me nervous — if Anthony was tapping the Velasquez phone he might recognize my voice, even when I pretended to be a drunk trying to call Tucson's Saguaro Avenue bowling alley. Nonetheless, plans were made for Maria's parents to move to Miami, though they consented more out of concern for Maria than fear for their own safety.

So I spent days consulting with Maria and Jennifer about the move and arranging the more mundane details of Joe's funeral. The Mexicans came, as well as many of his fellow workers, and far off in a corner of the church I caught a glimpse of the foreman. He looked guilt-ridden, ill and forlorn; and I couldn't join in the curses the Mexicans muttered as they stared at him, heads lowered, eyes blazing under wrinkled brows.

Maria looked less bereaved than the foreman — staring dry-eyed at Joe's ashes, occasionally reaching over to pat Joshua's head as he quietly wept. But her stoic calm was feigned — once or twice I saw her real emotion surface, not sadness but cold fury at a world that had casually wasted her husband's gifts, then buried him even before he was truly dead.

About two weeks before Christmas I dropped by Maria's school. I'd been to Miami the previous weekend, checking out rental houses for her parents. I'd walked through each house with my video camera running, and when I got back I'd given Maria the tape.

The students had already left when I arrived, but Maria was still in her classroom, grading homework and writing up lesson plans. Josh was sitting quietly in a corner, reading a book. I knocked on the open door and Maria motioned me out into the hall.

"Did you look at the video yet?" I asked.

"Yes, I did," Maria said, "and I don't know how to thank you. The tape was a great idea."

"Why do they want such a big house just for the two of them?"

Maria frowned. "It won't be just for the two of them."

"Is one of your sisters coming, too? I thought they were moving somewhere out West."

Maria bit her lip and looked away.

"No, my sisters aren't moving in with them," she said. "Josh and I are."

"Oh, really," I answered. I'd seen this coming, but somehow that wasn't making the news go down any easier.

"I've thought a lot about it," she continued, "and I'm sure it will be for the best. Joshua needs some family now that Joe is gone, and God knows I need some family, too."

I hadn't cried at Joe's funeral, but now I looked down the hall, fighting off tears.

"Peter, I don't know how to thank you for all you've done," Maria kept on, inexorable as the red Georgia mud that had killed her husband. "I can pay you back soon for your trips to Miami and Durham — Joe's life insurance check came this week — there wasn't any problem with the company at all."

"Forget it," I said. "I don't want your money."

"Come on, Peter! I insist. Though I can't begin to pay you back for all the help you've been to Joe and Josh and me. I know that knowing us . . . knowing me at least, has really messed up your life."

"Knowing Harold Anthony has messed up my life. Will you at least write?"

Maria edged a little further away.

"Sure," she said in a weak voice. "And Josh will write you. He was very upset when I told him we were moving — he asked if Uncle Peter was coming, too." She smiled up at me, her face a mask of bright and counterfeit cheer.

As for me — I wanted to take her in my arms like some cinema Don Juan, convince her through my own obsession to love me in return. Instead, I turned as if to leave. I'd actually taken a few steps down the hall when she called after me.

"Peter!"

I turned back.

"I want you to tell me something," she said. "Actually, I want you to say something, even if you have to lie."

"What?"

"I want you to say you did it all because you were such good friends with Joe. That's the only reason you've worried so much about us, isn't it?"

"Yes, I did it all for Joe," I lied.

"Thank you," she said, and opened her arms. I went to her and gave her a brief, brotherly hug.

"I'll miss you," I said as I straightened up.

"We'll miss you, too," said Maria.

After school got out for Christmas they left in a medium-sized Ryder truck, which Maria drove with surprising confidence. Joe's tools had been entrusted to Father Harding for later resale, but they took most of their second-hand furniture, clothes, Josh's books and toys, and twenty-two of Joe's guitars and lutes. Me they left behind.

But Josh was a boy of his word and wrote often, and for a five-year-old, at great length. I think anyone who doubts there's something unnatural about Joshua ought to read those letters. Indeed it might be good for Joshua to read them — it might derail some of his absurd modesty; it might even convince him that what I've written here is true.

Reading them myself I'm struck with a thought that's often galled me. Joshua could have been anything: a great artist or musician, a brilliant scientist, a millionaire ten times over. When I think of all the good things he's forgone, it breaks my heart. He works like a dog, lives like a monk, and anyone who's read two pages of history knows he's wasting his time. "The poor you will have with you always." Even Jesus knew that. Though they die by the millions, a never-ending resupply is born every morning.

And Joshua insists that each of them is worth as much as he. Well, I challenge you, Joshua, read this letter you wrote not long after your sixth birthday, and say with a straight face that you're an average human being.

Dear Uncle Peter,

Merry Christmas from Miami! I found that on a postcard at the store, and it seems like a good way to start a letter, even if it is already after Christmas. I'm sorry I didn't write you sooner. We've been very busy unpacking.

I like Miami so far, but it sure is hot here, at least for January. The beach is the best thing. I've seen the ocean on TV, but it's not the same. It's also fun that everybody in our neighborhood speaks Spanish.

I like my new school, but the teachers all want me to work on things that are too easy. I went to the library the first time this week. I found a neat book called The Lion, the Witch, and the Wardrobe, but the librarian wouldn't let me check it out at first. She said it was too hard. I told her that I'd already read the first chapter in the library, and that I thought I would be able to read the rest. She looked at me funny and opened it up somewhere in the middle and asked me to read it to her. I did for a while, and she sat there still looking kind of funny, and one of the other ladies who works there came over and listened too. After a while she asked me what I thought the book was about, and I told her it was about religion. One of the ladies looked like she was going to laugh, but the other one looked kind of surprised. She asked me to tell her how it was about religion, since the story was talking about a lion named Aslan and wolves and things like that. I told her that it was the same thing we get told about in church, except that the writer had changed all the names and made it look like a fairy-tale. She looked at me even more funny, then she told me I could check the book out after all. Then she went over and talked to my new teacher for a while.

Speaking of church, I have been reading the Bible, and I have lots of questions about it, but when I ask our catechism teacher any of them she gets upset. That makes me confused, because she always tells us what a good thing it is to read the Bible. I am up to the Book of Joshua, and I told the lady at church I wasn't sure I liked being named Joshua, because he seemed like an awfully bad man who killed lots of people. She got upset and said Joshua was a hero who just did what God told him to do.

My adventure at church made Momma laugh, which made me happy, because she is very sad most of the time now. She still misses Dad, but she likes being back with her parents. They are very nice, but they try to feed me so much I think I'm going to get fat. I still miss my father and I also miss you. I think Mom misses you too, but she doesn't like to talk about it. Maybe you should move to Miami. I think that would be a lot of fun.

Momma says it's time for me to go to bed now, and I don't have anything else to write about so I guess I will. Happy New Year!

Your friend,
Joshua

There it is — the typical scribblings of a kindergartner. Actually, Josh didn't scribble, he pounded out his letters on an old IMac. I'm sure a study of prodigies could find more adult-sounding letters, but even after you discount the eerily correct spelling and grammar you're confronted with the subject matter. Josh was always fascinated with religion, something I've not often encountered in the annals of wunderkinds. But even more startling was his childhood refusal to be led by anyone. If he hadn't been unfailingly polite I imagine a nun somewhere along the way would have strangled him. And he didn't restrict his heresies to Catholicism. Joshua was constantly after his mother to attend different churches. Though Maria drew the line at visiting a mosque, in most cases she indulged his wishes. Which is how Josh was able to write me of experiences like the following:

> . . . Last week I wanted to visit a new church, so I got Mom to take us to one we'd never been to before. It was a Southern Baptist church, and when I asked to go there Mom laughed and said, "They'll love you." When I asked why she told me she didn't have time to explain, but that I'd probably find out.
>
> Well, I tried not to, but I got this Sunday School teacher mad at me too. She said something about how anybody who didn't love Jesus wouldn't get to heaven, and I asked her if that meant all the Muslim and Chinese and Jewish children were going to go to hell. She got this really sad look on her face and said that unfortunately that was true, if they didn't accept Christ when they were adults there was nothing God could do for them. Then we sang a song about how Jesus loves the little children of the world.
>
> After we finished singing I asked why if Jesus was God and loved the little children he would send so many of them to hell when they grew up. She got very angry and said that was what was written in the Bible. I told her I'd read the Bible and that it had lots of things written in it and not all of them agreed. She turned kind of red and sent me out into the hall. I was worried Momma would be mad, but when she came out and found me in the hall she said, "Well, I warned you," and we went straight home.
>
> I have learned three new guitar pieces. Also, Grandma is teaching me how to cook. You ought to come here for a visit sometime soon. I miss you, and I think Momma misses you too.
>
> Joshua

When I glance back through Josh's letters, I'm struck by how many of them end that way. "Momma misses you." Or . . . "Momma is still very sad. I think you should come down and cheer her up."

But Momma wrote only a few times — perfunctory notes like the form letters people churn out at Christmas. Every line seemed to scream her fervent wish that I be satisfied with these little breadcrumbs of her life and stay away.

And stay away I did. I could have found a new position and moved to Miami — in fact I considered it often. But memories of Joe haunted me, my friend against whom I'd sinned in thought if not in deed. And besides, to chase after Maria again would be to lose the last shreds of my dignity, which, as far as Maria was concerned, was all it seemed I had left.

And what was life like without Maria?

Mostly, I worked. I upped my volunteer time at the charity clinic and took on more patients at my "real" job. I dropped my hobbies, didn't read, didn't write, put the guitar in the closet. One year after Maria left, my senior partner was commenting on my constant exhaustion, and by the next year my own physician was nagging about blood pressure, cholesterol, and stress. Then he quoted Benjamin Franklin's cheery aphorism that most men die suicides, only they use whiskey or work or bile or sorrow instead of a gun.

Maria never wrote, at least nothing I considered a letter, and she weaseled out of seeing me the two times I went to Miami. I could find nothing to replace her, no other reason for getting up in the morning. Sex, my old standby, stood no longer. I had two short and disastrous relationships with other women, and four even more disastrous trips to bed, trips where my dignity was salvaged only by a ready store of Viagra jokes.

When the phone rang late one afternoon in 2010 I was recovering from a typical two-day stretch. One of the junior partners at DeKalb had asked me to fill in while he went on an unexpected vacation, and I'd put in an eighteen-hour stint at the hospital, followed by a quick trip home, four hours in bed, and then a phone call summoning me back to do it all again. Afterwards, I'd planned to grab a quick six hours rest and work some more, but somehow my senior partner had gotten wind of this, called the junior partner on the phone, and told him to pack his golf-bags or mistress or whatever and get back to town so I could quit delivering babies in my sleep. Which was why I was taking a leisurely shower and wondering how to fill an unusually idle weekday. The prospect wasn't appealing, so I'd hurried to pick up the call, dripping and naked, for some reason hoping I'd have to go in to work anyway.

But it wasn't the hospital, and it wasn't my senior partner wanting to have a serious talk. It was Maria.

"Hello? Peter?" said a woman's voice. "Remember me?"

"Maria?" I said, wondering if I was dreaming.

"Yes, it's me. How are you doing?"

"I'm all right," I practically stuttered. "How's Miami?"

"I'm not in Miami. I'm here in Atlanta. Are you free tonight? Can we go out and have dinner?"

"Sure," I said. "Where are you?"

"At the Motel 6 in Stockbridge. Room 215."

"The Motel 6? You're on a budget, I take it."

"It's cheap and it's clean."

"It's certainly cheap. What are you doing in Atlanta?"

"Uh, why don't we talk about that later. Do you want to drive or should I? I've got a rental."

"I'll drive; I can pick you up, too. When do you want to go?"

"How about right now?"

"Sure."

"How long will it take you to get here?"

"About fifteen minutes."

"Great. I'll see you then. Bye!" And she hung up.

As I drove to Stockbridge my favorite body part stood to attention, inspired by thoughts of Maria dressed first in a Victoria's Secret negligee, then in nothing at all.

Halfway to the motel I had another, less pleasant vision: Beverly phoning me out of the blue, inviting me to dinner . . . and her wedding.

Maria must have been watching from the lobby, because as soon as I pulled into the parking lot, she came striding and waving towards the car.

She'd gained a little weight and there was now a touch of grey around her temples, but her hair was long again, well past her shoulders. I pulled into an open parking space and she hopped in before I could even lean over and open the door.

"Peter!" she said, "it's so good to see you!" She gave me a quick, one-armed hug, the stickshift between us.

"Hello, Maria," I replied, a little sedately. If it was so good to see me, why the obvious reluctance to even stay in touch? Why this sudden change?

"Peter," she said, "are you sure you want to go out? You look awful."

"Why, thank you."

"I'm sorry, I didn't mean it like that. I mean you look tired."

"Well, I just pulled a double shift. Where do you want to eat? It's still early; we might get in at the Pheasant."

"Peter, that's a little beyond my budget."

"It's my treat Maria, come on."

"But I don't want anything fancy. Is the Golden Lotus still open? I used to like to eat there."

"It's still open, but there are better places, even in South Atlanta."

"The Lotus will do just fine for me, if it's all right with you."

"Okay, the Lotus it is. Chinese Georgia style."

We got there a little after five, and because it was so early we had the place almost to ourselves. It was like talking in a church.

"How's Joshua doing?" I asked after we'd ordered some egg rolls and tea.

"Fine," she said.

"Still setting school on fire?"

She frowned. "He gets straight A's without studying at all, and of course he's in the gifted program, but they just don't know what to do with him."

"A mind like that, I suppose he can pretty well educate himself."

"I guess so. I just wish that . . . well, I just wish his teachers liked him a little better."

"Why would they dislike Josh? He's the nicest child I've ever seen."

"I know. Something about him just makes most adults very uneasy. I worry about him a lot."

I worried about him, too, but most of my unease centered on one man. Services from Harold Anthony's Church of Biblical Truth were now regularly broadcast on one of the religious channels. Anthony's recent sermons frequently warned that *in vitro* fertilization or human cloning would be behind the birth of the Antichrist. Occasionally he even dropped dark hints that the worst had already happened, that *He* was already here.

"And how are you doing?" I asked Maria.

She bit her lower lip this time, an old sign that she was trying to be tactful.

"All right," she said. "How are you?"

"I'm fine. I work more than I used to — I don't turn anything away anymore."

"How's your love life? Are you seeing someone?" She looked down, and I had the feeling that she'd gotten to the real point of her visit much sooner than she'd planned.

"Okay, I guess. No one regularly. How about you?"

My question made her look down again. Here it comes, I thought, she's about to tell me about her new fiancé, and she doesn't know how to start.

"Peter, I don't know how to talk to you about this," she finally said, and all the hurt of the past few years suddenly boiled up inside me.

"I suggest you just blurt it out. You've never minded being blunt before."

She straightened and looked me in the eyes for the first time since I'd picked her up. "All right, I'll just blurt it out. Peter, do you still love me?"

The question was so unexpected that I answered without thinking.

"Of course I still love you. I've always loved you."

Maria stared at the floor again, her face a study in guilt.

"Why don't I help you out," I said, determined to enjoy my role as martyr since that seemed to be the only enjoyment left me. "You're getting married, and you don't know how to break the news. Well, I've been rejected before and I'll survive it again. I just wish you'd had the decency to write sometimes."

She looked up and laughed. "Is that why you think I'm here? To tell you I'm marrying somebody else?"

"Well, isn't it?"

"Hell, no! I've got nothing against getting married again, but marrying you was what I had in mind."

I stared at her, stunned beyond words. She looked stunned too.

"Oh my God," she mumbled. "Did I just say what I think I said?"

"Yes, you did. And I accept your proposal. Let's get married."

She sank back in her chair, her brown face for once almost ashen.

"Somehow I'm not hungry anymore," she said.

"Me either," I replied. "Let's get out of here."

"I couldn't forget you," Maria said.

We were walking hand-in-hand down a trail at the Reynolds Nature Preserve, a hundred-and-forty wooded acres miraculously saved from metro Atlanta's suburban sprawl. It had been one of Joe and Maria's favorite spots.

"You tried awfully hard," I answered. "You've written me all of four letters and a Christmas card."

"But I wanted to write you all of the time. I wanted to see you all of the time. I've missed you terribly, and so has Joshua."

"Good for him. So why didn't you write?"

"Because thinking about you made me feel unfaithful to Joe."

"But . . . hell, I don't know of a kind way to say this . . . Joe's dead."

"I used to think about you when he was alive, too. I've never felt good about that. Not that I ever planned to do anything about it, but sometimes I couldn't help wondering . . ."

I stopped and turned towards her. We'd come to a lake. No one else was in sight, and the only evidence of the city was the murmur of traffic, far away. The sun was setting across the water, brilliant red and framed by the trees. I put my hands on either side of her face, bent down, and gave her a long, delicate kiss.

"Oh, God," she murmured.

"I thought a lot about you when Joe was alive, too," I said. "What I thought was that he was a lucky man."

She broke the embrace and turned away. "You know, Peter, you don't have the world's greatest track record with women. My mother said that was what should worry me, not that we were . . . friends . . . while Joe was alive. I'm not interested in some open relationship where you sleep around every now and then — I'm old-fashioned about that. I want a faithful husband and a father for Joshua."

"You think I can't be that?"

"I've wondered sometimes. I heard rumors about you in Tucson."

I laughed. "Look, Maria, in the past two years I have almost no track record with women. Dreaming about you kept getting in my way. And I can be old-fashioned, too. Watch, I'll prove it."

I got down on one knee. She laughed.

"Maria, will you marry me?" I asked.

"I thought I'd already asked you."

"You did, but this is official. Well, almost. I don't have a ring. What's your answer?"

She looked out across the water. I remained on one knee, looking up hopefully. Finally she smiled down at me.

"Yes, Peter. I'll marry you. I came up here to see if we could start a relationship again. This has been a little fast, but I can't say it wasn't what I wanted."

I stood up and gave her another kiss, this time with a little more heat in it.

"That feels so strange," she said.

"You mean it feels so good."

"That too."

We got married in Miami two weeks later, then took off for a short honeymoon in Bermuda. In less than a month I'd gained both a wife and a son.

Part IV

Chapter 1

In 2025 Joshua Grant dropped out of his third graduate program and went to India to work for the Missionaries of Charity, a religious order founded by the 20th-century nun Saint Teresa. Grant was officially only a lay worker, but his views had a quick and radical influence on the order. Within months of Grant's arrival the Missionaries were accepting Protestant volunteers; within a year, the Missionaries were asking the Vatican to allow them to induct Hindus, Buddhists, and Muslims as members of their religious community. In Rome, alarm changed to cries of heresy when the first collections of his "sermons" were published by Grant's followers.

But then Grant himself came to Rome, charmed the Catholic hierarchy, and negotiated an agreement. The Church would not condemn Grant's ecumenical views, but neither would Grant's non-Catholic followers claim any official connection to the Church. And so the Brethren of Charity were born.

It was an appropriate beginning for such a vaguely defined group. To enter, one makes only two promises: first, to love one's neighbor as oneself, and second, not to use the name or resources of the Brethren to denigrate another's religion. These promises may sound innocuous, but the vow not to denigrate other religions allows the different groups within the Brethren to work towards common goals, and the activist spin Grant applies to loving one's neighbor draws Brethren members into many political debates concerning relations between the First and Third World.

Since they strive to cross cultural and religious divides, the Brethren have been frequent targets of bombings, assassinations, and political repression, but the organization seems to thrive on persecution. The group's most dramatic influence has occurred in the Middle East. In Arab countries, Brethren members have popularized liberal Sufist interpretations of the Koran, and then used these religious arguments to fight discrimination against both women and Christian and Jewish minorities. In Israel, the Brethren's campaign of peaceful civil disobedience has eroded world tolerance of discriminatory Israeli laws and policies more thoroughly than years of more violent Palestinian resistance.

As a result, Joshua Grant and the Brethren are viewed as a threat by groups that can agree on nothing else; including conservative factions in Israel, repressive Arab governments, and both Islamic and Jewish extremists. As of this date Jewish extremists have taken no overt action against the group, but Islamic extremists have not been so cautious. However, several of their attempts to assassinate the Brethren's leader have gone so spectacularly awry that the *jihadists* have reputedly decided Allah has a special (and presumably grisly) fate in store for Grant, one with which mere bomb-carrying mortals should not meddle.

In the United States the Brethren were initially seen as a praiseworthy charity, but as Grant's political and religious views become better known the Brethren have again become the subject of angry debate. Grant is quick to defend his politics, but his religious prominence seems unintentional, the result of unofficial booklets purporting to contain his comments on matters divine. These booklets were not actually "written" by Grant; instead they are reputedly transcripts of what he has said in religious conversations and informal debates.

So what does Grant (who still calls himself a Christian) believe, at least according to his disciples who take notes? In a nutshell:

- The Bible and other religious texts are not divinely inspired. They are human discussions about the nature of God.
- The concept of Jesus as the Son of God cannot be rationally explained, defended, or understood. It is instead a poetic expression of the mystical relationship between God and Humanity.
- The doctrine of the Trinity is also not amenable to rational understanding. It expresses how human beings, like Christ, will experience a final union with God, a union in which all will be one and will still also be separate.
- Following Christ is the path to this final union, but following Christ means following his ethical teaching, not belief in a particular doctrinal system (including Grant's) or even belief in the historical existence of Jesus. "Misspelling the name of God," Grant has supposedly said, "hardly merits eternal damnation."
- As for damnation, Grant believes that repentance and salvation can take place after death. He is also intrigued by the concept of reincarnation.
- In order to bless mankind with free will, Grant believes God gave up most of his ability to know and control the future. The story of Jesus is thus a "true myth" about God's willing sacrifice of power.

Liberal Christian theologians speak well of Grant's musings, although some accuse him of plastering over complex issues with naive generalities. But to Christian fundamentalists, Grant's synthesis of Christian beliefs with elements of Hinduism, Buddhism and Sufism smells suspiciously like the false one-world religion foretold in the *Book of Revelation*.

— *Wall Street Journal Online*
May, 2031

Maria cooked breakfast this morning: three eggs and biscuits from a tin. She usually considers such biscuits a venial sin (they make more trash than home-made) but I convinced her that her illness excused this small extravagance. I couldn't convince her to have a restaurant deliver, nor could I convince her to let me cook — she said my eggs would kill her more surely than any disease. Joshua is flying in from India today and she hoped to follow up breakfast by making him some special treat, but fixing that simple meal exhausted her. Now she's lying on the sofa while I write in the other room.

Maria thinks I'm embarked on another crime novel. I've written two so far, both featuring Val West, private eye. Val's snappy repartee is based on Valerie Weselesky's patter, but Val has a taste for violence and priapic firearms that Valerie never shared. Both novels have sold moderately well, but they took me years to write. Maria is quite curious about my new "detective story," because I'm churning the pages out at lightning speed.

Of course, I *haven't* been writing a detective story; I've been answering Joshua's question. I realized yesterday that I'd covered everything Josh needs to know, but I can't seem to stop. Hence the above, and the below.

The bell rings at a little after one, earlier than I'd expected. Maria sits up at the sound and gets to the door before me. It's more energy than she's shown in weeks. She opens the door and throws herself into Joshua's arms.

"Mom! It's so good to see you!" he says, lifting her off her feet before quickly putting her down, as if he's suddenly remembered how ill she's been. I usually get an equally enthusiastic greeting, but there must be something off-putting in my body language, and I settle instead for a quick, one-armed hug. We go into the living room to talk, but when Maria offers to make some tea, Josh says that he intends to wait on her hand and foot. He goes off alone into the kitchen. I stay in the living room with Maria, but she hisses at me:

"Peter! Go keep him company!"

"I'm keeping you company."

"You see me all the time! Go talk to him!"

I walk meekly into the kitchen. Josh is heating water and arranging toast and cookies on a plate, the cookies apparently something he bought at the airport. He must have had some flowers hidden in his knapsack too; he's already got them in a vase.

I smile at him for a moment, too preoccupied for light conversation. He senses what's really on my mind, and speaks without looking up.

"I haven't forgotten my question, Peter. You are going to tell me, aren't you?"

"Yes. But it's a complicated story, so I've written it down."

"How long did that take?"

"Several weeks. It's about 80,000 words."

"Eighty thousand?"

"Like I said, it's complicated."

"Obviously. How's Mom doing? She's so thin."

"She's okay. She sleeps a lot, though. We'll have plenty of time to talk this evening."

"Is there anything she needs?"

"She needs you. When do you have to leave?"

Joshua frowns. Conflicts between family and saintly charity are one reason he's never married, but a man has to have a mother.

"I can stay two weeks," he says. "Then I'll probably need to go."

"Two whole weeks? Wow."

"Look, Bangladesh has been lucky this year: only one cyclone has hit. But they need money, not luck. If the World Court decides for them, they'll finally have some capital. You've heard about the suit, haven't you?"

"Of course. But do you really believe they'll see a penny of our money?"

"Why shouldn't they? The sea level is up two feet since 2000, and it will probably go up another two feet in the next twenty years. Europe, India and China are finally taking the problem seriously, but the U.S. is still pumping out CO2 like there's no tomorrow, and we put most of it into the atmosphere to begin with."

"But why do you think this particular case is so important?"

"Because we're at a turning point. The U.S. has been the world's only superpower for forty years now, and compared to other empires they haven't been too bad. Maybe the human race is learning something. But working in Bangladesh will show you we're not learning fast enough."

"And you think you can change that? The U.S. doesn't give a damn about the World Court, or the rest of the world for that matter. As far as that case is concerned, we'll find one crank scientist who'll say the sun's gotten hotter, or there's less dust in space. Or we'll ignore the verdict if we don't like it. How can the Court enforce anything?"

"Economic sanctions."

"Sure. They're going to try and run the world without one of its most powerful economies."

Joshua frowns and begins buttering some more toast.

"You're right, of course," he finally says. "If the U.S. won't give the aid the World Court can't make them do it. So I've made a decision.

Since everyone thinks I'm a preacher, I'll stay here for a while and preach. Maybe I can convince people that you don't love your neighbor by drowning him with your garbage. But I'll have to go to New York sooner or later."

"But you'll be able to do some work from here, won't you?"

"I hope so. But this is important. And Mom agrees with me."

"I know. She's told me. Constantly."

The food is ready. Josh puts the flowers on one side of a tray and the plates and cups on the other, lifts the tray like an experienced waiter, and then walks towards the living room. His frown has been replaced by a hearty smile — cheerfulness in the face of disaster is one of his specialties.

We spend a pleasant afternoon. Maria is as happy as I've seen her in months; Josh doesn't talk much about India, and what little he does say concerns the Brethren's sunnier affairs. Maria tells him that I'm hard at work on a new book, and that's she's sure I'm in the grip of some great inspiration. We avoid talking about her illness, but after a few hours Maria is plainly exhausted — she gets up to use the bathroom and nearly falls over. Josh plays nursemaid after that, and against her fervent protests helps her to the bedroom, then gets her a final cup of tea and a book. He comes out a few minutes later; Maria has fallen asleep almost instantly.

"So where is this great literary work?" he asks.

"It's in my study, on the old computer."

"Do you have a password? Not that it would guard much on that relic."

"You're probably right, but I have one anyway. Try 'water heater.' "

He looks at me, puzzled, then shakes his head and goes in to read. I wait in the living room for a few minutes, but the tension is too much — I want to hang over his shoulder; watch his reaction to every word. That would probably strain even Josh's patience, so I go out to the garage, get in my car, and drive to my office.

I'm not just going to kill time; I have other problems to attend to. On arriving, I take out my pocket computer and turn on the wall monitor. I'm not good with computers, and sure enough, I've filed something away and forgotten what I called it, which has me fussing and fuming for twenty minutes before I locate what I should have found in five. It's an Internet news shot of Joshua with a few of the more committed Brethren. Something about it has been bothering me all day. I know most of Josh's compatriots well, but there's an older man in this photo whom I've never seen. At least that was my first impression. On a second look the face seemed familiar, and just before Joshua arrived I had a sudden flash of insight. Having found the file, I e-mail it to a friend of mine, a fellow crime writer who calls himself Truman Coyote.

Truman is a computer nerd, (as are his detectives) and I often go to him for advice about the cyberworld. Truman practically lives at his computer and sure enough, in about twenty minutes I get a reply. A new, improved version of the photo fills the wall-screen, complete with a piece of freeware. At the bottom Truman adds some instructions for this nifty new tool he wants me to install on *my* computer. With the scrollbar I can age faces in the photo, or make them younger, or type in a number and view the vaguely familiar man as he would have appeared at twenty, thirty, forty, and fifty.

After the instructions Truman adds a few lines mocking my computer skills — the program is apparently a plaything for five-year-olds and he can't believe I couldn't find and install it myself. I ought to E him back a nasty reply, just to keep him from getting too cocky, but I don't bother. Instead, following his instructions, I bring up a row of heads on my wall monitor, a life-gallery of one man miraculously progressing from forty to his mid-seventies, heading steadily towards the end that will someday claim us all.

When I come back hours later Josh is in the kitchen, sitting in a straight-backed chair. Music is playing, something gloomy and Russian.

"What on earth are you listening to?" I ask.

"Mussorgsky. *Songs and Dances of Death.*"

"Cheery tune."

"It seems appropriate," he replies, "for the text, that is."

"Did you finish *my* text?" I ask.

"Yours is the one I was talking about."

"Oh."

"I suppose you think this is funny?" He stands, turns off the music, and holds up the old-fashioned CD I've saved the "manuscript" on.

"It's not meant to be."

"What is it meant to be?"

"It's meant to be the truth. If it reads like one of my detective books it's because that's how I'm used to writing."

"So you're telling me Joseph Grant wasn't my father, Maria isn't my mother, and I was cooked up in a test tube like the monster in some fourth-rate science-fiction movie? Do you have any idea what Harold Anthony and his zealots would say if they ever found this?"

"I can guess. What would you say if they'd attacked you with the truth when you didn't know it yourself?"

"So you maintain this all really happened?"

"Yes."

"And what evidence do you have?"

"I know that your mother had an *in-vitro* fertilization — she told me herself and I saw all the paperwork that went with it. I know that genetic tests I arranged showed Maria didn't share any of your DNA."

"And how do you know somebody at this 'clinic' didn't just grab the wrong Petri dish?"

"Because Eric Schroeder and Harold Anthony both told me you were cloned."

"And the source of the DNA? What evidence do you have about that?"

"Anthony Enterprises did tests on fragments of the Shroud, back in the 90's. It's a matter of public record."

"And they got a complete genome from an unfrozen biological sample that was either seven-hundred or two-thousand years old? That's another miracle, you know, it beats anyone else's best efforts by about nineteen hundred years!"

"I don't know why it worked, but it did. There've been eerie things about this business, all along."

Josh fixes me with one of his soul-searching gazes, but I stare straight back. You won't find a lie lurking in my heart, I think, not about this. When I refuse to look away, his anger is slowly replaced by an emotion I never thought to see in him. Joshua is afraid. He moves away from me and sits.

"All right, I'm sorry I accused you of lying," he finally says. "But this is nonsense. I don't feel in the least bit like Leonardo Da Vinci or some fourteenth-century conman. I could imagine myself as twin to some sweaty lab technician, but as for that other possibility, well, I'm not even going to consider it. Do you have any other reason for believing what this man Eric told you?"

"Yes. Unfortunately I do."

"What is it?"

I don't reply. Instead I wave him into my study, open the closet, and pick up a plastic bag. Inside is a wig, its long hair tied back into a ponytail; two other pieces of hair, and a tube of actor's makeup glue.

"Sit down near the mirror," I command.

Josh sits, too perplexed to object. I squeeze a little of the glue onto a small brush and anoint his face and upper lip. Then I attach the smaller pieces of hair fairly expertly — I've been practicing on myself. Finally I top it all off with the wig.

"What do you look like?" I ask.

"Like I'm dressed up for Halloween."

"I think you look like this." I pull out my pocket computer and type in a quick command. An image flashes onto the wall screen, the ghostly black-and-white figure of a bearded, pony-tailed man, naked, his hands crossed in front of his genitals.

"Do you see a resemblance?" I ask.

"Yes," Josh says shakily, looking back and forth from the monitor to the mirror. The image on the screen is from a photo negative of the Shroud, and with long hair and beard Joshua looks so much like the man on the wall that I want to run from the room. Josh does nothing so dramatic, but he does raise his own right hand, then stands up to hold it against the screen. Maria always said he'd inherited those long, capable fingers from Joe, but their real provenance seems dreadfully apparent now.

Joshua looks back at me, seeming far more ill than Maria did earlier this afternoon.

"I have to think about this," he says. "I'm going for a walk."

He's gone for hours. When Maria wakes up at nine she's surprised he's not there, but I cook up an excuse about his going off to see an Atlanta friend. It's not a very good story, but it works because Maria wants to believe it. I fix a really bad dinner, which Maria eats without complaint, and then we watch an idiotic old movie. Maria goes back to sleep at about eleven, and I breathe a sigh of relief, but unfortunately she wakes up again at 1:45. I tell her Josh called soon after she went to sleep, but this time she doesn't buy it.

"You're lying!" she says. "You don't know where he is, and it's two in the morning!"

"He can take care of himself," I say, without much conviction. "And it's 1:45."

"This isn't like him; he knows how I worry. The streets aren't safe this time of night."

It's such a feminine response, completely devoid of any real perspective, and I retaliate without thinking.

"You think he's in more danger out there than he is in Calcutta? Or working in Palestinian refugee camps, like he did last year for three months? Or meeting with the Syrian president and asking him to condemn the latest terrorist atrocity, with live news cams running, no less?"

"Thank you. I feel much better!" She stalks over and gets herself a glass of juice out of the refrigerator, then slams its door shut. "You've treated him like he was a rattlesnake ever since he went to India. Your own son . . ."

"He's *not* my son!"

"Josh was five when Joe died! You're the most father he's ever had!"

"He remembers Joe every bit as well as you do! He's my stepson, and he knows it."

"But he treats you like a father! Why can't you treat him like a son?"

"I never expected to have a son with an I.Q. of 250."

"That's ridiculous. Josh was something of a prodigy, I admit, but you make him sound like he's not human."

"I'm immensely proud of him."

"I know you are. But . . ." She grinds to a halt. "You had an argument, didn't you?"

"When do I ever argue with Josh?"

"You're not answering my question."

"And I won't. If Josh wants to tell you about it, he will."

I glance at her and see that she's grown pale.

"Are you all right?" I ask.

"Of course not. I've got leukemia, remember? Help me into the living room."

"Why don't you just go back to bed?" I ask.

"I won't be able to sleep until he gets back."

But she's underestimated her exhaustion; she's asleep on the couch in ten minutes.

Joshua finally returns about twenty minutes after four, easing through the front door as quietly as he can, startled to see me sitting in a chair waiting for him. He glances at a clock and grimaces.

"I had no idea it was so late," he murmurs.

"Your mother was worried about you."

"I'm sorry." He walks over to Maria's sleeping form and kisses her lightly on the cheek. She doesn't wake, but her breathing seems easier, her brows unknit, and she stirs slightly, smiling in her sleep.

"We need to talk," Josh says, and I follow him into the study.

"I really don't want to believe any of this," Joshua says, waving the CD, "but it does explain some things."

"Such as?"

"Your attitude towards me."

"What attitude is that?"

"You've treated me with a certain coldness ever since I went to India. You're not that way with other people."

"I've done my best."

"I know that, and if you believe what you've written, I guess it's been a struggle for you."

Joshua reaches over to my pocket computer, still resting on the table, and brings back the image of the Shroud.

"I've always had the feeling that I was a bit . . . unusual," he says. "It's a strange feeling to grow up with. And at times I have an odd certainty about things. I don't hear voices or see visions, but I just seem to know. I have that feeling about this."

"So you believe my story?"

"I believe that you believe it. So let's say I'm giving it . . . provisional credence."

"I'm glad, because it's true."

"But in two hundred pages you still haven't answered my question; you've just presented me with some possibilities. Now is the time to quit being diplomatic. Once and for all, who do you think I am?"

He's chosen his words carefully, and I'm equally cautious. I start to say something at least three times, and each time the image of the Shroud looms large in the corner of my sight.

"You're Joshua Grant," I finally say. "I don't care whose DNA you have, you've been a good son, and the most worthwhile human being I've ever known. None of this alters that in the least."

"You still haven't answered my question."

"I think you were cloned using DNA from the Shroud of Turin."

"And who do you think provided the DNA? Leonardo Da Vinci? A sweaty lab technician? Or the most disturbing possibility of all?"

"Joshua, I don't have any evidence to make that decision. I thought my story made that clear."

"I didn't ask you to be rational. I asked for an answer from your heart. Who am I?"

I don't want to look at his face, so I stare at the image on the wall instead. But somehow that's even worse. I close my eyes, and when I speak it sounds almost like a prayer.

"I believe there was once a man named Jesus, that he was executed by the Romans, that the Shroud of Turin was his burial cloth, and that you were cloned from his blood."

"And which of your three theological possibilities does that make me?"

"I'm not sure what you're talking about."

"Don't lie to me, Peter; you know precisely what I'm talking about. You listed three possible conclusions about someone in my theoretical position . . . for those who believe in the divinity of the original Jesus."

"I'm not sure I fall into that category."

"I'm not sure you don't, so for the sake of argument let's stick with your options: Jesus's second coming, divinely preordained; Jesus's twin brother, merely human — or the Antichrist. Which of the three do you think I am?"

"The second."

Josh is silent for a moment, then lets out a long, shuddering sigh, perhaps considering the disadvantages of carrying Jesus's DNA without any heavenly fringe benefits.

"In a way it doesn't make any difference," he finally says, answering a question no one visible has asked. He looks at the image on the wall as he speaks, and I notice that his eyes have almost regained their usual expression, a transcendent calm that seems not quite human. I can imagine that look on the face of Jesus, but I can also imagine it on the face of the Old Testament Joshua, calmly supervising the slaughter of Canaanite women and children.

"I hope you won't copy Jesus's most controversial behavior," I say. There's an edge to my voice, a tone I rarely take with Joshua.

"Which was?"

"Claiming to be the Son of God."

Joshua looks back at me rather sharply, then smiles, sadness returning to his eyes.

"You're forgetting an important qualification for would-be Messiahs."

"Which is?"

"You can't really want the job. Remember the Garden of Gethsemane?" He laughs.

"What if one of your disciples deifies you?"

"Why should that happen? Certainly you're not going to try and publish your story." He smiles again. "Excellently written though it is."

"Secrets have a way of getting out. There's already one doctor in India who knows there's something unusual about your relationship to your mother."

"So? He'll just assume I was adopted and my parents never told me. And isn't it against medical ethics to reveal information like that?"

"Of course it is, and if you're lucky whoever did the DNA test will keep his mouth shut. But he may mention it to one of his colleagues, who'll mention it to someone else, on down the line until it gets into one of the tabloids. Or he may sell it to them himself. And you and I aren't the only ones who know about the Shroud."

"Well, Harold Anthony knows, assuming your friend Eric Schroeder wasn't lying. But why should Anthony tie that story to me?"

"Because he's on the lookout for Maria Anthony's child, and he expects that child to be a religious or political figure. You're pretty conspicuous in both areas. That's why I've tried to keep my picture and your mother's out of the press. Unfortunately, I haven't been entirely successful."

"Would he recognize either of you after all these years?"

"If he's even suspicious all he has to do is take a picture and run it through one of those computer aging programs. Then he'll be able to see either one of us as we looked thirty years ago. He could also take a picture of you, digitally add long hair and a beard, and compare it to the Shroud negative. And that may not be your worst problem."

Josh's eyebrows rise wearily. "I could have a worse problem?"

"Unfortunately." I reach over to my pocket computer and change the image on the screen, back to the photo I e-mailed to Truman this morning. In a flash the monitor shows Joshua and the Brethren hierarchy frozen in mid-stride. "Who is this?" I ask, pointing at one of the figures.

"His name's John Baxter. He's only been with the Brethren a year or two, but he's rapidly becoming my right-hand man. I don't think you've ever met."

"Actually we have," I say. Another picture flashes onto the screen, a blow-up of John Baxter with red hair, computer-adjusted to forty-seven years of age.

"Joshua," I tell him, "say hello to Dr. Eric Schroeder."

Chapter 2

I wake early the next morning, but Joshua has been up long before me. Coffee is brewed and poured into a thermos, the kitchen cleaned, other chores done and done well. Josh sleeps on the floor when he comes home, but the sleeping bag and pillow he uses are back in the linen closet. Since he's not in the kitchen, I wonder for a moment if he's gone for a walk, but then I hear the soft click of computer keys in my study. I peer in and Joshua looks up.

"What are you doing?" I ask.

"Sending E-mails. I'm trying to get on some news and talk shows."

The wall monitor is off — Josh prefers the fold-out screen on his pocket computer because it uses less power. I glance over his shoulder and see a form letter and a long list of netcasters and news anchors. The idea, obviously, is to sound them out to see whether they'll air Joshua and the Brethren's unpopular opinions. I'm surprised to see a great many Christian fundamentalists listed, including Harold Anthony.

"You're trying to get on Anthony's show?" I ask, stunned.

"Why not? John thinks we might as well beard the lion in his den, and I agree with him. Even if I can't convince Anthony . . ."

"You can't, believe me."

"Well, I might convince some of his listeners, and our debate should be dramatic enough to get the Brethren more coverage. We don't have enough money to buy netcast time on one of the big channels."

"Hold it. You said this was John's idea? You mean John Baxter? Also known as Eric Schroeder?"

"Yes."

"Doesn't what I told you make you a little uneasy about taking his advice?"

"Not really. Why should it?"

"The fact that he very likely knows about your . . . DNA problem."

"Why do you assume that?"

"You think it's just coincidence he's attached himself to you?"

"Maybe."

"And maybe he's figured out who you are. Maybe the knowledge has driven him completely round the bend. You have every reason to be suspicious of his advice."

"I prefer to assume his intentions are good."

"You always assume people's intentions are good, and it's going to get you killed someday."

"So I should reject a good plan just because he proposed it?"

"Not necessarily, but . . ." I give up. Arguing with Joshua is like trying to nail jello to a tree. "Just be careful, all right?"

"I've tried careful," Josh replies. "Careful doesn't work."

So, while Joshua sits and types in the other room, planning to meet his worst enemies on their home-ground, I sit in the living room, trying to decide just what the hell Eric Schroeder is up to. I've already come to one conclusion: since he isn't dead, Valerie Weselesky was right; he arranged his own disappearance. I wouldn't be surprised if he was also behind the rumors that inspired someone to bomb the Institute.

As to how to find out more about "John Baxter," I'm clueless, but I know someone who probably can. I get out my pocket computer, turn on a wall monitor, and send Truman a quick e-mail. I get an answer within minutes. I click into my mailbox and read:

> Hi Peter
>
> I was sitting here writing and your message popped up. Your starting information is a little thin, but I can probably find something. And as usual, there will be a price!
>
> No, it won't be much, you cheap Brethren lunatic. I'm working on a new book, and my villain is a psychopathic doctor. Since I'm neither a physician nor a psychopath I need your expert advice in both capacities. As to Mr. Baxter's background, I'll get on it right away. In the meantime, could you give me a little information on the following?

"The following" is a list of questions about poisons decidedly outside an obstetrician's daily experience. It would be idiotic to expect an immediate answer about John Baxter, so I hop on the Internet to review my toxicology. I find some web-sites boasting a truly frightening amount of information, enough to make me wonder if the FBI monitors their log-ons.

Interesting stuff for a crime writer, however, and I'm ready for some distraction. I also enjoy speculating on the plot of Truman's book — from the poisons he's listed I suspect it will start with several hundred fictional Europeans barfing their way into oblivion. Maria wakes up before I'm halfway through Truman's questions, and I fix us all some breakfast. Maria doesn't ask Josh where he was last night, but Josh offers a vague excuse anyway, something about forgetting that his biological clock was still on Deshi time. Then he and I make Maria comfortable on the couch in the living room, where she tries to read a book and nods off to sleep.

When I sit back down at my computer several hours later I'm surprised to see that I already have a reply from Truman. I open it up, and sure enough, it's a surprisingly extensive overview of the life of Dr. John Baxter. My first reaction is awe — maybe the feats of Truman's cyber detectives aren't so exaggerated after all — my second is that either Truman or I have goofed big-time. Dr. Baxter has bona-fides extending back well before Eric Schroeder's disappearance.

But when I reread the information I notice some contradictions. Before 1999, Dr. Baxter was hardly one of medicine's brightest stars. Despite his American citizenship, he graduated from a Caribbean degree-mill, then worked in low-prestige positions, HMO grunt work mostly, up until sometime in 1999. Soon thereafter, I'm willing to bet, the first Dr. Baxter met an unfortunate end and Eric arranged to replace him. Why else would Dr. Baxter's career go into warp-drive in the space of three or four years? In 2000, "Baxter" has a new job in a charity clinic (shades of Valerie!) and in 2002 he starts work on a master's degree in paleontology. On paper it sounds implausible, but I can easily imagine Eric reading through ten basic textbooks at lightning speed, convincing a small Midwestern college to indulge his midlife crisis, then amazing everyone with his quick grasp of the biology used to analyze fossil DNA.

In 2005 "Baxter" marries, in 2006 he has a daughter, Judith, now well-known for her own work studying Native-American matrilineal descent via mitochondrial DNA. But in the small world of human bonediggers, her reputation is still eclipsed by her father's — despite Baxter's obvious distaste for publicity. In recent years Baxter has mostly given up his scientific work; instead he's devoted his time to humanitarian organizations, particularly the Brethren. Here too he's been happy to work behind the scenes — the picture I saw of him with Joshua marked one of the few occasions he's ever been photographed.

Which gives me another idea. I'm certain the current John Baxter is really Eric Schroeder, which means there was once another Dr. Baxter, a pre-1999 version who probably had no fear of cameras. A photo of Baxter Number One might well be useful. I zip off another e-mail to Truman. But days go by without an answer.

Joshua, meanwhile, isn't idle. He sends out dozens of e-mails and gets dozens of rejections, some reeking of distrust and hatred. But two Christian Netcasters invite Joshua on their shows: Nicholas Preston, pastor of the second largest Baptist church in Atlanta, and Charlton E. Larcen, host of a Bible-thumping, faith-healing, hellfire-and-damnation extravaganza.

"Excellent!" Josh says. "I like Dr. Preston."

"As I remember, he once called you one of the greatest dangers Christianity has ever faced."

"He said that about one of those 'books' I didn't actually write."

"And Charlton Larcen?"

"Well, I asked to be on his show, so it would be odd to refuse. Maybe we'll reach some new people."

"And listening to the music can be penance for your sins."

Joshua laughs. "Now, Peter. I don't think your namesake stands at the Pearly Gates giving humanities exams." He pauses, as if looking for a way to introduce a touchy subject. "Speaking of gatekeeping, do you or Mom mind if I invite a house guest? I need to get ready for these shows."

"Of course we don't mind."

"We'll stay out of the way; Mom needs her rest. As to who's going to help me, well, I'm not sure you'll be comfortable with that. But there's really no way for me to do without him right now, whatever his history."

"What history is that? Who are you talking about?"

"John Baxter. He's flying in from India tomorrow. If he can't stay here we'll both go to a hotel. But I'd rather not spend the Brethren's money that way; flying is expensive enough."

For a moment I'm speechless, my mind teaming with objections. Then I erupt.

"Josh, I've warned you about this man! Are you nuts?"

"Is it nuts to see someone whose help I need? Besides, I want to get his opinion on our other discussion."

"What other discussion?"

"The one about the Shroud."

I'm flabbergasted. "Why?"

"Well, let's suppose he is who you say he is. And let's also suppose that he doesn't know whose son I am, or of my possible connections with Harold Anthony and the Institute. Is it honest to hide that from him?"

"You're not trumpeting it to the rest of the world."

"The rest of the world has no pressing reason to know. This man, according to you at least, was involved in the whole affair. Besides . . ."

"Besides what?"

"Your story relies on your interpretation of some odd events and a DNA test. The only reason I've given it any credence is my faith in you. Maybe John can give me some proof, or maybe he can show us how the entire thing has been a misunderstanding. In any case, to hide the fact that I've heard the story is to lie to him. I won't do it."

"It's your funeral."

An unusually smart-ass reply for me, especially to Joshua, whom I habitually treat with a certain awe. But the words leap almost unbidden from my tongue.

I spend the next morning and early afternoon pottering around the house, trying to think of what I'll say to Eric, or John, or whatever the hell I'll end up calling him. Joshua got up early after going to bed late, but every time I see him he says how wonderful it was to finally get a good night's rest. He spends the morning meditating, reading the Bible and one of the Hindu *Upanishads* (in the original Hindi, of course), and praying. Then he gets on the computer and takes care of nearly two hundred e-mails (his daily load). At ten he's getting ready to take public transit to the airport to meet John. When I ask him why John can't get here himself, Josh reminds me that "John" is now in his seventies, which startles me: in my mind's eye he's still forty-nine or so, only slightly older than when he disappeared from Tucson. But seventy or not, John won't take a cab or let someone pick him up in a car, even my car, a hybrid that gets sixty miles to a gallon. He's a member of the Brethren; he needs to set an example; he doesn't want to waste gas or spew a single extra ounce of C02 on the peasants in Bangladesh.

Josh figures they'll be back in about four hours, but two in the afternoon comes and goes, as does three, and then four, and still no sign of them. I call the airport and find that "John's" flight was late, but not enough to cause a three-hour delay. I'm starting to get worried when I look out the front window and see Josh walking slowly up the sidewalk, followed by an older man dressed in blue jeans.

"They're here," I call out to Maria, and head for the door.

I open it just as they get to the front steps. It's my first look at Eric Schroeder in thirty-three years, but I have no doubt that it's him, though I'm shocked at how much he's changed. His face is a mass of lines, he's cadaverously thin, and he walks like an old man. Standing in the open doorway, I wonder how he'll react, whether they'll be some amazed moment of recognition (assuming he really doesn't know who Josh's "parents" are), or feigned ignorance.

But "John" surprises me. He breaks into a broad smile, hands his cane to Joshua, and spreads his arms in greeting.

"Peter!" he says, then totters forward to embrace me.

Maria has followed me to the door, and she's a little confused.

"So you're John Baxter," she says politely. "I didn't know you and Peter had met."

"Oh, Peter and I go way back," John says, stepping back and ignoring Maria's puzzled expression. "I've heard a lot about you, too, Mrs. Grant. I've looked forward to meeting you for a long time."

"It's Mrs. Lunsford, actually, but come in. Peter made some coffee."

"And iced tea," I add.

Joshua, Maria, and "John" sit in the living room, conversing pleasantly. Since he's supposed to be dead, I'd expected John to be ill at ease, but I'm the only one in the room who seems uncomfortable — I lean forward in my chair, elbows on my knees, trying not to glower. But though John's conversation is relaxed, he looks almost as sick as Maria. After a while I start wondering which one of them will give out first. But John is either healthier than he looks, or too stubborn to let his body order him around. It's Maria who tires, and John who notices.

"Mrs. Lunsford," he says, "it's very kind of you and Peter to put me up, but I understand you've been ill, and I don't want to wear you out. Joshua, why don't we get to work and let your mother rest?"

"I don't know, John," Josh answers. "I'm ready for a little longer break, myself." I look up in surprise. "Say," he continues, "since you and Peter are such old friends, why don't you go eat dinner someplace and catch up on old times?"

I look over at John, slightly panicked. John, for his part, smiles gently, knowing we've been maneuvered by a master.

"It'll take us an hour to get to any restaurants by the bus," I object.

"Then drive, Peter," Josh says. "Your car gets sixty miles per gallon, remember?"

"John" and I go out to the garage and get in the car, he a lot more slowly than I. For a moment I sympathize with the senior citizens who drive monstrous old Cadillacs: a big car is definitely easier to get in than the fuel-efficient rollerskate Maria insisted we buy. But John doesn't agree, because as soon as we're off he says, "Now this is a sensible automobile, if you've got to have one." We drive several blocks in silence, a contest of wills to see who'll speak first. I lose.

"I can't make up my mind what to call you," I say testily, "John or Eric."

"Why would you call me Eric?" he asks, with a wicked grin.

"Because that was your name before you drowned your car, back in the days when you and I worked for Harold Anthony."

"Whatever are you talking about?" he says, still smiling.

"Imagine my surprise to find out you weren't really dead."

"Well, I will be before too much longer, if that will make you any happier."

"You're not that old."

"No, I'm not, but neither am I in the best of health."

I don't even want to know what's wrong with him. I have the horrible suspicion he'll tell me something truly outlandish just to confirm my continuing gullibility.

"Were you as surprised to see me as I was to see you?" I ask, and suddenly he drops his charade.

"No," he says, "I've known who you are and where you've been for five years now. I was glad to find out you weren't really dead. I was hoping you'd return the favor."

He says it in a matter-of-fact tone, and somehow that affects me more than resentment or sadness. I glance over and realize he's not lying, whatever's wrong with him is serious; like most doctors I've developed an instinct for that. Tears well up in my eyes. I try to fight them back, but it's no use, and in a few moments I can't see well enough to drive. Luckily there's a parking lot handy, so I pull off the road.

"Dammit Eric," I say, "I was happy to find out you weren't dead, but I wasn't happy with you when you disappeared. You left me with a major problem."

"One you've handled brilliantly, I must say, marrying Maria to protect her."

"Very funny. You know how Joe died, don't you?"

"Some sort of construction accident, wasn't it? Listen, I didn't mean it like that. It's just that I can never resist a good joke. Or a bad one, for that matter."

A thought both horrifying and comforting comes to me then, my oldest fear and probably Josh's fondest hope, that the whole tale of shrouds and clones was merely Eric Schroeder's last and grandest whopper.

"But what you told me about Maria's baby," I say softly, "that wasn't a joke, was it?"

Eric, a.k.a. John, looks at me sadly.

"I should have known my reputation would get me into trouble. No, that was no joke, and I thank God you figured that out."

With that fear gone I'm done for; the tears come streaming down my cheeks, and John sits beside me patiently, every now and then patting my shoulder and saying, "Take it easy" or "I'm sorry." I finally get a hold of myself, and John tries to turn this maudlin senior-citizen moment into something a little more dignified.

"Well," he says, "tell me what you've been up to all these years."

"I thought you already knew."

"Actually, I do. What would you like to know about me?"

A glimmer of suspicion returns. "Lots of things," I say, "but one more than anything else. Why have you hooked up with Josh?"

"Well," John says, and for the first time I sense a carefully calculated reply. "I was on the lookout for Joshua, well for Maria's baby anyway, because I felt responsible for him. In a way, I'm as much his father as you or Joe. But I imagine your other questions aren't exactly made for brief conversation, and I'm hungry. Can we go to that restaurant?"

The last time I saw Eric, some thirty years ago, he was the one who got plastered and I was the one who tried to stay sober. At least that's the way I remember it. Tonight I polish off beer after beer and Eric or John or whatever sticks to his endless glasses of iced tea.

We start by trading stories about our supposed fatal accidents — he tells me how he'd scouted Tucson for a dip in the river road, made a deal with the "Bumpers" waitress to bring him club soda when he ordered gin-and-tonics, then timed his bar-room confession to coincide with predicted morning thunderstorms. I tell him about the exploding water heater, not even omitting my struggle to keep Valerie from warning Anthony's thugs.

"Shame it wasn't Anthony on that door!" he says.

"No one got hurt. At least not much."

"So you say. Anyway, I wish I'd seen it."

"So tell me," I ask, "did Valerie Weselesky engineer your disappearance, too?"

"Valerie what? Weechokowsky?"

"Weselesky."

"What kind of name is Weselesky?"

"Polish. I had her looking into your disappearance, but it's occurred to me since she might have been the one who set it up."

"Hell no! I did all that by myself."

"And John Baxter? Was he somebody who died just before 2000?"

"No. I just kind of invented him, it's a long story exactly how. Is that how you did it, found some stiff to take over for?"

"Yes indeed. The first me died putting up a TV antenna for my neighbor. Noble fellow that I was."

"You have my deepest sympathies."

"Thank you."

I tell him about Joe's untimely end and add several amusing tales of Josh's precocious childhood. He tells me about his ex-wife. "A great lady, actually, but she had no patience for all my traipsing around the world, so she divorced me. My daughter, though, that's another matter. She travels with me a lot these days. She likes Joshua, if you want to know the truth."

"What?" That Joshua might be developing a romantic entanglement is startling news.

"Yeah, I think there's a certain attraction there."

The thought of that slows me down for a second.

"Joshua is a fine young man, to say the least," Eric continues. "Although you can't take complete credit for that. I imagine his, uh . . . 'unusual heritage' has a lot to do with it."

With that, we both lapse into silence. The habit of decades is hard to break, but I suddenly realize that "John" is somebody I can talk with frankly about Joshua's "unusual heritage."

"So," I say cautiously, "who do you think Joshua really is?"

"What do you mean?" He looks at me a little oddly.

"When you told me about all this that night, back in Tucson I mean, you said Joshua's genes were probably from modern DNA, but that Anthony thought the DNA came from whoever forged the Shroud, maybe even from Leonardo da Vinci. What do you think now?"

John doesn't answer.

"Have you noticed how much he looks like it?" I ask.

"Like what?" he says gruffly.

"Like the image on the Shroud."

John looks down and toys with his food. If I've learned one thing from Joshua, it's how to use silence to wring the truth out of somebody, so I just sit there and stare. Finally John looks up, frowns, and speaks again.

"You were probably wondering why we were so late, I bet."

"Yes, I was."

"As soon as I got off the plane, Joshua said we needed to talk. We marched into some tacky coffee shop and he told me how his DNA didn't match up with Maria's, watching me like a hawk all the time. He's a hard person to lie to, have you ever noticed that?"

"Indeed I have."

"Well, of course the second that little story was out of his mouth, he asked me if I was surprised. Of course I said I was, but he wasn't fooled for a minute. Then he told me how you were under the definite impression that I was really Eric Schroeder. And I had to admit that much was true."

"All right, then what?"

"Then he asked me if the rest of your story was true: if Anthony Enterprises had really used DNA from the Shroud of Turin to clone an embryo, and so I told him that we had done precisely that, and that he was the result."

"How did he take it?"

"Like somebody who's heard something he didn't want to believe, but knew was true anyway. He went and found one of those little chapels they have at the airport, then sat down and asked me to come back in two hours. I take it you'd already broken the news to him?"

"Yes, but since I had no proof, I guess he wasn't exactly convinced. At least not rationally."

"I can't believe you even got him to even consider the possibility. How'd you do it?"

"I wrote the whole story down and gave it to him to read. Then I got a wig and a beard and had him wear those and look at a negative of the Shroud."

"So Josh's resemblance to that picture isn't my imagination."

"With long hair and a beard, it's not a resemblance; it's an identity. It frightened *me*, and I was expecting it."

John looks down at his plate, toys with his food again.

"You still haven't answered my question," I say.

"What question was that?"

"You know damn well. Exactly whose DNA is Joshua blessed with?"

"Well, whoever's image is on the Shroud, obviously."

"Come on, John-Eric, that doesn't answer my question. Who do you think Joshua is?"

John stirs his food one last time, then looks back up.

"He can learn a new language in three weeks, and then remember it for the next five years. He's mastered four different musical instruments and sings like an angel. His doodles ought to hang in the Metropolitan, and I get the unpleasant feeling that he knows as much genetics as I do, as much physics as Stephen Hawking, and more math than anybody but God himself. All that might make you think of Leonardo, but instead of making a name for himself he spends his time in the slums of Calcutta, or raising funds for AIDS orphans in Uganda, or eating moldy rice with starving Muslim farmers in Bangladesh. In addition he never lies, he never cheats, he doesn't screw around, he almost never loses his temper, and I've never seen him do or say a cruel or unkind thing to anyone. And when I've lied or cheated or been cruel, he can look into my eyes and see straight into my stinking little soul. Who the hell do you think he is?"

I don't answer.

"And you know what's really infuriating?" John sputters on. I shake my head no. "As smart and as good as Joshua is, and despite the fact that he's got some of the best-intentioned men and women in the world working with him, all of that talent and all of that good will aren't accomplishing anything. The U.S. runs the planet right now — with a lot of competition from the Chinese — and what do we do with our wealth and power and technology? We get fatter and fatter while others starve, we live longer and emptier lives, and we buy more and more expensive junk we don't need and don't have time to enjoy. In the process we're drowning the world in our garbage. Everybody hates us, but at the same time they want to be just like us, even if they have to murder, rob and enslave their neighbors to do it. And Joshua thinks he can reform the human race through reason and love."

"I don't know that he thinks that at all. All I know is that he thinks he has to try."

"Well, he's trying as hard as anybody possibly could, and it's not working. He needs something else, some power that works on stupid people, which means most people, or all that will happen is that someday soon some nut will gun him down in the street like a dog."

Now it's my turn to stare glumly down at my plate. "That's what I always liked about you, John," I say. "Your cheerful outlook."

"Have another beer," he replies.

We get back to the house at nine o'clock. Since I'm drunk John has to drive, and he hasn't driven in years. We avoid disaster until we're almost home, when John cuts the final corner too sharply and smashes the right front wheel into the curb. The car makes it into the garage, but there's an ominous clanking that's probably a broken CV joint.

We stumble into the house, and to my surprise, Maria is still awake, waiting for us alone in the living room.

"Where's Joshua?" John asks.

"He's in Peter's study writing," Maria says. "He asked if you could come help him when you got back." John goes into the other room, and Maria looks at me with a mild expression, about one part disapproval and two parts amusement.

"And how many beers did you have?" she asks.

"I don't remember. Too many, anyway."

She shakes her head.

"Boys will be boys," I say.

"Yeah, but you're an old man."

"Middle-aged."

"You're gonna live to be a hundred and forty? Not like that you won't. Come help me get into bed."

Although I'm not all that steady myself, I help her get to her feet, and the two of us totter into the bedroom.

"You've known him a long time, haven't you?" Maria says as soon as I shut the door.

"Sure."

"I mean you knew him back before we left Tucson."

I'm too drunk to lie. "We both worked for Harold Anthony. How'd you know?"

"Women's intuition," she says. I start to get ready for bed myself, but Maria has other ideas.

"No you don't, Buster. You sleep on the couch."

"So I had a little too much to drink! How often do I do that?"

"I'm not kicking you out because you're drunk; I'm kicking you out because you'll need to pee thirty-five times tonight. The couch."

I pick up my pillow and leave.

By four a.m. I've almost fulfilled Maria's prophecy. I feel awful and the need to urinate has woken me continually. Since I've already had my quota of aspirin, I sit up, grab my pocket computer off the coffee table, and turn on the wall monitor. For about ten minutes I watch NetV, but nothing strikes my fancy. I'm getting ready to turn it off when an icon blinks on the corner of the screen. I've got mail from Truman: a 1997 photo of one Dr. John Baxter, later to become the well-known paleontologist, do-gooder, and iced-tea gourmand. It doesn't look anything at all like Eric Schroeder, which means that Eric became John the same way I became Dr. Lunsford: he found a conveniently dead and totally obscure M.D. and took over his identity. But at dinner, Eric had denied doing any such thing, had, in fact, lied to me. I wonder why.

I can't think of any good reason, so I download the picture onto a spare flash-drive, hide it in the bottom of a drawer, and delete the file from the hard drive so that "John" can't stumble across it. Then I nod off into a restless and uneasy sleep.

Chapter 3

Josh and John are up early the next morning, and though they keep to the kitchen their every noise is like a nail pounding through my skull. After a while I sneak into my bedroom, lie down next to Maria, and pull a pillow over my head. At about 10:30 I finally feel human enough to get up. When I walk into the kitchen, Josh and John are sitting at the counter drinking coffee.

"Peter," Josh says, smiling, "how's your . . . headache?"

"I've felt better," I admit.

"We need your expert opinion. You watch a lot of NetV, and we want this to look professional."

"You want what to look professional?"

"Charlton Larcen wants a ten-minute video about Brethren missions in Bangladesh. We don't have much to work with, just some amateur video and news footage. We want to know if you think what we've come up with is appropriate."

When I see their video I can only shake my head. There's no way to make starving children photogenic, or to make pictures of bloated, two-weeks-drowned corpses anything but nauseating. Americans deal with pain this extreme by subconsciously denying its victims' humanity. John and Joshua listen to my criticisms, admit that I'm probably right, and send the video off anyway.

I can understand. A few years ago, I did a short stint in a Brethren mission in the middle of an ongoing famine. Three months was all I could stand. But even though I couldn't take it, I've been there; and I can guess that Joshua and John feel that toning down such a nightmare amounts to telling an unconscionable lie.

Several days pass before we hear from Charlton, but one afternoon he calls and tells Josh he's booked him for Sunday's show, three days away. Charlton offers to send a car to pick up Joshua and his "entourage" (i.e., John and me) early Sunday morning. To my surprise Josh accepts.

"John isn't up to much walking," Josh tells me when John is out of the room. "It was days before he got over that trip from the airport.

And the 'temple' . . ."

"Temple?"

"Larcen calls his church 'The Temple of the Holy Spirit,' and it's out in the suburbs where there's no bus or subway service. Since your car is in the shop there isn't a reasonable alternative."

But the "car" that arrives Sunday morning hardly fits the Brethren idea of "reasonable." It's a stretch limo that could easily seat twelve, but we are the only passengers. Joshua's expression darkens even more after we climb in and the driver tells us to "help ourselves to anything we want."

"This man is a minister?" Joshua says as we pull away.

"You mean the driver?" I answer. I can see where the afternoon is headed and for some perverse reason I'm finding it funny.

"I mean Charlton E. Larcen," Josh hisses. "How can he waste money on things like this?"

"You mean the car itself or what's in it?" I persist.

"Both. I wonder if his viewers know where their donations are going."

"What do you find excessive?" I ask. "This?" I lean to the side and open one leather-covered compartment, discovering a small refrigerator filled with appetizers, cold soft-drinks, a container of caviar, and a bottle of champagne. "This?" I open another compartment and find a well-stocked mini-bar. "This?" I pick up a remote and flick on the large monitor, which instantly begins running a video recording of Mr. Larcen himself. "Or this?" I push another button and the bombastic tones of a large orchestra and rock combo swell from the limo's Bose speakers, followed immediately by the even more tasteless bawling of one of the temple's star vocalists.

"Why do you find this amusing?" Joshua asks me.

"I don't, really. What's funny is that you're shocked by it. You've been in India too long, Joshua; American preachers always fleece their flocks."

"Peter," Joshua says, his eyebrows forming an angry ridge, "if being sophisticated means finding this funny, then I'd prefer to remain naive."

So I shut off the singer, the orchestra, and the Reverend Larcen. The rest of the drive passes in silence.

When we reach the Temple we're met by the Reverend's assistant, an unctuous young man who immediately hands us a detailed itinerary. First we're to attend the Temple's Sunday morning service, an intimate gathering of two to three thousand, watched on the Net by thousands more. The Reverend wants Joshua on the dais to help form "a critical mass of sanctity." After the service is lunch, then a "business meeting and rehearsal," which I assume will be a short discussion of where the microphones and cameras are, where to look, etc. — then the show itself. Joshua's to be decked out in robes for the service, and the assistant backstage makes a huge fuss over them: pulling a fold here, tucking in or pinning another there, until finally he's satisfied with "the way it hangs." Then he reminds Josh in kindergarten tones not to rub or pick his nose, not to yawn, and to "smile, smile, *smile!*" Josh is also drilled on when to applaud, when to "spontaneously" stand, when to sit down, and when to knowingly nod at telling points in the sermon.

The sanctuary is already almost full, but Larcen's assistant takes us to a small waiting area just off the main floor, not to the dais. Joshua takes his place in a line of similarly robed gentlemen. I know what's coming, but Joshua and John don't; they've been too busy to watch a complete example of the Reverend in action. The lights in the sanctuary dim, the forty-piece orchestra strikes up a soft but emotionally charged tremolo, and a voice comes over the speakers.

"Let's welcome this week's Apostles of Our Lord . . . the Temple's Assistant Pastor Dr. Stanley Osgood . . ." (kettledrums crescendo and trumpets play a short fanfare as Dr. Osgood takes his place on the dais) "our Minister of Music, Wilhelm Reger . . ." (the same orchestral effect, but a half-step higher, as Herr Reger takes his place to conduct the choir of eighty) "our missionary-of-the-week, Dr. Joshua Grant . . ." (the music swells again, and Josh is given a firm push from behind by Larcen's assistant) "our Youth Minister . . . Charles Rodgers . . ." (a man in his late twenties, dressed in a robe that's somehow more "casual" than the others; Mr. Rodgers waves to the audience on his way out) "and finally your friend and mine: The Reverend Charlton E. Larcen!"

The people in the sanctuary leap to their feet and applaud, the music finally cadences, the choir rises and bellows "Victory!" (kettledrums and trumpets follow, bashing out the same rhythm) "Victory!" (kettledrums and trumpets again, this time joined by orgasmic glissandos on the harp) "Victory!" (kettledrums, trumpets and harp finally resolve their chord, which dies down into a subdued violin tremolo, an effect which somehow reminds me of a *film noir's* post-coital cigarette.)

In the wings, safely off-camera, I giggle. John gives me a look of complete disgust, then a restrained grin, and then he's laughing too. Larcen's assistant turns toward us with a haughty glare, so John pulls out a handkerchief, fakes a coughing fit, then hauls me off in the direction of the nearest men's room.

"You're incorrigible!" he wheezes as soon as the door closes behind us.

"I just love good music," I tell him, which starts John laughing again. After a minute he finally stops, and looks at me as seriously as he can manage.

"Listen, we've got to quit. This is rude and you know it."

"All right," I say. "I know it's rude. But it sure is fun." John hits me lightly over the head with his rolled-up itinerary.

"You don't think Joshua finds it funny?" I finally ask.

"Maybe, but if he thinks the people in the sanctuary are getting something out of it, he won't let on that he's amused. We better quit or he's going to get mad at us."

I lean back against the sink and catch my breath.

"Josh is boiling today, isn't he?"

"Of course he is. This guy Larcen has crook written all over him. It's going to be a long afternoon."

John and I hang out in the backstage men's room for another fifteen or twenty minutes, then, sobriety restored, we decide to find a NetV monitor and watch the rest of the service. We don't have to look long — there are at least ten monitors spaced out evenly in the lobby, apparently put there so that anyone on the way to the big public restrooms will only miss a little of the Reverend Larcen's inspiring message.

"I'm surprised there aren't screens in the restrooms," John says waggishly, and after that, nothing will do except for us to investigate. Sure enough, there are monitors in the big public lavatories, booming the Rev's words and image out to the excrementally disadvantaged.

We head for the sanctuary wings just before the service ends, hoping to avoid the crowd and hook up again with Joshua. He's played little part in the service, although he was asked to stand when the Reverend praised "those tireless warriors of God who toil overseas, striving to save the heathen masses from eternal damnation." Josh stood, but the close-up quickly pulled back — my stepson's grim face looked like he was contemplating damnation for someone other than the heathen.

We find Josh without much trouble when the congregation files out. Then we head towards lunch: Josh and his entourage of two, the Reverend and his entourage of twenty-five. But before lunch (which, the Reverend loftily informs us, will be served in the Temple's "luxurious" executive dining room) the Rev decides to gives us the grand tour. We start in the lobby, and John and I both have the giggles again — wondering whether the tour will include the NetV monitors in the restrooms. But the Rev heads to the sanctuary itself, and once inside goes on at great length about the sound system, the pipe organ, the baptismal font (built into the back wall, thirty-five feet above the altar), and the gigantic video screens that simulcast the service, so that those in the furthest pews can catch the Rev's every grimace, smirk, frown, and beatific smile.

Joshua takes all this better than he did the limo, perhaps because the people who go to this church or watch the netcasted services obviously know and approve of this use of their money. But when we move further back, into the areas NetV never shows, Joshua's expression begins to change. The Rev doesn't stint himself, nor does he seem ashamed of the fact. We go into an underground garage and see three duplicate versions of the stretch limo we rode in this morning, plus the Rev's private cars, which include a fire-engine red Porsche and a Mercedes convertible. We visit the Rev's "office" — actually a suite of rooms featuring absurdly plush carpeting, a gigantic marble-topped conference table, and walls paneled with tropical hardwood. Then we visit the Rev's "communications center" — more utilitarian than his office, but stuffed with the latest in computers, high-definition monitors, and "tight-beam coherent-radio-wave satellite communications gear" for messages too sensitive for the Internet. And whenever Larcen speaks directly to Joshua there's an odd undertone, an assumption which at first eludes me but gradually becomes painfully clear. The Rev thinks that Joshua will approve of all this, that he too wants to "do well by doing good," as Larcen says at least twice.

The unpleasant surprises continue at lunch. I know Josh told these people he's a vegetarian, but somebody forgot and the meal starts with an enormous steak. Joshua isn't rabid on the subject of eating meat, but however he feels about others eating animals, he personally won't touch anything further up the evolutionary chain than a fish, which now presents him with a dilemma. He doesn't want to eat this hunk of flesh, but on the other hand, he'd rather that the poor cow not have died in vain. So he motions to one of the waiters as subtly as he can.

"Can I get you anything, sir?" the waiter asks.

"Yes, thank you," Josh answers softly. "I don't like steak. Why don't you give this to someone else or take it home for yourself?"

"Certainly sir," the waiter says. "Can I get you something else instead?"

"Another potato would be good," Josh says.

It's all done with a minimum of fuss, but it's hard to ignore, particularly when John does the same thing, and cowed a little myself, I follow his example. Reverend Larcen notices, and is offended.

"What's wrong, son?" he asks Joshua from across the table, "don't you like good American meat? You one of those weirdos thinks we should all eat tofu?"

Joshua looks up and gives the Reverend a weak smile.

"Dr. Larcen," he says, "I've gotten out of the habit of eating beef. The Hindus I work with frown on it."

"You think there's something wrong with this?"

"No, no, go on, enjoy your steak. I just don't care for it myself."

"I'm surprised you worry about what those idiot Hindus and Islams think. You're over there to convert them to your religion, not the other way around."

Josh looks down at his potato, but the word "idiot" hangs in the air.

"The Brethren are an ecumenical group, Reverend Larcen," he says after a moment of uneasy silence. "There's a preponderance of Christians and Hindus, but we have members from dozens of other religions. We may have friendly theological debates, but no one is out to convert anyone. At least not in the sense you're speaking of."

"Then what *are* you out to do? Besides stuffing food in people's mouths, that is."

"We're out to change the way people behave. We start with an ethical code based on principles we feel are common to all religions, all religions, that is, that assume that the Supreme Being is good. There aren't any Satan worshipers in the Brethren."

"Those Hindus and Buddhists and Muslims are worshipin' Satan, whether they know it or not."

"Personally, I believe God accepts all good intentions and prayers."

I half expect Larcen to start foaming at the mouth in reaction to this, but to my surprise he just slowly chews a piece of his steak, and then asks Joshua a fairly insightful question.

"A code of ethics based on all religions, eh? Do the Brethren women walk around in chadors? And do the men get to have four wives, like the Muslims?"

"Well, none of our Muslim members forced anyone to marry them, and I think the current Brethren polygamy record is two wives. But when it comes to basics most religions are remarkably similar. Their ethical weak point is usually that those outside the faith are seen as outside the protection of the religion's rules. So we teach that no one is a heathen or an infidel; that all men and women are our brothers and sisters, and born our spiritual equals."

"And that's where the Brethren name comes from, eh?" the Reverend asks. "Is not eating meat one of your rules?"

"No, it's not a rule. I don't eat meat because it bothers my Buddhist and Hindu friends. But it would hardly be kind of me to criticize your diet when I'm your guest."

As if in answer, the Reverend picks up another large bite of steak and inserts it slowly into his mouth. There's something mesmerizing about the way he chews, so for a few moments no one says anything, and then the Reverend speaks.

"It's a brilliant schtick, Brother Joshua, but I don't think it's ever gonna' make you much money." Joshua stares at him, seemingly baffled, although I suspect this slow comprehension is itself a virtuous act — perhaps Josh doesn't want to believe this conversation is about to go where I think it will. Or perhaps Josh is just giving the Reverend enough rope to hang himself with.

"What I mean is," the Reverend starts again, "you're appealing to the wrong instincts. You know what half the attraction of religion is? It's not just that people think they're goin' to heaven; it's that they think their neighbors ain't. It's like a country club: the more exclusive the place is the more people will pay to belong. You know, I've looked over the Brethren's books on the Internet, assuming, that is, that you're releasing the real figures."

"We are," Joshua says, and when I see the look in his eyes I almost expect lightning bolts to dart down from the heavens. "A charity that's ashamed to show where its money goes isn't worth giving to."

"Well, if those figures give a real picture of how much you're pulling in, considerin' the political connections you must have, then you ain't doing squat. And I say that's because your whole philosophy misses out on the two most powerful motivators there are."

"You've already told us about one, Reverend," Joshua says, "vanity. You said that was half the appeal of religion. What's the other half?"

"Fear, Brother Joshua, fear. As far as I can tell, your version of religion doesn't have any hell at all."

"I'm not a preacher, Mr. Larcen. But you're right; my personal version of religion doesn't have a hell. Not in the sense that you envision it, anyway."

"Well, in what sense do you envision it, Mr. Grant?"

"To be at peace with God requires choosing good over evil, and a willingness to do penance. Some souls may be too hardened to ever undertake either. To spend eternity in such a state might be described as hell. Or to put it another way, while I can't believe God will ever reject anyone eternally, I can believe some souls might eternally reject God."

"Well that's all very pretty, but it's too intellectual and more than a bit too Catholic for most folks — it sounds more like Limbo or Purgatory than Hell to me. And that's why I think you're not pulling in more money — you're taking the two most powerful motivators and waterin' 'em down when you ought to be heatin' 'em up. Now me: I tell people that God chose them, and guess what happens? They choose God! I put the fear of hell into 'em, and guess what happens? They send enough money to build me a little heaven right here on earth!"

"I see that."

"But I see some real potential in the Brethren, and I have a proposal for you."

"Which would be?"

"Start shifting some of your theological positions, and let me be your consultant for a year. Oh yeah, and quit putting your real bookkeeping on the Internet where every Tom, Dick and Abdul can see it. We'll combine the best features of both operations: my ability to bring in the contributions and your international connections, and we'll make a killin' for Christ. All I want is thirty percent of the increase in the contributions you receive. How about it?"

"I'll have to think about that for a while," Joshua says, "before I can give you my complete reaction."

"Well, you do that. Now we need to finish eatin', and then we'll tape the show."

* * *

Josh is remarkably amiable through the rest of lunch and after we move into the Temple's small NetV studio. He's particularly friendly with the technicians, a group apparently hired for their NetV skills rather than any personal devotion to the Reverend. The Rev, on the other hand, is surprisingly rude to these mere employees; he snarls at the smallest delay, makes unfunny jokes about their salaries, says they're all "gay boys" who'll get their rear ends reamed by something decidedly unpleasant in the world to come.

"So we'll record this show at precisely the time last week's show is Netcast?" Josh asks the head techy, a scruffy fellow who reminds me of Frank Zappa, although his name tag reveals the far duller moniker of Matt Wilson.

"Yes, sir."

"Is there any particular advantage to that?"

"Not really."

"Interesting coincidence, then."

Mr. Wilson looks around to see if anybody's paying attention. Apparently he's read about the Brethren; he's already expressed admiration for Josh's work and seems equally impressed with Joshua in the flesh. When he sees that the Reverend is occupied, he leans closer to Joshua and says softly:

"Actually, there's one advantage. For some reason the Reverend likes to claim this show runs live."

"What does the time we record have to do with that?"

"Well, I've been there when people ask him if we netcast live. And the Rev doesn't exactly lie, all he says is 'We tape the show for our archives, but let me assure you, the show goes out over the Net at the exact same time those recorders are running.' "

"Praise the Lord," says another techy.

"But this studio can do a live Netcast?" Joshua says.

"Oh sure. We'd just have to flip a few switches."

"How many cameras do you use?"

"Usually just two. Talk shows don't need fancy camera work."

"Is either camera handheld?"

"No, but I can get an extra cameraman to do some hand-held shots if you'd like. Does the Reverend want that today?"

"No, but I think it might be useful. Could you have that extra cameraman standing by when we start?"

"Sure thing," Matt Wilson says.

* * *

About fifteen minutes later the technicians tell us they're ready. The Reverend takes his place on one side of the little stage, and after some cheesy intro music he gives a little spiel about how money sent to Larcen Ministries is donated to outreach programs around the world. Then he walks to the other side of the stage, where, sure enough, a large globe resides. As he spins it a computer-generated globe also spins on the video screen behind him. The Reverend smiles and begins to speak.

"Today we're going to look at one of the most important programs we fund: The Brethren of Charity, and the work they do in Bangladesh and India. We have with us today the Brethren's founder, Dr. Joshua Grant, and we'll be hearin' from him the good news about this important facet of our Christian ministries. Let's go now to New Delhi, India, and see some of the work of our Lord!"

The music swells, the Reverend smiles, and the computer-generated world behind him slows its rotation, stops with India centered, and then rushes toward us until India fills the screen. A little arrow materializes and centers on a dot representing New Delhi.

"Cut," somebody says, and the Reverend drops his smile and walks away from the globe. "Okay you little froo-froos!" he yells, "What's next? Where's Mr. Grant?"

"Over here, Reverend," Joshua says. He's been sitting in a chair next to Matt the technician, talking about something. John and I are sitting nearby.

"The Brethren video runs next, Reverend," Matt says.

"Do we need to see the whole thing today?" the Rev asks.

"We don't have to, sir," says Matt, "but it wouldn't hurt. I'd like to make sure we made the changes you wanted."

"You better have gotten it the way I want it, as much as I pay you. After the video you cut straight to Brother Joshua and me, right?"

"Yes, Reverend. Mr. Grant, you need to sit up there in the chair on the left." Joshua stands and walks onto the stage; he and the Reverend sit and stare up at the screen, and John and Joshua's video begins to play.

"Why did you have to change anything?" John asks.

"The Reverend thought it needed a little more work," the technician says.

The remastered video is indeed a piece of work. They've kept John and Josh's opening: a thirty-second view of New Delhi's modern business district backed with music on sitar and tabla. But the next scene — originally meant as a stark contrast to the opening — has been changed utterly. Joshua's narration is gone, replaced by the Reverend's sententious tones, views of the children of some of the Brethren themselves, and the sounds of an immense choir warbling "Amazing Grace." Josh and John had included these well-fed, happy children to dramatize the personal sacrifices Brethren members make — most of the clips weren't even shot in India. What the Rev has done is to take the more foreign-looking of these kids and substitute them for starving Deshis and Indians. The narration goes on and on about how the Brethren have taken these poor waifs, fed them, clothed them, and snatched their souls away from the evil and pagan cults of "the dark subcontinent." All, of course, with the generous financial help of Temple of the Holy Spirit Ministries.

"We've never seen a penny of their money," John mutters to me.

It's all painfully tasteless, and completely false to the work and message of Joshua and the Brethren. But it's over in less than five minutes, and near the end the technicians fade into a reaction shot of Joshua and the Reverend seated on the stage, both smiling benignly up at the screen.

That's right, Joshua is smiling, a big grin that lights up his face.

"Brother Joshua," the Reverend says, "it warms my heart to see the good works you're doing in the land of the Godless."

"I'm glad to hear that, Reverend," Joshua replies. "Unfortunately, it chills *my* heart to sit next to a thief and a liar like you."

This is so unexpected that the Reverend sits there, still smiling, for at least five seconds. Then the smile fades, and the Reverend yells angrily towards the control booth:

"Cut, you idiots!" He turns towards Joshua. "I take it you've decided not to accept my business proposal?"

"You mean your offer to skim off thirty-percent of the increased income you bring to the Brethren, on the sole condition that I sell out every scruple I've ever had? 'We'll make a killing for Christ,' was how you put it, I believe."

"Listen, if you didn't like my offer, or if you don't want to do the show, why didn't you just say so!"

"No, no! I'm enjoying my appearance on your program immensely."

"Like hell you are. You're crazy if you think I'm gonna' let two seconds of this out on the Net."

Joshua glances down at his watch. "Actually, Reverend, we're about seven minutes into your show right now. Today I convinced the technicians to do the program live."

The Rev is a little slow on the uptake, but then he looks into the booth and sees Matt Wilson smiling just as broadly as Joshua. "Cut!" he yells again, but the two cameramen on stage keep their lenses on him, and then there's the man with the handheld videocam, safely tucked away in the locked control room. The Reverend runs over to one of the stage cameras and tries to wrestle the techy out of the seat. When this proves impossible he starts yanking cords. A few lights go out.

"While Reverend Larcen makes his feelings known," Joshua says, "I'd like to say to our viewers that the children you've just seen were the thin but healthy children of Brethren members. The truth in India and Bangladesh is more grim, and none of the money you've given to the honorable Reverend has ever reached us. Today I'd like you to see where your money has really gone."

The Reverend gives up on the cords and rushes at Joshua. He's a big man, but most of it's fat, and every ounce on Joshua's skinny frame is muscle or bone. Joshua dodges his charge, and the Reverend trips and falls neatly into a corner of the sound stage.

"Why don't we begin the tour while the Reverend calls security?" Joshua calls out. As Larsen runs from the room, Matt unlocks the control booth, then hands Joshua a big ring of keys, and John, myself, and the man with the hand-cam follow him out the door. The two dolly-cam operators look at each other, shrug, and then tag along as well.

The Reverend had shown us around the Temple earlier that morning, but Joshua also seems to have some other, more accurate source of information. Without hesitation he leads us into room after room that I'm sure the Reverend considers utterly secret.

"First, let's drop in on the Reverend's private screening facilities," Joshua says to the camera, and unlocks a door that looks like the entrance to a broom closet. It opens instead into a short hallway, which ends in another door, which Joshua also unlocks without even fumbling with the big ring of keys. We follow him into a plushly carpeted room dominated by a circular velvet-covered water-bed (with overhead mirror) and a huge video screen. Joshua walks over to a shelf, slides back a door, and motions for the cameraman to focus on the screen of the laptop computer inside.

"Perhaps this is some of the Reverend's research into the evils of pornography," Joshua graciously theorizes as he wakes the sleeping machine, double clicks an icon, then uncovers a list of videos the Rev has downloaded. The titles have nothing to do with religion. "Let's see how he fortifies himself for battling these buxom minions of Satan." He opens another cabinet and reveals a small refrigerator, stocked with caviar and champagne. Joshua picks up a bottle and looks at the label. "Vintage Dom Perignon!" he exclaims, "currently selling for around six-hundred-and-fifty dollars a bottle! And beluga caviar, selling for about five-thousand dollars a jar! But let's be charitable — perhaps the Reverend miraculously transformed sardines and apple juice!" He motions for the cameraman to leave, and the man turns and heads back out to the hall. Joshua turns to follow, no longer smiling, and just before he closes the door he takes the bottle in his hand and hurls it into the video screen.

He leads us next to a large room, its walls lined with cardboard boxes and most of its floorspace taken up by tables.

"Here we have the storeroom for the Reverend's 'Miraculous Water from Lourdes,' " Joshua says. "You know Reverend Larcen doesn't feel the Virgin Mary's blessing is enough for this water, so he also prays over each bottle individually, and then puts the label on with his own hands. We know that's true because the labels are crooked, wrinkled, and smudged, certainly not something machinery would do. Since the Reverend can only pray over a hundred bottles a week, the Temple supposedly holds a kind of bottle lottery, and a lucky few are mailed this wonderful liquid, contingent, of course, upon a one-hundred-fifty dollar love-offering to Larcen Ministries. I wonder why the Reverend needs so many chairs and tables if he does all this hand work by himself? And I wonder why he needs to store so many thousands of bottles if he only mails a hundred a week?" Joshua walks over to a stack of boxes, lifts one down and puts it on a table. "And I also wonder why this box . . ." he opens it and pulls out a tiny, unlabeled bottle, "is marked Mountain Springs Water Company, Helena, Montana?" He turns the box so the camera can see the company name, then sweeps it off the table, upends it, and dumps about fifty tiny bottles out onto the floor. Then he stalks out of the room, cameraman in tow.

Next we tour Larsen's garage, where Josh walks down the line of Jaguars, Porsches, and Mercedes, keys in hand, scraping a jagged scratch down each one's buffed and immaculate finish. Then it's off to Larcen's private office, its walls lined with paintings and prints in impressive gilt frames. "Is this real?" Joshua asks, pointing to a painting a little brass wallplate says is by John Twachtmann, a 19th-century American impressionist who's been much in vogue. "Of course not," his secretary spits out, "it's a reproduction." Joshua nudges the frame and an alarm whoops, leading Joshua to speculate as to why Larcen guards his Wal-Mart prints so zealously. I hold my breath, remembering what happened to the video-screen and autos. But Joshua spares the painting.

Ten minutes later, the security guards finally corner us, and though they're a sad-looking quartet, so old and fat that I think they'd have a hard time arresting even John, Joshua submits peacefully. He sits down in the lobby and in less than a minute has drawn two of them into a conversation about their families. The policemen who show up five minutes later are less friendly. They refuse to arrest the cameramen, (since they work in the place, or did until today) but they do arrest John, Joshua and me for trespassing, destruction of property, and disturbing the peace.

Chapter 4

"My friends, you may think that the United States is immune from the calamities that afflict the rest of the world, but I'm sorry to tell you that God's dark angels will not pass this land by much longer. The pornographers, adulterers, homosexuals, and socialists will soon gain complete control, and after that God will rain down his judgment upon our land, as well as the rest of this tired old Earth! And all sorts of horrors are waiting out there beyond our borders. Did you know that in Africa there are new forms of AIDS that can be carried by mosquitoes? Did you know that New York City — that pimply Babylon on the face of the once God-fearing U.S. of A — did you know that in fifty years New York City may well be drowned under the rising sea? Did you know that cancer rates worldwide have gone up eight-hundred percent in the last thirty years? And that diseases like tuberculosis and meningitis are making a comeback, and none of our wonder drugs can stop them?

"My friends, these are what the college professors call rhetorical questions, which is just a fancy way of sayin' that I know that you know these things — you watch the news just like I do. But I know something else. I know that if you've been saved by the Lord Jesus Christ, you don't have to worry. The *Book of Revelation* tells of dreadful things to come, but it also says that the Chosen of Christ will not suffer through any of them! Soon we will all be in Heaven, snatched up in an instant, safe from the bloody hooves and dire weapons of the Four Horsemen!"

— The Reverend Charlton E. Larcen
from a sermon, May 2031

According to a recent INN poll, sixty-seven percent of American adults describe themselves as fundamentalist Christians, and fifty-five percent believe in the rapture of believers and an imminent Apocalypse.

— INN report
January, 2030

It's possibly the strangest coalition in living memory: ultra-orthodox Israeli Jews and American Evangelicals. What could possibly bring two such disparate groups together? Nothing less than the most contentious issue in Israel today: the planned rebuilding of the Temple in Jerusalem. Ultra-orthodox Jews want to worship and sacrifice there, and the Christians see a rebuilt Temple as a prophecy fulfilled: one of the last events that must happen in this world before they're transported to Paradise in the next.

According to public opinion polls, most Jewish Israelis are against rebuilding the Temple. But the more liberal Israeli factions, crippled by a series of internecine feuds, currently lack power in the Knesset, while the conservative parties are cooperating on this issue with near unanimity.

Meanwhile, Israel's large Islamic minority sees the coalition as their worst nightmare come true.

— *All Things Considered*
NPR, November 2032

Five hours later, we are free.

"What is my congregation going to say?" our liberator exclaims. "I had to give the bondsman half my monthly salary! I can't believe I'm doing this!"

I can't believe it either. It would have been no surprise to be sprung by Maria, or to spend the night in jail. But instead of sitting in a cell, hoping for honor or pity among thieves, I'm slouched comfortably in the back seat of Nicholas Preston's big Mercedes. Nicholas Preston! The pastor of Atlanta's second largest Southern Baptist Church! The earthquake that freed Peter and Paul was a miracle puny in comparison.

"Well, you certainly have our heartfelt gratitude," Joshua says, "if that's worth anything."

Preston shakes his head, then mumbles one more time, "I can't believe it."

"I can't believe you got us out so fast," Joshua says. Preston scowls at Joshua, but then his expression softens.

"I called a judge who hates Charlton Larcen. He bumped you forward onto the day's last bail hearing. But Joshua! What on earth were you trying to do?"

Joshua shakes his head and laughs.

"I don't know, Nicholas," he says, "something just came over me. You saw the Netcast, didn't you? I had a horrible feeling it wasn't going out and that we'd been arrested for nothing."

"Of course I saw it. Larcen's show runs live."

"Well, it did today at least."

"Anyway, when you started breaking things I got on the phone, because I knew right then where you'd end up." He looks over at Joshua again, trying to seem stern, but in a second he's laughing too. "Not that the old fraud didn't deserve it."

"See? Maybe I accomplished something."

"I doubt it. Most of Larcen's viewers don't see anything wrong with a minister being rich. I liked the business with the videos and the Lourdes water, but he'll weasel out of that, too."

"Well, somebody needs to get mad. Particularly when he lies about sending donations on to real relief groups. Why haven't the ministers in this town done something about him?"

"Because exposing one preacher as a fraud makes us all look like frauds. You know, you're a good man, but your faith is weak. I know that God will take care of Charlton someday, but you had to try and do it yourself. Sometimes I fear for your soul."

Joshua isn't frightened. He laughs and lays his hand on Preston's shoulder.

"Nicholas," he says, "you're a good man, and I'm not afraid for your soul. I'll scare up some money tomorrow so I can pay you back." Nicholas looks troubled at this, perhaps thinking of how many Deshi children that money could feed. "And as for faith," Josh continues, "it's yours that's weak."

"My faith is like a rock!"

"No it's not, Nicholas. Your faith is like a house of cards — you're afraid the least breath of reason will blow it down."

Nicholas gives a soft "humpphh!" but doesn't answer.

When we walk in the door Maria jumps up off the sofa and throws her arms around Joshua.

"Mother," Joshua says, "I'm all right!"

"I know what the jails here are like," she says, "I was so worried!"

"Come on, Mother! You're worried about me spending a few hours in an *American* jail?"

Somehow this doesn't have the expected effect, and Maria hangs in Joshua's arms, crying some more. I stand on the doorstep, wondering why there are no tears for me, while Josh gently urges his mother into the living room, sits her down on the couch, and looks at her sternly.

"It won't do you any good to get so upset," he says. "We're all fine, though I think John's malaria has come back. Where're your tablets, John?"

"In my backpack. I can't believe I forgot to bring them today."

"Come lie down and I'll get them for you. And Mother, wouldn't you like a cup of tea?"

Maria nods meekly, and Josh helps John to the back room, then heads into the kitchen.

"You weren't worried about *me*?" I ask Maria.

"No. Not really."

"Why not?" I persist. She sees my pained look and leans forward to give me a hug.

"I don't know why, but you come out of everything all right," she says. "I never worry about you. I'm sorry, but it's the truth."

The next morning, Joshua eats breakfast with a sour look, perhaps wondering whether tearing up Larcen's church was really a good idea. And the first news isn't good — Nicholas Preston phones to say his show no longer wants Joshua, although when Josh asks him where to E repayment of the bondsman's fee, Preston does a surprising thing: he tells Josh to consider the money a gift to the Brethren.

"Half your monthly salary?" Josh asks. "Are you sure you can afford that, Nicholas?"

"I was exaggerating; it wasn't quite half. And I can afford it."

"Well, we thank you," Josh says.

Better news comes later in the afternoon — Charlton Larcen will not press charges. Apparently several hundred viewers punched "save" after the Reverend's first damaging admissions, and the media already have copies. A trial would get Joshua's Temple exposé on every news program in the country. A few programs have netcast it already, and calls start coming in just after lunch.

"Joshua," John says after the fourth one, "you ought to be smiling! You've gotten the Brethren a million dollars of free publicity!"

"But is it the sort of publicity we want?" Josh asks. "People may just assume I'm a lunatic. How many rejections have come in today from the Christian networks?"

"Lots," John admits. "But we still haven't heard from the biggest."

"No word from Anthony?"

"None."

"Why don't we keep it that way?" I interrupt angrily.

"Peter," John says, "I know you're worried, but there's no way we can ignore Harold Anthony. He's a big deal with the more radical conservatives. If we can get on his show we have to do it."

"Anthony's viewers are nuts! How do you hope to influence them?"

"We're not hoping to influence them. We're trying to split the conservatives by making the liberal conservatives . . ."

"Liberal conservatives?"

". . . all right, the moderate conservatives. We're hoping to get the moderates to reject Anthony's bullshit."

I don't buy John's plan, in fact, I'm not convinced that he's told me his plan. He was once a consummate liar. He seems in a cold sweat again this morning, and somehow I doubt it's from malaria.

"Josh," I ask hopefully, "do you really think this will work?"

And Josh treats me again to that faraway look.

"No," he admits, "at least not the way John describes it. But I do know one thing. I have to go on Harold Anthony's program."

This plan might well have been hatched by lemmings. Shaking my head, I leave Josh and John at the kitchen table and go off to watch NetV.

Flashes from planet Earth, via the wonderful worldwide web:

The U.N. fossil-fuels tariff comes up for another vote this week, and an odd rumor is making the rounds. Rather than voting against the measure, supposedly this time the U.S. will abstain. Without a U.S. Security Council veto, the proposal will then pass. The rumor gives no explanation as to why President Patterson's administration would make such an about-face, and most sources consider it utter moonshine.

The Euro-U.S. alliance is only putting up a token defense against Bangladesh's suit in the World Court. Everyone knows the Deshis will win — the scientific facts are clear and the World Court has become increasingly unfriendly to the U.S. More interesting is the question of who will pay — guesses are that the United States won't fork over a red cent, the Europeans, Chinese, and Indians will negotiate some token payment, and the Japanese (who aren't named in the suit) will nobly give away more cash than anyone in order to buy influence on the subcontinent. Informed opinion concludes that the Deshis won't get enough money to do anything meaningful, and that baksheesh will eat up what they do get.

Not that the American public gives a damn. The really big news (apart from gossip about manufactured celebrities) concerns efforts to rebuild the temple in Israel.

I ignore this last story for almost an hour, my mind on Bangladesh instead of the Middle East. But as I roll from one program to another, a name brings me up short. Not sure I've heard correctly, I back up too far, and then overshoot my mark again. But about a minute later I find it. The segment on the temple is over, so I get off NetV's pre-selections onto the genuine Net; hit the URL listing, and download the entire program. Then I do a quick word search and zoom to the correct segment. It lasts about five minutes, not much reward for all the trouble of tracking it down. But in my inefficient way I've learned something that's probably news even to Joshua. Harold Anthony is going to Jerusalem.

"Which explains why he hasn't answered our e-mail," John says, "he's probably been too busy. You say he's moving his show to Israel too?"

"Uh-huh. They're going to do Holy Land specials and try to whip up sentiment in the U.S. for rebuilding the Temple."

"I thought the Israeli government had vetoed rebuilding the Temple."

"The present Israeli government," John reminds me in a patronizing tone, "is a coalition made up of nearly twenty feuding factions. Some policies last less than five or six weeks."

"Don't they know this will bring the Palestinians up in arms?"

"Of course they do. But the faction pushing the temple doesn't care. They want to make Israel a complete theocracy, and friction with the Islamic community makes that more likely, not less."

"Well," I say hopefully, "I guess this means you won't be trying to get on Anthony's show."

"Why not?" Joshua says. "According to you I should feel right at home in the Holy Land."

Chapter 5

Maria has a doctor's appointment early the next morning, and getting there turns out to be quite a production. Joshua comes along, of course, but John comes too — his malaria is acting up and he needs to see a doctor himself. Since neither Maria nor John is up to the subway, we take our little gas-electric car, just back from the mechanic. At the hospital Maria relays good news — she's dying only slightly faster than the rest of us. John must have gotten a shot or some new medication — by the time we're ready to leave he seems positively perky.

"We need some groceries," Maria says as we start back.

"Where are we gonna' put 'em?" I ask.

"In the trunk, of course."

"I hope you're not buying much." The trunk on our car is only slightly larger than the glove-compartments on the SUV's and maxivans roaring by on the freeway.

"We've got to eat," Maria persists.

So despite the prospect of packing groceries around Josh and John in the back seat, Maria prevails, and we stop by a store on the way home.

It's not one of the boutique groceries that cater to those who still cook as a hobby, this place is for those too poor to have their regular meals sent in. We're about fifth in line, and as we wait I look at the tabloids near the register, expecting the usual baloney about lustful aliens, Satan popping out of volcanoes, and angels sighted in outer space. But one of this week's headlines is all too credible, at least to me. I yank the magazine out of its slot.

Christ Walks The Earth Today!
Scientists Say Jesus Was Cloned In The Year 2000!

By now our groceries are going down the belt, and I toss the tabloid face down on the black rubber. Maria sees the whole thing.

"Widening your reading horizons?" she asks.

The second we get home, I grab the tabloid and go to my study.

The paper's lurid prose tells a tale suspiciously similar to Joshua's conception, complete with DNA from the Shroud of Turin, an accident that kills most of the scientists behind the cloning, and a new Mary blissfully unaware of the cosmic nature of her child, until, that is, the pint-size deity starts popping out miracles. The article is short, so I'm able to finish it before Josh and Maria have done with the groceries, but when I look up from its pages I see John standing over me.

"What's going on?" he asks.

For some reason I feel reluctant to show him, but it's nothing I can pin down, so I close the magazine and hand it over. He looks at the cover and grunts.

"Page twenty-two," I tell him, and he leafs to the story.

"Are you really worried about this?" he asks, scanning.

"Aren't you?"

"No. It's the *National Investigator*, for crying out loud. They do cloning stories all the time."

"But it's so accurate! It's like they've been talking to somebody who knows!"

"Oh come on!"

"You think it's just coincidence? They have the right year, the right source for the DNA, they even know that the scientists involved are dead."

"Look, if they're going to imagine Jesus back on earth, cloning would be the way to do it, and there's really only one reasonable source for the DNA. And they don't even have the right year — Joshua was cloned in '99, he was born in 2000."

"Big difference!"

"And the scientists have to be dead for the story to work — you ought to know that; you write stories yourself. A secret like that's too big for ten or twelve people to keep, so they have to bump most of them off. It's just art imitating life — the writers are creating a plausible scenario."

"Since when did the *National Investigator* worry about plausible scenarios?"

"I don't know, maybe they've gotten some better writers lately."

"I wonder if Joshua will agree with you."

"Don't bother him. He's got enough to worry about."

But I'm not convinced. I walk out into the hall and call towards the kitchen.

"Josh! Can you come here?"

I turn and see John scowling, but I don't care. When Joshua comes back I shut the door behind him and point to the magazine.

"You need to read that," I say.

Joshua picks it up. He smiles at the headline, but when he gets to the story his brow furrows.

"What do you think?" I ask.

"It does strike close to home," he says softly.

"But consider the source!" John says. "This sort of thing is their stock-in-trade!"

"But still . . ."

"It's nonsense," John says. "We can't let it change our plans."

"Oh, that's not an issue," Joshua says firmly. "I'm going on Anthony's show even if he knows. About me, that is."

Exasperated, I stalk out of the study and flop down into a living-room chair, just as Maria comes in from putting away the last of the groceries.

"Fat lot of help you are," she tells me.

On Tuesday the U.N. carbon-tariff comes up for a vote, so John mournfully dials up the obscure web-site that netcasts U.N. proceedings. The site has no commentary, no explanations, nothing but the events themselves. But John stays glued to the monitor, and when the resolution comes up for its annual U.S. rejection he calls me into the living room.

"Why do you bother?" I ask him.

"As a gesture of respect. You should watch, too."

I snort and go into the kitchen for a cup of coffee. I just happen to walk into the living room again as the roll-call gets to the U.S.

"The United States of America?" the chair asks.

"The United States abstains," our ambassador answers, so calmly that his words nearly bypass my brain. The vote has the same delayed effect in the U.N. chamber — it's fully five seconds before the astonished buzz begins. The chair is as nonplused as anyone; he bangs his gavel and looks towards the U.S. desk.

"Excuse me, Mr. Ambassador," he says. "For the record. On U.N. resolution 749, concerning a proposed tariff on carbon-based fuels — the United States of America abstains?"

"The United States abstains," the ambassador repeats.

The buzz in the chamber increases in volume, and the chair bangs his gavel vigorously to get the voting started again. John looks back at me, stunned.

"Go to a news channel!" I say. "Quick!" John switches onto INN, but apparently we're ahead of the curve — the newscaster is running through a list of bland domestic events.

"Don't tell me they're gonna' wait for the ten o'clock summary," I say.

"Of course not. This guy doesn't know what's happened yet. Just wait, they'll break in for it in a minute or two. Get Joshua in here."

I call back to him, and he comes from my study, where he's been working through his daily load of e-mails.

"What's up?" he asks.

"The U.S. abstained," John barks.

"Abstained from what?"

"Abstained from voting on the U.N. carbon tariff."

"You're kidding!"

"No, I'm not. The U.S. abstained, nobody else on the Security Council voted against it, and they've lost their chance now."

Joshua is interested but calm. Maria walks in from the bedroom, but there's no need to fill her in, apparently she's been following the entire conversation through the half-open door.

"What does it mean?" she asks.

"Probably nothing," Joshua says. "The U.N. doesn't have a mechanism to collect tariffs, the Senate will insist this is a treaty they haven't voted on, and the oil companies will refuse to pay. The Arabs could collect the tariff themselves, but that's more unlikely than this vote was."

"The Arabs voted for the resolution," I point out.

"Only because they expected it not to pass," John says.

"If it's useless, then why all the excitement?" Maria asks.

"It's a complete about-face for this administration," John says. "I wonder what the hell's gonna' happen next."

"Shhh," says Josh, "I think this newscaster's just gotten the message."

Which isn't exactly correct. The morning anchor doesn't tell us of the event himself, instead he announces a late-breaking story, then switches us to one of his colleagues at U.N. headquarters. The next newsman tells us what's happened, rather badly, and then we see a two-minute clip that shows the vote, then the on-the-scene reporter comes back and answers some questions relayed from the anchorman. This all takes about ten minutes, long enough for somebody at INN to scare up an expert, who proceeds to tell us nothing we didn't know before. We're about to turn off the monitor in disgust when some new information finally comes in. The White House has announced a press conference, to be netcast in two hours.

We have some lunch and then tune in at 12:30 as President Patterson strides out into the White House briefing room, stands behind the podium, and motions for quiet.

"Ladies and Gentlemen of the Press, I have a few brief comments to make about today's vote in the United Nations.

"First let me state that our ambassador was acting under my personal orders in not vetoing U.N. resolution 749. Our intention was for the resolution to pass, which it has. This administration will aid the U.N. in collecting the tariff with the full power of the Executive branch. Questions?"

There are a host of them.

"Mr. President," one reporter asks, "do you think your actions in this matter are constitutional?

"I imagine the Supreme Court will tell me that within three or four weeks," Patterson shoots back.

"Mr. President," another says, "have you fully considered the economic consequences if this tariff is enforced and collected?"

"I expect the price for petroleum products and coal-based energy will double overnight."

"And the economic consequences of that?"

"The economic consequences will be severe, but I'm convinced this tariff is necessary."

"Mr. President," another asks, his tone almost querulous. "This vote was unexpected, to say the least. Why such an abrupt turnaround in your administration's policy?"

At this the President pauses for a few seconds. Then he points to one of the reporters, an older woman who's been uncharacteristically quiet.

"Ms. Ivan, I think you can answer that for the gentleman, can't you?"

Ms. Ivan is surprised, to say the least.

"Pardon me, Mr. President?" she says.

"Ms. Ivan, we were talking about this very subject off the record about a week and a half ago. I'd like to put that conversation on the record, if you don't mind."

"All right, Mr. President. I asked if you'd considered the political consequences of this vote, and you said, 'Fuck the politics, the icecaps are melting.' "

The room erupts into laughter, and the camera turns immediately back to Patterson for a reaction shot. For a moment he turns red, but the moment passes quickly, and then he smiles broadly along with everyone else.

"Actually, Ms. Ivan," he says dryly, "I was expecting an edited version."

More laughter.

"Anyway," Patterson continues, "I think Ms. Ivan's quote about says it all. I've become convinced by the latest scientific evidence that this is a problem we should have addressed fifty years ago. I'm equally convinced that the U.N. tariff is a logical first step to address the problem as it stands now. My administration is currently at work on other steps to ameliorate the effects of climate change. We should be presenting a complete package for Congress's attention in five or six weeks. Ladies and gentlemen, thank you for your time." And he turns and walks out the door, leaving a stunned silence behind him.

John turns off the NetV as soon as the President leaves the pressroom. I would probably have done the same thing myself — I doubt any of the media talking heads will say anything new — but it irritates me a little, this tendency of John's to take charge.

"Well," Maria says, "that was certainly interesting. What on Earth is going on?" She turns towards Josh, expecting an answer, but he just stares at the blank set, deep in thought.

"I'm not buying it," John says gruffly, "I've never trusted that stupid bastard. He must have something up his sleeve."

Josh stirs from his reverie.

"He's anything but a bastard. I didn't vote for him, but I've always thought he had a certain integrity. I just wish he'd picked a different vice-president. And John . . ."

"Yes?"

"Turn the news back on."

The words are innocuous, but as I watch the two of them I sense a struggle related to something more than the NetV. John frowns, then turns the monitor back on. We all watch for the next hour, silent and still.

* * *

John takes his temporary banishment from power well, so well, in fact, that I suspect this happens to him often. His expression reminds me of some wise elder counselor dealing with a petulant prince. In the afternoon he goes off to my study to work alone. I glance at his computer and see he's sending an e-mail, but it has nothing to do with Joshua or the Brethren. His daughter Judith is working with DNA from some Native-American graves and wants his advice.

By dinnertime John seems to be back in Josh's good graces — they discuss Patterson's press conference in civil tones and make plans for Josh's appearance on *The World In Brief*, the first of several news shows that booked him after his escapade in Larcen's temple. They even talk about John's daughter. Joshua hardly seems love-smitten, but it does sound as if they have a warm friendship. But the conversation quickly drifts back to Patterson: the news from Washington strikes Joshua as amazingly good in one way; he thinks it likely that Patterson will advocate payment of some reparations to Bangladesh. Even the food is unusually good, perhaps because Joshua and Maria tactfully relieved me of kitchen duty. But the best thing about dinner is Maria herself. I haven't seen her eat so well since long before we realized she was ill; her eyes have some of their old sparkle, and when we talk about Judith, she even teases.

"Your daughter sounds like a very respectable young lady," she says to John, "not to mention extremely bright."

"She is indeed," John replies, then goes off into the kitchen to refill his iced tea. The moment he's out of earshot, Maria leans over and stage whispers to Joshua.

"Just one problem with respectable young women, Josh."

"What?"

"The chaste must be chased."

"Thank you. I'll remember that."

Maria giggles at her pun, but pushes her quest for grandchildren no further.

Her good spirits last until well after dinner, and instead of going to sleep early, she stays up with the rest of us. I'm so happy to see her feeling well that as we get into bed I give her a quick but fervent kiss.

"I'm feeling better, Peter, but I don't think I'm quite ready for that," she says, mistaking the sparkle in my eyes.

"I just wanted a kiss," I say, "that's all."

"That's all? Well there's a first. Maybe *you* should see a doctor."

* * *

As either reward or torment I sleep and dream of our newlywed days, when Maria and I would sit impatiently on the sofa, watching TV until we were sure Joshua slept, then make for the bedroom, strewing clothes behind us like Hansel-and-Gretel breadcrumbs. Josh had stumbled in on a few of those nights, frightened by dreams, sending us scrambling for nightgowns and underwear. But Josh's nightmares were spooky as well as unromantic, often presaging plane crashes, sinking ferries, floods, or bombings covered in the next morning's news.

So it's with a sense of *déjà vu* that I wake at two a.m. and hear Joshua stirring, not sure if the sound is real or my sleepy memory of nights twenty-three years past. At least this time I don't have to get decent — I went to bed in an old man's pajamas, and Maria is wearing a flannel nightgown only a grandfather could love. All I have to do is slip out of bed, quietly open the door, and walk down the short hall to the living room. The NetV is on, and Joshua is staring at the screen.

"Josh," I ask, "is anything wrong?"

"They've killed him," he says. "President Patterson is dead."

Chapter 6

"Inside job? It reeks of an inside job."

— FBI Director Robert Craig, one day before submitting his resignation for "personal reasons."

The official line on the assassination is that the gunman, identified later as David Johannson of Lansing, Michigan; somehow managed to separate himself from a tour, slip unnoticed into the White House living quarters, and hide in a closet adjoining the small kitchen where President Patterson frequently ate a late-night snack. After shooting the President, Johannson exchanged fire with Secret Service agents and was killed trying to escape.

Corey Jeffers, head of the Secret Service, declined to speculate on how Johannson managed to evade the tight security that guards the residential areas of the White House, saying only that a complete review of procedures was already underway. NewsNet has been unable to confirm rumors that a Secret Service agent saw Johannson earlier in the day with Vice-President Armstrong, and was told by the Vice-President, "He's with me."

Johannson's motives are currently unclear, but NewsNet has learned that he was a member of at least one apocalyptic Christian fundamentalist organization."

—*NewsNet Magazine*
Lead website article
December 2032

President Armstrong: "No, I will not enforce U.N. resolution 749. For one thing, I have little doubt that the Supreme Court will rule that the resolution is a treaty, and the President cannot enter into treaties without the consent of two-thirds of the Senate. For another, nowhere is it stated in their charter that the U.N. can collect tariffs. My third objection is the most basic of all — I have always been opposed to this resolution. There is still no definitive proof that global warming is linked to the burning of fossil fuels. I will oppose U.S. payment of damages awarded to Bangladesh by the World Court for the same reason. Next question."

James Douglas, INN news: "Mr. President. Meteorologists say that 2033's cyclone season will be unusually violent, and that the Indian subcontinent will probably be struck by at least three storms of major proportions. In view of this and other global calamities, do you foresee any increase in our funding of foreign aid, which is currently at its lowest level as a percentage of the federal budget since the Great Depression?"

President Armstrong: "No, I do not. America is tired of the ceaseless begging of the Third World. Private charity is open to anyone who wants to give his or her hard-earned money away."

Mr. Douglas: "But Mr. President. Private charitable donations to other countries are also at their lowest levels since the Great Depression."

President Armstrong: "Well, as I said: Americans are tired of the ceaseless begging of the Third World."

— Official transcript,
Presidential News Conference
December 2032

"Friends, I tell you, the connection between this resolution and the coming government of the Antichrist is as simple as 1, 2, 3.

"To prove it, let's look at the three digits of the resolution — 7, 4, 9 — and their relation to the expression 1, 2, 3: the most common numerical way of sayin' that somethin' is perfectly obvious. Seven minus one is six. Four plus two is six. And nine minus three is six again. And *Revelations* warns us that 666 is the number of the beast. God is wavin' this one right in our faces, but the sinners of this world — Satan's patsies — are too blind to see it."

— The Reverend Charlton E. Larcen
NetV sermon, January 2033

Daniel Will: "Mr. Grant, you have been highly critical of other religious leaders' involvement in politics, but in recent years you've hardly been silent on political issues yourself. How do you reconcile this contradiction?"

Joshua Grant: "I don't think there is a contradiction. I don't see myself as a religious leader, for one thing. And though I've spoken out on political issues which have moral implications, I haven't supported particular candidates or parties, nor have I raised funds for any candidate or party."

Mr. Will: "Why is U.N. resolution 749 a moral issue?"

Mr. Grant: "The resolution itself isn't. It would be a defensible moral stance to be against the resolution, if we were willing to address the problem in some other manner. What isn't moral is the increasing callousness of the U.S. to the rest of the world, particularly our refusal to admit that our consumer habits are resulting in a widespread loss of life in other countries. And I don't know that secondhand, I've seen the effects myself in Bangladesh."

Mr. Will: "Mr. Grant, I'm hardly a Biblical scholar, but I'm fairly sure that carbon dioxide emission is not condemned in the Ten Commandments. Without getting into a long Biblical discussion, can you quote anything in the Bible that supports your position?"

Mr. Grant: "Well, 'love your neighbor' leaps to mind."

Mr. Will: "But even there you'll get some arguments. Harold Anthony, for one, points out that the people of Bangladesh are hardly our neighbors."

Mr. Grant: "I can get on the Internet and talk instantaneously with computer users in any city on Earth, get information in minutes from half the world's libraries, shop from companies in Hong Kong and Tahiti. That neighbor excuse might have worked for a Christian living in the Roman Empire: but it hardly applies today. Everyone on the planet is our neighbor."

Mr. Will: "And what's your reaction to those who say the climate changes are the result of natural processes beyond human control?"

Mr. Grant: "Why the climate is changing shouldn't matter. The Christian thing to do when your neighbor is drowning or starving is to do everything in your power to help. The Christian thing to do when your actions *might* be harming your neighbor is to change the way you behave."

Regina Brewster: "Mr. Grant, speaking of changes, I'd like to change the subject. For all your talk of religion, you're a man the majority of Christians in this country love to hate. Why is that?"

Mr. Grant: "Christians who love to hate? What type of Christians are those?"

Ms. Brewster: "Well, perhaps my wording was a little inappropriate. But you can hardly deny that to fundamentalists, the group that now makes up the overwhelming majority of those who profess to be Christians, you are rapidly becoming public enemy number one. They claim your religious writings undermine the authority of the Bible; that your ecumenical views will lead to a single world religion; and that your sympathies with the aims of the U.N. and the environmentalists come dangerously close to advocating a single world government, all things they say are signs of the imminent reign of the Antichrist. What's your reaction to these criticisms?"

Mr. Grant: "As to undermining the Bible; I've never heard a fundamentalist preach on Jesus and the Pharisees, and perhaps they ought to reread those verses. As to the possibility of a single world religion; I think God loves everyone, regardless of their religion. And concerning a single world government; well, the world wouldn't need much governing if we all behaved more like Christ. Maybe they should try that and quit worrying about the U.N."

Ms. Brewster: "And what about the Rapture?"

Mr. Grant: "Jesus once said that those who were first on earth would be last in the Kingdom of God. Present-day Americans are citizens of the richest and most powerful nation in the history of mankind. In view of what Jesus said, well, I don't think we should count on taking an express elevator to Paradise anytime soon."

— *The World in Brief*
Internet News Network

"What frightens me is that they didn't ask about Patterson," Joshua says.

We're sitting in my living room, Joshua, John, Maria and myself, plus two now-frequent visitors — Matt Wilson (former NetV technician for Larcen Ministries) and Nicholas Preston. At their request we've just finished watching Josh's INN appearance, which took place about a week after President Patterson's murder. It's been a popular episode, generating enough hits to stay posted on the INN archive long after it aired.

I don't mind Nicholas being here, but Matt is another matter. He's not rude or irritating, in fact he's almost invisible, sitting for hours and saying nothing — but I'm spooked that he found us so easily. Joshua may be a celebrity, but I've done my best to keep Maria and myself out of the public spotlight. My best is apparently pretty poor; Matt tracked us down with ease, different last name and all, ringing our doorbell one afternoon and asking for Joshua as calmly as an eight-year-old inquiring after a new playmate.

"Why does it frighten you that they didn't ask about Patterson?" I ask Josh. "You're a relief worker, not an expert on assassination."

"But his death will have a huge impact on the Brethren. Besides supporting the fuel tariff, Patterson was also going to support payment of the Bangladesh settlement, as well as increasing foreign aid. I was expecting a slew of questions about the new president."

"They were afraid," John says.

"Afraid of what?" I ask.

"Afraid of getting killed."

Joshua looks skeptical, and Maria snorts. But Nicholas nods.

"Unfortunately, you're right," he says, and John glares at him — Nicholas is an ally he doesn't want. "This is as close as we've ever come to a coup in this country, and it's going to succeed because there's one thing the founding fathers didn't safeguard against."

"Which was?" John asks acidly.

"Public opinion. No U.S. politician does anything without checking a poll first, and the media makes more money when they're telling the public what it wants to hear. Nobody's making a fuss because the public's reaction to the assassination has been a huge sigh of relief — 'Oh, Thank the Lord! Gas will still be cheap!' "

"What about your congregation?" Matthew asks.

"As bad as the rest of them," Nicholas says, and frowns at the floor. Nicholas preached a scorching sermon soon after the assassination, excoriating the American public for its indifference to Patterson's murder. After the sermon, many in his congregation refused to shake his hand, and a small but powerful minority are now petitioning for his ouster.

"Serves you right," John mutters, so softly I doubt Nicholas can hear him. But Josh hears, even though he's further away, and he shoots John a warning look.

"Have you heard anything from Anthony's show yet?" Nicholas asks, perhaps as a tactful way to change the subject, but probably also out of genuine interest.

"No," Josh says.

"That may be just as well," Nicholas continues. "Israel is a dangerous place to be right now, and I don't think the Reverend Anthony is . . . well . . ." Nicholas pauses, perhaps surprised by the words coming out of his own mouth. "I sometimes think that Dr. Anthony is a bit . . . extreme."

"Oh really?" John says. "I figured you'd be a great fan."

"I am not," Nicholas says sternly. "Some of his interpretations of scripture are even more outlandish than Joshua's, and I suspect they're made from less praiseworthy motives."

"You mean you think he's a kook," Matthew says. Matt has become our court jester — he can utter unpleasant truths without offense.

"I just feel it's important," Joshua persists, "important to go on Anthony's show, I mean. Even if that does involve going to Israel."

"Joshua, it's too dangerous now," Nicholas says. "The situation with the Temple is getting more tense every day."

"It's not that bad," Joshua replies, but I recognize this as the only sort of lie he ever allows himself: misdirection meant to spare feelings or prevent worry. I sensed the same impulse this morning as we watched the news — he reacted to each of John's gloomy presentiments with an unenthusiastic, "Let's not get carried away, John." But the news seemed worrisome even to me: President Armstrong promised U.S. support for the Israelis' recent decision to rebuild the Temple, calling the project "an undertaking well within Israel's rights as a sovereign nation." He then pledged U.S. troops as "peacekeepers." All in all it seems a bad time to tour the Holy Land, though I take a little comfort in the thought that the Israelis may well deny Joshua a visa.

"What do you think the Arabs will do about the Temple?" I ask.

"Riot, of course," John says.

"No, I don't mean the Palestinians; I mean the other Arabs, the Saudis, the Jordanians, the Egyptians."

"Forty years ago they might have invaded," John says, "but I don't think that will happen now. The Israelis are too strong, particularly with several thousand American troops there."

"What difference would four or five thousand American soldiers make?"

"Well, they're a sign that we'd be willing to send 50,000 more. The Arabs will make a lot of noise, they may send a few deluded lunatics carrying suicide bombs, but they won't do anything really effective. You watch."

"But John," Joshua says. "You're forgetting. The Arabs have the oil."

"Never happen," John says skeptically.

"What will never happen?" I ask John.

"They'll never try another embargo."

But it's an interesting possibility. The Arabs artificially lowered oil production several times in the twentieth century, but the embargoes broke down; the big bucks always tempted somebody to pump more, and the tactic of embargo has now almost faded from popular memory. Still, if one enjoys politics it's an interesting scenario, and John, Nicholas, and I get into quite a discussion about it. But Joshua and Maria soon desert us, she to rest and he to work.

Later in the afternoon I hear Josh and John arguing loudly in the kitchen.

"But he hasn't said you can come on the show yet, Joshua! You don't have the authority to spend Brethren funds that way!"

"The authority just isn't spelled out. I have discretion for emergencies."

"So where's the emergency?"

"Believe me, it's an emergency. We have to get on Anthony's program."

"What are you going to do? Just show up in Jerusalem and knock on the studio door?"

"If I have to, yes. All I know is that we have to go soon."

"You seem to know a lot lately that nobody could know."

"I'm playing a hunch."

"Does your hunch say that the Israelis will approve all our visas on one week's notice?"

"Yes."

"And why did you get so many tickets! Air travel is cheaper than when *I* was thirty-three, but it's not that cheap!"

"I bought tickets only for those I need: you, my mother and Peter, Nicholas and Matthew."

"Nicholas and Matthew! What do we need them for? Why do we need your parents, for that matter? Have you even asked them? These tickets are for a week from tomorrow!"

"They have to come. Trust me."

"I'd love to trust you, but you haven't given me a single good reason."

"Trust doesn't work that way, John. I didn't ask you to trust my reasons, I asked you to trust me."

This hits home. For several seconds John doesn't reply, and then I hear a muffled "all right." A few minutes later I hear the front door shut — Joshua is off on another of his interminable walks. John comes hesitantly into my study the moment Josh has left, sits down on my small sofa, and looks over as if he wants to say something.

"Well?" I finally ask.

"Peter . . ." he says, "did you ever start something that spun totally out of control?"

It's not what I was expecting, and neither is the reply that pops out of my mouth. "No," I say, "I react, I don't initiate. It's the secret to my many failures."

John gives a sad little laugh. "Being effective isn't all it's cracked up to be."

I don't have the slightest idea what he's talking about. But when he stands, he looks as if I've dispensed some sage counsel. Then he walks over, squeezes my shoulder, and leaves.

I was reading my e-mail when John came in, and a new message popped up on the screen as we talked. As he shuts the door I open that message, and like the blade on a guillotine, everything slides into place.

To: Peter Jacobson the e-mail begins, then

From: The Reverend Harold Anthony,

then the message itself:

Peter!

It's been a long time! We have a lot of catching up to do.

As to our most immediate business, tell your sheep of a stepson that we'll be glad to have him on our show. But as you know, we've recently moved operations to Jerusalem, so you'll all have to buy tickets to the Holy Land. (Unless, of course, Joshua has sprouted angel's wings and no longer needs an airplane.)

Give me a call as soon as you get into town!

The Beast's loving GrandDad

Harold Anthony

I'm tempted to erase it at once, to never let Josh know I've seen the damn thing, but I know it won't do any good. Joshua will fly to Israel with or without me, he'll get in touch with Anthony whether he sees this message or not, he'll go on Anthony's show no matter what I do. Better that he know just what he's getting into. I carefully save the message on the hard drive, and then, after a few moments' thought, print out a copy on paper as well.

Hours later, Joshua returns, and I call him and John in to tell them the news.

"Sheep of a stepson?" John asks. "Is he making some joke with Christian imagery?"

"Dolly," I mutter.

"Excuse me?" John says.

"Dolly the sheep," Joshua says dryly, "the first cloned mammal." John hits his forehead lightly with the heel of his hand, muttering something about the onset of senility. "He called you Peter Jacobson," Josh points out.

"So he knows," I say. "He knows everything."

"Maybe he's always known," Joshua replies, neither upset nor surprised. He looks away from the computer screen with the air of a man moving on to the next item in his grocery list. "I'm going to talk to Mother about Israel," he says, and leaves.

As soon as Josh is out of the room, John turns towards me and hisses:

"We've got to convince him not to go! I know it was my idea at first, but it's too dangerous now!"

"John," I reply, "I've known Joshua longer than you have. If those visas come through, you better pack your bags."

Chapter 7

Joshua's bought six tickets, but John was right, my stepson has somehow neglected to ask us if we want to go to Israel. No doubt Maria will go, sick as she is, and where she goes I go. Matthew also will be no problem — in a few short weeks Josh has become the focus of his life. But Nicholas Preston is another matter, and Joshua knows it. Without even mentioning a trip, he calls Nicholas and invites him over for breakfast.

"Go where?" Nicholas erupts the next morning, spraying a mouthful of coffee like a spouting whale.

"I want you to go with us to Israel. I've already bought your ticket."

"Well you better try and get your money back! My visa is good for the rest of the year, but I can't imagine the Israelis will give *you* one after all the trouble you've stirred up over there."

"What trouble is that?"

"The protests!"

"You think the Israelis prefer suicide bombers to peaceful civil disobedience?"

"The ones in power now might, and you know it."

"Well, my visa was approved this morning, so I guess you're wrong." Josh glances at me, smiling. I look back in disbelief, then sadly realize he's telling the truth.

"But I can't just leave," Nicholas says. "I've got a church to run."

"You won't have a church to run soon," Josh replies. It's the most tactless thing I've ever heard him say, and Nicholas looks stunned. "I'm sorry," Josh continues, "but we both know it's true. They're going to ask you to leave."

For a moment I think Nicholas will break into tears. "I've been called to help those people."

"And you have. But this is more important than your church, more important than your career, more important than your family. I need you."

"What right do you have to order me around?"

Joshua isn't fazed in the least. "Nicholas," he asks, "has God ever spoken to you?"

"Of course He has."

"Nicholas," Joshua asks again, fixing him with that knowing stare. "Has God ever *really* spoken to you?"

Nicholas's expression darkens, hovers somewhere between loathing and fear. As a "born-again" Christian, he's supposedly had some unmistakable religious experience, but looking at his expression, I wonder. As for Joshua, it's as if he knew precisely which button to push, what one question out of a thousand would uncover a painful wound.

"No!" he says angrily. "I want Him to speak to me; but so far the Almighty has been resolutely silent."

"I think He speaks to you all the time, and you don't realize it because He speaks in your own voice. I can't order you to do anything, but I will give you some advice: you should go someplace quiet and listen — maybe your own good voice will tell you the right thing to do."

Nicholas seems moved for a moment, but then some sterner thought enters his mind. He stands and places his coffee cup on the table with exaggerated caution. "Joshua," he says, "if the Devil himself asked me to pray, I'd do it, because I'd know the Devil had just made a big mistake. I'll call you if I have any sudden epiphanies." He looks towards Maria, gives her a nod that turns into a mock bow, and struts out the front door.

"Joshua!" Maria says. "That was cruel, what you said about his church!"

"No it wasn't," Josh answers. "It won't hurt any more now than it will next week or next month. And I need him."

"He'll never speak to you again!"

"He'll call back in an hour."

And fifty-five minutes later I pick up the phone and hear a contrite Nicholas ask for Joshua. I hand Josh the handset, and a moment later he smiles, says, "Thank you so much, Nicholas," then turns to us all.

"He's coming," Joshua says.

With the question of Nicholas out of the way, the only real problem left is Maria and me. I pack neither quickly nor lightly, and Maria's doctor isn't thrilled about her hopping on an airplane. She sends me a long list of medicines Maria can or cannot take, foods she should avoid, rules not to break. And then she says something disturbing.

"There's one good thing about Mrs. Lunsford going to Israel."

"What's that?"

"She can see Micah Leisner. I don't know if you've heard of him, but he's a well-known leukemia specialist. I'll get you his address. He lives in Tel Aviv."

"Why does she need to see another oncologist? I thought you people had this thing on the run."

"Well, your wife's case has been rather unusual, and Dr. Leisner knows as much about leukemia as anyone on the planet. Aah, here we go. I'm sending you his e-mail and address."

A soft beep as the information passes through the phone lines to my computer.

"Got it," I say.

"Dr. Leisner may want to do some more tests, and he may want the results of the tests we've done here. There's a release form; I'll send it for Maria's signature."

Another beep, another number on my mail-box icon. I open this one and type in the password for Maria's e-signature.

"And one final problem," the doctor continues, "I doubt that your health plan will cover the consultation."

"Do you have a guess as to how much it will cost?"

"A couple of thousand, no more. Though if he needs to run other tests it will be considerably more, maybe as much as ten or fifteen."

"We can handle that. What about treatment?"

"Anything additional that he recommends I'll recommend also, so your health plan here should cover it. But there's no way to waffle on the consultation; Dr. Leisner is definitely not on your plan's provider list. Why are you going to Israel, anyway?"

"It's a long story. If you really think she should stay home, I'll try to convince her. But I don't think it will do any good."

"Well, if it wasn't for the chance to see Dr. Leisner, I would advise her not to go. But seeing him in person is worth the exertion of a plane ride."

"I see."

"Be careful over there yourself. Israel's not the safest place in the world right now."

"So I've been told."

The good doctor's misgivings rattle through my brain all night. Even obstetricians know this routine: the refusal to say the word "terminal," the equally obvious reluctance to be truly encouraging, the ass-covering desire to spread the blame when the end inevitably comes. I've been breathing easier for weeks, but now I lie in bed listening to my thumping heart, wondering about Maria's mortality, and, God help me, my own.

But the morning we're to fly out it's hard to believe there's anything wrong with her. *I* shuffle like a zombie headed back to the grave; *she's* bubbling like a teenager. Her good spirits are easily explained — the prospect of seeing Israel thrills her and she thinks my fear of Anthony is overblown. But when she turns up the stereo, then dances through our bedroom and throws me a naughty look (packing one final item, a sheer black nightgown) explanations are too timid for the miracle I feel.

"Is that klezmer music?" I ask as she sashays past.

"Of course."

"Could we turn it down a little?"

"Aww, getting too old to listen to something new?"

"I'd like to keep the hearing in my good ear, at least."

"Poor baby," she says, grabbing a remote and reducing the volume ever so slightly.

There's no relief in the living room — she has the music blaring out there too, and I also have to endure Joshua's amused glances at the pile of luggage we're accumulating. Matthew and Nicholas have already arrived — they sit flanking the bags, Matt smiling and juking slightly to the music, Nicholas somber and stiff. John made some noises about taking public transit to the airport, but in consideration of Maria Josh accepted Nicholas's offer to take one of his three cars. I never thought I'd see Josh ride in a luxury SUV, but I should have known that if he ever did it would be packed like a sardine can.

"I'm not sure this will all fit," Nicholas says gloomily.

Josh gives the pile of suitcases and backpacks a quick look. Used to Indian and Deshi concepts of crowding, he probably thinks we could carry two more passengers, a goat, and three chickens. "No problem," he says, and shoulders the first load out to the car. And he's proven right, even if I do end up with two carry-on bags and Maria's purse on my lap.

Things go less smoothly at the airport. I'd heard that security on Israeli planes was exceptionally tight, but the reality exceeds the rumors. They unpack and search our carry-on luggage, run metal detectors over Maria, and pat the men in our party down, checking for guns and knives. Then all the passengers wait for several hours, presumably while the bags destined for the luggage compartment undergo similar treatment.

There's more waiting to be done on the plane, but the flight attendants are friendly and the liquor is cheap, so no one raises a fuss as we sit on the runway for another thirty-five minutes. We finally get in the air at about two p.m. Atlanta time, and I promptly feel sick, courtesy of sleep deprivation, turbulence, and Jim Beam miniatures. The seat-belt sign stays lit for what seems an eternity, so I sit by the aisle discretely clutching a barf bag, almost wishing for some terrorist bomb to blast us the rest of the way to heaven. When we pass the coast the sign finally goes off and the turbulence ends as well, and when I finally make it into the bathroom I don't need to puke at all.

Our seats aren't together — Maria and I are in one row, Josh and Matthew in another, and John and Nicholas are seated separately towards the back of the plane. But John has gotten lucky; due to somebody's missed connection he has an empty spot next to him, and as I head up towards Maria he beckons me to sit down. His pocket computer is out.

"Have you been following the news?" he asks as I sit.

"No, I've been trying not to vomit. Don't you ever rest?"

"No. Unlike Joshua, I need some outside source to tell me what's going on."

"And what is going on?"

"The Saudi ambassador met with President Armstrong this morning, and the Saudis have scheduled a press conference this evening."

"So what do you think will happen then?"

"I think the Saudis will express their disgust at the Israelis for building the Temple. Then they'll ask for a U.N. resolution condemning Israel, which will pass easily and then be vetoed by the United States."

"And for this you're staying awake?" I ask, then look forward to see what the others are doing. Maria is engrossed in travel brochures, Nicholas is reading his Bible, Joshua is staring out the window, deep in thought, and Matthew is scribbling in a notebook, something he does often. I'd like to go sit by Maria again, because at the moment I'm sick to death of world affairs.

But since John seems upset I stay as he flits from one news

program to another. I learn that none of the media pundits think the Arab oil states will do anything drastic, indeed, none of them even bother to discuss the possibility. Instead there's a great deal of talk about the Temple. The Israeli government has promised the new building will in no way endanger the Dome of the Rock, perhaps the second-most sacred spot in Islam, but the Israeli government has so many warring factions nowadays that no one trusts official pronouncements, especially when a leader of an extreme Jewish sect says Yahweh will be satisfied with nothing less than an accurately-sited recreation of the temple of Solomon. To build that would require razing the Dome. However, this particular Jewish "priest" (rabbi no longer, now that the Temple is to return) doesn't foresee wrecking balls or controlled blasting; he's sure Yahweh will remove the offending structure Himself. The Muslims are equally sure Allah will do no such thing, but they're worried the Israelis may decide to help Yahweh along, perhaps with the aid of one or two micro-nukes, a weapon which (according to wild rumors) has recently been invented by the Mossad. Reputed to be smaller than a man's wallet, a micro-nuke supposedly has the explosive power of several tons of TNT. American and European physicists scoff at the notion, but, as the Arabs enjoy pointing out, physicists have been wrong before.

I guess it's all very interesting to a news junkie like John, but I'm so tired the now-gentle motion of the plane lulls me to sleep. I wake up about twenty minutes later, when John nudges me less than gently with his elbow.

"Hey! If you're gonna' sleep, go sit somewhere else," he says testily. "You snore. I can't hear what's happening on my shows."

I start to suggest what he can do with his shows, but the thought of Josh's preternaturally sharp hearing dissuades me, so I get up groggily and sway back to the empty seat next to Maria.

"John says I snore," I tell her. "Why don't you go back and straighten him out?"

"You do snore. I've been complaining about it for years."

"I went to a sleep clinic three times. They said I don't have any such problem."

"You should invite them over to our house some night."

I'd straighten Maria out but sleep suddenly seems more important.

"Wake me up when we get to Jerusalem," I say.

"Tel Aviv. We're flying into Tel Aviv."

"Wherever."

* * *

I wake up long before we reach Tel Aviv or even the Mediterranean. The cabin is dark and quiet; most of the passengers are either asleep or trying to sleep. There are a few die-hard insomniacs, however, and as I look around the plane I see that John and Joshua are among them. They're sitting together now, conversing in earnest whispers. Alert after my snooze, I unbuckle my seat belt and walk back. There's another empty seat in the row behind them, next to a women who's simultaneously reading a novel and listening to something on the airplane headphones. I make a small gesture in her direction, asking permission to sit, but when she ignores me I sit anyway.

"Well, gentlemen," I ask, leaning out into the aisle. "Anything exciting happening?"

"As a matter of fact, there is," John says quietly.

"What?"

"The Saudis are going to enforce Resolution 749," Joshua answers. "They're going to demand tariff payment on every barrel before they'll let it be pumped onto the tankers. Kuwait, the Emirates, Iraq, and Iran are expected to do the same. No doubt it's a sort of revenge against the U.S. for us helping the Israelis build the temple."

Still sleepy, this takes me a moment to comprehend. As best I can remember, nobody was expecting any such development — everyone assumed the Arabs would never let their religion cost them that much money.

"And the U.S. can't weasel out of it somehow?" I ask.

"There were problems with Patterson's plan to collect the tariff in the U.S.," John says. "But the Arabs can collect it. It's their oil; they can sell it for whatever the market will bear. The tariff will triple the cost of gasoline overnight, because the U.S. oil companies pumped most of our reserves dry in the 20's. Americans are gonna' start drivin' mopeds, and the U.N.'s gonna' be rich, assuming, that is, that the Arab governments actually give them the tariff money."

I start to congratulate Joshua: a great deal of that tariff money should be going to Bangladesh. Seawalls won't go up by the next cyclone season, but eighty million bucks for concrete storm shelters could work wonders. But Joshua seems anything but ecstatic. Since he's been back in Atlanta he's put on a little weight, gotten some well-deserved rest. But the face that looks back across the seat belongs in flooded Bangladesh or AIDS-stricken Africa; its great hollow eyes seem to carry the burdens of the world.

"What's wrong?" I ask. "I thought you'd be happy about this."

"I keep thinking about what they did to Patterson," Joshua replies.

I go back to my seat and try to get some sleep, Resolution 749 or no. But just before I nod off, I notice a change in the sound of the engines. We're flying much faster, fuel consumption be damned. Someone in the Promised Land wants their planes home soon.

Chapter 8

Daniel Will, INN News: "Ambassador Saíd, some of my more cynical colleagues feel your government's decision to enforce Resolution 749 is a blatant attempt to make the United States withdraw its support for the new Jewish temple. How would you respond?"

Ambassador Saíd: "We are collecting the tariff for two reasons, neither of which is connected to the Israeli government's recent actions. The first is obvious: we wish to protect the environment. The second is equally obvious: as a member nation of the U.N. we wish to support its wise policies. We encourage the governments of the United States and Israel to also respect U.N. policy, particularly in regard to the 2028 U.N. resolution recognizing the area surrounding the Dome of the Rock as equally sacred to Judaism, Islam, and Christianity."

Will: "So there is no *quid quo pro* here, no carrot and stick?"

Saíd: "Excuse me?"

Will: "In other words, there is no implied reward or punishment in relation to American policy?"

Saíd: "Mr. Will, I am no prophet. If the U.S. changes its current stance in regard to the Israeli Temple, I cannot predict what will happen as a result. But let me assure you, we are concerned about global warming. Saudi Arabia is hot enough."

— *The World In Brief*
Internet News Network

Hours later, it seems that all my worries will come to an end. Through Maria's window I can see the lights of Tel Aviv and a stunning full moon. As we bank towards the city the plane hits a pocket of rough air, then another patch of turbulence so extreme I wonder if we've glanced off something solid. Shuddering still, the plane continues to roll and I find myself looking straight down at the moonlit waves of the Mediterranean. After another violent shock the plane whips back in the other direction, the lights of Tel Aviv flashing past Maria's window before giving way to a view of the stars. We hang this way for what seems an eternity, and I can feel my rear end floating inches above the seat. Engines screaming, the plane finally rolls level. It's hard to judge in the middle of the night, but the view out Maria's window seems radically different — I'm willing to bet we've lost five thousand feet in ten seconds.

Though we started this maneuver with most of the passengers half asleep, there were yelps and a few outright screams as the plane thrashed around. Now that we're flying straight there's a low murmur of frightened voices, and one man calls out frantically: "My wife has hit her head!" Several rows in front of us, a flight attendant goes to help.

"I don't fly much," Maria says, "but I know that's not routine. How bad was it?"

"Pretty damn bad," I say.

But nothing vital has broken. Five minutes later we're on the ground, and ten minutes later we're getting off the plane. As we're filing out the front door, I can hear the pilot and co-pilot talking loudly in Hebrew. I sidle up to Josh in the ramp to the terminal and ask for a translation.

"It was fairly obscene," he laughs. "Want the edited version?"

"Sure."

"He said the Seraphim nearly knocked us out of the sky."

"Seraphim?"

"An Israeli nickname for a C-6A. It's a *big* military cargo plane. Apparently we hit one's wake."

"Wake?"

"Its turbulence. The pilot is very angry. We were routed too close to its flight path. Like I said, it's a big plane."

"He must be pretty angry to talk like that where we could hear. You can't be the only passenger who speaks Hebrew."

"Often I would be — flights this time of year are usually crammed with American tourists. But there's quite a few Israelis on this one."

"I wonder why."

"Getting home before the storm hits, I guess."

"What storm? Weren't all the American troops flown in last week?"

"Yes. We sent two C-6's over."

"Would two be enough for 1000 troops and their supplies?"

"More than enough, unless they needed tanks and artillery. And a police force shouldn't need tanks and artillery."

"Then why more C-6's?"

"I was wondering that myself."

By the time we get our luggage through customs Maria is wobbly with fatigue and John isn't much better, so Josh decides to get them a cab. Since it's 4:30 in the morning this takes a while, and when a cab finally shows, Josh asks Matt to ride with Maria and John, presumably to tote luggage at the other end.

"Shame we can't all fit in," Nicholas says.

"They don't make cabs that big here, Nicholas," says Joshua, ignoring the hint that we hire another. "The rest of us can take the bus. The first one should be here in about half an hour."

The bus shows up shortly before five. It's mostly bringing workers to the airport, so we have plenty of room on our ride back into Tel Aviv. As we pass the city limits Joshua points out several large contingents of American soldiers. I think they're Israelis — if they're not I don't see how there can be any American troops left over for Jerusalem. But Josh is adamant, he says he knows his uniforms and these are Americans.

After about forty minutes on the bus, followed by a five-minute walk, we arrive at the house of one Martha Greenbaum, one of the small but growing number of Jewish Israelis who have joined the Brethren. Joshua has never met Ms. Greenbaum, but when he asked if she knew of a place we could stay she offered to put us up herself. She's about my age, thin, lively, and a little stunned that fate has brought her Joshua Grant as a houseguest.

I've been in many Brethren homes, so I'm not stunned that we'll be sleeping on the floor, or that the only cooling comes from old-fashioned overhead fans, nor am I surprised to find only one NetV monitor, instead of wall-sized screens in every room. Nicholas, however, can't stop a look of dismay from flitting over his face — I'll bet he's used to tourist hotels cooled to a polar bear's taste, big wall-screens visible from a king-size bed, coffeemaker, small fridge, and room-service button ready to hand. But he makes no complaint when Martha shows us to a back room with five futons laid out on a hard-tiled floor. We all lie down and sleep like the dead.

"You're right, Dr. Grant, there are American soldiers everywhere, many more than the news reports say. And more seem to be arriving every day."

I pour myself some more tea. It's about two in the afternoon, local time, and we're having a late lunch after sleeping off our jet lag. Joshua looks alert and ready to work, Matthew looks fresh and eager as well, and I don't feel too bad myself. At least I hope I look better than Maria, John, and Nicholas, all of whom seem in need of four or five more hours sleep. I'm particularly worried about Maria — she got up dizzy, and needed to lean on my arm as we came in to eat. But Martha! Martha is the type of old woman who'll dance on our graves.

I suppress a laugh when she calls Joshua doctor; he doesn't have a doctorate in anything. Certainly Martha knows this, but she's obviously in awe of him, and he's too polite to correct her more than once. So Dr. Grant it is.

"Then the news reports we've heard," Josh asks, "that the U.S. was only sending a thousand troops, they were wrong?"

"I haven't been driving around counting them, Dr. Grant, but I'd guess there were more than a thousand American soldiers just in Tel Aviv, so there must be twice as many in Jerusalem. That's where everyone is expecting the real trouble."

"I'm surprised there hasn't been more about it on the news," John says, "although I'm twelve hours behind. I haven't seen any NetV since we were on the plane."

"There seems to be something wrong with the Internet," Martha says, "I can't get half the sites I usually do, particularly news sites. I thought it might be my computer but a couple of my friends said they were having trouble, too."

"You don't think . . ." I start to say, but John cuts me off.

"Come on Peter; you can't censor the Internet. It was designed for communications in a nuclear war. If you block one route to a site it just finds another one."

"I don't know," Joshua says, "Ninety percent of Net users go through three or four big companies. What server do you use, Martha?"

"USWeb, Dr. Grant."

"See?"

Matthew nods, but John is skeptical. "I bet we won't have any trouble with our computers."

"Well, why don't the three of us look at Martha's? Is that all right, Ms. Greenbaum?"

"Certainly, Dr. Grant," she says hesitantly. "The rest of us can go into the kitchen so you can concentrate."

Conversation is sparse in the kitchen — some of the awe Martha feels for Joshua rubs off on the rest of us, although there seems to be a subtle hierarchy. Martha treats Maria the way a Catholic would treat the Virgin Mary if she dropped down from heaven for tea and toast; I'm only Joshua's stepfather, but Martha still makes me feel like a minor prophet. But Martha doesn't quite know what to make of Nicholas.

Her first shock comes when she finds he's not a member of the Brethren, her second when he lets slip that he's a Southern Baptist minister. Even after a short acquaintance, I feel certain that the words "right wing" and "fundamentalist" can be applied to neither Martha's religion nor her politics, so it's hardly surprising that she treats Nicholas like an ill-mannered child in need of instruction, occasionally glancing at Maria or me for approval.

"Is your church very large, Mr. Preston?" she asks him tentatively.

"I had a congregation of nearly three thousand," he says. "It was the second biggest church in Atlanta."

"Had?"

"I'm still officially the minister, but they'll dump me as soon as we get back from this crazy trip."

"I don't see anything crazy about it," Martha bristles. "Maybe Dr. Grant can show my fellow Jews just what sort of idiots they're hooking up with."

"And what idiots would that be?"

"Bible-thumping Americans."

Nicholas's answer is surprisingly mild.

"Ma'am," he says, "my apologies. If the trip is crazy it's crazy in a noble way. Joshua ought to be doing it, even though I don't think it's got a bat's chance in hell of succeeding."

Just then Joshua strides in.

"Can we borrow your computer?" he asks me. I take it out of my pocket and hand it to him. "We'll need you, too," he continues. Baffled, I follow him into the living room.

"You must be hard up if you need my help," I say.

John snorts from a corner. "Josh is hoping your love of obsolescence will pay off. When's the last time you updated your browser?"

"I don't know. A year or two ago, I guess."

"Which means two or three years ago, I'll bet. Give it a try, Josh."

Joshua clicks my computer on and the desktop flashes onto Martha's screen. But instead of clicking on my Net or NetV icons, Joshua burrows into a systems folder I never knew existed.

"I'm dialing manually and accessing a university server that John has privileges on," Joshua explains. "Actually, it's a demonstration program for a networking class — a basic server minus the bells and whistles. John, if you were the U.S. government, what sites would you go after first?"

"Saudi news?"

"Unfortunately, we have to get the URL exactly; this server doesn't give you any help." Joshua types in a long string of letters, punches the enter key, and quickly gets a low bong and the cryptic message Error x3645. He changes a letter or two with the same results.

"Try *two* back-slashes," Matthew suggests, and suddenly we're in. A man speaking in Arabic pops up on the screen.

"The question I have now is: are we in because we used Peter's old program, or because we tried my backdoor server?" John wonders.

"Why would an old program help?" I ask.

"Because nobody would craft a virus for a three-year-old browser," Matt says.

For a second I wonder how we're going to learn anything from a news program in Arabic. But I've forgotten about my stepson.

"Nothing interesting so far," he says after listening a minute or two.

"When did you learn Arabic?" I ask in some awe. Joshua shrugs; either he can't remember or he regards the question as unimportant. The program continues for about five minutes, and suddenly the announcer shifts slightly in his seat. Even I can tell that he's started a new story.

"Here we go," Joshua says softly. Three minutes later he shakes his head and shuts down my computer.

"Well?" John asks.

"The Saudis claim the U.S. is starting a massive buildup in Israel, that we're flying in tanks, fighters, bombers, and thousands of troops. They've put their own armed forces on full alert. The Emirates, Iran, Syria, and Iraq have done the same. They're also talking about a U.S. plot to sabotage the Internet — did you see the scrolled words in Arabic at the bottom? That was a request for any Saudi who could receive the Netcast to let the authorities know what software they're using. And last but not least, the Saudi government maintains that the Internet sabotage was carried out by computer-savvy members of the Brethren of Charity, working in league with the evil forces of the American CIA."

"And you heard nothing about this when you went on the Net with Martha's computer?" I asked.

"Martha's computer crashed the second anything about the Middle East was mentioned. So did John's. We're full of theories, but I like Matthew's the best. He thinks a virus was placed in the speech-recognition software, one that could be activated by an e-mailed command. He thinks a virus like that could crash individual computers whenever certain keywords or word combinations were said or printed. Peter's computer might have worked because the virus was inserted in a recent upgrade."

"And nobody else would notice this?"

"You mean the keywords? I'm sure a lot of people have noticed, but they're having an awfully hard time communicating with each other."

"Okay, enough about the Internet. Why are we sending tanks and fighter planes over here?"

John looks stunned at my innocence. "Come off it, Peter."

"All right, so I'm stupid or jet-lagged or both. Tell me."

"Either we're trying to scare the oil states into not enforcing 749, or we're planning to invade them. Take your pick." He laughs softly. "I wonder if the Israelis knew just what they were signing up for when they let us send troops. Probably not."

I turn to Joshua, hoping that he has a happier interpretation of events.

"John's right," Joshua says, before I can even ask.

I stay and watch the three of them try and debug their computers for about forty-five minutes. They don't get very far. Matthew is a computer specialist, but he's not a troubleshooter; he builds sites and runs live action over the Net. Joshua and John are almost as computer savvy as Matthew, but none of them have access to basic source codes, and their only tools are four pocket computers. They succeed only in ruling out several promising theories by sending each other e-mails. Any mention of troop buildups and the Middle East doesn't go through.

At about four o'clock Maria comes in and tells us she's going back to bed. Her ashen face tears my mind away from invasions and oil, and I decide to call Dr. Leisner's office to confirm tomorrow's three p.m. appointment. His secretary asks me to hold the line and I find myself talking to Leisner himself.

"Ah, Dr. Lunsford," he says. "I hope you had a good flight."

"The landing was a little rough."

"Make sure your wife gets plenty of rest; traveling is hard on anyone, and she needs to be particularly careful."

"I will," I say, and then wait — somehow I have the impression there's more to come.

"Dr. Lunsford," he finally says, "forgive my being inquisitive, but are you by any chance related to Joshua Grant, the well-known Joshua Grant, that is?"

"Yes. He's my stepson," I answer without thinking. It would probably have been wiser to lie — I know nothing about Dr. Leisner's politics. "How did you guess that?" I ask, my tone a little belligerent.

"Well, your wife's physician E'd me test records, and mixed in was a form listing relatives, next of kin, that sort of thing. I happened to see that her son was named Joshua, and I'd also heard that Mr. Grant had just come to Israel, so I wondered if the name was a coincidence."

"It's not."

"Dr. Lunsford, tensions are running very high in our country right now . . ."

Here it comes, I think, he's going to tell me he can't see Maria. But I'm wrong.

"Please be careful," he finishes.

"I will."

"Shalom," he replies, and hangs up.

A standard Israeli farewell, but I sense an extra dose of sincerity. "Shalom," I reply to the dead line, and put down the receiver myself.

By nine that night I feel as bad as Maria looks. I've gotten plenty of sleep, I've been taking vitamins to help with jet lag, and by the logic of time zones I ought to be wide awake. But, as Maria often reminds me, I'm not getting any younger, and at 9:30 I leave a lively political discussion to the others and join her on the futons in the back room.

I wake up early the next morning confused and not quite sure where I am. Around me, everyone else is still fast asleep. I grab some clothes from my backpack, then head off towards Martha's bathroom to change out of my pajamas. Down the hall I catch the sounds of someone moving around in the kitchen and the smell of coffee. Martha, at least, is awake.

I walk towards the kitchen to join her, visions of eggs, toast, coffee, and bacon dancing through my head, even though I haven't eaten bacon in years and I'm unlikely to get any from even the most unkosher Israeli Jew. When I turn the corner I don't see any bacon, but Martha apparently knows that Americans are used to big breakfasts. There's a big pitcher of orange juice, some sort of sweetbread in the oven, and a bowl full of eggs waiting to be cooked. Martha smiles and bids me good morning, then hands me a warm cup of coffee. It's not extravagantly early, a little before eight, but Martha expresses surprise to see me up — most people just over from the U.S. sleep till at least nine, she says. We sit and talk for about twenty minutes, waiting for the others to wake. I'm just tucking into my third roll when there's a knock at the front door. Martha looks puzzled, shrugs, and goes to answer it.

"Martha Greenbaum?" asks a polite but firm voice. I stand and look towards the front door, and see a man in a nondescript shirt and tie looking in over Martha's shoulder.

"Yes," Martha says, still sounding a bit baffled.

"Major Levi, Mossad," the man says. "May we come in?" When Martha doesn't answer he steps past her and into the front room, followed by two soldiers and another man dressed in the same ominously generic fashion. Martha stands her ground, jaw thrust forward. "How can I help you gentlemen?" she asks.

"You have some house guests?" the other man asks in return. "One Joshua Grant, his mother, Maria Grant Lunsford; her husband, Dr. Peter Lunsford; Nicholas Preston, Dr. John Baxter, and Matthew Wilson?"

"Yes."

"We would like to talk to Mr. Grant, Dr. Baxter, Mr. Wilson, and Dr. Lunsford, please. Immediately."

"Are they under arrest?"

"Not at the moment."

They don't seem to have spotted me yet, and for a moment I have the ridiculous urge to run out the back door. But then I hear Joshua's voice calling, "I'll be there in a minute." In less than thirty seconds he steps out of the bathroom and strides past the kitchen into the front room. Feeling foolish and frightened at the same time, I follow.

"What can I do for you?" he asks.

"Who is this?" one of the men says, pointing at me.

"That's my stepfather, Dr. Peter Lunsford," Josh answers.

"Are John Baxter and Matthew Wilson here?"

"They should be out in a second. They were just getting up when I left the room, and certainly they've heard their names by now. And could you speak more quietly? My mother's been ill and she needs her rest. What's this all about?"

"We'd like to discuss some e-mails the four of you sent yesterday."

"The four of us?" Josh says softly. I'm as baffled as he is — I didn't send any e-mails.

"The four of you," the shorter Mossad man says.

"By what right were you reading our e-mail?" Joshua asks. "That used to require a court order under Israeli law."

"It still does, and we have one."

"I'd like to see it."

"Not on your life."

"Then why do you need to talk to my stepfather? He didn't send any e-mails."

The two detectives or secret agents or whatever the hell they are walk over to a corner of the room and discuss this in low voices while flipping through some papers. After a minute or so Joshua says:

"We did borrow Dr. Lunsford's computer. Perhaps we used some software registered in his name, but I can assure you he didn't send any e-mails yesterday."

One of the "detectives" turns.

"Our orders are to bring him in."

"Gentlemen, he came to Israel to be with my mother. She has an appointment to meet with a Dr. Leisner today — he's a Tel Aviv oncologist, perhaps you've heard of him. My stepfather doesn't have a political bone in his body, and my mother needs him. Won't you be satisfied with three of us?"

The detectives consult again, one of them occasionally grumbling softly. Suddenly the shorter one turns and says, "All right. Dr. Lunsford can stay."

About that time John and Matthew shuffle up to the front room, escorted by one of the soldiers. John seems almost happy — perhaps he's looking forward to martyrdom — but Matthew looks worried for the first time since he's hooked up with us.

"Sir," Martha says loudly, "I'll ask you again. Are my guests under arrest?"

"No," the shorter man says. "We just want to ask them a few questions."

"And you can't ask them here?"

"No. They've got to come down to headquarters."

"Then my lawyer will meet them there. Just to make sure you ask your questions politely." The detectives scowl, the soldiers look deadpan and inhuman as soldiers do, and Josh, John, and Matthew are led out the front door.

When it shuts I turn to Martha hopefully. "Is your lawyer good?" I ask.

Martha sighs. "The only lawyer I know is my nephew. Since he's family I like to think he's good, but he only passed the bar six weeks ago. I'll give him a call and see what he can do."

Miraculously, Maria sleeps through it all.

She wakes up about an hour later, and though she looks better than she did last night, she still walks like an old, old woman, putting her feet down as if they were made of glass. Nicholas, sitting beside Martha and me at the kitchen table, stirs uneasily, then gets up to help her, but she waves him off, then sits wearily in the chair next to mine. Martha walks to the counter and returns with a tray of sweetbread, tea and coffee; but Maria only takes a few tiny bites of a roll and a few sips of tea, then stares absently at the far wall. After a few minutes she asks:

"Where's Joshua?"

I'd love to hide it from her, but there's no chance.

"Some men from Israeli security came this morning," I tell her. "They wanted to ask Josh a few questions. John and Matthew, too."

"Why didn't you go and keep an eye on them!" she asks heatedly.

"That wasn't an option. Martha's lawyer is checking up on the situation."

Maria's knuckles tighten on the old china cup she's holding — for a second I'm afraid it will break in her hands. I can't think of a thing to say that will comfort her, but Nicholas can.

"Don't worry, Mrs. Lunsford. They're all American citizens, and this is Israel, not some crazy Arab country. They'll be just fine."

There's our real religion, stated bluntly. We're rich Americans: the chosen of God, the boss's son, the teacher's pet, the boxer whose opponent will soon take a dive. Surely nothing can touch us. We go through life half-convinced that even death will pass us by.

Maria finds it no more convincing than I do, but she appreciates Nicholas's intentions. She smiles a little and eases her grip on the cup.

"Thank you, Nicholas. I hope you're right."

* * *

As an obstetrician, I'm used to waiting, accustomed to not being entirely in control. A surgeon would be tearing around Tel Aviv, anxious to take command, desperate to do something. But by one o'clock I can sip tea in Martha's kitchen, comfortable that what can be done has been done — Martha has called her nephew, and I've been to the U.S. embassy to tell them what they certainly know already: that Joshua was picked up by the Israelis. I expected that to take hours, but to my surprise I was seen by a high-level diplomat almost immediately. He was extremely polite, completely useless, and gave every indication of feeling guilty about something.

Nicholas, to my surprise, volunteered for the most dangerous task and has yet to return. He's out notifying the press, or at least what he can find of it. With the Internet so screwed up, we both thought the more adventurous reporters might have already found Joshua, John, and Matthew . . . in the cell next to theirs.

But Maria doesn't view our impotence quite so philosophically. When I get back from the embassy she plies me with questions. While I eat a good lunch; she picks at her food, glaring at me occasionally as if to ask how I could possibly eat. Then she makes some noises about canceling her appointment with Dr. Leisner. I won't hear of it.

By 2:15 it's time to go. When I was out earlier I had a cabbie drive me over to Leisner's office, so I know it's fifteen minutes away, probably less since the cabbie said traffic was light until three-thirty. The same cabbie should be arriving here any minute now, lured by the promise of a big tip.

"Are you ready?" I ask Maria when she reappears in the kitchen, purse in hand.

"Yes. I still think we should stay. What if Josh and the others get home while we're gone?"

"Then Martha will fix them something to eat and they can tell us all about it over desert."

"What if they need us to raise bail?"

"They won't actually arrest them unless they want to keep them in jail, in which case bail will be out of the question, anyway. You know what I think?"

"Yes. You've told me five or six times already."

"I'll tell you a seventh then, because you're not listening. I think this is just the Mossad's way of letting Josh know they're watching him. I bet the three of them will be here when we get back from the doctor's."

"I hope you're right."

But I hope I'm wrong. The more I think about it, the more I realize Josh might be safer if he spent a few weeks in a Tel Aviv jail. Though I don't entirely trust the Israelis, I trust Harold Anthony far less, and the longer Joshua goes without seeing him, the better the chance they will never meet at all.

We get to Dr. Leisner's office quite early. I'm expecting a long and dull wait — certain that Israeli doctors run far behind schedule just like doctors at home, but to my surprise the nurse calls Maria at precisely five after three. I start to follow her back into the examining rooms, but the nurse will have none of it.

"Dr. Leisner prefers to see his patients alone," she says. "We'll call you back for a talk later."

"But I'm her husband."

"Husbands are often a problem."

"But I'm a doctor, too. An M.D. I mean."

"M.D. husbands are *always* a problem. Please sit down."

Back in the reception area half of the magazines are in Hebrew and the NetV crashes continually. I can't use my own computer because the Mossad has it, and an oncologist's waiting room is not the place to make small talk with other patients and their families. So I get my long, dull wait after all.

At four thirty-five the nurse walks out and motions for me to follow.

With no distractions, every minute in the waiting room has increased my certainty that I'm going to hear dreadful news. But when I walk back into the good doctor's private office, one look at Maria sets me at ease. She's smiling and relaxed, although she still looks tired and pale. I sit down beside her and she pats my hand.

Dr. Leisner comes in after me and sits at his desk. He's a healthy-looking sort himself; tanned, slim and in his early forties, just bald enough to seem intellectual. He has a neat well-trimmed beard with no sideburns, and his entire effect is almost a caricature of Hollywood's idea of a gifted foreign physician. He shuffles a few papers and then looks at me sadly.

"I wish I had better news," he says.

"What do you mean?" I ask, looking over at Maria. She's still smiling, but for the first time I detect a rueful edge to her expression, like a little girl caught with her hand in the cookie jar.

"As I've already told your wife," he continues, "I don't think a second round of treatment will do much good. It might buy an extra two or three months, but they wouldn't be pleasant ones."

"I don't understand."

"I'm going to die, Peter," Maria says. "Of course you are too, but the doctor here thinks I'll be going a lot sooner."

Her voice has the tone of someone talking about the imminent demise of a goldfish. For a second I wonder if it's all just a bizarre joke, then a wave of denial strikes.

"What do you mean!" I sputter, "they can treat leukemia now! Nobody at home says you're going to die!"

"Peter, my doctor at home has never been exactly optimistic. I just asked her to put a good face on things until she was completely sure."

"But there are at least twenty new drugs for leukemia. Why won't one of those work? Just what did you find in an hour-and-a-half that convinced you there's nothing to be done?"

A flash of annoyance flits through Leisner's eyes, then is quickly suppressed. He seems to weigh his next words carefully.

"Dr. Lunsford, you must have noticed that your wife's treatment has been somewhat . . . shall we say . . . old fashioned."

"So?"

"This hasn't been the fault of your wife's physician — it's just that there really wasn't anything else to try."

"I don't understand."

"I think you don't want to understand; I wouldn't want to either, if I were in your position. But as a doctor, you know that leukemia is a catch-all term for all sorts of blood malignancies. You know these new drugs aren't drugs at all — they're genetic therapies for blood cells with known defects, we just call them drugs out of long habit. Each treatment has been tailored to correct the particular genetic error causing the malignancy. Some sorts of leukemia are more common than others, and naturally those were the first ones that scientists targeted. Your wife's leukemia is extremely unusual; in fact I've never seen a blood malignancy quite like it. At the moment there's no genetic therapy that fits."

"Then someone should find one!"

"Dr. Lunsford, if you think rationally you'll understand that's impossible. It would take a research team working full tilt for five or six months just to make a start, and even then, since your wife's case is to my knowledge unique . . ."

He doesn't finish, but he doesn't have to. He was about to say that even if Maria could be kept alive long enough for someone to find a cure, no bio-tech firm could spend millions to save one patient.

"Are you sure no one's ever seen this type of leukemia before?" I ask.

"Dr. Lunsford, I did two things in my hour and a half today — I had my nurse draw blood, and then I bumped your wife's sample to the head of the line at the hospital lab. The technician there found clear evidence that the leukemia is coming back. They were willing to analyze the sample immediately because your wife's case is so unusual. But I've spent a lot of time on this. When I got Mrs. Lunsford's records three days ago I found none of the usual DNA markers for leukemia, so I sent the information to several of my colleagues to see if they knew anything I didn't. No one did. We discussed running new tests to try and find precisely what genetic error is expressed in the cancerous cells, but of course that would be far worse than looking for a needle in a haystack — statistically the problem is enormous, and even if we found the defective gene we'd have no treatment ready to correct it."

"Did you see any abnormalities in the genome segments analyzed in the U.S?"

"Of course we saw abnormalities. Everyone shows a few abnormalities, even when you analyze random parts of the code. But the human genome is far from completely understood — we may have mapped it but we still have no idea what much of it actually does. A great deal of it apparently does nothing."

"What the good doctor is saying is that any more work will be a waste of time," Maria says. She stirs in her seat as if ready to leave.

"Did anyone have any hunches?" I persist.

An odd look passes over his face, and for a moment I think he's about to lie and say no. But apparently the hunch was so interesting he's dying to mention it to someone, even a grieving husband.

"One of the older doctors did say something," he finally admits.

"What?" I growl.

"According to him, one of the abnormalities was in a part of the genome easily affected by retroviruses — back in the early bio-tech days a retrovirus was often used to . . ."

"I know all about that."

"Well, anyway, this older doctor said the abnormality looked like something you might have seen, oh, in a bio-tech warfare lab back at the turn of the century . . ." Leisner grinds to a halt, looking a bit guilty — this is not a discussion he ought to be having with a terminal patient and her husband, and he knows it. He's probably wondering why I've been so persistent.

"Dr. Lunsford," he says after an uneasy silence, "your wife and I were discussing additional treatment, and I do have some recommendations."

"I thought there was nothing you could do."

"There's nothing we can do to change the outcome, but I can recommend several drugs to make the disease less debilitating. I've already written a prescription for one and had it sent over; you can pick it up on your way out. It should help with the exhaustion. And I'll be in touch with your doctor in the States, Mrs. Lunsford, and she can discuss some of my other recommendations with you there. I understand you're only in Israel for a short visit."

"Yes," Maria says.

"I was hoping to meet your son. I'm surprised he didn't come with you."

"He was unavoidably detained," I say.

"Give him my regards," the good doctor says. "And Mrs. Lunsford, I'll be praying for you. I'm sorry that's all I can do."

The last sentence seems familiar, and as we wait for a cab outside I remember where I'd heard it before. Another good doctor said that to me a few days before they buried Joe.

Maria cries easily over other people's troubles, but on the way back to Martha's she sits beside me dry-eyed, quietly staring out at the unfamiliar city. She turns to me once and says:

"I've always wanted to be unique. I guess you should be careful what you wish for."

It could be a line straight out of some ancient Humphrey Bogart movie, and it brings tears stinging to my eyes. I'm trying hard not to lose it completely, trying desperately to hold off my despair with rage. When Leisner described the nature of Maria's leukemia, there was suddenly no doubt in my mind that Harold Anthony was behind it — that soon he would succeed in killing my wife the same way he killed Joe's mother. At his behest the Clinic doctors must have planted a defect in Maria's marrow cells back in '99, and a once-rare carcinogen has now become common enough to set those cells to their deadly work. I don't care whether Anthony has provided the second part of this equation by accident or design — he arranged the first part thirty-three years ago; and to me he's responsible as surely as if he put a knife through Maria's heart.

For a fleeting instant Joshua comes to mind: what he would think of the plan sprouting malignantly in my brain, how he would say that my hatred was too great a burden to put on any one man's head. But oh, Joshua! Anthony has become more than a man to me — his name alone is a talisman of evil.

If only I could be Jesus on the cross, and Anthony the thief, destined but for my mercy to an eternity of fire, blistered flesh and pitchfork-wielding demons. I'd wait until Harold the Once-Great looked in his agony towards me, until he pleaded: "Will you remember me when you come into your kingdom?"

And then, I would consign him to the lowest pit of damnation.

Chapter 9

"Later, he was asked by the Pharisees when the kingdom of God was coming, and he gave them this reply:

"The kingdom of God never comes by watching for it. Men cannot say, 'Look, here it is,' or 'There it is,' for the kingdom of God is inside you."

— *The Gospel of Luke,* 17.20

We walk in through Martha's door, and Joshua, John, and Matthew are sitting at the kitchen table, eating sweet rolls. It's as if my afternoon prediction has conjured them out of the coffeepot.

"Joshua!" Maria exclaims, and wraps her arms around his shoulders. I'm left with John and Matthew.

"So, how long did they hold you?" I ask.

"We got back about four o'clock," John answers through a mouthful of sweet roll.

"Did they question you all that time?"

"Mostly they just left us in a locked room. Matthew was getting worried, but I've been in worse jails."

I look curiously at Matthew. He smiles wryly, then asks, "Is it my imagination, or do you guys get arrested a lot?"

"No, it's not your imagination," I reply, just as Maria finally releases Joshua. Quietly, in a voice not meant to be heard by anyone else, he asks her what the doctor said.

"He didn't tell me a thing I didn't know already," Maria answers gaily, which is literally true, though it functions as an utter lie. Joshua seems to be fooled, however, and he asks me in an easy voice:

"By the way, you didn't have anything . . . sensitive . . . on your computer, did you?"

"If you mean my latest book, no I didn't. I've been writing it on my old Mac back in Atlanta, remember? Anthony's e-mail was on there, that's probably the worst of it. Was it really as routine as John says? Your visit to the Mossad, that is."

"The Mossad and the CIA, I think. They did intercept our e-mails. John and I were sending each other messages about the Middle East, trying to get them through by calling the Middle East the Muddle Feast or Israel Ishmael, things like that. They thought it might be some sort of code."

"A little obvious for a code."

"That's what they concluded, too, except for one agent who insisted we were trying to look incompetent."

"We are so cunning," John cuts in.

The festive atmosphere is more than I can stomach. "I have a headache," I tell them, "I'm going into the living room." Then I walk out of the kitchen and sit on a ratty old wicker couch, away from the three prodigals. There's an overhead light and a small lamp, but I leave both off, since tears are suddenly coursing down my cheeks. But I'm alone for only a few moments. Joshua has followed me.

"Peter, is something wrong?" he asks.

I don't answer — I just sit there blubbering.

"Was it the doctor's visit?" Joshua persists. I look back at him and say bluntly:

"Your mother's going to die. The doctor gives her about two or three months."

"She just said she was fine. Why would she hide it from me?"

"She doesn't want to distract you from your work. And she wasn't lying. She just said the doctor didn't tell her anything new. Apparently she's known there's not much hope for months now."

"And there's nothing the doctors can do?"

"According to that jerk we went to see," I spit out, "all anyone can offer her are prayers."

Joshua looks sadly at me, but his voice is oddly unaffected as he says:

"I'll be praying for her, too, Peter. Remember that."

But I don't want his prayers. What I want is a gun.

Later that night, I lie awake on my futon. Joshua can't sleep either — he's in the front room reading or praying or something similarly useless. Maria, on the other hand, is resting peacefully beside me. She hasn't seemed at all upset since we got back from the doctor's, in fact later in the evening she sat down happily with her sightseeing brochures. I asked her how she could possibly play tourist at a time like this, and she cheerily told me that it was the only time she had, so she was going to make the best of it, war and leukemia be damned.

But Harold Anthony is the only thing I want to see damned, and for that I need a gun. If I was back in the States there'd be no problem — Americans love their firearms. But the state of Israel is more circumspect: the army and militia may be armed to the teeth but the government keeps careful track of weapons; I imagine because they don't want the in-resident Muslims to get their hands on any more than they already have.

I decide the most likely source for a gun is an American soldier, one who's brought along a pistol or two in addition to his official arsenal. If what I've read about previous wars is true, there'll be quite a few enlisted men hiding something small, metallic, and deadly from their officers. Or if I'm really lucky, something small, ceramic and deadly: a gun that won't set off any metal detectors. And I have just what's needed to tempt a good ol' boy soldier into bending a few regs — since I was worried about paying Dr. Leisner, I took an unusual amount of cash with me on this trip.

But finding this hypothetical soldier may not be easy. I imagine the American troops here aren't horribly accessible; those functioning as police will probably be under orders not to mix with civilians, and if some are actually here as an invasion force they're probably hidden away on an army base. I finally decide to walk up to a group guarding a corner and simply ask for directions. With luck, they'll then explain that they're American soldiers, not Israelis, which will give me a chance to boast that I'm an American, too, by gawd! Perhaps I'll get gunned down first, mistaken for a mad Arab bomber, but I think there's a better-than-slim chance I'll get a few words alone with some lowly private. I'll probably have to pull this stunt several times before I meet the right lowly private, but I can think of nothing better.

And step two? I'll figure that out when and if step one succeeds.

I wake up late the next morning, alone on my futon. From the front of the house I hear voices and smell breakfast — so I swing the door shut and get dressed in the back room. When I walk into the kitchen I find that everyone else has eaten, but they're all sitting around the big table, except Matthew and Martha, who are cheerily washing the dishes. Josh is sitting by Maria, covering her hand with his.

"You almost slept through breakfast," Martha says. "Fix yourself a plate."

I get some eggs and coffee while the others discuss plans for the day. Joshua has been e-mailing Anthony since we got to Israel, but Anthony hasn't replied.

"He'll get in touch soon," Josh says when John asks how long we'll wait to hear something.

"But what if he doesn't?" John persists hopefully.

"He will," Josh answers.

"My son, the prophet," Maria jokes, and John stiffens. Eric Schroeder took pride in his rationalism, but John Baxter seems a little less certain that the world operates on a strictly scientific basis.

"So you don't think we'll be going to Jerusalem soon?" I ask.

"Not for a few days," Josh replies.

"So I have time to do a little sightseeing?" Maria asks.

"If a war doesn't break out first," John says.

"That's not going to happen just yet," says Joshua the prophet. "Maybe it won't happen at all."

"And you'll come keep us company?"

"I can't today, Mother," Josh says. "Martha has asked me to come speak at her synagogue. Not at a service, of course — I don't think they're that reformed."

"Not quite," Martha says.

"You could call it a lecture, although I've been told all my lectures end up sounding like sermons. Anyway, it's this evening, and I have to think about what I'm going to say. I'll be glad to go with you tomorrow."

"All right," Maria says, "Peter and I will just do a little trip today."

Maria's little trip turns out to be fairly ambitious. Tel Aviv boasts a great many Roman ruins, interesting and (I hope) less flooded with awe-struck American tourists than the famous attractions near Jerusalem. We head off to see what's advertised as the remains of "a remarkably well-preserved Roman bathhouse, theater, and upper-class residence."

It's ungodly hot, and when we get a cab its air conditioner puts out a feeble breeze that smells like the men's room in a sardine factory. Luckily the trip takes less than a half hour, and I pay the cabbie off, rejecting his offer to wait for a "very small" fee.

"It 'ees very hard to get a cab out here," the man says in Arabic-accented English, "and the fee 'ees really very small."

I glance around. Three other cabs sit idle in the little parking lot. Of course, they may be waiting for somebody else, also for a "very small" fee, but I can see a city bus stop thirty yards away. The city bus I rode on with Joshua had air conditioning considerably colder and less fragrant than this cab's. "I'll pass," I say, and walk off to catch up with Maria.

"You call what you gave him a tip?" she asks.

"You call that a cab?" I answer.

There's a small museum that goes with the ruins, and we head there first to cool off. The displays are impressive, featuring artifacts dug up in the area and pocket computer commentaries available in Hebrew and English. Also French, Italian, Spanish, Portuguese, Japanese, and Chinese. "No Arabic?" I ask the attendant, and she looks at me quizzically before asking, "Do you speak Arabic?"

"No," I answer, "I was just wondering."

"We have Arabic commentaries on paper," she says with a touch of disdain, leaving me to wonder if only Jewish Israelis and tourists visit the place, or if Muslim Israelis rarely have pocket computers, or if they're afraid that Arabs won't return the cheap little flash drives the commentaries come on.

I'm more impressed with the museum than the ruins. The only things standing are a few columns, and the overall effect is like wandering through a life-sized, bas-relief blueprint.

"What do you think?" Maria asks me, as we stroll around outside.

"It's okay," I say vaguely. "What do you think?"

"I don't know. Somehow I was expecting something a little less . . . ruinous."

Which strikes me as quite funny, so I stop and give her a quick and very sweaty hug.

"I'm getting tired," she says. "Let's head back."

Inside the museum, the attendant helps me call a cab company, which promises to have a driver there in ten minutes. But twenty minutes go by with no cab, and by then the attendant is gone on her lunch break, and the lone guard refuses to help. I try to call a cab myself, but succeed only in getting busy signals and error messages. Then I go out and try to hail a cab, but there are none to be seen. Feeling a touch desperate, I come back inside, pull out my computer, and look up the city bus routes. As best I can tell, we can get within a few minutes' walk of Martha's with only one transfer. If nothing else, we can take the bus back into the city and hail a cab there.

Forty-five minutes later, Maria turns to me and growls, "We're lost. Admit it."

We're sitting in the back of a very crowded, very old bus. Apparently Tel Aviv saves the best buses for the airport run, because this one has no more air-conditioning than a camel.

"We are not lost!" I insist. "Trips always seem to take longer in a strange city."

Maria's not convinced. "I was watching the scenery all the way from Martha's to the museum, and let me tell you, this doesn't look anything like the neighborhood near Martha's."

"We haven't gotten to that neighborhood yet."

"Then show me where we are on that little map of yours."

I have my pocket computer open on my lap, displaying a map from the Tel Aviv public transit website. As the bus bounces around a corner, I point out what I think is the area near Martha's on the computer's fold-out screen.

"That's Martha's," I say, and then move my finger down the screen about an inch, "and I think we're about here."

"And why do you think we're about there? I can see the GPS isn't working, but have you seen a cross-street that matches up with something on that thing?"

"I thought I did."

"How long ago?"

"About ten minutes."

Maria sits back and mutters something in Spanish. I'm not as good at the language as Joe was, a fact she takes advantage of often.

"What was that?" I ask. She repeats it, still in Spanish.

"In English," I insist.

"I said you're suffering from male directional arrogance."

"I'll bet you did."

"Where's that piece of paper with Martha's address?" she asks. I pull it from my wallet, and she takes it and stands.

"Where are you going?" I ask.

"To see if we're on the right bus."

When Maria finally gets a chance to talk to the driver, he looks at the slip of paper with Martha's address, frowns, and then shrugs his shoulders. After a few moments' thought, he says something to Maria, after which she also frowns, then waves her hand at me to come forward. We get off at the next stop. Ten minutes later and we're still there, sitting on a bench waiting for yet another bus, so we can retrace the five or six miles we've come in the wrong direction. At least the bench is enclosed — surrounded on three sides by a shelter made of brushed steel and semi-opaque Plexiglas.

"When the next bus gets here," Maria says, "I'm going to show the driver the address first thing and ask him to tell us when to get off."

"All right," I say sheepishly. I'm half expecting Maria to add a few more caustic comments, but she doesn't. She's pale and very tired.

"What do you think about this neighborhood?" I ask.

"The driver said it was safe. He said most of Tel Aviv's safe."

Perhaps, but I'm still uneasy. The houses and apartment blocks around us look as pale and tired as Maria: paint peeling, litter scattered on the street. Further down the block I can see soldiers guarding the next bus stop.

"I wonder why they're guarding *that* one?" I ask.

"The driver said they're guarding it because that's where the orthos got on."

"Orthos?"

"Orthodox Jews. You know, the ones that dress funny."

"My, aren't you mastering the lingo. So which bus stop is this?"

"The one where most of the Arabs get on. The driver suggested we walk down to the other one."

"So why are we here?"

"Because that stop's wasn't on his route and I'm tired of walking. This is Tel Aviv, not Jerusalem. This isn't the part of Israel where Arabs throw rocks at the police."

Her tone is slightly panicky, and I realize she's not sure she can make it down the street. Which is why I don't mention several obvious flaws in her logic: such as the fact that somebody thought the situation tense enough to require that soldiers guard bus-stops.

"Why do the orthodox Jews live next door to the Arabs?" I wonder aloud.

"Martha told me the orthos have big families and they don't make a lot of money. Which also describes the Arabs. Maybe they both end up in the cheaper neighborhoods."

Which makes a sort of perverted sense. Of course circumstances would conspire to put the most radically Jewish Jews in close proximity to poor Arabs, usually the most radically Muslim Muslims. After all, we live in the best of all possible worlds. I glance nervously at the graffiti on a nearby wall. Stars of David abound, along with the clenched fist symbol of the United Arab Alliance. Many of the fists and all of the stars have been painted over with crude red or black strips, underlined by what I imagine are curses in Arabic and Hebrew.

"Are you sure you don't want to walk to that other bus stop?" I ask.

Maria looks around one last time. “I’m so tired,” she says in a sad voice, and leans her head on my shoulder.

Five minutes later we’re no longer alone. A woman in a chador walks around the corner of the bus shelter and sees us sitting on the bench. She stops, surprised, and retreats to lean against the building behind us.

“The bus must be coming soon,” Maria says.

Which is probably true, since the Arab woman is soon joined by three others, as well as two men. Each one peeks around the corner of the shelter, gives us a good look, and then retreats to stand behind; the men keeping their distance from the women like good Muslims. I can see them clearly through a gap in the Plexiglas.

“I don’t feel good about this,” I mutter.

“Don’t like being a minority, eh?” Maria says.

“Not today, I don’t.”

Just then I hear a bus approaching and I look up hopefully. But this bus is heading up a cross street about twenty yards away — a different route than our bus took. When it comes to our street it heads in the wrong direction. I can see its passengers clearly, mostly sad-looking men in black, several of whom stare at us as the bus makes its turn and then pulls away.

“Shit,” Maria says wearily.

The bus slows to a halt at the next stop, and ten or fifteen of the men in black suits and old-fashioned hats get off. They mill around for a few moments, and then, to my surprise, six of them start walking toward us. Glancing through the Plexiglas, I see the Arab men standing just behind the bench, facing the approaching Jews in an uneasy phalanx. The women move further back, tense, set looks on what little I can see of their faces.

In less than two minutes the Jewish men arrive. They look uneasily at the Arabs standing behind the bus stop, and then one of them strides up to Maria and me and says loudly:

“You’re Americans aren’t you? You need to leave this bus stop at once. It’s not safe here.”

“And why isn’t it safe here?” another voice barks. Its owner is a tall, slender Arab dressed in blue jeans and a light cotton shirt. The Jewish man doesn’t answer him; instead he speaks to us again.

“The Arabs hate Americans because they are our allies. You are in a very dangerous situation.”

“I don’t hate Americans,” the Arab man says. “I like nothing better than to show them we are not all terrorists. Maybe then they'll quit supporting fools like you. Have we bothered you, sir?"

"No, not at all," I say.

"And you, American lady?"

"Certainly not," Maria says.

"This woman is my mother's age," the Arab man continues. "What sort of pigs do you think we are, that we would bother her?" He takes a step closer. The Jewish man moves in as well, and then, to my utter surprise, leans down and grabs Maria's arm and pulls her to her feet.

"You must come with us!" he says and begins to walk away, dragging Maria with him.

"I am a Sufi, a man of peace," the Arab barks at him, "but for you I could make an exception!" The other men are behind him now, glaring at the black-hatted Jews. The Jewish man pauses in his abduction of my wife and finally deigns to speak directly to the Arab.

"The Temple will rise again, and your prophet's house will crumble into dust like the walls of Jericho!"

I don't really see who throws the first rock. It's not the Arab who spoke — he turns away just as the stones begin to fly, a weary expression on his face. It's not the young Jew either, he's too busy pulling Maria up the hill. Just as I catch up with them, Maria raises her foot and brings her heel down hard on his instep. If she'd been in her prime he wouldn't have walked for an hour, and even in her weakened state the maneuver is effective enough to let me come up and shove him to the pavement. Then I take Maria's arm and we head up the hill towards the bus stop with the soldiers. For half a minute we're ahead of the Jewish men, who've stayed behind to trade rocks with the Arabs. But more Arabs start coming into the street, as if called by magic, and the orthos quickly decide to give up the fight. In a matter of seconds they've passed us and are headed back to the safety of their own neighborhood.

None of the rocks seem to be aimed at Maria and me — but as the Jewish men pull ahead of us some of the stones fall short. We're about thirty yards from the soldiers when Maria stumbles and falls. I bend down beside her and see a small cut on her forehead.

"I'm all right," she says, struggling to get up.

"Like hell you are. Did you get hit by a rock?"

"I don't know. I think I just fainted. I'm so tired."

"Great." I look up, half expecting to see a mob of angry Arabs closing in. Instead, I see soldiers breaking out riot shields and heading down the street. They sweep past, and right behind them come two others, one carrying a small first-aid kit.

"Are you all right, Ma'am?" the first asks with a decidedly Southern accent. I've found my Americans.

"I just fainted," Maria says. "They weren't throwing rocks at us."

"Looked like rocks to me," the second answers.

"I mean they weren't trying to hit us," Maria insists. "They were throwing them at the Jewish men."

"Don't you worry, Ma'am," the first one says, "we'll take care of them Arabs. A little tear gas'll do 'em good. Let us help you get back to our post."

They gently take hold of Maria's arms, help her to her feet, and halfway carry her back up to their "post." I follow uselessly behind.

"Goddamn Arabs," the first medic says as he puts a bandage on the small scrape on Maria's head. "Throwin' rocks at a woman. We ought to shoot 'em all."

"They didn't start it," Maria says, "and I hit my head on a rock on the ground. I fainted."

The first medic isn't listening. "Of course they're all gonna' fry someday soon. The judgment's comin.' "

"And what about your Jewish friends?" Maria says testily.

"They're gonna' see the light in the last days, Ma'am, you watch. It's in the Bible. But these Islams, they're in for it. You wait and see." Maria shakes her head wearily and looks off down the street, too tired to argue. I'm pretty angry myself, and I almost take up the cause for her, encouraged by the disgusted expression on the face of the second medic during his fellow soldier's spiel. But then I remember the gun. I move a few steps away and beckon the first medic.

"I want to thank you boys," I tell him in an overdone Southern accent. "We came to see the Holy Land; we hoped we might even be raptured from here. But I don't want to get killed by a bunch of dirty Arabs before that happens."

"Just doin' my job, sir," the medic says.

"I wish I coulda' brought some protection, but they kinda' frown on takin' guns on airplanes."

The soldier nods his head in agreement.

"You wouldn't happen to know where I could get myself a little handgun, would you?" I continue in a low voice, "I can pay a good price," I add, "seein' as how guns are kinda' in short supply here."

The soldier looks at me, astonished.

"Shit, Mister!" he hisses. "You think I'm crazy? You know how many rules I'd be breakin' if I got you a gun? I'd spend the rest of my life in the stockade. What if you took that gun and *shot* somebody? Shit!" He moves a step away and sways back and forth, trying to come to a decision. Then, eyeing me as if I'm a madman, he sidles over to one of the officers. They talk for a moment, then the soldier points at me. The officer looks, then shakes his head. I wait uneasily, expecting the soldier to come back with a pair of handcuffs. But nothing happens. Wearing a surly expression, the medic returns and takes one more look at Maria's bandage, then goes off to some other pressing military business. A moment later, the officer walks over.

"Can I see your passport sir?" he asks. I hand it over. He looks at it carefully, then stares at me for a moment.

"I'm going to have one of my men drive you to your hotel, sir," he finally says. "Where are you and your wife staying?"

"Actually, we're not at a hotel," I answer, sans accent. "We're staying with an Israeli friend." The officer looks a little surprised, but after a moment he digests this unexpected news. "I see," he says. "You have the address, I hope." I pull it out of my front pocket, and he hands it to a soldier who walked over with him, but had been standing respectfully a couple of paces behind. "Can you walk, Ma'am?" the officer asks Maria. She nods and gets slowly to her feet. The officer takes her arm, and we head towards a HumVee parked on the sidewalk. Then he helps Maria into the backseat, closes the door behind her, and stands beside me as the driver walks around and hops in on the other side.

"You been following the news, sir?" the officer asks.

"Some."

"Situation's getting kind of tense over here."

"I've noticed. But the situation's often tense over here."

"Yep." He has a Southwestern drawl, and deep in his brain probably sees himself as a new millennium cowboy, a misplaced paladin of the Western plains. He sidles closer. "But just between you and me, sir, all hell is fixin' to break loose now. You're right to think you might need some protection." And then, like a miracle, there's a sudden heavy weight in my trousers pocket. I don't put my hand down to feel it, afraid that if I do this apparition may somehow disappear.

"What do I owe you?" I ask hesitantly.

"Nothin'. I was keeping it for a throwaway. I figured there'd be less questions if any Arabs we shot turned out to be armed. But turns out nobody's gonna' be askin' questions — we're gonna' be shootin' Arabs left and right in a few more days. You need it more than I do." He opens the door, and I hop in awkwardly beside Maria.

"God bless you mister," the officer says, and shuts the door behind us.

And so I ride home, a lump of tension in my chest almost as big as the lump in my pants pocket, a lump which luckily happens to be on the side away from Maria. I ought to be ecstatic — I've gotten my gun, gotten it with almost supernatural ease. But when the driver pulls to a stop in front of Martha's house, an old saying runs through my head, something to the effect that when God is a little angry with you, He thwarts your heart's desires.

And when He's really pissed, He lets you have them right away.

Chapter 10

"In the Christian *Book of Revelation* Jesus's disciple John called Rome the Whore of Babylon, and warned that this mighty city would someday fall before the power of Christ. And in a way John's prophecy was fulfilled: in three hundred years pagan Rome was no more, and the Emperor Constantine worshipped Christ, and through Christ, the God of the Jews.

"Of course many Christians take issue with this reading of *Revelation*. They say the book is a prophecy of *our* time, and they curse as Babylon whichever nation has most recently aroused their displeasure. But today's Pharisees always overlook one modern state when they bestow this dubious honor. Like Rome and Babylon of old, this country is the pre-eminent power of its day. It is wealthy, corrupt, and failing of its promise. Once it was the hope of the world, but its morals have spiraled downward. Thousands have drowned or starved to pay the price of its tinsel enjoyments, and in a few days thousands more may be slaughtered more directly by its soldiers, who have been lied to by their leaders and sent to Israel, ostensibly to 'keep the peace.' And Israel, a land whose name means 'those who have wrestled with God and won,' may soon be at this New Babylon's side.

"Notice that I say 'may be.' The United States may have become the new Babylon, and its leaders may tell us their plan is the sure road to survival, but I tell you mere survival is no worthy goal for any true child of God. You have a choice. Embrace the new Babylon, and do what is safe; or risk the love and mercy of God, and do what is right."

— Joshua Grant, in a speech at the
Bethel Reform Synagogue, Tel Aviv

When we walk in the door, Martha clucks like an old mother hen, John looks worried and important, and Matthew hangs back, wordlessly waiting to help. Only Joshua seems unconcerned. He stands in a corner, eyes fixed on me, as if he already senses I have something to hide.

"Where have you been!" Martha says. "I knew we shouldn't have let you go. Even Tel Aviv isn't safe right now. Oh my goodness! What happened to your head?"

"It's nothing," Maria answers, heading wearily for a chair.

"Are you sure?" John asks. "Maybe I better take a look at it."

"Peter already did," she answers. "He's a doctor too, remember?"

"Where did the bandage come from?"

"An American medic put it on."

"How'd you hurt yourself?"

"I fell down."

"How'd you fall down?"

"The usual way, John!" She pauses. "Oh, you'll find out anyway. We were near a little fight some Jews and Arabs had."

"A little fight!" Martha exclaims.

"A civic disagreement," Maria says. "But nobody was trying to hurt *us!*"

"What about you, Peter?" Joshua asks. "Are you all right?"

"I'm fine," I growl. "Why do you ask?"

"I don't know. You just look . . ." He pauses. "You look tense."

"Of course I look tense. We were in the middle of a mob throwing rocks."

"It wasn't a mob!" Maria snaps.

"What would you call it?"

"Oh I don't know!" She looks around the room. "Really, it was nothing. Don't worry about us, we're fine."

"Well, what happened?" John persists.

"You tell them, Peter," Maria says.

I look around, wondering if I should make a trip to the bathroom, then try and hide the gun on my way back.

"Come on, Peter," John persists.

"It was nothing, really," I say, echoing Maria in my haste to get the story done. "We went out to see that old Roman bathhouse, and we couldn't find a cab, so we decided to take the bus instead." I pause, expecting Maria to tell how I stiffed the odoriferous cabbie. But for once she keeps her silence.

"Anyway," I continue, "we missed our stop or something — and the bus driver said we'd have to catch a different bus. He let us out at a bus stop that was mostly used by Arabs, and some Jewish men decided to rescue us, even though we didn't need rescuing. Somebody started throwing rocks and we got caught in the middle."

"What's this about American medics?" John asked.

"There were some American soldiers at the next bus stop up the street. They broke up the fight, put a bandage on Maria's head, and gave us a ride home."

"And that's all that happened?" Joshua asks, staring intently at me.

"Isn't that enough? Listen, you'll have to excuse me."

* * *

When I come out of the bathroom, I'm dismayed to find Josh waiting.

"Peter," he says, "I want to ask you something."

"Ask away," I say, still anxious to hide the gun.

"I want to ask you in private."

I sigh and head towards the bedroom. When we get there he follows me in and quietly closes the door.

"Peter," he says, "I read your 'book,' so I know how Joe's mother died. And I know you think Harold Anthony had something to do with it."

"Having read my book," I answer testily, "don't you think so, too?"

"I'm not sure. I only have your version of events."

"Well, I'm sure. And Joe was sure, too."

"You think Anthony's responsible for Mother's cancer, don't you?"

My rising anger is tempered only slightly by the weight of the gun in my pocket. "Of course I think he's responsible!" I snap.

"You have no proof, you know. Cancer rates have gone up threefold in the last forty years. It could be a coincidence."

"Do you really believe that?" I hiss. "Are you really going to defend that fucking monster? Don't you have any more love for your mother than that?"

"I love everyone, my mother included."

"You're supposed to love *her* a hell of a lot more than everyone! Can't you understand that?"

"I don't know that I do."

I want to punch him right in his sanctimonious face. What good is his love if it's the same for everyone?

"Peter," Joshua continues, a veritable Sisyphus of virtue, "why are you cultivating this obsessive hatred of Harold Anthony? He's more to be pitied than anything else."

"Pitied? What the hell for?"

"Can't you see the fear he lives under? All of his talk about God's love . . . he doesn't believe it. At heart Anthony believes the universe is arbitrary and evil, and he thinks that God is too."

"Does that justify what he did to Maria?"

"What you think he did to Maria. Besides, I didn't come in here for Anthony's sake, or Maria's sake, or even my own sake. I came to help you."

"Help me do what?"

"Help you remember to love your enemies."

"I'm afraid love is the last emotion I feel for Harold Anthony right now."

"Well, if you can't feel love, try pity. Think of all you've had in your life: a good marriage, the love of parents, friends, and family. Has Anthony had any of that?"

"If not, he has only himself to blame."

"No one has only himself to blame; no one has only himself to credit. Think of what your hatred is doing to you, if nothing else."

I stare at my stepson. Why I am suddenly the beneficiary of this maudlin sermon? With a start it comes to me: he knows about the gun; he knows what I plan to do with it. I look into his eyes dreading and hoping for some confirmation. But Joshua's eyes seem fixed on some other world, and I cannot bear to hold his gaze.

"All right," I say, "I'll think about it. Is there anything else?"

"No," Joshua replies sadly, then turns and walks off down the hall.

I wait a few seconds to make sure he's not coming back, and then yank my suitcase from the closet and unlatch it, looking for a good hiding place. A small, zippered toiletries compartment is the best I can do. I take the gun out of my pocket. It's not ceramic, but otherwise it's a passable assassin's weapon, a small .22-caliber pistol with a short barrel and a five-shot clip. The safety is on, which is fortunate, because the good lieutenant has given it to me loaded. I don't waste much time examining it, I just roll it up in a pair of boxer shorts and cram underwear and gun into my suitcase. I hear a sound behind me, and realize that in my haste I haven't shut the bedroom door. John is standing in the doorway, but if he wonders what I'm doing he doesn't give any sign.

"Did he tell you?" he asks.

"Tell me what?"

"That Anthony called while you were gone. We're going to Jerusalem tomorrow. We're going on the show the day after that."

Later that evening, after the other four have fallen asleep, John and I try to persuade Joshua not to go on Anthony's show. I argue with much heat and little hope, but John, though he claims to be on my side, speaks with an odd lack of conviction, as though he half agrees with Joshua.

"Listen," I say near the end of our debate, "the people in Anthony's Jerusalem audience are his hard-core followers, the sort of zealots who torched Valerie Weselesky's VW with her in it. And from what John says about that 'little talk' you gave at Martha's synagogue today, I bet the Israeli government and our own won't lift a finger to protect you. You can bet the Mossad or the CIA had somebody there."

"I know that," Josh replies calmly.

"Then let me ask you one more time: Why are you doing this? Are you trying to get yourself killed?"

Josh says nothing, but his expression slips, and the ghost of a little boy I once loved stares out, sad and dreadfully afraid.

"You're hoping they'll do something to you, aren't you?" I ask.

He straightens; the hardness returns to his eyes.

"I'm not hoping for that at all, Peter. That Anthony will see some sense is what I'm hoping for."

"And what are the odds of that?"

"Not good. But I have to try. I have to make it clear to him and everybody watching where he's headed, and where we're all going with him."

"And how will getting yourself killed make that clear?"

"I'm hoping it won't come to that. But if it does, who knows what my death will accomplish? Who could have foreseen the consequences of Thomas à Becket's murder, or even Jesus's own? All I know is that I have to go."

"But . . ."

"You're acting like your Biblical namesake, Peter, so I'll act like mine. Go to bed and leave me alone."

So John and I head back towards the bedroom where Nicholas, Matthew, and Martha are already asleep. Maria is in Martha's bedroom — at Martha's insistence — sleeping on the one real mattress in the house. Joshua, meanwhile, is still out in the front room — reading or praying or whatever he often does in the lonely hours of the night. For some reason I have a mulish desire to actually outlast him, and I sit reading on my futon, the screen on my computer at its dimmest setting. But sometime before midnight my eyes slide closed and the next thing I know I'm awakened by a soft but persistent knocking.

Joshua beats me to the front door. The clock in the main room reads 4:45. I can't imagine who would come so early, but the knocker's identity surprises me nonetheless. He's one of the men who arrested Joshua: Major Levi, now bleary-eyed and tieless.

"Major Levi," Joshua says softly, "what a pleasant surprise."

"Listen," Levi says, stepping into the house, "we have about forty-five minutes if we're lucky, less if we're not. Dr. Grant, you must leave immediately."

"Leave?" Joshua asks. "Leave where? Tel Aviv? Israel? This house?"

"If only you *would* leave Israel! But I suppose there's little hope of that."

"No hope at all," Joshua replies.

"We've been reading all your e-mail, you know, and tapping the phone. You insist on going to Jerusalem and appearing on this maniac preacher's program?"

"Yes, I do."

"Then you must leave Tel Aviv immediately, so at least your blood will not be on our hands. This house is being watched — and when you leave for Jerusalem they are going to have you killed on the way. They'll make it look like an Arab extremist attack. Apparently that is why they wanted you to come to Israel in the first place, though please believe me; we did not know it when we approved your visa."

"Who are 'they'?" I ask.

"Your CIA, of course, egged on by this murdering war-monger, this fake, this President Armstrong! But most people in the Mossad want nothing to do with it, and even those too frightened to say anything are dropping hints that they would not be sorry to see you escape."

"And no one is watching the house right now?" Joshua says.

"I am supposed to be watching the house, myself and two others who are also disgusted with this plan. We hope to get you to Jerusalem before anyone else realizes you're gone."

"And what will happen to you and your friends?"

"At worst, we will be kicked out of the Mossad, which will bother me very little right now."

"Why are you doing this?"

"Something I read in one of your books, Mr. Grant. You said that sometimes there are only two choices: to be the criminal or the victim. And I thought: just this once, when the Palestinians say they want peace, we Israelis should be good *schlimazels* and believe them."

"And how do I figure into that equation?"

"Well," Levi laughs. "If Joshua Grant is dead, who will we blame if it all goes wrong?"

"Joshua," I say, "this man arrested you two days ago. You're going to trust him now?"

"Yes," Joshua says. "What do we need to do, Major?"

"How many are going with you to Jerusalem?"

"Five," Joshua says, "Peter here, John, Matt, Nicholas, and my mother."

"Why so many?"

"I need them. Don't ask me to explain."

"It's a good thing I arranged for two cars. My wife can drive you and your parents; your friends can go in the other car. Then I will go back on watch. My replacement gets here at 5:30, maybe sooner. He's a brown-nosed sort — it would be just like him to show up early. We must hurry."

When I wake Maria I don't give her Levi's full explanation, I just tell her that one faction in the Mossad wants to arrest Joshua again, and that another suggests we leave for Jerusalem immediately. When I see Martha in the hall I tell her the same story. She marches into the kitchen, and in the eight minutes or so it takes everyone to throw on some clothes she manages to brew some coffee, pour it in a thermos, and hand it to Joshua on his way out.

"Shalom, Dr. Grant," she says to him.

"Shalom to you, too, Martha," Josh replies.

"Miss Greenbaum, everybody," Levi says, "remember: I was never here. Dr. Grant planned to leave very early all along, right?"

"All right," Martha says, glowering. "But if I hear you've arrested him again, I'll remember your face, your name, and everything else. You can count on it."

Levi shakes his head, too tired and tense to argue, and we leave the house. Across the street, comically obvious, a parked car holds two men, slumped in attitudes of deep slumber.

Levi's wife and oldest son are parked about two blocks away. We get there with only one incident.

"Walk normally!" Levi hisses at me.

"How am I not walking normally?"

"You're . . . how does one say? . . . on your tippy toes!"

So I try to walk "normally," feeling as if I'm now slamming my heels into the pavement.

"That's worse," Levi says, disgusted. "Forget I said anything."

The cars are nondescript: two rental Toyotas. One is a convertible, its top raised. Joshua, Maria and I scramble into it; John, Nicholas, and Matthew are directed by Levi into the other. As soon as we hop into our car, Maria, in the front seat, leans over and pats the driver's hand.

"Mrs. Levi," she says, "I want to thank you. I know this must be dangerous for you."

"Thank my husband," she says tersely, "I told him not to bother. I think your son is going to get himself killed anyway." And then with a jerk she accelerates from the curb.

After that, conversation lags. Maria sits quietly, pursing her lips, probably trying to reconcile "your son is going to get himself killed anyway" with the story I told her before we left the house. Joshua stares out the window, sad eyes taking in the passing suburban landscape. It's left to me to think about practical matters.

"What happens next, Mrs. Levi?" I ask.

She doesn't answer immediately, but when we come to a stoplight she glances into the back seat. Her expression has softened a little.

"Dr. Grant is to go into hiding, but first he is to make a spectacle of himself."

"Why?"

"My husband's worst fear is that Dr. Grant will be killed and the murder will be blamed on Israeli Arabs or Israeli Jews. So we have arranged a little celebration when he comes into the city, with a few moderate Arabs and Jews doing the yelling, and we have invited a few sympathetic reporters. With luck, the celebration will make people suspicious if your CIA kills Dr. Grant and then tries to blame it on someone else. Also with luck, Dr. Grant can slip away before the celebration is noticed by one of the several dozen other groups that want him dead."

"Wouldn't it be safer if Joshua just went into hiding now?"

"Certainly. But if Dr. Grant wants to be safe, why does he preach inflammatory sermons in synagogues watched by the secret police? Why does he tell crazy Arab Imams that Allah will not be pleased with the way they treat women and Jews? Why does he expect huge, corrupt corporations to care about something besides money? Why did he not stay and run his little missions in India? Why does he not take the next plane home?"

"What if we don't like this plan?"

"Then I will stop the car and you can get out and take your chances. Is that what you want?"

Joshua awakes from his reverie. "No," he says, "your plan is excellent, Mrs. Levi. And I apologize for forgetting my manners. Thank you for your help. And may God bless you."

"God bless you too, Joshua Grant." She laughs. "You will need it."

I'm not really nervous until we come to our first checkpoint, about ten miles from the old city. Once one could pass from the "original" Israel, (the pre-1967 border, that is) into Jerusalem without any examination at all — the Israeli government wanted to make it clear that they considered all of Jerusalem a part of modern Israel. But those days are long gone — the tensions in the city have become too extreme for such philosophic niceties.

"What happens now?" I ask Mrs. Levi as we join the long line of cars waiting behind the swinging wooden crossbar.

"Either we pass through or we get arrested. It all depends on whether they think you're still at home in Tel Aviv."

A dreadful thought occurs to me. "Didn't they have the house bugged?"

"Oh, of course," Mrs. Levi says cheerfully. "But my husband has been very busy. The bugs transmit information in microbursts. The microbursts are decoded and stored in a computer, so one of my husband's Mossad friends who is good with computers has arranged for yesterday to play as today. They would have caught us in minutes otherwise."

I find this less than reassuring, and as we approach the roadblock my heartbeat accelerates, finally tripping along so fast that I add fear of a coronary to my other worries. Seemingly at random, the soldiers at the gate are pulling some cars to the side of the road, where other soldiers open trunks, inspect luggage, search the occupants.

"I hope no one was foolish enough to bring a gun," Mrs. Levi says in a joking tone, obviously assuming no one has. But my little pistol is still tucked away in the small suitcase I packed for Maria and myself; even a casual search will find it.

We're there. Mrs. Levi rolls down her window and hands over our false papers. The soldier glances at them without a hint of suspicion, and waves us through.

"Ah, there they are!" Mrs. Levi says about ten minutes later.

We're in the suburbs of modern Jerusalem, a few kilometers away from the old city, and Mrs. Levi has been driving slowly, checking for tails. Now she pulls into the parking lot of an Israeli convenience store and pulls out a cell phone. She quickly punches in a number, talks to someone for a few seconds in Hebrew, then puts the phone away. About forty seconds later her son pulls up behind us.

"We need to do some rearranging," Mrs. Levi says. "It would be best if no one rode in this car but myself and Mr. Grant. The other car only seats five, so perhaps your wife can sit on your lap, Mr. Lunsford."

"Wait a minute," Maria protests, "why shouldn't we stay in this car?"

"Well, for one thing . . ." Mrs. Levi improvises, "we hope to have a few reporters there. NetNews is up and running again and my husband doesn't want the cameramen to get confused and take pictures of Mr. Lunsford instead of . . ."

"You're really worried that someone will attack my son, aren't you?" Maria says.

"There's a possibility of that," Mrs. Levi admits. "But if it were much of a possibility, my husband would not have arranged this demonstration. But still, the two of you should ride in the other car."

"No!" Maria says. "You should ride in the other car, Mrs. Levi. Peter can drive."

"Mother, no one should ride with me," Joshua protests. "I can drive."

"Now how is that going to look?" Maria says, "Have you ever seen a parade where the guest of honor drives himself? Say, why don't you ride in the other car, too, Peter? I can drive."

"No," I say, trying to put down my fear. "I'll stay here with the two of you."

Mrs. Levi warns us halfheartedly that we might get lost, but Joshua says we can follow the other car until we're almost there, and then pull in front. The other car can flash its lights when it's time. She objects that we might get separated, but Josh assures her that he knows Jerusalem well, and can get to the correct neighborhood without help if she will give him the name of the street. Finally she hops out and gets in the other car, I come around and get in the driver's seat, and her son pulls out of the parking lot onto the street.

"So, where are we going?" I ask Joshua as I pull out behind.

"Into the Old City, a neighborhood in the Christian quarter near the Jaffa Gate."

"The Christian Quarter? I thought this was a Jewish and Arab demonstration."

"The Christian quarter is neutral territory. A slight increase in the number of Arabs visiting there isn't likely to raise an alarm."

"I didn't think you could drive into the Old City."

"They widened the Jaffa Gate in 1898 so the Kaiser Wilhelm could ride in with a properly impressive entourage. There's a small road that runs right through the wall."

We reach the top of a small hill and I get my first good look at the Old City of Jerusalem: gold-topped domes and towers rising into the air, with thousands of trees growing up between the buildings.

"I didn't know it would be so beautiful," I mumble. As if in answer, I hear Joshua speaking Hebrew softly behind me.

"What did you say?" Maria asks, but Joshua makes no reply.

Chapter 11

"Ten measures of beauty gave God to the world:
Nine to Jerusalem and one to the rest
Ten measures of sorrow gave God to the world:
Nine to Jerusalem and one to the rest."

— *The Talmud*

As we near the Jaffa Gate I almost panic; the traffic has slowed to a crawl and I'm afraid we're going to run into another checkpoint. Looking for soldiers, I don't see the speed bumps, and we bounce over the first so hard my head hits the cloth ceiling.

"Roll back the top, Peter," Joshua tells me as we pass under the wall, "we're almost there."

"Roll back the top? Are you crazy?"

"Why do you think Major Levi got a convertible? Roll down the top!"

My hand is shaking, but I reach forward and push the button that retracts the roof. The sudden rush of wind makes me expect a bullet to come zinging by at any moment, and when the car driven by Levi's son slows I almost rear end it. We turn right into a narrow side-street, lined with old two- and three-story stone and stucco buildings. The street seems choked with people. Ahead of me, Levi's son flashes his lights.

"This is it," Joshua says. "Pull around him and stop."

I pull to the left of the other car, and as I pass, Levi's son calls out, "We didn't expect so many! Keep moving slowly and they'll get out of the way!" I pull in front of him and stop the car.

"What are you doing? Keep moving!" Levi's son yells, and suddenly Joshua vaults out of our car and heads off down the street, walking with long powerful strides, waving his right hand in greeting to the crowd. Before I can do anything they close in behind him.

As years go by, I suspect the tales of Joshua's entrance into Jerusalem will grow ever more fanciful. Some will say he was accompanied by angelic music; that his raiment shone with unearthly radiance; that a donkey miraculously appeared and calmly waited to be ridden through the throng. Others will say that cloven hooves peeked out from Joshua's sandaled feet; that his person reeked of death and corruption; that innocent children were struck dead by his baleful gaze. Some may say they were cured of arthritis by the brush of Joshua's cloak, or saw clearly for the first time in decades; others may blame tumors or backaches on his dire presence. All may say the crowd laid down palm branches, and that may well be true: palm branches are a Jerusalem custom; thrown down for Allenby and the Kaiser as well as Jesus. And all may claim that the crowd numbered in the tens of thousands, although six or eight hundred would suffice to block that narrow street. Thousands will probably claim to have been there, and some may wish it so strongly they will one day believe it themselves.

As for the forces of mundane reality, an INN cameraman and reporter are there, but they've positioned themselves poorly, and mostly they get footage of the backs of the crowd. My vantage point is just as bad, and I'm also busy trying to follow the panicky directions of Major Levi's son, who leaps out of his car just seconds after Joshua, then halts beside me.

"Why did he do that!" he screams.

"He didn't want us to be in danger," I yell back over the rhythmic chants of the crowd.

"In a car at least he would be hard to stab! You can run people down in a car!"

"Well, he's not in a car, and we can't drive in there to get him. What should we do next?"

"We'll drive around and meet him when he comes out the other end of the block!" He reaches into the pocket of his tight jeans and wrestles out a thin phone. "Here, take this! We will call you if we get separated. Follow me!"

It works better in theory than fact. A few cars and a great many people on foot are coming in behind us and Levi's son foolishly tries to turn around rather than just backing up, which delays us two or three minutes. Back on the main road, we miss a turn and end up in slow-moving traffic on a one-way street. As we come to one halt after another, I can see Levi's son banging on the roof, making classic hand gestures at the other drivers. Once or twice I can even hear him shouting in Hebrew. I can't see his mother over Matt, Nicholas, and John in the back seat, but I have a feeling she's not making the situation any calmer. It's almost fifteen minutes before we pull to a stop further south on the street where Joshua hopped out. It's one-way to the south, but Levi's son rightly assumes anyone trying to come down it will be blocked by the demonstration, so he blithely heads north. In less than a minute we see the edge of the crowd and he pulls to a halt. Then he jumps out and stands by my car.

"They sound happy, at least," I say.

"Maybe they're happy because they've killed him."

"I thought your father was rounding up people friendly to Joshua."

"I don't know *who* we've rounded up. We never expected this many."

"What are they saying?"

"If I spoke Arabic I could tell you."

I turn and look at Maria, expecting to see her dissolving in tears of panic or rage. But she's wearing one of Joshua's expressions, a kind of beatific calm, as if she's already seen the future, good and bad, and made her peace with it.

"He'll be all right," she says. "No one there wants to hurt him."

Levi's son scowls, disbelieving. But a moment later he smiles as the rhythmic chant changes to Hebrew. The crowd is moving closer to us, but thinning out at the same time. Suddenly it parts and I see Joshua. He faces the crowd, makes a deep salaam, then turns back and walks towards our car. Amazingly, no one follows. Levi's son stares at Joshua as one might stare at a ghost, but Josh doesn't say a word, just opens the door and sits down by Maria. Levi's son gets back in the other car, and we drive away.

"Why did you do that?" I yell over the roar of the wind.

"Do what?" Joshua yells. Even with the top down I can hear a hint of satisfaction in his voice.

"Jump out of the car. That made it about ten times easier for somebody to kill you."

"It seemed like the thing to do," is all he will say.

We stop at a park in West Jerusalem, just outside the Old City. Gathered around some picnic tables, Joshua's explanation seems even less satisfactory to Mrs. Levi than it did to me.

"That's all you can say?" she yells. " 'It seemed like the thing to do'?"

"That's all I will say," Josh replies.

"Do you know how incredibly foolish that was, jumping out of the car like that?" Joshua doesn't answer, but John puts his two cents in.

"Mrs. Levi, of course it was dangerous. But how much more dangerous was it than your husband's original plan?"

And now Mrs. Levi doesn't answer.

"It was only slightly more dangerous, wasn't it?" John persists. "And the extra danger was to Joshua — in fact his jumping out of the car made things a great deal safer for the rest of us. So why are you complaining?"

John's words are persuasive, but if anything, Mrs. Levi looks angrier.

"Listen," she says, "who is running this show, as you say in the United States? If you will not do what we tell you, why should we help?"

John starts to speak, but Joshua cuts him off.

"Mrs. Levi," he says, "there are things I must do, with or without your help."

She stands, angrier still, and beckons to her son. He starts to get up, then slowly sinks back down onto the picnic bench.

"Go home, mother," he says.

"Of course I'm going home, and you're coming with me. We will take the cars and leave these lunatics on their own."

"No, mother. You take a taxi to one of the big hotels, then get a *sherrut* back to Tel Aviv. We will park the cars somewhere. The Americans may have the license-plate numbers by now. Go home."

"You are staying with these fools?"

"Yes, mother, I am."

"Why?"

Levi's son pauses for a moment, perhaps not sure of his reasons himself. But then he smiles.

"It seems like the thing to do," he says.

And so Joshua gains yet another convert. Even before his mother has stomped out of sight, Levi's son asks:

"What next, Rabbi?"

Perhaps it's just the sort of slip that has Catholic children calling Baptist preachers "father," but it chills me. How many times was Jesus called "rabbi" in the gospels? More than once, I'm sure, and now I sit in a Jerusalem park and hear the same word applied to my stepson.

"Your father arranged a place for me to stay tonight, I take it?" Joshua replies, a question for a question.

"Yes."

"Then we should go there."

Chapter 12

"He hath scattered the proud in the imagination of their hearts,
He hath put down the mighty from their seats,
And exalted them of low degree;
He hath filled the hungry with good things,
And the rich he hath sent empty away."
— *The Gospel of Luke 1.51-53*

"Dr. Grant," Levi's son asks, "is it true you believe all religions are equal?"

We're in an upstairs room somewhere in the Christian Quarter, a room decorated in Middle Eastern style, with low tables and cushions instead of chairs. It's early evening, about nine o'clock. In front of Joshua is a platter piled high with food: bread, tabuli, fruit, rice, and vegetables. Joshua picks up a roll and takes a bite before answering.

"If by equal you mean the same, then I don't think that. I wouldn't bother being a Christian if I thought all religions were the same. And you wouldn't bother being a Jew."

"Then what do you think of Jews?"

Joshua picks up the bottle in front of him, conspicuously labeled "Made in Israel," pours himself another glassful, and takes a large swallow.

"I think you make very good wine," he says.

The room is in a house owned by an acquaintance of Levi's, a Christian from an old Jerusalem family. He once spied for the Mossad, but became disturbed at the increasing power of Jewish fundamentalists in Israel. Levi's son brought us here in the early afternoon, then he and Matthew drove the two rental cars to West Jerusalem and abandoned them on a suburban street. While they were walking back, our host drove the rest of us to a small Christian church where everyone but me took communion. On the way he told us how he used to argue with Levi, until one afternoon Levi told him he could do more good if he kept his opinions to himself, as Levi was doing. And his keeping quiet has paid off, because now we have a host who's not on any Mossad list of liberal "activists."

"What do you think of our religion, I mean?" Levi's son persists.

"I don't know. Study and pray and come to your own conclusions."

"And God will not punish me for my conclusions?"

"Why ask me? Do you think I have a direct line to the Almighty?"

Levi's son pauses. "Of course not," he stammers, "what I meant was . . . what do you believe?"

"I believe those seeking a good and merciful God will find what they seek, because God will listen to their prayers regardless of what name they use. And perhaps those who are really seeking Satan will find him also, whether they die calling on Rama, Allah, Yahweh, or even Jesus."

I look up, startled. The first sentence is Brethren "doctrine," but the second sounds unusually bitter, as does the reference to Satan, poetic though it may be. But Joshua doesn't elaborate, he just reaches forward, takes another bite of his roll, follows that up with another healthy swig of wine.

"You may say you're a Christian, Dr. Grant," our host chimes in, "but you talk about religion like a Jew. Christians discuss religion to make converts, Jews do it for entertainment."

"A sweeping generalization," Joshua says.

"Which you have not refuted," our host points out.

"I was hoping you hadn't noticed. All right, I'll admit it, I'm really Jewish."

Everyone laughs but John and me, perhaps because we know how Jewish Josh really is. Or perhaps our lack of humor just reflects our mood: John has been abstracted the entire evening, and I've settled into a profound funk. Joshua has been unusually outgoing, but there's a strained quality to his good spirits: he's like a man on death row, eating his last meal, saying his goodbyes, trying not to think about what happens at midnight. Maria's mood seems brittle as well — she's smiling and giggling, but every few minutes she leans over, shivering, and squeezes against me.

But Joshua's newer disciples are well fooled. Nicholas keeps looking at the furniture like a tourist in a Moroccan restaurant, Matthew has drunk too much wine and is for once talkative and silly, and Levi's son sits reverently beside Joshua, trolling for pearls of wisdom.

"So, Dr. Grant, why do you think Christianity is superior to Judaism?" he asks.

Joshua looks at him a little sadly, his smile fading for just an instant.

"When you ask me that," he says, "do you mean Christianity as it's usually practiced, or as I think it should be?"

"As you think it should be."

"Ah, there you give my religion an unfair advantage." His smile has returned. "I prefer Christ's life and message to those of Moses and the prophets."

Levi's son stops and ponders that for a moment. Joshua, meanwhile, picks up another roll and has another gulp of wine.

"Rabbi," Levi's son finally says, and this time the word seems a sudden challenge. "Certainly the life of Jesus was not like that of Moses. But how was his message so different?"

For a few seconds the only answer he gets is the sight of the rabbi chewing. Then, very deliberately, Josh swallows his bread and puts down his wine.

"Jesus said what's in your heart is more important than your outward actions or obedience to rules. And he told us to love our enemies. Before Jesus, that wasn't exactly stressed by Judaism."

"What about Jesus being the Son of God?"

"A Son of God who told us all to address God as 'Father.' In fact, some linguists say the word Jesus used should be translated as 'Papa' or 'Dad.' " Joshua laughs into his glass. " 'Our Daddy, who art in Heaven . . .' I wonder how that would go over with Harold Anthony?"

"So your version of Christianity doesn't consider Jesus God?"

"My 'version' would consider following Jesus's advice as more important than resolving just who he was. You know, everyone seems to think I'm a preacher now, and I've thought of a good story about Jesus, but I haven't had a chance to tell it to anyone. Shall I bore you with it?"

Levi's son nods. He's becoming less reverential, almost amused; a prophet who swills wine is a little out of his experience. It's a little out of mine, also: I've never seen Joshua drink so much, nor heard the subtle slurring that's crept into his speech.

"Once there was a wise and good landlord," says Joshua, "who owned many estates scattered all over the world. Word reached him that the tenants at one estate argued and fought, that some went hungry while others grew fat, that some fouled the fields of others with their garbage, that at times the tenants did not even stop at murder. So the good landlord sent one of his servants to remind these tenants how they should live. But the tenants sent the servant back; beaten, bruised and unheeded. So the landlord sent another servant, then another, and another, always with the same result. Finally this good landlord thought: 'Perhaps my instructions have lost something in the translation.' So he sent his son to the farm to straighten things out.

"At first the tenants listened to the landlord's son better than they had to his servants: for the son set a faultless example, he spoke clearly and with authority, and his message was of love and good to hear. But then the tenants began to argue. Some said: 'This man says he is our master's son, but how do we know that?'

"The son felt that the wonderful nature of his words was proof enough of their origin, but some of the tenants were in dire need, so in the end he did all he could to help them. But his kind and amazing acts did not stop the arguments. 'Miracles!' said some, 'We have been given a sign!' 'Forgeries!' said others, 'tricks of the devil!' And the tenants began to fight again. Finally, some said: 'Look at all the trouble this man has caused. We're worse off than before.' And they waylaid the son, beat and stabbed him, and left him for dead, hanging on a tree beside the road. But when they came back later his body was gone.

"After that, some tenants said: 'He was a liar, whatever honey-coated words came from his mouth.' And others said, 'He was just like those sent before, but he shouldn't have been killed. He spoke the truth.' And still others said, 'Truly he was the landlord's son, and he has been miraculously reborn. We should worship him.' And for many long years after that, each group fought the other, and while many actually worshipped the son, few remembered his words, and fewer still used them to guide their lives."

It's a good story, one of Joshua's better efforts, and I can tell he likes it. As soon as he's finished, he pours himself another half-glass of wine, downs it in one swallow, then smiles. The smile might be taken as pride in another man. But in Joshua it doubtless reflects nothing more than honest pleasure at a job well done. His glass empty, he reaches for the bottle again.

"Joshua . . ." Maria says hesitantly.

"Yes, Mother?" Josh answers, bottle in hand.

"Don't you think you've had enough? We're getting up pretty early tomorrow."

Josh looks ruefully at the bottle beside him, from which he alone has been drinking. It's almost gone. He shakes his head.

"I hadn't noticed . . ." he mumbles.

"Well, I have," his mother says, "and I keep on thinking of the hangover you're going to have after all that wine. Red wine, no less, and that's the worst, let me tell you."

Josh looks at her, smile definitely gone now, and puts the bottle back on the table. But then he reconsiders and picks it up again.

"You're right, Mother," he says, "but we can't go to bed without one more toast."

The rest of us rise. I wonder what on earth this will be about. We've already toasted our host, the Brethren, the United States, the State of Israel, etc. etc. But I'm too tired to argue, so I pick up my glass and half fill it from one of the bottles resting on the low table. Everyone else does the same.

"I give you," Joshua says softly, raising his glass high, "Harold Anthony!"

The glass is at my lips before I really hear the words. "Harold Anthony!" I yelp. "Why are we toasting Harold Anthony?"

"Because," Joshua says calmly, "I've prayed for my grandfather, but I've never drunk to him. I thought it was worth a try."

I look around the room, expecting to see that Maria and John will be as offended by the toast as I am. But I'm disappointed. Maria seems baffled only by *my* behavior, and John is staring sadly down into his glass. I look furiously at the others, and Matthew returns my gaze, while Nicholas looks sheepishly at the floor.

"Jesus wasn't joking when he said to love your enemies, Peter," Joshua says. "Did you think that was just pabulum for Sunday school?"

"I never went to Sunday school," I spit back. "And I grew up loving people a lot better than some of those you call Christians."

I glare at Nicholas as I say it, and Nicholas starts to say something in his own defense — but he senses that logic isn't involved here and holds back his anger. Joshua looks at me again, and I writhe under his gaze.

"I made the toast for your sake as much as Harold Anthony's," he says. "If you can't love him, can you at least pray that he'll receive God's love?"

I try to imagine something good coming to Anthony, but a vision of Valerie's charred corpse explodes in my brain. I try again, but can only think of Joe's wasted life and Maria's haggard body beside me, soon to join her first and truest love in the grave.

"I'm sorry, Joshua," I say. "I won't toast Harold Anthony, and I won't pray for him."

"Why not?"

"Call it loyalty to my friends, particularly the ones whose lives Harold Anthony made a living hell."

Josh eyes me sadly. "Let's hope your loyalty fares better tomorrow than it did 2000 years ago, Peter." Then he looks at the others and raises his glass a second time. "To Harold Anthony!" They all drink. There's a moment's awkward silence, then Nicholas stands, mumbles something about being tired, and walks off to his room. One by one the others follow: Matthew, John, Levi's son, then Joshua and our host, until finally only Maria and I are left.

"That was a very poor joke," Maria says.

"What was?" I snap, wondering if I've said anything this evening that could possibly be considered humorous.

"What Joshua said to you just then. You know, about Peter. His not-so-veiled Biblical reference."

"Oh." I haven't really thought about it; my brain is too full of rage.

"Try to relax," Maria says. "It won't do any good worrying."

"You think there's nothing to worry about? When you're dying of cancer and your son is planning to walk into a den of maniacs?"

"And your worrying will change that?"

"Somebody ought to talk him out of it."

"You tried, remember? Besides, he's doing what he thinks is right."

"He's going to get himself killed!"

"I said he was doing what was right, not what was safe. Maybe you should follow his example for once," she says, and walks off down the hall.

Maria and I have a room to ourselves for the first time since we've come to Israel. But there's no bed; just thin pads, pillows and rugs on a hardwood floor.

I take my time in the tiny bathroom, half hoping that Maria will be asleep when I come out. Despite her soft tones, I expect she'll still be angry, and I'm too tired and heartsick to face even her silent disapproval. But when I come into our room she turns and embraces me.

"Let's not fight," she says, "tonight of all nights."

And later, I'm surprised to feel her leg rubbing gently against mine: an old signal for lovemaking.

* * *

We wake to the smell of Turkish coffee, stronger even than Joe once liked, strong enough to make the dead walk one last time. It's two in the morning, time to get ready for Harold Anthony's show, scheduled for four a.m. in Israel so it can air live in the U.S. at eight p.m. The day I'd hoped to never see has come.

Our alarm is set to ring in five minutes, but I briefly consider shutting it off and letting Maria sleep. She's been adamant about going to the show, but if I can get out of the room without waking her there's a chance she'll sleep through the whole affair. But senior-citizen love betrays me — one of her legs is still wrapped sweetly around mine. The second I move she stirs also.

"What time is it?" she mumbles.

"Two a.m. Well, not quite. Maybe five till."

"I guess we might as well get up. Five more minutes of sleep won't do us any good." She untangles herself and sits up groggily. "Jeez," she says, "is that coffee I smell or are they tarring a roof?"

"It's Turkish coffee," I tell her.

"A cup of that should perk me right up."

"A cup of that and one of the good doctor's pills might kill you." Leisner's medication has certainly given Maria more energy, but I suspect it's nothing more than a new and sophisticated type of speed.

"You're an old granny," she says.

"You didn't think so last night."

"That doesn't count. Your gonads may think they're eighteen, but the rest of you acts like a scared old lady."

I turn on the one dim light in the room and we get dressed. I thought I'd dealt with my fear, but suddenly I'm shivering, and Maria is weeping, her bravado collapsed at long last.

"I'm so frightened," she says.

"It's all right," I say, crouching down beside her. "You don't have to go. Josh will understand."

"But I'm frightened for *him!* Something's going to happen, I know it! Damn it all, he knows it! And we're going anyway!"

"Then tell him! Tell him you need him! Tell him you don't want him to go! You've never really done that."

"It wouldn't do any good," she says, suddenly calmer, and I know she's right. She pushes me gently away, gets up and walks towards the stairs.

I close the door, walk over to our small bag, and stare at the zippered pocket that hides my gun. For a good five minutes I kneel there, thinking.

When I finally arrive in the kitchen, I find the others ahead of me, halfway through a quick breakfast of bread and coffee.

"Hurry up, Peter," John says cheerfully. "Have some of this Turkish brew. Hey, Joshua, does the Bible ever mention coffee?"

Josh doesn't answer; his mind is elsewhere.

"How are we getting there," I ask, "now that we've abandoned the cars?"

"Our host has kindly offered to drive us in his van," says John.

"It seats seven?"

"It fits seven. He's taken out the back seats." Nicholas frowns, perhaps thinking of his big Mercedes with the leather upholstery, back in Atlanta. "Scarf that bread down, Peter," John continues, still oddly chipper, "and take a shot of coffee. We need to get going."

But as we pull away in the van, John suddenly becomes quiet. As for me, Turkish coffee is burning a hole in my stomach and I'm shivering so hard my teeth chatter. My shakes are due to more than the cold Jerusalem morning — unlike Maria, I'm afraid to die, and if Levi is right, any moment a rocket might come screaming out of an alley, or a spray of bullets erupt from a passing car.

Whether the others are plagued by similar fears I can't tell, but no one says anything as we drive through the Jaffa Gate and out of the Old City. The only sound is the whine of the engine and an occasional slurp — Maria has brought her coffee. We've given her the one passenger seat in deference to her illness, and as we come into West Jerusalem I realize why she hasn't objected — if a hail of bullets does rip through the van, the only spot as dangerous as the driver's seat will be where's she sitting now.

"There it is," John says.

We round one last corner and I see our goal, the Jerusalem Temple of the Warriors of God. It's a big building, though still smaller than the grandiose arenas Anthony's erected back in the States. It's reminiscent of the old Anthony Institute: the same sort of cool clean lines, the same abstract geometry overwhelming the antlike figures scurrying through its big glass doors. Floodlights bathe it in a sterile white glow, and its large parking lot (an expensive American oddity in Jerusalem) is rapidly filling with cars and charter buses. There are no checkpoints visible, no Israeli or American soldiers. The Mossad and the CIA must know we're headed here, but apparently they've decided not to keep Joshua from appearing, and I find it unsettling that their goals and Joshua's should suddenly coincide.

"What do we do now?" John asks.

"Go in with everyone else," Josh replies. He says a few words in Arabic to our host, who pulls a little closer to the building and then stops. Joshua opens the sliding side door and we all hop out, then Josh turns and helps Maria down from her seat. We join the crowd heading toward the front entrance.

I'm praying for a gigantic anticlimax. With giddy elation I can see it coming: since we've made no special arrangements, we'll walk into the building with everyone else and suffer through a long, ridiculous, religious spiel without even being noticed. Then we'll go home and take a well-deserved nap.

But it's not to be. As we come in the front entrance (unguarded by any visible metal detectors) six broad-shouldered men in identical suits head our way. Their leader walks up to Joshua.

"Dr. Grant?" he asks simply.

"Yes," Joshua replies.

"Come with us, please." And we all turn and meekly follow.

In the nightmares I've had of this day, the bad things always happen in crowds. But as we follow Anthony's flunkies through the back of the building, I remember that President Patterson was murdered in a kitchen, and Martin Luther King was shot taking the air on a motel balcony. But no assassin jumps from a dark corner, and Anthony's henchmen do nothing more than take us to a backstage green room, where a smiling young woman pats a little powder on Joshua's face.

"Dr. Anthony knew all six of you would be coming," she tells us, "but he only wants Dr. Grant on stage. The rest of you can sit in the front row of the audience. The show will be going out over the net in about ten minutes. Bob here will show you to your seats."

For a moment this all sounds so reasonable that I start to rise. Nicholas, oddly enough, is the first to object.

"I'm not so sure that's a good idea, young lady. I don't think Dr. Grant should be back here by himself."

"Well, the security men will be staying," the sweet young thing replies. "Except for Bob, of course."

"But . . ." Nicholas says hesitantly, "it's the security men I'm worried about. What do you say, Joshua?"

Josh looks up at Bob and his bulky friends, then glances at John and me, seventyish; Maria, his terminally ill mother; Nicholas, a soft and slightly overweight preacher, and small and wiry Matthew, a runner perhaps, but no fighter. Josh shakes his head and smiles.

"Why don't you stay, Nicholas? The rest of you might as well go and sit down."

So the rest of us leave, following Bob over to a side door and into seats in the front of the Temple's sanctuary/studio. The house is packed, but the stage is almost bare, a vacant expanse of floor with two chairs parked forlornly in the middle. A large cross hangs on a side wall, and a beautiful stained-glass rose window hangs in a frame suspended over the stage nearby. I end up seated next to John, so I lean over and whisper:

"Why Nicholas?"

"He's the best witness, I guess, if something bad happens. A Baptist minister's more likely to be believed than you or me."

Which makes a certain cock-eyed sense. But I'm still restless. So I turn in my seat and look as people fill the few remaining spaces in the studio. Most of them are what I expected: Americans, to be sure, but younger than Anthony's stateside audience. The front rows in particular seem to be packed with earnest young men, gazing up at the stage with a wide-eyed expectation that reminds me of old Nazi propaganda films. The audience also sports a fair number of orthodox Jews in stiff black costumes, and Hasidic Jews with long dreadlocks and funny caps, all seated together in one corner. Lately, the Christian right has been hinting that most Jews will be saved after the Rapture, and Anthony has taken to inviting prominent rabbis and their followers to his netcasts. They're not expected to participate, and there are no overt attempts at conversion. The Jews, for their part, seem inclined to indulge these foreigners, so long as they continue to support rebuilding the Jewish Temple.

After about five minutes an extremely attractive young lady comes out with an armful of old-fashioned cue cards. APPLAUSE!! says one in cherry-red letters, STOP APPLAUSE!! says another, and KEEP APPLAUDING!! says a third. The audience (except for the Jews) obediently responds. Then we get to try our hand at a more surprising trio of instructions: BOO! then CATCALLS!!, and finally CALM DOWN!!

Then the sweet young thing is replaced by an obese man in an out-of-fashion suit. He reminds me of a once-popular type of Southern preacher: hard charging and loud, a man whose girth somehow proves his sanctity.

"WARRIORS OF GOD!" he bellows with no preliminary, "ARE YOU READY?!"

"WE'RE READY?!" the crowd shouts back.

"ARE YOU READY TO FIGHT FOR CHRIST?!!"

"WE'RE READY!!" the crowd replies, much louder. Many stand. I turn and look at the Jews, wondering if they're ready to fight for Christ, too.

"ARE YOU READY TO WRESTLE WITH SATAN?!!"

"WE'RE READY!!" More people are standing now, some glaring at us as we sit silent and conspicuous in the front row.

"ARE YOU READY TO GIVE YOUR LIVES TO CHRIST?!!"

"WE'RE READY!!" the crowd replies.

"ARE YOU READY TO DIE FOR CHRIST?!!"

"WE'RE READY!!" the crowd roars, then bursts into applause. And here in Jerusalem, a city dripping with the blood of those murdered in God's name, I stand and join the herd, afraid that these happy masses might be as ready to kill for their savior as to die for him.

A moment later the show begins. A kettledrum rolls in the studio orchestra while an amplified voice intones "Remember, the Faithful must be as Warriors of God . . ." Then a choir of twenty or so stands and begins "Onward Christian Soldiers." The audience sings too, nearly drowning out the choristers and the flamboyant piano accompaniment, but not the brass section, which lights into the trumpet-calls with a vengeance. When the song finally crashes through its final Amen, the amplified voice — like a cinema God booming down from the clouds — solemnly asks us to welcome "the host of our show, the Reverend Harold Anthony!"

Pandemonium erupts, but a happy chaos, a fit greeting from these fallen angels. Anthony walks to the middle of the stage and stands there with a sheepish grin, aping the demeanor of countless talk show hosts. "Aw, shucks," his smile simpers, "all this fuss for me?" And yet it rings utterly false, as carefully scripted as the applause itself, which goes on and on as the pretty girl holds up her KEEP APPLAUDING!! sign. When she finally pulls it down and the applause starts to die away, there's a quick flash of the old Anthony — a tight-lipped smirk that seems to say: "Enough of this nonsense. Now we have some real business to transact, if you fools are up to it."

But "Thank you, thank you," is what Anthony says out loud, and when he continues there's a quaver in his voice. "We have an interesting and unusual show for you tonight, with just one guest: a gentleman with whom I have often disagreed, sometimes violently. He has come here to show me the error of my ways. I hope instead to convince you of the error of his. Ladies and gentlemen, I give you the founder of the Brethren of Charity, Dr. Joshua Grant!"

There's a smattering of applause, but as the name sinks in it sputters and comes to a halt. When Joshua walks out, there's a tentative hiss, several boos, and suddenly the audience is in an uproar. The pretty girl holds aloft her CATCALLS!! sign, but this crowd needs no encouragement. Wadded programs rain onto the stage, but Joshua ignores them and sits in one of the chairs without being asked, leaving Anthony standing alone and forlorn.

The demonstration continues for a good three minutes, leading me to wonder about Anthony's Internet viewers. The act of booing may entertain, but watching it must quickly become tedious. Anthony's media consultant apparently agrees, because security men appear and spread out in the hall. They work their way towards the stage, stopping by each aisle-seat to impart friendly advice and what looks like an exceedingly painful armhold. Word spreads; order is restored. In a dead silence Anthony turns and looks at Joshua, and I realize that my old nemesis is deathly afraid. For a brief instant it seems as if Anthony might even flee the stage, but with a visible effort he gets hold of his emotions, walks toward the other chair, and sits down.

"Well, Mr. Grant," he says, "I must say I'm surprised to see you here tonight. I didn't think you'd have the nerve. What lies masquerading as truth do you have to tell us?"

"No lies. You know, my father once told me something about lies . . . "

"Your father! Your stepfather, you mean."

"No, I mean my father, Joseph Anthony. He said the worst lies are the ones you tell yourself."

And suddenly Anthony can't continue — even from here I can see his tears. It makes no sense: Anthony knows who I am, he must know I married Maria; that Joe came with her to Atlanta; that he died there, not on some nameless Arizona mountain. But Anthony looks unsure now, and I can only think that Joshua has repeated something Joe once said, something Anthony remembers with fondness or pain. And when Anthony speaks again his voice is gentle, and it frames an old man's tremulous question.

"But your father, he died when you were very young, didn't he?"

"Yes, but I remember him well."

"What was he like?"

"He was the kindest man I ever knew. Too kind for this world."

"What did he do for a living?"

"Well, he was a framer most of the time, a construction carpenter that is, but what he really liked was making instruments."

"Instruments?"

"Musical instruments. Mandolins, lutes, guitars. Especially guitars."

Hearing this, Anthony chokes up again, and looks out towards the audience. And there, sitting in the front row, he sees Maria. The bittersweet look on his face sours, becomes all bitterness: a mad, hopeless fury. He whips his head back and turns on Joshua.

"He wasn't really your father, you know."

"He wasn't my biological father, perhaps. But he was my father nonetheless."

"No he wasn't. Satan is your father."

"God is my father, and yours, although I don't think you've listened to Him for many long years."

"Lies, lies, more lies."

"The only lies here are the ones you tell yourself. Your son was right."

At this Anthony grows angrier still. "All right," he says, "all right." But everything is not all right; he's just so apoplectic he can't say anything else. "All right," he tries one more time, then waves his hand angrily at a stagehand who runs out to hand him a glass of water.

"All right," he finally sputters, "I'll let you have your say. Ten minutes . . . for ten minutes you can tell my audience anything you want them to hear. But after that, you have to stay and hear what I have to say about you. Then we'll let the audience decide."

"I don't need ten minutes. Jesus said it in a way even a child can comprehend. He told us to love everyone as we love ourselves, to never sleep easy while even one of our brothers or sisters lives in need or despair."

"And you would have us clothe, feed and comfort the enemies of God's word on this earth? Muslims and Buddhists and atheists?"

"Yes."

"You would ally yourself with others who seek to carry out your aims, even if they don't believe in the word of God?"

"If they seek to carry out those aims above all else, then they believe in the word of God. And they believe in Jesus, because they believe in the essence of His word."

"You would have us pursue political policies that weaken Christian countries, the guardians of God's truth, in order to feed and clothe those whose godless children might someday rise and destroy us?"

"If they are hungry and naked, yes."

"And you realize that your aims are impossible, that a world where no one is hungry or downtrodden is filled with insane contradictions?"

"Yes. Jesus didn't command us to succeed, he commanded us to try."

"Are you saying Jesus was a communist?"

"Jesus endorsed no political system."

"But you don't deny that communism has had many evil results?"

"So has capitalism. Any system run by evil men will cause evil. But if we were all truly Christians only God would need to rule over us."

"The God of the Holy Bible?"

"The God hidden in our hearts."

"But our hearts are evil."

"Our hearts contain both good and evil. That's what makes us human."

"What if the God hidden in our hearts is evil?"

"Then it isn't God we've found there. We've really gone in search of something else."

"And that's the core of your religious philosophy? Love your neighbor, remember that everybody's your neighbor, and never be truly content until your neighbors are content also? No other considerations whatsoever?"

"Yes."

"What about loving God?"

"I cannot do one without doing the other."

"What about the prophecies of *Revelation*?"

"They're open to a thousand different interpretations. Yours makes less sense than most."

"What about the wrath of God? What about the God of judgment?"

"To dwell with God will be to know the truth about everything, including ourselves. Facing that truth will be punishment enough."

"Not horribly original for a great religious thinker, are you?"

"I've never made any claims of originality."

Anthony stares at Josh for a moment, waiting for something more, but nothing more is forthcoming. Joshua merely stares back, leaving Anthony without a convenient segue into his own agenda.

"All right," he finally says, "All right. You've just heard the lame, wishy-washy religious philosophy of Joshua Grant. I bet many of you don't find anything dangerous in it, nor do you find anything dangerous in Mr. Grant here. Well, tonight we're going to show you just how wrong you are."

And suddenly Anthony and Joshua's seats are moving, seemingly gliding as their section of stage floor slides to one side. The lights fade, and at the back of the stage a huge video screen descends, accompanied by a soft tremolo from the orchestra's violins. Floating above it all comes Anthony's voice, now subtly enhanced, a bit of reverb added perhaps, a touch of bass.

"You know, friends," he says, "the Bible hints that the Antichrist will resemble Our Lord in a great many ways, in fact, the Bible makes it clear that many people blessed with intelligence but cursed with a flawed faith will be fooled into thinking that he is the returned Christ. Which leads me to wonder, how will the Antichrist accomplish this? In how many ways will his life resemble Our Lord and Savior's?"

The strings become more urgent, and I notice that the lighting on Joshua now comes from a lower angle, and is tinged with red.

"Joshua," Anthony asks, his voice now sweet and light, "what were your parent's names?"

"Joe and Maria," Joshua answers. They've done something to his microphone too, his amplified voice has an odd, metallic ring.

"Joseph and Maria. An interesting coincidence, isn't that? If we put both names in English they become Joseph and Mary, don't they?"

"There must be thousands of couples with the same names."

"I'm sure there are. But still, it's interesting, isn't it?"

"To you perhaps."

"And Joshua. Isn't Jesus just a Greek version of that very name?"

"Yes. And there must be thousands of people named Joshua in the U.S."

"But there probably aren't all that many families where all three names occur, do you think?"

"Perhaps."

"Were Joseph and Maria your real parents? Your biological parents, I mean?"

"I was a test-tube baby, if that's what you're getting at."

There's a low rumble from the audience. Anthony has preached for years that *in-vitro* fertilization is a sin; that babies thus conceived are unusually susceptible to Satan's tinkering.

"Actually, Mr. Grant," Anthony says, "that's not precisely what I was getting at. What I mean is, even though your mother gave birth to you, you're not actually related to her in any genetic sense, are you?"

Joshua doesn't reply.

"Come now, Mr. Grant," Anthony prods, "you told us earlier that you never lie. Isn't what I said true?"

"Yes," Joshua sighs. "I recently found out that I'm not genetically related to my mother."

"How do you explain that? How could you not be related to the woman who bore you?"

"This all starts to sound very melodramatic. The truth is, I don't really know. The hospital might have switched babies."

"But you were born in a small facility staffed by midwives, and your mother was the only delivery that evening."

"Perhaps there was a mistake in the *in-vitro* process. Perhaps the doctors inserted the wrong embryo into my mother's womb."

"So there's no denying that your birth was more than a little unusual?"

"I suppose not."

"What I'd like to investigate is just how unusual it was. I think the real story is far wilder than what you've just told us."

"Maybe so. But if you have any proof I'd like to hear it. I'm curious myself."

"Actually, Mr. Grant, we do have proof, devastating proof in fact." Anthony stands, strides to the middle of the stage. A subtle spotlight follows him as he turns to speak to the audience.

"The man you're about to see on our video tells an interesting story," Anthony says, "as does the second player in our drama tonight. While the first's motives might be less than pure, we took extraordinary care to insure that the second gave us an unbiased opinion. My friends, let's start by listening to Dr. Rajiv Patel."

The video screen comes to life and we see a brown-skinned man in white doctor's garb. For a second I wonder what's coming, then I realize that this must be the Indian doctor who analyzed Joshua's blood when Joshua wanted to donate bone marrow for Maria.

"So you're certain that the sample came from Joshua Grant?" an off-camera voice says.

"Yes, I am. When I first got back the results, I thought there must be some mistake, so I had Mr. Grant come back and give me a second sample. But there was no mistake. Mr. Grant is not his mother's son."

"And what did you do with this information?"

"I tried to sell it to one of your country's less reputable newspapers. Somehow your organization found out and offered me more money."

"And what did you do with the sample, at our request?"

"I mailed it anonymously to the name you gave me. I did, however, identify the sample with a code number, so that there would be no question of confusion in her lab."

"And you're willing to swear in a court of law that the sample you mailed is from Joshua Grant, the well-known founder of the Brethren of Charity?"

"I am."

"And to whom did you mail the sample?"

"To a Dr. Judith Baxter, in Pierre, South Dakota."

And the screen fades to black.

Anthony walks to the middle of the stage as the lights come back up, smiles in his folksy way.

"Now friends," he says, "you've probably never heard of Dr. Judith Baxter. She specializes in a rather obscure branch of biology known as forensic anthropology. In a nutshell, she does DNA analysis on human fossils. She can take an eight- or nine-hundred-year-old bone or smear of blood and tell you all about the person it came from, how long ago they lived, what racial group they belonged to, things like that. In addition to being a respected scientist in her field, she's also the daughter of one of Joshua Grant's closest advisors, Dr. John Baxter, who happens to be sitting in our audience tonight, and I understand that she's also quite friendly with Mr. Grant himself. We picked her to do this analysis because she's an expert in her field, and also because we couldn't think of a person less likely to be biased in our favor. Let's hear what she has to say about this sample."

The lights dim again, the screen descends, and I get my first good look at John's daughter. She's a redhead like him, and she might be pretty if she cared to comb her hair or wear something other than a stained white lab coat, shirt, and blue jeans. She gives the camera a lame, self-conscious smile and a little wave before she starts to speak.

"Hello out there, whoever you are. As you requested when you sent in your sample, I'm giving a summary of my report in video form, but I want to remind you that I'm not exactly a NetV star, so if you think you've gotten a crummy performance for your very generous payment, I'm sorry." She clears her throat nervously and looks at the notebook on her lap.

"The sample identified as number 666 was *very* interesting, and frankly I'd love to know more about it, since it casts serious doubt on testing procedures which I've worked on for ten years, procedures that have been completely verified by every method of cross-checking imaginable. Until now, that is.

"The sample appears to be blood taken quite recently; when it arrived in my lab it showed almost no signs of biological degradation. I have dated the sample based on mitochondrial drift — which is the natural mutation rate in genetic material passed unchanged from mother to offspring — and the date I keep on getting is about the year 0 C.E. A bone or blood stain of this age would make sense, but unfrozen blood does not stay fresh for two thousand years. I can only hope that you got this sample from some recently thawed corpse from Iceland or something like that, although even then I would expect far more deterioration than has occurred.

"Some other things you asked me to check for were racial background, which I would identify as Semitic, i.e. Arab or Jewish, and sex, which is male. In closing, I'd like to thank you for sending me a very interesting and disturbing sample, and I'd also like to ask you: please tell me who you got it from!"

And Judith fades away.

"Mr. Grant!" Anthony says as the lights come back up. "You certainly do seem to be surrounded by amazing coincidences! Do you have any explanation for why the blood coursing through your veins is two-thousand years old?"

"No, but I bet you do," Joshua says. He looks sick, and I suspect he'd be very pale if it weren't for the subtle red tinge they've given his lighting. I wonder how much he's shocked by this final "proof."

"You're quite right, there, Mr. Grant," Anthony says, "I do have an explanation. It's not one I'm proud of, but I do have it."

I move to the edge of my seat, suddenly baffled by the test results and perversely interested in what will come next. Will Anthony reveal his part in Joshua's conception? Or will he shift the blame to somebody else?

"Most of you know," Anthony begins, "that before I saw the light of Our Lord Jesus I was a scientist myself. I owned and ran one of the most powerful biotechnology firms in the world. And in my arrogant humanistic pride I was determined to discredit Christianity in any way I could. Back in the early 1990's my company got hold of some minute cloth samples from an amazing relic called the Shroud of Turin, which many Christians still believe is the burial cloth of Our Lord Jesus. I was hoping to discredit this relic, and I had my researchers analyze some of the stains on the cloth, thinking that they would be some sort of painter's pigment. To my vast surprise, they turned out to be genuine blood, although in the 1990's we had no way of biologically determining its age.

"I had my researchers downplay this discovery as much as they could, and then moved on to other projects. But one of the Institute scientists began a truly devilish undertaking, entirely on his own initiative. He decided to extract DNA from this sample and attempt to use it in a human clone. Now, remember folks, this was back in the twentieth century. No one had ever cloned a human before, and certainly no one had ever tried to generate a clone from such an ancient and extremely small sample. The odds against its success were so great that it could never have worked without either divine or diabolical intervention.

"But it did work, in fact, the procedure went without a hitch. The egg began to divide, still in a Petri dish, of course, but ready to be implanted in any female of child-bearing years. And, unbeknownst to me, it was implanted, in the evil woman who had ensnared my beloved son Joseph into marrying her. What became of this child? Well, all the principal players in this scheme from hell itself are here tonight. Look in the front row and you'll see three of them. Maria Grant, Joshua Grant's supposed mother, but really Beelzebub's broodmare; her lover Peter Jacobson, the man who cuckolded and then murdered my son; and Dr. John Baxter, alias Dr. Eric Schroeder, the man who had the awful presumption to attempt to clone our Lord Jesus Christ!"

At Anthony's last sentence, a low rumble of consternation starts in the audience, interspersed with isolated cries of "Christ Jesus!?" and "Lord save us!"

"And of course, my friends and fellow warriors of God," Anthony continues, his voice ringing out above the noise, "that means that before you stands Joshua Grant, cloned from DNA extracted from the Shroud of Turin, a man whose blood appears two-thousand years old, the supposed son of a Caucasian father and Hispanic mother, but Jewish nonetheless. Mr. Grant, do you have any answer to this?"

"Yes," Joshua says, standing. "What proof do we have for this story beside your word?"

To my horror, the lights dim slightly again, naturally attracting attention to the video screen. I know what's coming, and I can't believe that Joshua doesn't too.

"What proof?" Anthony asks, as the negative image of the Shroud fills half the screen and a photo of Joshua fills the other. "Look behind you." Both images are enlarged, until only two faces remain. Then the Joshua on the screen suddenly shuts its eyes and begins to grow a beard and long hair, tied in a ponytail behind. In seconds, two identical faces are before us.

"Proof enough, Mr. Grant? Why don't you tell us what you really are."

"I'm a man, just like you," Josh answers.

"A man who favors one world religion."

"No. I'm a man who believes God forgives mistaken beliefs."

"A man who favors dictatorial, one-world government."

"I believe in world-wide brotherhood, yes."

"A man who mouths words of peace . . ."

I sense a presence behind me, and I'm pulled up out of my seat and shoved forward. Three security guards surround me.

". . . but whose disciples carry murder in their hearts," Anthony finishes.

Anthony's guards have my arms twisted behind my back, but I seem to have grown another right hand, and it's holding a gun. It squeezes off two shots, and Harold Anthony collapses just before his beefy Praetorians pull me to the floor. As I fall, my head slams into the arm of my chair, and the last thing I hear before blacking out is the sound of the crowd surging forward.

Chapter 13

"Were you there, when they crucified my Lord?"

— Spiritual

For a few seconds consciousness flees, and then a forlorn mantra runs through my brain.

"My gun is in the car!" I think as the pale fog starts to lift. "I was afraid to bring it inside! My gun is in the car!"

The guards and the crowd have forgotten me. Though I've just been set up to look like an assassin, they're gathered on the stage. Off to one side lies Anthony, rolling on the floor as if in pain, but all the mob's attention is focused on a huddled bloody mess of a man, hiding his head as they beat him. For an instant his hands are pulled aside and I see Joshua's bruised and battered face. Then someone kicks him in the mouth, and his head snaps out of view. I back slowly away, then sideways till I find the aisle. Turning, I try to walk inconspicuously towards the exit.

But not everyone has rushed the stage to bludgeon the Anti-Christ. Many in the audience are trying to get out of the studio, away from the horror that's taking place beneath the big video screen, and on it, too — someone has pointed a NetV camera at this execution, and its image has been routed to the screen, appalling violence rendered three times bigger than life. And a few brave souls are trying to stop it. Like the homely woman who grabs my collar as I push into the crowd heading for the door.

"They're going to kill him! We've got to stop them!" she says, then takes another look at my face. "You were with him, weren't you!" she asks, suddenly hopeful. "Help me!"

"Not me, lady!" I yell at her. "Get your fat ass out of my way!"

Or the pretty girl, barely out of her teens, mascara streaked by tears, who's grabbing people one after another. She's wearing a tight, knit shirt, and as she works her way towards me, a thought leaps into my brain, a vision of fondling her shapely young breasts. The vision infuriates me, and when she approaches I don't even wait for her to ask whether I know Joshua.

"Leave me alone!" I bark. "It's none of my business!"

I'm at the back of the crowd, and my aisle's exit is jammed. So I cut across a row of seats, hoping the other aisle will be better. One of the Jews, a young man who looks a little like Josh even in a beard and black curls, is bypassing the jammed aisles by going over the seats.

"Help me!" he calls across two rows.

His resemblance to Joshua stops me, and as I wait in the middle of the aisle he vaults into my row.

"We can't do anything," I protest. "There are too many of them!"

"We can stop them!"

"What do you care?" I ask, whining. Behind him, I see most of the older Jews also working their way towards the stage, though more slowly than this athletic young man.

"Don't you see what they're doing?" he says, pointing forward. Some of the mob on stage are pulling down the huge cross from the wall. "We've got to stop them; they've lost their minds!" he says, then looks at my face. "Aren't you one of his friends? The cameras showed his friends on the front row just before we heard the shots. Weren't you one of them?"

I don't answer; I'm too busy weighing my options. Three people now have recognized me, but no one has identified me as the man who supposedly shot Harold Anthony. So maybe Anthony's setup didn't work, maybe somebody goofed on a camera angle, maybe everyone could see that it was a guard who held the gun, a guard who aimed to miss. Maybe this crowd won't tear me limb from limb the second they catch on to who I am.

But then again, maybe they will.

"I don't know what you're talking about," I tell the young Jew, and shove myself rudely into the throng jamming through the exits.

A few minutes later and I'm outside. I was probably lucky to be in the back of the crowd; an exit door is smeared with blood, and a trampled body lies on the hard, cold floor of the lobby. The scene outside is almost as dangerous. Fleeing drivers are tearing through the pre-dawn gloom, swearing, blasting their horns at pedestrians too slow to leap out of the way. As I sprint to the first row of cars I hear crunching metal as two of these maniacs collide. Off in the distance there are sirens.

Unfortunately, I have no idea where our van is parked. I dodge speeding cars for at least five minutes before I finally spot it, out towards the edge of the lot.

"What's going on?" our host asks as I pull the door open.

And then a strange thing happens. There's a sudden silence, and I look back towards the temple, back to the east. The sun is rising at the edge of an ominous sky, and a rooster greets it, a pastoral sound oddly out of place in the suburban landscape around us. Shame and self-loathing comes over me, and I sink down to the pavement instead of hopping into the van.

"What's going on?" our host repeats, then he gets out of his seat, walks around the van and kneels beside me.

"They're killing him in there," I say.

"Killing who?"

"Joshua."

The man sighs, not entirely surprised. "What about the others?" he asks, and I realize that Maria hasn't come out; none of them have.

"They must still be in there," I say. Without another word our host turns and runs towards the temple.

And suddenly, my shame is gone, replaced by rising anger; and the only loathing I feel is for Harold Anthony. He made it look like I'd shot him, but no doubt he's hiding comfortably in the back of his phony church, listening to the idiots he's whipped into a frenzy tear Joshua limb from limb. Well — I think — I'll show him I'm no longer a man of talk and no action. I hop into the van and reach under the passenger seat, up in the springs, where I've hidden my gun.

As I head back towards the temple, I see more people leaving, mostly men, spread far apart, all with a dazed look, as if their hands have just done something their brains can't comprehend. These must be those who have just beaten Joshua, either killed him or left him for dead. They seem drained of violence now, but I don't want to chance it, so I make for the back of the building, hoping to find another open entrance.

The first three doors are locked, but the fourth is not, and I enter and wander through and past kitchens, offices, production rooms, a small chapel. And then I turn a corner and know where I am: next to the green room where an hour ago a pretty girl patted makeup on Joshua's face. I stand there a moment, then turn and walk reluctantly to the big studio.

The mob has taken the large cross from the side wall and leaned it against the video screen, smashing the stained-glass window in the process, so that thousands of blood-red shards glitter menacingly on the floor. Joshua is hanging upside down on the cross, feet splayed on the crossbar, both hands pinned together on the vertical, the same lag-screws that once fixed the cross to the wall now passing through his flesh into the wood. And at the foot of the cross stands Maria, barefoot and bleeding.

"He's dead, isn't he?" she says through her tears. "I watched him die."

I walk closer to my stepson. His hands are nailed about five feet above the floor. I feel for a pulse, but there's none, and I can see a large dent in his forehead, the sort of skull fracture no one survives. His face is surprisingly peaceful.

"He's dead," I tell Maria, wondering if we should try to take him down.

"Leave him there," calls a voice from across the hall. I turn and see John, with Matthew and Nicholas trailing behind. "Let the whole world see what they've done to him," John says again. He's been beaten too; he has one prominent black eye and blood streams from his nose. Matthew and Nicholas are in better shape, and Matthew, silent as usual, walks up to Maria, lifts her, and carries her gently over the broken glass to the side of the stage.

"We've got to get out of here," I say, "the police will be coming."

"They won't do anything to the rest of us," John says confidently. "Not today."

And at the mention of the police I remember the gun in my pocket, and the one thing I want to do before I die. I trot over the broken glass, back into the wings, looking for Harold Anthony.

Later, the authorities will have many excuses for why it took them so long to get to the temple. At first they'll claim that no one called until a half-hour had passed. But undercover Mossad and CIA agents will come forward to tell how they'd pulled out their phones as the mob rushed the stage, had screamed themselves hoarse trying to get police to the scene. Then the authorities will claim that the ambulance and police vans were hit by fleeing cars, but they won't be able to come up with an accident report or a crumpled ambulance. Finally they'll claim there was a delay in putting together a riot team, blissfully denying the well-known fact that Jerusalem keeps at least three such units on constant alert. None of the excuses will hit upon the truth: the American government wanted Joshua dead, they kept the Israelis from doing anything to save him, and they don't really want to catch those responsible.

And as I stalk through the back corridors of Anthony's temple, I wonder if anyone will ever spend a day in jail for murdering Joshua. Anthony can claim that he instigated nothing; that he'd been lucky to escape with his own life, that even though he hadn't been shot he'd fallen to the floor from fear and fainted. And how does one prosecute a mob? Yes, I was there, each will say, but I didn't kick him, I only watched; I went backstage for the toolbox, but I didn't know why they wanted it; I tried to stop them.

And maybe some of them did.

And so — I tell myself, stoking my anger — the man who really murdered Joshua will get off scot-free, will go home and bend the truth in his "sermons" and in another six months, Joshua will be the villain of his own demise. And the evils Joshua foresaw will still come to pass: millions will drown or starve as the oceans rise, more millions die in wars fought for nothing, as the rich and the poor and the Muslim and the Christian and the Hindu and the Jew alike find in God only an excuse for their mindless hatred. God will be with "us," he will be against "them"; "we" the chosen people, the predestined of Jehovah, the sword of Allah, the righteous ones; allied against "they" the great Satan, the worldwide Zionist conspiracy, the fundamentalist Muslim fanatics, the Democrats, the Republicans, the evil forces of secular humanism, forever and ever, Amen.

And where is my great Satan! I'm expecting the police to be here at any moment, men who will take a dim view of my putting five or six bullets into Harold Anthony's head and testicles. In a panic, I finally push open a plain steel door and step outside.

The sunrise is gone, replaced by a drizzling, miserable rain. I look around in surprise, then lunge back at the door, realizing too late that it will lock behind me. And there, kneeling in the mud, is Harold Anthony. He has a long, ragged gash on his forehead.

"What the hell happened to you?" I ask, stupidly.

"The bullet grazed me. You must have hit the guard's arm as he fired."

"So he missed by a little less than he was supposed to?" I say, and lift my gun to finish the job. But Anthony doesn't jump to his feet, doesn't run, doesn't even grovel. He just looks at me and says:

"Go ahead. Shoot."

I hesitate. "You want me to shoot you?"

"You're the instrument of God's vengeance. Kill me for my sins."

"What sins?"

He looks at me for a long instant, rain and blood streaming down his face and hands. "He wasn't the one," he finally groans.

"What are you talking about?"

"Joshua. Your stepson! He wasn't the one! He couldn't have been the one!"

"The one what!" I say, wondering why I don't just pull the trigger and get it over with.

"The Beast! The Antichrist!" And he gets to his feet as if to preach. "He would have smitten them! Don't you understand? The Beast hasn't established his rule! There are signs, oh God yes, there are signs aplenty that the Beast is out there, but it's not time for the Antichrist to die! Not now! I was trying to expose him; I had no hope of killing him, not yet. I thought he would blast anyone who attacked him; I thought he would give unmistakable signs that he came from the devil. I thought thousands, millions would repent when they saw it!"

"You bastard!" I spit back. "I've got news for you. Joshua wasn't the Beast; he wasn't the Antichrist. All you did was kill a man, the gentlest and best man I've ever known. I don't care what screwy route he took to get born. He was just a man!"

"I know! I see that now! Oh, God, God, what have I done!" And he puts his face in his hands again, bows toward the mud, rocking back and forth as he wails his sorrow.

I don't buy it. Anthony was always a quick thinker. He probably came up with this incredible sham repentance the second he saw me walk out the door. He killed Gluckmann, he killed Joe's mother, he killed Valerie, he's all but killed Maria. Why should another murder trouble his soul? I raise the pistol one more time.

But I can't do it, can't pull the trigger. For a moment, disgusted at my weakness, I consider pointing the gun at myself, but then I think of Maria, sobbing somewhere in the building behind me. Shaking my head, I drop the gun into the mud and grind it down with my heel.

"You bastard," I say weakly, and then turn and walk away through the rain.

Chapter 14

The Israeli government categorically denied that there were any plans to arrest or deport Joshua Grant prior to his assassination, and added that they are investigating the murder with "every means at their disposal." As of yet, no arrests have been made.

—*INN News Roundup*

The Armstrong administration has categorically denied the story, but NetNews sources report that a pledge with nearly three thousand signatures was delivered to army commanders in the Middle East earlier today. The pledge supposedly stated that the officers and soldiers who had signed would willingly face court-martial and imprisonment rather than (quote) "participate in an invasion that violates both U.S. and international law" (end-quote).

In a related story, government spokesmen denied that they had ever made plans for an invasion of Arab oil states in the Middle East. "Certainly we would like the oil tariff lifted," President Armstrong told the media, "but we have no plans nor have we ever had any plans to cause its revocation by military force."

—*INN News Roundup*

What your about to see is what really happened, don't let any scumbags in the government tell you any different. This is the real video downloaded by one of Harold Anthony's Netcast technicians before the CIA got there and took the computers away. By the way, our last sight got ten million hits before the government shut it down, so don't worry about getting arrested for finding us, the jails aren't that big.

This is really graphic stuff, so keep your kids away till their old enough to know the truth."

—*Joshualivesgovsux.com*

"Praise God from whom all blessings come.
Praise Josh His accidental son"

—*Joshan hymn*

"I tell you, whoever does not accept the kingdom of God like a child will not enter it at all."

—*The Gospel of Luke* 18.17

"When I became a man I put away childish things."

—*I Corinthians* 13.11-12

Six months later, millions have seen Joshua's death, but I'm not among them.

It's not for lack of opportunity. I could wait for Maria to go to bed, wander into my study, vault onto the Net, and hunt up one of the several hundred illicit websites that replay the last episode of Harold Anthony's "Warriors of God." After I'd read the messages I could just move the cursor over and push the play button. And afterwards, I'd probably go get the gun I bought when Maria and I made it back to the U.S., put its muzzle in my mouth, and pull the trigger.

I've surfed to those websites countless times, but I can never get up the nerve to push that little mouse button. In fact, the one time I hit a site that started the video automatically, I nearly smashed the computer in my haste to shut it down. Though part of me thinks the footage will prove I couldn't have saved him, another part fears I will learn just the opposite: that I killed Joshua just as surely as those who beat him and then used a power screwdriver to pin his limbs to Anthony's teakwood cross.

The U.S. government says the footage is faked, but everybody knows it was really salvaged from Anthony's computers, supposedly downloaded by a repentant technician with a backdoor log-on. Our government also says Anthony gave instructions to stop filming if things got out of hand, and there is some proof of that — the final minutes of "Warriors of God" did not go out live over the Net. But many insist the CIA or some equally sinister U.S. entity itself killed the live feed, and then sat and watched through their own line, and did nothing.

And the government has no hope of killing the rumors. Every day I hear a new one, and being close to the center of things, I know that many of them are true. It's true, for instance, that Joshua's body was lost, probably mistakenly buried along with those shot in the "riots" that broke out after his death. The ashes Maria and I scattered near the Dead Sea came from burnt olive branches, an appropriate touch, she thought, for a man of peace.

"Riots," by the way, is the outgoing Israeli government's term. I've heard whispers that say the demonstrations were mostly peaceful, and that it was Israeli Christians, Muslims, *and* Jews who surged on to the streets to protest Joshua's murder; only to be shot at by panicked American soldiers, primed by lies to expect an insurrection.

Meanwhile, several Arab states have officially made the Brethren of Charity an illegal organization, an act which has inspired even more of their citizens to join.

In the U.S., Joshua is rapidly becoming a secular saint, on up there with Martin Luther King and JFK. Secular saints must be firmly grounded in reality, so people now claim there's no resemblance between Joshua's face and the ghostly shadow on the Shroud of Turin. As for Anthony's genetic, scientific, "proof": even people who don't know a mitochondria from a Krispy Kreme Donut will tell you that if Josh was cloned, his mitochondrial DNA would have come from the 20th-century woman who donated the ovum, and therefore; the test Judith Baxter ran should have shown nothing unusual or "ancient" at all. And of course they're right, although oddly enough, no one (including me) can come up with a purely rational explanation for what Judith Baxter *did* find hidden in Joshua's blood.

But behind the public denials there are private whispers. I had a long Netphone talk with John two weeks ago, a talk that started out friendly and almost degenerated into a shouting match. In the end, I accused him of knowing precisely what was going to happen on Anthony's show, and of setting much of it in motion himself. For a second he looked like he wanted to hit me, but then an odd look settled over his face, as if he were about to reveal a great secret.

"I've seen him, you know. Since he died."

"What do you mean?" I scoffed. "Are you having visions now?"

"It didn't seem like a vision," he said.

A week later I had another "discussion" with John, and I could sense the whispers building. Harold Anthony dropped out of sight after Joshua's death, but as I predicted, no one tried to bring any charges against him. I'd hoped that Anthony's remorse was real and that he'd go home and shoot himself, since I wasn't quite up to it. Instead, he went back to the States and began dismantling CIN, selling everything at a huge loss and then giving the proceeds to charities he once wouldn't have touched, including the Brethren. And now John tells me he's showed up at a Brethren relief center in Bangladesh, unannounced and unattended, carrying only a backpack. He's made himself useful performing the most menial tasks. According to John, hours go by without his saying a word, and he works like a dog.

"You let him stay?" I asked.

"I figured that's what Joshua would want," John told me, and I had to shut up, because I knew John was right: that's exactly what Joshua would have wanted. But I was surprised by the reverent tone of John's voice. The old John often tried to use Joshua for his own ends. But this new John sometimes hints that Joshua Grant was something more than a mere man, even something more than a man with remarkable gifts and an extremely unusual pedigree.

And others do more than hint. The Joshans, a small offshoot of the Brethren, have come out and said it: Joshua was Jesus, the Second Coming, and now we must await a third. Their theology is still inchoate, still forming, already a tortured mess. But then, whose isn't?

And of course, there are still those who say Josh was Christ's evil twin, although few are mad enough to endorse his upside-down crucifixion. They're losing ground rapidly, so they hunt desperately for some bad fruit from Joshua's life, some scandal to taint his increasingly sainted name. So far, they've found nothing, so they've resorted to hints that the Joshans are right about one thing: Joshua Grant will be coming back. And since he did nothing evil while he was here, those who vilify him hope for his return almost as fervently as those who now sing corny hymns in his honor.

But I still see nothing supernatural in the whole story, or at least nothing undeniably supernatural. Nothing, not even Maria.

She's still ill, and she's still alive — her leukemia repeatedly progresses, then goes into remission. Her stateside oncologist shakes her head and mutters gloomily, but she's quit prescribing any treatment other than an occasional dose of Dr. Leisner's stimulants. Leisner himself wasn't entirely surprised when we told him how his most famous patient was faring.

"I told you the illness was unique," he said. "Apparently that has its good side, too."

And Maria won't talk to me about it. Though she was always a most unusual Catholic, she never lost touch with her church, and lately she goes to Mass almost every morning, carefully observing their odd little rituals. People in the church sidle away when they see her coming, in awe as much as fear. Occasionally those who are sick find an excuse to touch her.

On the subject of Joshua, Maria has also become curiously reticent. She accepted my apology for hiding what I knew of his conception with stunning tranquility, commenting only that if she had been in my place she might have done the same. And though she likes to share fond memories of Joshua's childhood, when I try to discuss the odd tack the Joshans are taking, she chooses her words carefully, as if she's hiding a secret.

"Don't tell me you've seen him, too," I ask. "Like John, I mean."

"John saw him?"

"In a hallucination or a dream, he wouldn't say which."

And tears well in Maria's eyes as she looks down and makes the sign of the cross.

And so I sit awake, late at night, and ponder the life of my stepson. Who was he? I ask, and then wonder whether the question can be answered about any of us. Who am I, for instance? Maria's faithful husband; or the cheating lecher once married to Beverly Jacobson? Charity doctor for coke-sniffing teen mothers, or money-grubbing hack publicist for Harold Anthony? The hero who tried to save Ed Devaney, or the coward who three times denied knowing Joshua Grant as they murdered him not fifty feet away?

But while I'm a mass of contradictions, Joshua's life seems a record of unearthly consistency. Even his death has worked out well, (for almost everybody but him, that is). In the U.S. the carbon tariffs have doubled the price of gasoline and the economy has spiraled downward, but public opinion has turned against a war for cheap oil; the Armstrong administration even brags about American-paid tariffs saving thousands of lives in Bangladesh. In Israel moderates and liberals have come into power, preaching peace and reconciliation; and the Palestinians have put away their desperate hatred to see where it will all lead. All over the world Joshua's death has made it fashionable to tolerate one's enemies, though actually loving them is perhaps still too much to ask.

But if that is what Joshua meant to the world, I'm left with a different question. Who was he to me? How should I mourn him? I look for an answer in the notes that Brethren members have written down from Joshua's "idle" conversations, and after a long search my eyes fall on this:

"We were meant to weep for Christ as well as worship him, but when we weep for Christ as God, and forget that Christ was also our brother, our tears fall into a heavenly abyss."

And there comes a day when I wake early to the smell of strong coffee, walk into the kitchen, and find Joshua sitting at the table, as calm as can be.

"Good morning, Peter," he says. "Have a cup."

I slowly pull out a chair and sit beside him, careful not to look away. There's no otherworldly glow, no hint of ghostlike transparency. No saintly robes, either: he's dressed in a pair of battered old jeans and a knit shirt, standard Saturday morning wear at home.

"You're alive!" I say, stupidly.

"Well, maybe not in the sense you mean. But the part of me that matters is alive. No one really dies."

"Then the Joshans are right?"

"Now why do you say that? If no one ever dies, how is my presence more remarkable than anyone else's? Anyone 'dead' that is." He pours me some coffee and favors me with a carefree smile before I realize he hasn't answered my question.

"You noticed," he says.

"Noticed what?"

"That I didn't answer your question."

"Yes, I did notice." I sit, waiting for his next words. But a long time goes by, and Josh just sips his coffee, and encourages me with gestures to take a sip of mine. After two minutes I can't take it any longer.

"Joshua," I ask, "why are you here?"

"Well," he says, "first, I wanted to thank you for not shooting Harold Anthony."

That he knows I almost shot Harold the Great isn't surprising; it's easy to believe someone back from the dead might have special sources of knowledge. But a chill comes over me nonetheless, a sick feeling as I remember how that day ended for Joshua.

"Why do you care about Harold Anthony?" I ask weakly.

"He has potential," Josh says blithely. "I have high hopes for him." I just shake my head.

"I'm glad he'll be of use to someone," I say, thinking of the gun in my closet. "Why else are you here?"

"To give you the secrets of the universe, the hidden meaning of life, the keys to the kingdom!"

Humor was one of the few things lacking in the old Josh, and I wonder for an instant just who this is sitting in my kitchen. I catch not the faintest whiff of brimstone, but a fragmentary quote by somebody, Rilke perhaps, flits through my brain. Something about beauty being nothing more than the edge of a terror we're barely able to withstand.

"The secrets of the universe," I say, visions of my pistol playing behind my eyes. "Okay, I'll bite."

He sets his coffee on the table, eases smoothly into lotus position on the floor.

"Which secret do you want first?" he asks.

"Tell me how to be happy."

"That's simple. The Buddha told people how to do that 2500 years ago."

"Tell me again."

"Want less."

"That's it?"

"It works, if you can do it, that is."

"All right, tell me how to be happy and good."

"Want less, give more."

"Four words are the secret of the universe. It figures." I look at his smiling face and suddenly recall . . .

"Wait a second, I've heard that. Some children's picture book you used to like, some crazy thing with dinosaurs and people and paintings."

"You know, you're right, though I think I changed it a little. But if a stegosaurus can handle it, you'd think people could too."

"Four words that aren't even your own. Some guru you are."

"Well, the most important part is so simple a child can understand. But I'll elaborate."

He waves a hand in the air and produces a prized possession of Joe's, an old "Calvin and Hobbes" cartoon, carefully framed. As they plunge downhill in a wagon, the six-year-old with the morals of Attila and the vocabulary of Daniel Webster worries that nothing matters. His stuffed tiger, as mysteriously alive as Joshua himself, cowers behind him. But as they bounce off a rock Calvin switches tracks as abruptly as his wagon. What if everything matters?

"Very funny," I say, handing the cartoon back to him.

And then I think of a universe where everything matters: my impatience with parents and friends and the boring old man next door, my contempt for waiters and mechanics and maids, the talents I've frittered away, the talents I've let rot unappreciated in others, the lives I might have saved or made better if I'd only cared, the space on this world I've filled with the useless void of my being. Nothing unusual, but even so an endless list of sorrows, an ocean of tears, an Everest of debt owed even before I deserted Joshua in Jerusalem.

Finally, of course, there are the lucky women in my life. Beverly, betrayed by me in her own bed; and Maria, who I left standing alone as her son died upside down on a cross.

And what do I have to balance against all this? I can think of nothing. Suddenly I'm on my feet and Joshua is in my arms.

"I'm sorry," I'm mumbling, my tear-stained face buried against his shoulder, "Please forgive me. I'll try and do better, I swear it."

"You'll do no better on your own," Joshua says. "Knowing what to do isn't the hard part. People have always known. They just keep on looking for an answer that's easier to swallow."

"I let them kill you!"

"I was born to die. So were you."

"I should have done something!"

"Yes, you should, even if it was only to die beside me. So do better next time. Don't turn your back when the opportunity comes. Pray for strength, not power. And remember that all will be healed in the end."

"And when will that be?"

"Maybe in ten million years. And maybe tomorrow. Why not make plans for both?"

He steps back and looks at me fondly. "I have high hopes for you, too, Peter," he says, and embraces me again.

And then my arms are empty, and he is gone.

About the Author

In addition to writing, Bill Hearn teaches, composes, and performs on guitar, banjo, mandolin, ukulele, lute, and theorbo. Bill's collection of original ukulele pieces and arrangements: *101 Easy Ukulele Solos,* published by Mel Bay, is available through music stores and online.

I hope you enjoyed ***Maria's Child***. If you would like to recommend it or buy a copy for a friend or relative, the novel is easily ordered direct from Amazon books as either a paperback or e-book. Either scan or forward the QR code below . . .

or go to:

https://www.amazon.com/Marias-Child-Bill-Hearn/dp/B09TR5L23S

for a link that will allow you to order the book in either print or e-book versions.

If you would like to rate or review this book, go to the product page on Amazon and look for the rating stars. You can also rate the book on Goodreads if you are a member. Ratings are very helpful to first-time authors.

If you got this book from a Little Free Library Box, please return it someday, but take your time if you're a leisurely reader.

Thank you!

Bill Hearn

Bill Hearn

Made in the USA
Columbia, SC
10 May 2022

60096856R00219